PRAISE FOR THE NOVELS OF SAMANTHA YOUNG

Before Jamaica Lane

"Young's third book in the On Dublin Street series will entice readers in every possible way. It's flirty, romantic, and passionate. . . . The perfect mix of giddiness along with that dizzying feeling one experiences during the first stages of love [is] exact and ever so sweet."   —*Romantic Times*

Down London Road

"Ridiculously incendiary chemistry."   —Dear Author

"Heartwarming, sizzling, and captivating. . . . [Young's characters] are complex, a little flawed, and at their core good people struggling to make it in this crazy world. . . . Young creates steamy scenes that sizzle with just the right amount of details."   —Caffeinated Book Reviewer

"Ms. Young dives deep into the psyche of what makes a person tick emotionally, what stirs their vulnerability, and ultimately provides them the courage to be better individuals as well as partners. . . . The one thing you can count on from Ms. Young is some of the best steamy, sexual chemistry."   —Fiction Vixen Book Reviews

"A deceptively complex romantic contemporary romance that will have you laughing, crying, and swooning with delight."   —Smexy Books

continued . . .

"Just as hot and sexy as the first book. . . . Smart and sexy, Young writes stories that stay with you long after you flip that last page."

—Under the Covers

"Passion, romance, angst, LUST, major heat, mistakes, personal growth, and the power of love all combine perfectly in *Down London Road*."

—Bookish Temptations

"*Down London Road* delivers on all fronts—charismatic characters, witty dialogue, blazing-hot sex scenes, and real-life issues make this book an easy one to devour. Samantha Young is not an author you should miss out on!"

—Fresh Fiction

"Another flirty, modern, and sexy story. . . . Thanks to the characters' special connection and snappy dialogue, readers will feel the pull of Young's story from the get-go and root for a happy ending."

—*RT Book Reviews*

On Dublin Street

"This book had some funny dialogue, some amazingly hot sex scenes, and emotional drama. Did I mention the amazing sex scenes?"

—Dear Author

"This is a really sexy book and I loved the heroine's journey to find herself and grow strong. Highly recommend this one." —*USA Today*

"This book is fun. Sexy. A little dark. While the hero is extremely dominant, he also shows his softer side just when she needs it."

—Smexy Books

"Every page sizzles when these two get together, but this book is so much more than a hot romp. This book has heart—and lots of it. . . . If you want a book that will lure you in, grab you by the scruff of the neck, and never let you go until you finish reading the last page, then *On Dublin Street* is the book for you."

—TotallyBookedBlog

"Brilliantly written with just the right amount of hotness, sexiness, and romance and everything else in between."

—Once Upon a Twilight

"The chemistry between Jocelyn and Braden was on fire. The characters were believable and more importantly they were lovable . . . one of the best books I have read in 2012!"

—Rainy Day Reads

"This book has it all . . . romance, fabulously written heat, family, friendship, heartbreak, longing, hope, and an ending that is completely satisfying."

—Bookish Temptations

"Lots of heart makes this book an absolute page-turner."

—*RT Book Reviews*

ALSO BY SAMANTHA YOUNG

On Dublin Street
Down London Road
Before Jamaica Lane
Until Fountain Bridge (Penguin digital Special)
Castle Hill (Penguin digital Special)

FALL FROM INDIA PLACE

SAMANTHA YOUNG

NEW AMERICAN LIBRARY

New American Library
Published by the Penguin Group
Penguin Group (USA) LLC, 375 Hudson Street,
New York, New York 10014

USA | Canada | UK | Ireland | Australia | New Zealand | India | South Africa | China
penguin.com
A Penguin Random House Company

First published by New American Library,
a division of Penguin Group (USA) LLC

First Printing, June 2014

 REGISTERED TRADEMARK—MARCA REGISTRADA

LIBRARY OF CONGRESS CATALOGING-IN-PUBLICATION DATA:
Young, Samantha.
Fall from India Place/Samantha Young.
p. cm.
ISBN 978-0-451-46940-3 (pbk.)
1. Man-woman relationships—Fiction. I. Title.
PR6125.O943F36 2014
823'.92—dc23   2014000855

Printed in the United States of America
1   3   5   7   9   10   8   6   4   2

Set in Garamond

For Kate and Shanine.
And for Mr. Neil Innes.
You're the best teachers I've ever known.
You inspire me. You inspired Hannah.

Remember tonight, for it is the beginning of always.

—ATTRIBUTED TO DANTE ALIGHIERI

Fall from India Place

CHAPTER 1

Edinburgh
October

I'd made a promise to myself when I stepped onto the cobbled streets of Edinburgh on the way to my first teaching job that I'd be the kind of teacher who would do whatever it took to reach my students. Never mind that now keeping that promise meant embarrassing myself and them with my fantastically awful drawing skills.

Removing my badly drawn illustrations from the projector, I replaced them with two sentences.

I glanced up at the small class of six adults, ranging in age from twenty-four to fifty-two, and gave them a wry smile. "Though I hate to deprive you of my artistic genius, I think I'd better get rid of those."

Portia, my fifty-two-year-old student, who had enough good cheer to lighten the often nervous atmosphere in the small classroom, grinned at me, while Duncan, a thirty-three-year-old mechanic, snorted. My other four students continued to stare at me wide-eyed and slightly scared, as though everything I said and did was a test.

"Now that you've learned these sight words and hopefully connected to them through my terrible attempts at drawing, I want you to become familiar with how they fit in an everyday sentence. For the rest of our time this evening I want you to write these two sentences ten times each." I watched Lorraine, my very, *very* anxious and prickly twenty-four-year-old student, gnaw at her lip, and winced at the thought of what she might do to said lip after my next instruction. I continued. "I've got two small booklets here for each of you. One is filled with sight words, the other with sentences made up entirely of sight words. I want you to choose ten sentences and write those sentences out ten times each and bring them with you next week."

Lorraine blanched and I immediately felt my chest squeeze with empathy. Lorraine was a prime example of why I'd decided to volunteer to teach an adult literacy course at my local community center. Some people, like my friend Suzanne, thought I was absolutely nuts to take on a volunteer teaching job during my probationary year as a high school English teacher. And maybe I was. My workload for school was insane. However, I shared the literacy class with another volunteer, so it was only one night out of my week—and it was something that really made me feel like I was making a difference. Sometimes it was harder to see the impact I made in high school, and I knew that there would be an awful lot of days ahead of me when I wouldn't feel like I was leaving much of an impression. However, volunteering gave me that sense of satisfaction every single time. The adults I was teaching were mostly unemployed, with the exception of Portia and Duncan. Duncan's employer had asked him to improve his reading and writing skills. Portia had somehow managed to get through life on a very basic understanding of literacy and numeracy (until one day she decided she wanted more), but the others were struggling to maintain employment because of their lack of language and communication skills.

I knew illiteracy was still a big deal in this country, but since I came from an educated family, and was a massive bookworm, it was something I had never been touched by. Until last year.

There was one moment during my teacher training year that would always stand out: I was in contact with a student's father who had been visibly shaken when asked to look at his child's work. Sweat beaded on his forehead as he confessed in a halting voice that he couldn't read it. Then, when I asked him to sign a permission slip that would allow us to take his daughter with us for the class trip to see *Twelfth Night* in the theater, his hand badly trembled as he made a squiggle on the signature line.

The utter fear and humiliation in his expression due to his illiteracy really hit me emotionally. I could feel the sting of tears in my eyes for him. A grown man made to feel weak and helpless by letters on a page? I didn't like having to witness his struggle, and later that night I started looking into local literacy courses. I put out some inquiries and a month or so later St. Stephen's Centre, my local community center, had contacted me because they had just lost one of their volunteer teachers.

Despite the fact that the small class seemed a bit dubious about having a woman younger than they were as a teacher, I really felt we were getting somewhere.

"Hannah, your head is blocking the word between 'wash' and 'cold,'" Duncan said teasingly.

"Is that your polite way of telling me I've got a big head?" I said, moving off to the side so they could all see the board.

He grinned. "Nah, I'd say it's just the right size. It's a very nice head."

"Why, thank you. I grew it myself," I drawled cockily.

He groaned at the daft joke, but his eyes were filled with mirth as Portia hee-hawed behind him.

Smiling, I let my eyes roam over the heads bent low to their jotters, pencils moving at different speeds, from the painstakingly slow and deeply grooved print to the fairly fast and sweeping handwriting. The smile died on my lips at the sight of Lorraine. She kept looking around at the others, panic in her eyes as she saw them getting on with the work.

She caught me looking and glowered, then lowered her eyes to her jotter.

I was losing her. I felt it in my gut.

Once I called time up, I walked over to Lorraine before she could bolt. "Can you stay back for a few minutes?"

She narrowed her eyes and licked her lips nervously. "Eh, why?"

"Please?"

She didn't reply, but she also didn't leave.

"Thanks for tonight, Hannah!" Portia called over to me, her voice probably carrying all the way down into Reception. I always spoke a little more loudly than I had to in class because I had a feeling Portia had a slight hearing problem and was unwilling to admit to it. She was a glamorous woman who benefited either from great genes or fabulous anti-aging creams, and anyone could tell she took a lot of pride in her appearance. Admitting to illiteracy was one thing, but admitting to being hard of hearing would signify her age, and I doubted she wanted anyone to think she was older than she felt inside.

"You're very welcome," I called back fondly, smiling and waving good-bye to the others as they thanked me and left.

Turning back to Lorraine, I was completely prepared for it when she crossed her arms over her chest and snapped, "I dinnae see the point in me stickin' aroond since am done wi' this shite."

"I had a feeling you'd say that."

She rolled her eyes. "Aye, I bet ye did. Whitever." She started to walk toward the door.

"You leave and you'll be right back at square one. Unemployable."

"No fer a fuckin' cleanin' jobe."

"And is that what you want?"

Lorraine whirled around, her eyes spitting fire as she sneered, "Whit? Is that no gid enough fer ye? Aye? Too fuckin' gid tae be a cleaner? Look at ye. Whit the hell dae ye ken aboot hard graft and huvin' nae money? And am supposed tae learn fae ye? I dinnae think sae."

Calmly, I took in her dark hair scraped back into a scraggly ponytail, her cheap makeup, her inexpensive and untidy shirt and trousers, and the thin waterproof jacket she wore over them. Finally, I saw the scuffed boots that had seen too many rough days on her feet.

Lorraine was only two years older than me, but there was a hardness in her eyes that made her appear much older. I didn't know anything about her life, but I did know she was lashing out at me because she was scared.

Who knows? Maybe she was also lashing out at me because of the way I talked, looked, dressed, and held myself. I was educated. I was confident. Two things she was not. Sometimes that's enough for someone to take a dislike to you. Was I the wrong person to teach Lorraine? Perhaps. But I wasn't quite ready to give up.

"Working hard comes in all forms, Lorraine," I told her quietly, careful to keep the kindness out of my voice in case she made the assumption I was being condescending. "The cleaners in the high school where I teach work their arses off tidying up after those kids." I wrinkled my nose. "I don't even want to think about what they find in the boys' toilets.

"But I work my arse off *teaching* those very same kids—lesson plans, piles of marking that eat into my evenings and weekends, spending my own personal money on resources because the school never seems to have enough in the budget, and I work on the lesson plans for this class and I teach this class for free. I know what it's like to work hard. It's not as physically tiring as cleaning, but it's mentally draining." I took a step toward her. "You're used to physical hard graft, Lorraine. This stuff"—I gestured to the board—"this is completely out of your comfort zone. I understand that. But that's why I'm here. I'm here to teach you to read and write so you can apply for a job that you actually want, and you wouldn't be here if you wanted to be a cleaner.

"Although, on a side note I'm guessing you'd still need reading and writing skills for that job. There are applications to fill out, client checklists to read through . . ." I saw her lips pinch and got back to the point. "You don't like me, fine, I could give a shit. I don't need you to like me. I need you to listen to me when I say I'm not here to embarrass you or make you feel bad about yourself. I'm here to teach you. You don't need to like me to learn what I have to teach. You *do* need to like yourself enough to believe you deserve more out of life."

Silence fell between us.

Slowly, the tension in her shoulders seemed to disappear as they slumped from the tips of her ears back into place.

"Can you do that?" I pushed her with the question.

Lorraine swallowed and gave me a jerky nod.

"I'll see you next class, then?"

"Aye."

I sighed inwardly, feeling my own tension melt. "If you need me to go over anything, or sit with you one-on-one, just say so. There is no one in this class that is rooting for you to fail. They're all in the same boat. *They* get it, even if you think I don't."

"Aye, aye, okay." She rolled her eyes and turned on her heel to walk out. "Calm the beans."

Okay, so sometimes it *was* like teaching a high school English class.

I grinned, collected my things, and headed for the door. Switching off the lights, I nodded to myself. Every time I walked out of a classroom at the end of the day, I wanted to feel like I'd won something and that therefore so had the people I was teaching. Sometimes, unfortunately, I just felt exhausted and stressed.

Tonight I felt like Lorraine and I had won.

In a good mood, and determined to take some "me time," I texted two of my friends from university, Suzanne and Michaela, and arranged for Friday night cocktails the next evening.

It was clear from the moment we met up that night that Suzanne was in the mood to party and pick up a stranger for a random hookup. She eyed the men as though she were searching for the best piece of meat at a buffet. Her eyes swung back to me as we sat at our table in a bar on George IV Bridge, and she grinned when I burst out laughing at her.

Michaela rolled her eyes at Suzanne and sipped quietly from her drink.

I'd met the girls at Edinburgh University after moving into Pollock Halls and then we'd gotten a flat together in second year. Michaela moved in with her boyfriend, Colin, in third year and I moved into a smaller flat with Suzanne. Then we'd gone our separate ways accommodations-wise after graduation. Suzanne was originally from Aberdeen, but after graduation she'd gotten a position at a large financial company in the city. She made pretty good money, so she could afford a one-bedroom flat in Marchmont. I, on the other hand, was extremely lucky. My big sister, Ellie, and her half brother, Braden, whom I thought of as a big brother, were well off, and for my graduation they'd bought me a chic two-bedroom flat on Clarence Street in Stockbridge. It did not escape my notice that this put me in the middle between my parents' house on St. Bernard's Crescent to my west, and Braden and his wife, Joss's house and Ellie and her husband, Adam's house, to my east on Dublin Street and Scotland Street. They were all just a short walking distance from me.

My family was overprotective. They always had been. Unfortunately, this meant I felt the need to dodge their protective instincts from time to time. However, the flat was a different matter altogether. It was the most amazing, outlandish graduation gift—a gift I could never have afforded on my teacher's pay. I was overwhelmed and eternally grateful to them for it. And honestly I was happy it was so close to my family. I had a growing bunch of nieces and nephews that I loved just as much as I loved their parents.

"See anything you like?" I asked Suzanne as I surveyed the talent. There were a couple of good-looking guys standing by the bar.

"Of course she does," Michaela teased. "She probably sees five."

Suzanne huffed. "Well, some of us didn't find our one true love when we were eighteen. *Some* of us have a lot of frogs to kiss before we find our prince. And some of us like it that way."

Michaela and I laughed. It was true that Michaela accompanied us on our nights out only to keep in touch with us. She was happily engaged to Colin, a Scottish student she fell in love with in first year of university. She'd decided not to return to her hometown of Shropshire, England, in favor of attending Moray House teacher training in Edinburgh with me. Like me, she was working toward qualifying as an English teacher.

My two friends couldn't have been more different. Suzanne was loud, flirtatious, and an assertive drama queen. Michaela was the quietest of the three of us. She was sweet and loyal, and she cared a great deal about her new students. If I wanted a good time and a distraction, I sought out Suzanne, but if I just wanted someone to talk to, I picked up the phone and called Michaela.

"How are the kids?" Michaela asked me, and I knew she was referring to family and not school.

"Really good."

"And more to come." She grinned.

"Ugh, I don't know how they do it." Suzanne shuddered. "You'd think they'd have learned their lesson with the one."

"Well, it's Jo's first one, actually." Not that that would change Suzanne's opinion that children were unpleasant little creatures she wanted nothing to do with.

Johanna MacCabe was probably my closest girlfriend, despite our seven-year age difference. When Braden met his wife, Joss, she brought into our little family her good friend Jo Walker, and Jo soon met the love of her life, Cameron MacCabe. The two of them had been married for two years and Jo was pregnant with their first child.

She wasn't the only one who was pregnant. My sister, Ellie, and her husband, Adam, were expecting their second child. They already had an adorable two-year-old son called William and were hoping to give me a niece this time around.

"She's nuts." Suzanne made a face. "But look at who I'm talking to. Teachers. Who on earth in their right mind would decide to become a teacher? Oh"—her eyes widened at something over my shoulder—"he's yummy."

Michaela and I shared a knowing look and I turned to stare as inconspicuously as possible at whoever had caught Suzanne's eye.

"And she's off!" Michaela giggled, pulling my gaze away from the tall guy with the bulging biceps who was exactly Suzanne's type, to watch her cross the bar with an exaggerated swing to her slim hips. "I don't know how she can do this every other weekend. A different guy."

Suzanne was way into the double digits when it came to the number of men she'd slept with. But I wasn't there to judge. She could do what she pleased as long as she was safe about it. I, on the other hand, didn't do the whole sleeping-around thing. Honestly, I didn't do the whole sex thing. The last and only time it happened, I'd gotten burned. So I had no intention of falling into bed with a guy until I was absolutely positive there was a connection between us that we *both* felt.

At that moment I was content with my life as it was. I was too busy for anything more than a bar flirtation and I was completely okay with that. I was young. I had time. Suzanne seemed to be on a mission to try out every single freaking frog she could get her hands on until she finally found that elusive prince.

Suzanne strode back to our table with the guy and his two friends in tow. They sat down and introduced themselves. Unfortunately, the guy she was interested in, Seb, quickly turned his attention from her to me. Thankfully one of his friends seemed more than into Suzanne.

Seb was really nice. He asked me a lot of questions about myself and I reciprocated. We laughed and chatted about everyday nonsense, and the guys bought us another round of drinks.

After a few hours had passed, our new friends started talking about hitting a club. Michaela didn't look too sure, and I wasn't about to leave her behind, so Suzanne and I went to freshen up in the ladies' toilets while Michaela mulled it over.

We were standing at the sinks, reapplying blusher and lipstick, when Suzanne mused, "So . . . Seb is delicious. Does he warrant a break from the longest dry spell in history or are you going to pull the Hannah Tease on this one as well?"

I grunted. "The Hannah Tease?"

She gave me a look that said, *Like you don't know.* "The Hannah Tease. The gorgeous Hannah Nichols always snags the hottest of the hot, flirts her arse off with him for a few hours, but leaves him to go home with blue balls and no phone number."

"I'm not teasing anyone," I objected. "If I'm not interested I don't put it out there that I am. It's harmless light banter. That's it."

This time the look she gave me was one that she'd begun to give me on a regular basis. It was an impatient expression that said she didn't understand me. Not one bit. "What the hell is wrong with you? And when are you going to get over the past and finally get under someone new?"

I shook my head, pretending I didn't know what she was talking about. "Have you ever considered I might be happy? Isn't that the whole point to all this? To be happy? And I am. I love my job, I love my family, and I love my friends. I have a good life, Suzanne."

She snorted this time. "Yeah, keep telling yourself that."

I felt my blood heat in indignation. "What is your problem tonight? Is it because of Seb? Because you're welcome to him."

This time Suzanne turned on me with narrowed eyes. "Oh, I could have him if I wanted to, don't worry."

"Then what's the attitude about?"

"Ugh, don't talk to me like I'm one of your kids. You know, you've gotten really boring lately."

I laughed incredulously at the turn our conversation had taken. Suzanne wasn't the most tactful person, and she had a tendency to snap impatiently at people, but tonight she was turning her reserve of nastiness on me, which she'd never done before. "In my defense, you are acting like a child."

"Eh, whatever." She threw her hands up in despair, like the consummate drama queen she was. "Let's just see if Michaela wants to go clubbing . . ." I felt sure she was going to say something else, but in the end she just pinched her lips together and stormed out of the toilets.

I was leaving the toilets when I got a text from Lucy, a friend from teacher training, asking if I fancied joining her for a drink. She was around the corner at a pub on the Royal Mile with a few friends and knew I was out tonight. I texted her back, then casually made my way over to my friends.

"Michaela has decided to come with us," Suzanne said cheerily, like she hadn't just verbally bitch-slapped me in the toilets.

I squeezed Michaela's shoulder and smiled at them all. "You guys have a good night. I have somewhere I need to be."

Ignoring Suzanne's sputtering, I sauntered out of there, away from the drama and the gorgeous boys, and spent the rest of the evening getting drunk with people who didn't care if I was single or married, skinny or fat, ambitious or laid-back. They were just out to relax and de-stress from work, and that was all I was looking for too.

Life was good. I certainly didn't need anyone trying to tell me it wasn't because they themselves were discontented.

CHAPTER 2

The next morning I woke up to get ready for Jo and Ellie's baby shower. My mum, Elodie, was hosting it at my parents' house for all the girls, while the men looked after the kids.

I'd just switched off my hairdryer and was sitting down to do my makeup when my door buzzer went off. Not expecting anyone, I wondered if one of the girls had decided to drop in on me before the baby shower.

"Hello?" I called into the entry phone.

"It's me," a familiar deep and masculine voice said.

Pleased by the unexpected visit, I answered, "Come on up."

When I opened my door Cole Walker smiled at me and strode inside. I turned my cheek for his kiss and offered him a coffee.

"Sure." He followed me into my kitchen.

Cole Walker was Jo's little brother. He was a year younger than me, but you'd never know it. I'd never met a guy so close to my age as mature as Cole. For as long as I'd known him he'd been that way. He acted more like a thirty-year-old than the twenty-one-year-old he was.

We'd been friends because our families were close, but the year I turned seventeen we'd grown closer. So close, I considered him my best friend. I often thought it was a shame there wasn't any sexual chemistry between us, because Cole was seriously one of the best guys I'd ever met and he would make anyone a fantastic boyfriend.

Despite being a little hotheaded, especially when it came to anyone hurting or even pissing off someone he cared about, Cole was the least judgmental person I knew. There were occasions when he could be cocky and come off as intimidating to those who didn't know him well, but I knew him to be down-to-earth, easy to talk to, intelligent, creative, compassionate, loyal, and sensible, despite what his appearance might suggest to people inclined to judge a book by its cover.

A few inches over six feet, Cole was broad-shouldered and athletically built—he had an amazing body, honed in martial arts classes and weekly visits to the gym. He had messy strawberry blond hair that his sister was always nagging at him to cut, gorgeous green eyes, and a handsome face that was usually scruffy and in need of a shave. It wasn't his natural good looks that raised eyebrows, although he did turn heads. It was the tattoos. He had lyrics tattooed on his inner right wrist, and black feathers on the back of his right shoulder that reached over and down his upper biceps, the feathers leading to an eagle that was flying, wings outstretched. In its talons dangled an old-fashioned pocket watch. He had yet to cover his left arm, although he was working on ideas for a sleeve.

He also had the same tattoo as Cam. They were best mates. Cole designed it when he was fifteen. It was a "J&C" that was visible in among this almost tribal-like design of vines and curlicues. Cam had it on his chest. When he was eighteen Cole had the same tattoo inked on the side of his neck where his pulse throbbed.

I knew how much that tattoo meant to him. For Cam the "J&C" symbolized not only his relationship with Jo but his relationship with Cole as well. For Cole, the "J&C" was Jo and Cam. Cole had had a pretty shitty time of it at home with his alcoholic mum, Fiona. She was never there for him. Jo had raised him. When Cole was fourteen Jo discovered their mother was beating him, and not long after that they moved in with Cameron and left their mum alone in the flat upstairs.

Fiona had passed away of a heart attack almost two years ago. I imagined it hadn't been easy for Cole, for many reasons. I'd tried to talk to him about it, but it was the one subject he didn't want to touch. As far as he was concerned, Jo was his mother and sister rolled into one and Cameron had saved their lives. They were all he needed.

"What are you doing here?" I asked as I made his coffee. "Shouldn't you be at work?"

Cole was a student at Edinburgh College of Art, but he'd been working since he was sixteen years old at INKarnate, an award-winning tattoo studio in Leith. Stu Motherwell had been running the parlor for more than twenty-five years and Cole had started off as an errand boy so he could get a feel for the place. When he was eighteen he started a part-time apprenticeship there. I knew Stu treated Cole like a son, and relied heavily on him.

I didn't think it would be too long before Cole was helping to run the place.

"Late start," Cole replied, taking the coffee with a "Thanks." "I start in thirty minutes but I thought I'd pop in to see you first."

I leaned back against the counter, staring up at him. "Why? Is everything okay?"

He gazed back at me for a few long seconds. "That's what I'm here to ask you. With everything that's going on . . ."

Understanding what he was getting at, I smiled reassuringly. "Things are good. Honest."

He frowned. "I haven't heard from you much lately and . . ." He shrugged.

"Cole, I'm run off my feet with school and volunteering. I'm stressing a little and I'm sort of failing at every other aspect of life because of it."

"You sure that's it?"

I crossed my heart. "Promise."

His eyes moved past me to the kitchen table, where the presents for the shower sat all wrapped up and ready to go. I saw him clock the packet of condoms I'd put beside them to give to Ellie and Jo as a joke. Cole snorted. "I do not envy you today."

"Two hormonal women and a packet of condoms? Isn't that like a Friday night for you?" I teased.

He laughed because we both knew I was far off the mark.

Cole wasn't really the player type. Sure, I knew he wasn't an angel, but he preferred to be in a relationship. Right now he was dating an art history student called Steph.

"At least I need condoms." He smiled, not unkindly.

I made a face. "So it's been a while."

"Correction: It's been too long." He frowned. "You ever going to give someone a chance?"

"Look, I just don't want to sleep with random people. I'm not Suzanne, Cole."

"I never said you were. Not all guys are just looking to hook up with you and then leave you in the morning." His expression softened. "You're not the kind of girl you want to leave, Hannah. Give one of them a chance to prove it to you. You've never been in a relationship. How can you knock it until you try it?"

I laughed. "I'm not knocking it. I'm just happy by myself right now. But speaking of couplings . . . how *is* the old ball and chain?"

Cole sighed. "Stressing. I promised her I'd head over to her flat after work to help her on her paper."

"Aw." I mocked him playfully. "You're such a good boyfriend."

Cole downed the last of his coffee and put the mug in my sink. He leaned over and pressed a kiss to my cheek. "Next time you see Steph, will you tell her that?"

"Trouble in paradise?" I asked, walking him to the front door.

"She's become a nagger."

"I'm sure she'll be fine once she stops stressing."

"Hmm." He smiled back at me as he stepped outside. "Enjoy the shower."

"Enjoy tutoring," I replied, grinning saucily. "Who knows? Things might get a little . . . *educational*." I waggled my eyebrows.

Cole laughed as he took the stairs two at a time. "One can only hope."

As soon as I walked through the door of my parents' house I heard the cacophony of female conversation coming from the sitting room.

My dad stepped into the hallway as I was closing the front door, his eyes lighting up at the sight of me.

"Hey, Dad." I walked into his open arms, melting into his hug.

"Hi, sweetheart." He kissed my hair and pulled back to smile into my face. "Long time no see."

I winced. "I'm sorry I haven't popped around lately. I've been bogged down with work."

My dad was a classical history professor at Edinburgh University. He was intelligent, passionate about his subject, laid-back, and most of all perceptive as hell. His eyes narrowed as he took me in. "Are you sure that's all it is?"

"Of course. I'm fine, honest."

"You would tell me if you weren't?"

I suppose he had every right to worry that I might keep problems from him. I had a track record of doing that. For once I was honest. "I'm past it."

"Clark! Can you get these canapés, please?" My mum's voice could be heard yelling from the kitchen.

Dad's eyes grew round with mock horror. "I'm trying to escape. Help."

I laughed. "Go." I gestured to the door. "I'll distract her."

He sighed in relief, kissed my cheek, and dashed out the front door.

Mum marched into the hall a second later. "Oh, Hannah." She smiled, coming toward me with open arms. "It's good to see you, sweetie." She hugged me tight. "Have you seen your dad by any chance?"

"Um, he left."

Mum pulled back, frowning. "He's supposed to be helping."

"Mum, he's the only man here. I don't think it's really fair to ask him to stay when all the other menfolk don't have to."

She gave a huff at that but didn't argue. "Would you help me, then?"

I held up my gifts. "First, where do I put these?"

"Sitting room."

I wandered into the sitting room as Mum went back to the kitchen and was immediately set upon by my sister and friends. Ellie reached me first. Just as when she'd been pregnant with William, she not only had a fairly large bump but her cheeks were chubby and her lips fuller. She was absolutely adorable, even if she would disagree. "Hannah." She tugged me toward her and I awkwardly hugged her, trying not to squash her bump.

"You look beautiful, Els." I kissed my sister's cheek and pulled back to stare down at the bump. "You're even bigger this time around."

Els groaned. "Don't remind me. Jo makes me feel like a heifer."

Jo laughed, gently brushing Ellie aside so she could hug me. "I feel like I haven't seen you in forever," she groaned, giving me a squeeze.

Except for the neat bump, Jo didn't look much different—she was gorgeous, as always. I wondered how many women in the room hated her for being able to look glamorous while pregnant. "I've been so busy. I'm sorry."

"Don't be." She smiled reassuringly at me. "I know how hard you work."

"Right, my turn." A musical American accent hit my ears, seconds before Olivia Sawyer embraced me. "It's been ages," she complained, her eyes teasing so I'd know she wasn't really grousing about my absence. "Your hair is so much longer than last time we saw each other."

Olivia, or Liv, as we all called her, was a curvy, attractive brunette who was practically a sister to Jo. Liv's dad, Mick, had been like a close uncle to Jo when she was young. He left for America to be with a kid—Liv—that he hadn't known about until she was thirteen, and returned to Scotland seven years ago when his wife, Liv's mother, died. Liv came with him to rebuild their lives. Mick and Jo worked together in his painting and decorating company, and Dad got Liv a job at the University of Edinburgh's main campus library. She got her own happy ending when she married one of the sexiest men I'd ever met, Nate Sawyer. He was Cam's best friend.

The group was so tightly connected we were all like one big family.

"Work." I shrugged unhappily. "Being a probationer takes a lot out of me." It didn't help that Liv and Nate had moved farther outside of Edinburgh to a house that could accommodate their growing family. They had a four-year-old daughter, Lily, and a one-year-old daughter, January. "I take it Nate has the kids?"

"The men have all the kids." Joss grinned, coming toward me with a flute of Buck's Fizz. "Honey." She kissed my cheek affectionately. "It's good to see you."

"You too." I grinned suddenly at the imagery that had popped into my head. "Are all the guys together with the kids?"

Joss chuckled. "Yeah. They took them to the zoo."

I burst out laughing. "Four men and five young children. The guys are totally outnumbered."

Braden was dad to the almost-six-year-old Beth and three-year-old Luke. Joss was an American who had come to Edinburgh to study. Tragically, she'd lost her entire family when she was fourteen—her mother, Sarah, her father, Luke, and her baby sister, Beth. Sarah had been Scottish, so Joss decided to start over in her motherland. After graduation she moved in with Ellie, met Braden, and began an affair with him that quickly grew into so much more. They'd been married for seven years and were two of the happiest people I knew.

"We'll see who comes back in one piece," Joss muttered dryly.

After joking with them all for a bit, I could hear Mum calling me, so I hurried into the kitchen and gave her a hand sorting out the buffet.

We all settled in the sitting room, oohing and aahing over the presents and laughing when Jo threw the packet of condoms at me.

I let them all chat, sitting there, just enjoying the happy atmosphere and the excitement of the upcoming births. Jo and Ellie were both almost seven months pregnant. Neither wanted to know what the sex of the baby was, so everyone had mostly gone neutral with the presents.

A few hours later, a little buzzed from the Buck's Fizz and needing some water, I quietly disappeared into the kitchen. I was trailed by Joss.

"Hey." I smiled at her over my shoulder as I filled my glass with water from the fridge.

Joss gave me an appraising look. "You seem tired. Are you okay?"

"Late night. And I'm exhausted at the thought of another two babies," I said teasingly. "I'm not going to have a life with all the babysitting I'm going to be doing."

Joss groaned. "I hear you. After all the babysitting Jo and Cam have done for me, I'm going to have to reciprocate. Beth, Luke, *and* a baby? It's going to cripple me."

"Ach, let Braden do it."

Joss laughed, but a masculine voice called out, "Let Braden do what?"

We both turned to the doorway to see Braden towering inside it. In his arms was Luke and hurtling toward her mother was Beth.

"Mummy, I sat on a penguin!" she shrieked, throwing her arms around Joss's legs.

Joss caught her, but her eyes were wide on Braden.

He chuckled. "Not a real one."

"Oh, thank God." Joss reached down and lifted her skinny, tousled-haired girl into her arms. "I thought we had a lawsuit on our hands." She rubbed her nose against Beth's. "Did you have fun with the animals, honey?"

Beth nodded and turned her head to look at her dad. Whatever she was about to say was abruptly halted when she spotted me. "Hannah!" she squealed.

Beth immediately scrambled out of Joss's arms and threw herself at me, whereupon Joss walked over to kiss her son's head and her husband's lips. I bent down to catch Beth, who chattered to me excitedly as the noise level in the house rose. I heard what I could only imagine was baby January crying, and William giggling. Pushing past Joss's leg was the beautiful, dark-haired, olive-skinned Lily. She ran at Beth and me, a stuffed tiger dangling from her small hand.

I caught her too, as Braden and Joss moved out of the doorway to allow a harried-looking Nate into the room. When he saw me with Lily, he relaxed and threw Braden a relieved look. "I handed Jan over to Liv. She's the baby whisperer."

We heard sudden laughter coming from the sitting room.

"William." Braden smiled. "A comedian in the making."

"Hannah!" Beth pulled on my hand, drawing my attention back to her. "We saw lions."

"And tiggers, Nanna," Lily added softly, pronouncing my name the only way she knew how, before chewing on the paw of her stuffed toy.

"What the hell . . ." We heard a loud, familiar voice speaking in a tone of confusion and dismay. A few seconds later my little brother, Declan, came into the kitchen, his hand clasped in his girlfriend's. Dec was eighteen and had been dating Penny since he was sixteen. I wasn't as close with him as I'd like to be, but I think that had much to do with his age and the fact that he spent most of his time with Penny.

His eyes swept the room and he looked beyond flummoxed. "Is this Sunday?"

I laughed. He was referring to my mum's famous Sunday lunches. Not everyone could make Sunday lunch every week, but on the occasions we did, the house was loud and full to bursting. "No. It's Ellie and Jo's baby shower."

Dec grunted moodily. "As if we need more people in this family."

"Hey," Joss admonished, "you should be grateful you have this."

"Yeah, yeah." He gave her a half grin. "It'd just be nice to come home to an empty house every once in a while."

"Hmm." I stood up, holding on to the girls' tiny hands. "We all know why." I looked at Penny pointedly and then winked at my brother.

He rolled his eyes. "There's something seriously wrong with you." He gently nudged the ever quiet and now blushing Penny out the door. "We'll be upstairs."

"Don't do anything I *would* do!" I called after him as Braden, Nate, and Joss laughed.

Nate shook his head at me. "You're mean to him."

I made a mock-shocked face and looked down at the girls. "Do you hear that? Auntie Hannah isn't mean, is she?"

Beth shook her head adamantly, while Lily nodded, clearly confused by the question.

CHAPTER 3

The house was quiet once everyone but my little brother and Penny had scampered. Although there had been many offers to help Mum clean up, in the end I helped her shoo them out and I stayed behind to offer my services, despite the pile of marking waiting for me in my flat.

I was just putting away some newly washed and dried dishes when Mum said my name almost tentatively. Wary at her apprehensive tone, I turned around, my eyebrow raised in question.

She was fiddling a little nervously with a sponge she'd been using to wipe down the counters. "Your dad and I have something we need to ask you."

I sighed, crossing my arms over my chest. "If it's to help you get rid of another body I told you last time I was done with that."

Mum cracked a smile. "Funny," she said dryly. "No . . . well . . ."

"Come on, Mum, spit it out."

She blew out air between her lips. "I'm worried about telling you because I don't want you to feel like we're shoving you aside."

"See this?" I pointed to my face. "This is what 'confused' looks like."

Mum gave a small huff of laughter. "I'm trying to tell you we've turned your room into a nursery."

I shrugged. "Well, that makes sense. You have the kids staying over here more than I ever do."

Mum seemed to deflate. "You're not upset?"

"No, Mum." I laughed. "I'm a grown woman with a very nice flat just up the road. It even has a bedroom in it. Two, actually."

She rolled her eyes. "Make fun all you want, but I'm still your mother and you're still my baby and I didn't want you to feel like we were ousting you from the house. We've got a single bed in the nursery so you can stay whenever you need to, and of course at Christmastime."

Shaking my head at the unnecessary worry in her eyes, I walked over to her, arms outstretched, and pulled her into a tight hug. "I can't believe you were worrying over telling me this."

She melted into me. "It's what mums do."

After a while I pulled back. "I take it you didn't get rid of my stuff, though?"

"No. We boxed it up. I thought maybe you could go through it just now and decide what you want to keep and what you want to throw out."

I really should have been getting back home to start work, but Mum and Dad never asked much of me and I knew it would help them out if I got organized as quickly as possible. "Okay. Oh, Sunday lunch might be out for me tomorrow. Got a pile of marking."

"Oh, well, just leave the boxes for now, sweetheart."

"Nah." I waved her off, heading toward the stairs. "I was probably going to have to miss it anyway."

Although I knew I would be walking into a different room from the one I'd left behind, it surprisingly winded me a little to see the cream walls painted a warm buttercream yellow, to see that my double bed had been removed and replaced with a beautiful whitewashed cot and a single bed. The posters I'd left up on the walls were all down, the books I'd left were packed away, and the photographs of my friends were boxed up too.

I stared at the boxes stacked on the floor at the far end of the room. My childhood was inside them, my developing personality, my teen years. I smiled as I walked toward them.

An hour or so later I'd pushed aside boxes of clothes that could go to charity, Dad had returned home and come upstairs to say hello and leave me with a cup of tea and a biscuit, and I was just ripping open a box I assumed was filled with books because it was heavy.

I found some books inside, but I also found diaries. My heart thudded a little at the sight of them, and I lifted them out to put them aside, with no intention of reading them. Ever. I was just lowering them to the "to keep" pile when a photograph floated out of the leaves of a black journal from my later teen years.

My heart no longer thudded.

It pounded.

Eight years ago

My English teacher had held me back after class to talk about entering my short story in a local competition. The thought freaked me out. My writing . . . on display like that to people who would judge whether it was good enough or not? I said no, thanks.

So why was I kicking myself as I hurried out of the school entrance toward the gate? I glanced around, noting that nearly everyone was gone. I'd missed the bus. It looked like I was walking home.

I hung my head, heaving a sigh.

Why had I said no to Mrs. Ellis? If she thought the story was good enough for the competition I should have just gone for it. Ugh. Sometimes I hated being this shy. Sometimes I even wondered why I couldn't change that somehow. It didn't seem to be getting me anywhere.

Frustrated at myself, I moved through the gates, catching sight of three older boys kicking a football against the school wall and talking. I recognized one of them.

Marco.

I didn't know what his surname was because he was in fifth year and I was a third-year. I only knew of him because he was so popular his name had made its way down the years. And also because he was hard to miss. Really tall. Really good-looking. I'd heard he was foreign, but there were so many rumors flying around about where he was from, I didn't know for sure.

Looking away quickly so I didn't get spotted ogling him, I turned left and started heading for home. I'd taken only about four steps when my feet faltered on the fifth and sixth.

Up ahead, smoking, yelling, laughing, and swearing at one another were Jenks and his crew. They were in my year. We'd had first-year classes together, but things had changed, since we'd gotten to choose which classes we wanted to take as our high school careers progressed. My friends and I were smart and didn't care to pretend that we weren't. Jenks and his friends had picked on us since first year. To begin with it had just been in class, calling us "teacher's pet," "geeks," and "swots." Lately, because they couldn't get to us in class, they'd taken to verbally abusing us as we got on the bus, or when they saw us in the corridors. The verbal abuse had gotten slowly cruder and nastier.

I glanced up the road to make sure there weren't any cars coming, then dashed across the street to avoid the boys.

Unfortunately, Jenks wasn't in the mood to avoid me.

I was looking at my feet, head down, when I heard him yell my name.

As if it knew something I didn't, my heart started hammering hard against my ribs.

Looking up, I was filled with dread as a grinning Jenks casually swaggered across the street toward me, his two friends following him with nasty smirks on their faces.

"Whit's up, geek?" Jenks stopped in my path and I moved around him.

He grabbed my arm, pulling me to a stop.

I did my best not to show fear as he stepped into my personal space, his eyes moving down my body in a way that made me feel nauseous. "I said whit's up, geek?"

"Nothing." I shook my head and tried to move away, but the three of them blocked me. "Look, I'm late for home." I wished my voice were stronger. I wished I could set them down or beat them or just somehow get them to stop thinking they could intimidate me.

"We just want tae talk." Jenks sneered at me. "So fuckin' stuck up. But ye always were."

Jenks's friend Aaron punched him playfully in the arm. "She got fuckin' tasty, though. I'd shag it."

I blanched, taking a step back.

Jenks grunted, glaring at me. "She's still a fuckin' swot." He took a step toward me. "Maybe a guid pumpin' would loosin ye up, though, eh?" He reached a hand out to grab at my waist and I stepped out of range.

I felt the blood rush in my ears at the decidedly dark turn of their bullying. "I'm going home." I tried to inject authority into my voice, but the words came out in a trembling tone.

They laughed and Jenks grabbed for me again.

My shriek of alarm was immediately quieted at the sight of Jenks crashing like a rag doll into Aaron. They almost fell to the ground, only barely catching each other. Their other friend, Rube, stumbled back, too, and my eyes went from them to the person who had shoved Jenks.

My gaze traveled upward in surprise.

Towering over us all was Marco.

A very angry Marco.

His menacing glower was fixated on Jenks.

"Whit the fuck?" Jenks pushed himself off Aaron and scowled up at Marco. "Who the fuck dae ye think ye are?"

I was astounded that he'd be so aggressive with Marco. Even Rube and Aaron looked unsure.

"Get out of here," Marco said quietly, calmly, his words soft and rounded with an accent. "I see you try this shit again and you'll be dealing with me."

Jenks opened his mouth as if to fight, but Marco was suddenly flanked by two friends. Seeing they were definitely not going to win against the older boys, Jenks spat at Marco's feet and marched away, fists clenched at his sides.

I shuddered at my near escape.

"You missed the bus?"

Taken aback, I realized Marco had directed the question to me. His voice was *rough, gravelly. I stared up into his blue-green eyes, eyes that were startlingly beautiful against his dark lashes and caramel skin, and I forgot to breathe for a minute.*

He was gorgeous. And there was something about him . . . an aura around him that made me wish I were closer to him.

I nodded, still too awestruck to speak.

His eyebrows drew together. "Where do you live?"

Not awestruck enough to be stupid, I gave this person I didn't know a suspicious look. To my surprise his lips twitched like he wanted to laugh. He held up his hands as if in surrender. "I'm not going to hurt you."

Going with my gut instinct, I replied, "Stockbridge. St. Bernard's Crescent."

He glanced back at his friends. "I'll see you later."

They gave me curious looks but nodded and turned away, walking up the street in the opposite direction.

I was left standing in the street alone with Marco—alone with a six-foot-something seventeen-year-old boy after having been accosted by mean boys. I should have been afraid, but when our eyes met again, I felt the complete opposite. I felt safe.

"Come on," he said gruffly, walking past me.

Baffled by my feelings, I hurried to catch up to him. "What are you doing?"

"Walking you home. I don't trust those idiots not to come back. They bother you a lot?"

"At school sometimes. They pick on my friends and me, but they've never tried to . . ." I grew quiet. I couldn't quite say the words out loud. I actually couldn't believe they'd even threatened me with rape, much less that they might follow through.

I looked up at Marco to find him giving me a dark, warning look. "You need to be careful. Jenks is a soulless little shit. He shouldn't have been here. He's suspended from school."

"Really? For what?"

He studied me a moment before finally deciding to tell me. "The police are investigating him. He's been accused of raping a girl."

My mouth fell open as my heart sped up again. "Honestly? Why haven't I heard of this?"

Marco shrugged. "Don't know. Just be careful though, okay?"

I nodded. I would definitely be careful from now on. I felt a little sick.

We fell quiet as we walked side by side toward my house. I was tall for my age, but still nowhere near Marco's height. He was athletically built, with strong forearms showcased by his rolled-up shirtsleeves. His size made me feel strangely protected and, for the first time ever, dainty.

Intrigued by my brooding would-be rescuer, I found that my curiosity overcame the self-consciousness I usually felt around people I didn't know. I tucked my short blond hair behind my ears and looked up at him again.

"Where are you from? America or Canada?"

Marco looked down at me, bemusement in his expression. "Most folks just assume I'm American."

There was a question in his tone, so I answered, "I read a lot and, well, you know, a lot of Scottish people immigrated to Canada, so it would make cultural sense that you might be a Scottish-Canadian."

He studied me, a small smile playing in the corners of his mouth. "How old are you?"

"Fourteen."

"You're pretty smart."

I grinned at him. "That's what they tell me."

This made Marco laugh. Triumph swelled in my chest. I'd never seen him laugh and felt sure he didn't do it often, since there was something kind of sad in the back of his eyes. "You look older than fourteen." His gaze flicked over me quickly. "You're not in any of my classes, so I knew you had to be younger. I didn't think that much younger, though."

I liked that he thought I looked older. I didn't like the fact that he thought fourteen was young. Technically, I was fourteen and a half. I wanted to say that to him but was afraid it might come off as childish. I pondered how to casually slip it into conversation but came up blank.

Realizing we hadn't spoken for at least thirty seconds, I said, "So . . . are you Canadian?"

"Nah. American. Depending on the area, a Canadian accent is different from an American accent. And then there are different accents in different places in the U.S. You just have to listen carefully. I'm from Chicago."

Soaking up this new information, I replied, "That's really cool."

He shrugged, shoving his hands into his trouser pockets.

"Why did you move here?"

Marco was quiet so long I didn't think he was going to answer. I was feeling an irrational amount of disappointment over that when he suddenly said, "My grandparents sent me to live with my uncle and his wife."

That one sentence told me a lot without really telling me anything. I guessed that meant his parents weren't in the picture, and that made me wonder why. The sad possibilities made me feel bad for him. I also wondered why he'd been sent away. Sensing that the first question might upset him more than the second, I went with the latter.

"Did you get into a lot of trouble there?"

He raised an eyebrow at me. "Are you writing my biography?"

Having been surrounded by sarcastic adults my whole life, I was immune to any kind of teasing. I stared him straight in the eye. "So what if I am?"

Marco smirked at my response. "Yeah. I was getting in trouble. They thought it might be better for me here."

"And is it?"

He shrugged again, a small frown furrowing his brow.

Realizing he didn't want to talk about it, I changed the subject. "Your name is Marco, right?"

"D'Alessandro. I see my reputation precedes me," he replied, a wry little smile on his perfect lips.

It occurred to me that Marco didn't talk like the kind of boys he hung around with at school. And it wasn't about his accent. I'd overheard them enough to know that they took pride in being rough in speech, sometimes overplaying Scottish slang and swearing so much their mothers' ears would have bled if they'd ever overheard them. They avoided sounding intelligent, whether deliberately or as a consequence of a collective lack of brain cells.

"Not to sound like a bitch or anything, but I don't think I've heard anyone in the crowd you hang with use a word like 'precede.' "

He grunted. "One of us needs to know how to read and write. You never know when crime might involve those basic tools of communication."

Although he was joking, I could hear the edge in his tone and felt stupid. "Sorry. That sounded really judgmental."

"Maybe. But I guess you're not wrong." He slid me a look and it was as if he saw right through me. "Some of us aren't great at school. I'm not great at school."

Another question popped into my head; I couldn't help myself. I'd never been so curious about anyone before. Then again, I'd never gotten butterflies from just being in someone's presence before. "What are you great at?"

A cloud passed over his features. "I don't know."

"You must be good at something," I insisted. I couldn't imagine that Marco didn't have some kind of talent. There was just something so special about him. I didn't even know what it was, but I knew it. I just knew it.

"Design and tech."

I stared at his hands, feeling somewhat envious. I'd been rubbish in design and tech. I tried to make a Perspex clock in the shape of a star and it ended up looking like . . . well . . . a star that had been in a car crash. My metal coat pegs almost caused me a fatality of the thumb and my wooden pencil case didn't close correctly. "You must be really good at it to be taking it in fifth year."

He didn't say anything, just scowled at a leaf that skittered by on the pavement.

Hmm. "So what do you want to be?"

He shot a quizzical look my way. "What do you want to be?"

"It changes every few months," I answered in consternation. My friends all knew what they wanted to be when they were older. I still hadn't made up my mind between a writer, a teacher, a doctor, or a librarian. "I really need to focus."

"Maybe you should be a reporter."

I snorted at his teasing. "The twenty questions? Right. Sorry."

"It doesn't bother me." His eyebrows drew together, as if he were surprised by his own confession.

Encouraged, I jumped to my next question. "D'Alessandro? Like the restaurant?" There was an Italian restaurant with that name, only a five-minute walk from my house.

"It's my uncle's."

"Great food," I said honestly.

Again, he didn't respond.

I got the feeling he didn't want to chat about anything related to family. "I heard the pizza in Chicago is the best."

That received a grin. "You heard right."

"Do you miss your friends there?"

He was quiet again, so I thought he wasn't going to answer this one either. I was thinking it was a no-go on any really personal questions, but then . . . "I didn't really have friends. Not good ones anyway."

Our footsteps slowed as we found ourselves on my street. I squinted against the sunlight peeking through a cloud as I looked up at him. "I hope you've found good ones here."

When he looked at me my heart almost puttered to a stop at the warmth in his eyes. "You got a name?" he asked softly.

I shivered, not understanding my body's reaction to him. "Hannah Nichols."

He smiled, drawing to a stop to hold out his large hand.

Feeling the butterflies riot in my belly, I determinedly ignored them and placed my small hand in his. I tried to hide my reaction to the tingling that shot up my arm from where we touched. I wanted to tighten my grip and had to mentally stop myself from doing so.

"Nice to meet you, Hannah."

"You too. Thanks for helping me out with Jenks. And for walking me home."

"Not a problem." He let go of my hand and I instantly bemoaned the loss of his touch. He took a step back, preparing to leave, but I grew still at the suddenly stern expression on his face. "Try not to miss the bus again."

He disappeared down the street before I could say anything, and I stared after his broad back, feeling so many things I'd never felt before.

After walking into my house, only to spend the evening distracted, I came to one conclusion: I had my first crush. On Marco D'Alessandro.

I should have joined the debate team. I shook my head, marching toward the main exit of the school and cursing my shyness to hell. At the beginning of the year my politics teacher had asked me to join the school debate team, and because I was sure I'd never be able to speak up and articulate in person what I was so good at saying on paper, I'd turned the offer down.

Now I'd missed the bus because I'd come across the team working in an empty music classroom and had stopped to listen to them. I'd been filled with the sudden urge to just stride in, introduce myself, and start airing my opinions. I had loads of opinions inside of me. I also had this fear that one day they'd just explode out of me, wreaking havoc and leaving disaster in their wake.

There were so many things I was missing out on because of how damn quiet I was. And in truth, I wasn't really that quiet anymore. I said what I thought at home, consequences be damned.

I frowned back in the direction of the school as I opened the exit door. It was definitely time for a change. I could feel it coming.

With a sigh of regret, I hurried forward, my eyes searching out Marco and finding him waiting alone by the gate for me.

For whatever reason, over the past year Marco had waited at the gate most days, watching me get on the bus. There had been several times I'd been late and he'd walked me home. Most of those times my lateness was not my fault, but I do admit to being deliberately late a few times in the last couple of months just so I could be around him.

I was addicted to the feeling inside me when we were together, or even when I was thinking about him—and I thought about him a lot. He didn't make me feel like a shy, awkward nerd. And to my delighted surprise, I discovered that I could make Marco—this boy who was definitely prone to brooding—laugh. He laughed at my jokes and teasing and he constantly remarked on how smart I was, as if it was something to respect rather than to mock. When I looked at him, my belly would flip, my pulse would race, and I'd get this delicious tingling all over my body.

I wanted him to kiss me so badly.

I couldn't tell if he felt the same way. I was fifteen now and five foot nine. Boys at school had started paying me more attention since I'd grown boobs and my hips had filled out. But I didn't know if Marco had noticed those things.

He'd surprised me over the last year. He wasn't the most talkative person on the planet, but he was patient with my questions even if he didn't answer a lot of them. He let me chat about the books I was reading and the music I was listening to and actually seemed interested when I did.

He'd also been there for me when I told him about the time my family went through one of its most difficult situations. When I was thirteen my big sister, Ellie, was diagnosed with a brain tumor, and although it turned out to be benign, the whole thing scared the crap out of us all. As had the brain surgery she'd had to have. I'd never really talked about it with anyone, or the effect it had on me, but Marco listened to me and somehow managed to give me comfort in his silence.

As well as discovering that he was a great confidant, I'd also discovered that he wasn't as terrible at school as he'd made out. Although some of his friends found themselves in trouble at school, Marco was quiet and kept out of the drama. His height and broad build had made other students wary of him. His good looks and the fact that he was American had made him popular. And his brooding intensity had given him a reputation for being utterly cool, and so all these things combined had garnered him respect. I knew he wasn't a typical bad boy, no matter what rumors I heard. He studied and he worked with a tutor. He'd passed his exams last year, excelling in design and tech, maths, and P.E. He had an English tutor and his grades were passable.

"Why were you late this time?" he asked, falling into step beside me.

I shrugged, not really wanting to talk about the fact that I was failing at life. "Should I be worried?"

The fact that he might care enough to be concerned for me made me feel all squishy and warm inside. I gave him a soft smile. "No."

His eyebrows rose. "You're really not going to tell me?"

I chuckled, kicking a stone out of my way. "You don't tell me stuff."

Marco seemed to process this. "Well, what do you want to know?"

Deciding that today was a good day to try to be brave, I asked, "Why don't you talk about your family?"

He gave me a look as if to say, "I should have known you'd go there." "I don't really get along with them," he admitted.

"All of them?" Since I came from a close family, the idea that Marco was estranged from his didn't sit well with me. I knew how happy my family made me. I wanted Marco to be equally happy.

"Nonna, maybe—my grandma," he replied. "Not Nonno—my grandfather. And not my uncle Gio. His wife is nice. Him, not so much."

I didn't like the sound of that at all and I wanted to know more, but this was more information than I'd gotten out of him in the past, so I decided not to push my luck. "I'm late because I was listening in on the debate team. My politics teacher asked me to join at the beginning of the year. I said no and now I wish I hadn't. I need to grow some balls, Marco." I sighed.

"You've already got them. You just to need use them. This supposed shyness of yours is all in your head."

"And how did you get so smart?"

Marco gave a short bark of laughter and drew to a halt. I stopped with him, my eyes widening slightly as he stared at me intently. "You're the first person to ever say that to me." He shook his head. "I'm not smart, Hannah."

Ignoring the shiver that chased down my spine as it did anytime he said my name, I gave him a disapproving look and skirted around him to sit down on the steps of the Georgian apartment building we were outside of. I looked up at him, my expression completely serious. "You don't have to be book smart to be clever, Marco."

Marco stared down at me for a few seconds and then sighed as he lowered his tall body onto the step next to me. His arm brushed mine and heat rushed up it, exploding through me. My cheeks flushed furiously, but Marco didn't notice. He *gazed out into the street, seeming lost in thought. Finally he asked quietly, "And you think I'm clever?"*

"Yes," I answered without hesitating.

I did think he was clever. And talented. And so much more than he even realized.

His lips twitched. "I don't think I've said anything clever to you."

"You have a dry, clever sense of humor. You get my jokes," I cracked, nudging him with my arm. While he smiled at me in return, I continued. "You always think before you speak. Some of the most intelligent people in the world haven't learned how to do that."

His eyes washed over me and my insides dipped like I was on a roller coaster. We'd never been this close to each other before.

"I bet your parents tell you you're smart all the time," he muttered.

"Yeah, they want me to believe in myself."

"That's good. You should believe in yourself."

I made an impulsive decision right at that moment and my palms began to sweat as the blood rushed in my ears. "I think believing in yourself means having to be brave sometimes."

Before Marco could reply to that, I leaned forward and pressed my lips against his. My heart was slamming so hard in my chest I could barely hear anything over the sound of its beating. Marco stiffened beneath my kiss, but I didn't pull back. Instead I put more pressure behind it. Seconds later, I felt the heat of Marco's hand on my waist and his lips moved against mine.

I didn't have time to feel relieved or triumphant because he was kissing me back, taking control of the kiss, and sending my hormones into overdrive. My skin was flushed, my lips tingling, and all I wanted was to sink deeper into him and feel his hands all over my body.

My hands suddenly had a life of their own, one coming to rest on his knee, while the other cupped the nape of his neck.

He squeezed my waist and I sighed involuntarily, my lips parting on the sound. Almost instantly I felt the touch of Marco's tongue against mine, and the surprising bolt of lust that hit me between the legs made me stiffen in shock.

Just like that, I found myself pushed away as Marco abruptly stood up.

I looked up at him, panting for breath, watching him rub his hands over his short, dark hair and drag them down over his face. Then he dropped his hands and his taut features were revealed to me as he lowered his incredulous gaze.

Before I could say a word Marco strode down the steps and disappeared up the street.

CHAPTER 4

The fourth-year class erupted into boisterous conversation as soon as the bell rang. Chairs scraped against the wooden floor, jotters were stuffed into backpacks, and friends who had been separated in my seating plan reunited as they headed toward the door.

I had finished a year of teacher training at the beginning of the summer, and now I was two months into my probation year. Once this year ended, I'd be fully qualified. After that came the really hard part—finding a permanent teaching position.

I felt confident that I knew what I was doing, but every now and then someone would remind me I was just starting out and there would be this moment of panic. I couldn't let that kind of self-doubt win, and I definitely couldn't let it show. Kids were like predators—show a sign of weakness and they'd take you down.

My eyes caught Jarrod Fisher's as he lazily put away his things. His friends, two of my problem kids in this class, stood by his desk, waiting on him. From what I had heard they followed Jarrod's example, but in my class Jarrod wasn't a nuisance, though his friends were obnoxious brats. I'd heard stories from the other teachers, however, that Jarrod could be a menace. He swore, he talked back, and he disrupted lessons.

I wondered what was causing him to clash with those teachers. I got his cheeky side, but never an aggressive manner.

"Jarrod, may I speak with you, please?" I asked, and then gestured to his friends to leave the room along with the rest of the students.

As per usual they ignored me, looking to their ringleader.

As per usual I didn't let that fly. "Boys. Out. Now."

The boys threw me dirty looks but turned and walked out of the classroom. Jarrod stood up, stretching out his tall body. He grabbed his backpack and came over to me slowly, a small smirk playing on his lips. At fifteen he was already well over six feet. With his dark skin and light eyes he'd reminded me of a certain someone from my past the moment he'd entered my class. After I discovered the photo two nights ago, that resemblance seemed somehow more pronounced. Of course, Jarrod was less brooding, but perhaps just as angry underneath his cocky charm. Sometimes it was difficult not to wonder what caused that anger in a boy so young. Sometimes it was difficult to try not to care about that and just teach him English.

"What's up, Miss Nichols?" He slouched against my desk, completely at ease with me.

"I'll be handing back the first draft of your personal essays tomorrow, but I wanted you to know that you did exceptionally well." I studied him, knowing there was more to this cocky boy than met the eye. There had to be. I knew that after reading such a wonderful essay about his little brother. "You're very insightful, Jarrod."

His eyes widened slightly. "Seriously?"

"I've written notes. You can look it over tomorrow. I just wanted you to know that I enjoyed it." I gave him a knowing look. "If you would work like that in all your classes, you'd do well. You should start thinking about university."

The spark that had lit in his eyes at my praise died, but he offered me a cheeky smile. "And why would I do that? That'd be no challenge for the teachers."

I gave him a look of reproach. "Jarrod."

He shrugged. "They piss me off. Mr. Rutherford does it deliberately. I'm not going to sit there and take it."

I didn't know if that was true or not, but since Mr. Rutherford, a maths teacher, rubbed me the wrong way whenever we crossed paths, I couldn't find the words to disagree with Jarrod.

Instead I went with, "Don't swear. And don't let anyone stand in the way of your future. You're a really smart kid. You should do something with it."

"If you say so, Miss Nichols."

"I do say so. Maybe the other teachers would as well if you'd stop smart-arsing them."

He cocked his head to the side. "Did *you* just swear?" he teased.

Knowing I'd be in trouble if he decided to report me, I cursed myself inwardly. Sometimes it was hard to separate teaching the kids and volunteering with the adults. When I swore in front of my literacy class it was no big deal. Swearing in front of youngsters? Not so professional. I shook my head in innocence. "I don't recall doing so, no."

Jarrod laughed. "Look, the other teachers aren't like you. They're immune to my charm. That's the problem. End of story."

"Oh, Jarrod." I gave him a mock-pitying look. "I'm not charmed by you. You *aren't* that charming. What I am is pleasantly surprised by your abilities."

"Whatever you say, Miss." He winked at me and then swaggered out of the room as if life was one big joke. It was all a pretense. I saw through his crap.

Although I felt we had a rapport, I did worry about whether my advice and encouragement were penetrating the barriers he had built up around himself. I knew all about building walls. Sometimes you needed those walls to keep folks out because letting them in broke down the glue that was holding essential pieces of yourself together . . . but there were times when you needed to learn when to let those walls down, to let people in because *they* were the glue that held you together.

Perhaps I'd have a better chance at getting through to Jarrod if I were better at recognizing the difference myself. I'd learned quite young that there was a massive divide between theory and practice.

Sometimes I just couldn't quite pull myself out of theory.

I had my reasons.

I reached down for my bag, ready to pack up and return home to do my marking there. Shoving a folder into the large handbag, I heard a crinkle and knew exactly what had happened. I'd crumpled the photograph.

Hands shaking, I reached in and tugged at the photo, pulling it out and smoothing it flat with the tips of my fingers. Why had I kept it? Why had I brought it to school?

Staring at the photograph of me—the younger, cockier, romantic sixteen-year-old me—as I smiled into the camera for the selfie I'd taken with my friend Marco, the boy I'd fallen for hard, I wondered not for the first time where that version of me had gone.

It was funny . . . I sometimes wondered if I lost her because of Marco, and yet I think I hadn't found her until I met him.

I couldn't explain how I knew there was something wrong when Marco texted me to meet him. It's not like he hadn't done that before. I'd met him several times at a library to help him with his Higher English work—a course he didn't need to take because he already had an apprenticeship with a joiner in Edinburgh. That didn't seem to be enough for Marco, though. It was like he was challenging himself, trying to prove to himself he could do what other people told him he couldn't. He'd surprised me over the last year and a half with his quiet determination.

It wasn't always about schoolwork. Sometimes he texted me to meet him at a shop or a restaurant only to spend the next few hours wandering the streets of Edinburgh with him, me chattering away while he mostly listened. That kiss, that impulsive kiss, so long ago was never discussed. He'd avoided me for a month after that kiss. But kissing him and being rejected had actually been somewhat liberat-

ing. Okay, it hurt like hell and I felt humiliated, but after a while I began to realize that the world hadn't ended. I'd done something for me, something brave, and I'd made it out okay. It had changed my perspective. I spoke up in class now, and I stood up for myself and for my friends against petty name-calling. I entered my short story in the junior writing competition my English teachers had urged me toward, and I joined the debate team.

That was sort of why Marco started speaking to me again. I, of course, missed the bus after my first meeting with the team, and when I walked outside, there he was. He never said a word to me about the kiss. He just pretended like it had never happened.

As long as I got to spend time with him, though, I was able to shove my disappointment deep down inside myself.

Usually I was filled with excitement when on my way to meet him. However, this time I was filled with a sense of foreboding as I walked in the early dusk toward Douglas Gardens.

The small gardens that ran alongside the Water of Leith were empty. Except for the large figure sitting on a bench.

"Marco?" I asked quietly.

He gave me a nod as I approached, and as I got closer his features came into better focus, as did the red swelling under his left eye. I sucked in a breath and hurried toward him, sitting down close. Without thinking I reached a hand toward his face, my fingertips tracing the skin just underneath the developing bruise.

"What happened?"

He looked lost. I felt a painful ache in my chest for him. "Some people are afraid of me. Because of my height, my build, the rumors, my reputation." His mouth quirked up at the corner in disdain. "And some see it as a challenge. Me as a challenge."

Infuriated for him, I lowered my hand to rest on his shoulder. "What did your uncle say when he saw?"

Marco snorted. "Hannah, who do you think did this?"

I didn't know what I wanted to do more: cry for him, or bring a world of pain down on his uncle. There would never come a time when I would understand how an adult could abuse a child under their protection because I'd never known anything but absolute love and devotion. I knew Cole had suffered at the hands of his mother and Jo at the hands of her father. I'd felt helpless upon hearing that. I felt helpless again.

"Has he . . . has he done this before?"

He shook his head. "And probably never will again. Aunt Gabby went ballistic at him. She told him she'd leave him if he ever touched me again."

I squeezed his shoulder. "I like your aunt Gabby."

That got a smile out of him. "Yeah, she's cool."

"Did you tell your grandparents what he did?"

"Hannah—" He smiled sadly. "Nonno pretty much hates me. He could give a crap. I was bad news in Chicago. I hung around guys that were getting into really ugly stuff. That's why my grandparents sent me away."

Intrigued, I leaned forward. "Why do you think your granddad hates you?"

My mum's dad had died before I was born, but my dad's father was still alive and he always showered me with love the few times a year I got to see him. I couldn't understand a grandparent hating his grandchild.

"I'm half African American. My Italian grandfather can't stand the fact that his precious daughter slept with a black guy."

My lips parted in shock. "He's racist?"

Marco shrugged. "My dad could have been Japanese, Jewish, or Mexican and it would have pissed Nonno off. What mattered was that my dad wasn't Italian and my parents weren't married when my mother got pregnant. Nonno is really old-fashioned and a total traditionalist."

You could call it whatever you wanted. There was no excuse for mistreating a child ever, and for it to be based on simple genetics? I was furious for Marco. "Was he awful to you?"

Marco shrugged again, but this time he met my gaze when he said, "My mom pretty much disowned my dad and my grandparents wouldn't let him near me. He gave up, took off before I was even one. My mom stuck around for a few years, but she couldn't take being a mom. She was only seventeen when she had me. And she couldn't take the fact that her dad, who she'd once idolized, couldn't stand the sight of her and the massive disappointment she represented. So she took off too. Left me with them."

My stomach felt heavy. "How bad was it?"

He looked me straight in the eye and I knew by his expression he wasn't going to tell me. By not telling me, though, he left my imagination to work overtime and I felt nothing aside from fury at his grandfather and a need to protect Marco. "Nonna's great. She tried to make up for . . . everything else. And most of the Italian side of the family are great. Unfortunately, I didn't get to live with them."

"So you got in trouble and they sent you here to your uncle?"

He nodded, a scowl forming on his handsome face. "My mom's big brother. My aunt Gabby is Scottish Italian, but her dad is originally from Chicago. She came for a visit years ago and my uncle Gio fell for her. They came up with the idea for the restaurant, her parents had capital, he moved here with her, and D'Alessandro's was born."

Silence fell between us and I suddenly felt awkward touching him. I dropped my hand and settled back against the bench. My eyes moved down the long sprawl of his legs, and I thought that if he'd wanted to, Marco could have fought back. He didn't. Out of respect or refusal to be brought down to his uncle's level, I didn't know. I just knew it made me care about him even more.

"Is this why you texted me?" My voice sounded loud in the darkening gardens.

"Nah. I texted you to hang out with me. To talk."

I laughed softly. "You? Talk?"

I felt warm all over at the sight of his grin. "I talk. I just did, didn't I?"

"I suppose. But you're really more of a listener."

"Whatever." He shook his head at me, still grinning.

Wanting to keep him smiling, I attempted some easier conversation. "Well, you said talk, so I'm going to make you talk more."

"Yeah?"

I nodded, turning to the side and stretching my arm out along the back of the bench. Marco shifted slightly, turning his body in toward mine. "Let me see . . . okay. What's your favorite song?"

"'Dirt Off Your Shoulder'—Jay Z."

I burst out laughing and his smile widened. "You're lying."

He shrugged.

"Seriously? Favorite song?"

Marco sighed, rubbing his hand over his head. He seemed almost self-conscious as he replied, "'Hurt' by Nine Inch Nails."

"I've never heard of it." But I'd definitely be YouTube-ing it when I got home.

"It's good. Real, you know." He shifted again so he was sitting to the side, facing me. "Nonna's neighbor died and her son inherited the house. He was a big Nine Inch Nails fan. He'd blast that music, pissing off Nonno and half the neighborhood. Nonno sent me over one afternoon when I was twelve to tell the guy to shut it off. But when I got there 'Hurt' was playing. I'd never really paid that much attention to lyrics until that moment. Didn't get how they could be like a letter someone wrote to you . . . to let you know you weren't alone."

For some reason this brought tears to my eyes. I'd never wanted to protect someone the way I wanted to protect him. I thought if he saw, he would resent it. But sitting there with him, looking into his eyes as he looked into mine, I knew Marco could discern how I felt about him. And for once he didn't walk away. Instead, his expression softened, his eyes warmed, and he asked, "What's your favorite song?"

I beat back the wetness in my eyes and smiled. "I grew up listening to Bob Dylan. My mum's a huge fan. Have you listened to him?"

Marco shook his head. "Not really."

"'Blowin' in the Wind.' That's my favorite song. It's kind of a sad song, but it doesn't remind me of sad times. It reminds me of day trips to the Highlands with the whole family, or lazing around on a Saturday afternoon, just Mum and me. I suppose sometimes it's the memories associated with the song rather than the song itself that makes it a favorite."

"That sounds cool. I'm glad you have a cool family, Hannah. You deserve that."

I frowned at the seeming insinuation behind his words. "So do you, Marco."

When he didn't reply, I pushed the frustration over not being able to help him with his family life aside, and asked, "Favorite movie?"

I saw his cheek lift into a smile again and I relaxed. "Training Day."

"I haven't seen it."

"We'll fix that oversight. What about you?"

"My favorite movie? Or my real favorite movie?"

He chuckled. "Both."

"The movie I tell everyone is my favorite is Dead Poets Society. *It's a great movie, but it's really my mum's favorite movie."*

"And yours?"

I felt my cheeks heat a little. "Okay, you can't tell anyone."

He laughed. "How bad is this?"

"It's Finding Nemo."

Marco grinned. "It's not that bad."

"Out of all the movies of all time, I choose Finding Nemo. *An animation," I reminded him.*

He shrugged. "I chose Training Day. *It's not what everyone else holds up as a great movie—your favorite movie is one you enjoy a lot. A movie you can watch over and over again because for whatever reason you get something out of it."*

"You're right. You're completely right. From now on I'm owning up to Finding Nemo."

"Oh, I never said that," he teased. "Keep that shit to yourself until you're out of high school."

"Hey!" I punched him playfully on the arm and he burst out laughing. Watching him, knowing I'd lifted his mood, made me feel like someone had wrapped us up in a warm cocoon. The connection between us had strengthened. "Next question. Favorite book?"

Marco grimaced comically. "Like I read."

"You've at least read something, right?"

He laughed and deflected the question. "What's your favorite book?"

"To Kill a Mockingbird."

Something I didn't understand glittered in the back of his eyes. "Nice choice."

"Aha, you've read it!"

Marco smiled and shrugged.

"I don't know if shrugging constitutes an answer where you come from, Chicago Boy, but here it doesn't qualify."

"Them be a whole lot of big words, smart girl. Ma small brain ain't be knowing what yer talkin' about."

I burst out into surprised laughter. Marco was often sarcastic and he enjoyed the ironic, but this side of him, this joking side of him, was rare to see. "Stop avoiding the question."

I waited for him to stop grinning. As the smile slipped from his face, there was something new and intense in his expression. Our eyes held and the air thickened between us. "To Kill a Mockingbird," he told me softly.

His confession seared me to my very soul. It might not seem like something to anyone else that we shared the same favorite book but right then, in the growing dark, it felt like everything.

"If you could go on the perfect date, where would it be?" What I really wanted to ask was who it would be with.

I knew the question would cause him some unease, but I think that's what I was pushing for. Pushing for answers about what was between us.

His brows drew together as he looked down at me. "I told you I don't date," he replied quietly.

The answer was unsurprising, but still I felt a pang of disappointment.

"You?" Marco did surprise me by asking.

I gave him a small smile. Perfect date. With him. Where? "It sounds really cheesy, but I remember reading this teen romance Ellie gave me and it was about this girl who meets a real-life prince and it's completely fantastical and utterly stupid really." I laughed nervously. "There's so many obstacles between them, but there's this scene where he takes her to this tiny cottage on his land, away from everything and everyone. They sit in front of a roaring fire, drinking and eating, sometimes talking, sometimes not. It was like there was no one else in the world but them and I don't know . . ." I trailed off, feeling my cheeks flush with embarrassment.

The heavy silence fell between us again.

"Why did you really ask me to meet you tonight, Marco?" I whispered, breaking it.

For once he didn't avoid the question. "Because," he whispered back, "when I'm with you it feels like everything's going to be okay. I can't explain it."

My pulse throbbed at his overwhelming confession and somehow my voice came out steady and soft. "You don't have to."

"That film was so rubbish," Sadie complained as we walked out of the theater and into the lobby of the cinema. "Such a boy movie."

"You were the one that voted with the guys on what film to go see," I reminded her.

"Yeah, because I want them to like me," she said in a "duh" voice, as though it should be obvious to me to change who I was in order to suit a boy. Ugh. Please.

If this was what being popular was all about, you could stick it.

Fifth year at high school was turning out a lot different than my last few years. My old friends had become scarce as I'd opened up and grown more confident, and my new friends were outgoing—they participated in a lot of extracurricular activities at school, but mostly they were utterly, completely, and totally boy crazy.

I was only crazy for one boy, but he'd graduated.

"Eh, Hannah?" Kieran, one of the guys in our group, walked over to me, looking a little nervous. "Can I talk to you?" He nodded toward a corner where we'd have a little privacy.

Sadie grinned mischievously. My stomach dropped a little when I realized where this was going.

Reluctantly, I followed Kieran over to the corner.

He stuffed his hands in his pockets, looked back at our friends, and then turned to me with a shaky smile. "So . . . I was, eh . . . I was wondering if you wanted to go out with me sometime?"

Crap. I hated this. I hated rejecting anybody. "Oh, Kieran, I'm really flattered." I smiled with a shrug. "But I think we should just be friends."

He frowned. "That's it?"

I nodded, wondering what else I was supposed to say.

He made this snorting, huffy sound and turned on his heel, striding angrily back to the guys. Whatever he said had them looking over at me in puzzlement.

I gritted my teeth, two seconds from deciding to walk away from every single one of them, when Sadie came hurrying over. She looked pissed off.

"What is your problem?" she asked, arms crossed over her chest. "Three of the guys have asked you out in the last two months, Hannah, and you've said no to every single one of them. They think you're a lesbian."

I rolled my eyes. "Of course they do. It's easier to believe that than the fact that I don't fancy any of them."

"Kieran is hot." Sadie pouted. "Do you think you're too good for him?"

Why were we friends again? "No. I just . . . I think I like older boys." It was mostly true and I was hoping it would get her off my back.

Thankfully, this was the right move. It was something Sadie could understand. Her expression cleared and she was just about to open her mouth to say something when a tall, familiar figure caught my attention.

My heart immediately started pounding.

Standing by the window, near the escalators, was Marco. My eyes followed the broad planes of his shoulders, then moved upward to his profile. My heart raced harder, a sharp ache piercing my chest as I realized he had a girl pinned against the railing near the window. The pain intensified as he bent his head to kiss the girl.

Really, really kiss her.

I think my heart shattered into a million pieces.

I looked at the floor, attempting to unsee things while I tried to catch my breath.

Marco and I had kept in touch since he'd graduated and moved on to Edinburgh College. He was working part-time at his apprenticeship while he did the carpentry and joinery course. I knew this because we still hung out. We talked on Facebook, texted each other, and every now and then he'd call me and I'd go meet him somewhere, like I'd done that night at Douglas Gardens. Nothing romantic ever happened, and he never said anything as sweet to me again as he had that night, but I had been beginning to hope the sexual tension I felt between us was mutual. I was sixteen now. Guys told me I was pretty and I knew I looked older than a lot of the girls my age because of my height and my figure. I was hoping Marco would see me differently. But nothing had changed.

I wasn't stupid. I knew there were other girls, because some of them had bragged at school about hooking up with him.

It was different seeing it with my very own eyes, though.

Sadie snapped her fingers in front of my nose. "Did you not hear me?"

I blinked, trying to breathe through the pain of unrequited torturous idiotic love. "What?" I asked sharply.

"I said I heard a rumor that Scott Wilder fancies you. He's older."

"Scott Wilder? The sixth-year?"

Sadie nodded excitely. "He told his friend Jamie and Jamie is Amanda Eaton's big brother. Jamie told Amanda, who told Vicky, and Vicky told me. Scott is so hot, Hannah. You'd be so lucky!"

And so it was with the burn of disappointment in my gut that I found myself saying, "Yeah. He is."

Sadie's eyes widened. "Oh, my God! I'm totally telling Vicky to tell Amanda."

Disappointment turned to anger, and I lifted my gaze and looked over at Marco as he put his arm around his date and walked her onto the escalator. "Don't bother," I told her. "I'll friend Scott on Facebook. We'll go from there."

I swore Mum and Dad to secrecy when I told them I was going out on a date. My family—as in Braden and Adam—could get really overprotective and I didn't know how they would react to the fact that I was dating. To my surprise, Mum and Dad were okay with it, and despite Dad's glaring an alarming amount at Scott when he picked me up for our date, they acted cool enough about the whole thing. Well, Mum did.

"You look great." Scott beamed at me as we walked away from my house.

It didn't feel right using Scott to get over Marco, but we'd talked a little lately and Scott actually seemed like a really nice guy. And I'd have to be dead to think he wasn't hot. He was good-looking and he was taller than me. That was always *a plus. I'd decided to give tonight a real shot and since he was taking me to D'Ales-sandro's for dinner, I also decided to dress up a little. I was wearing a shift dress that came to just above my knees and I'd looped a belt around my waist to give my figure definition. Heels would have worked with the look, but I'd gone with flats so I didn't end up towering over Scott. It felt a little strange going to Marco's uncle's restaurant for my first date, but since he didn't have a great relationship with his uncle, I knew there was no chance of bumping into him.*

"Thanks. You too." And he did look good. He was wearing a pair of suit trousers, a shirt, and a waistcoat. Very dapper.

He grinned at me and I wished, oh, how I wished, it had made my stomach flip like Marco's grin always did. "I've wanted to ask you out for ages."

I smiled. "Well, here we are."

"You're not like other girls, Hannah. You're so confident and smart and gorgeous. It's a little intimidating."

I made a face. "Believe me, I'm not intimidating."

Scott didn't look convinced.

I didn't want anyone putting me on a pedestal. Ever. "Okay. I snore." I nod-ded in earnest. "I can't lie flat on my back if I'm sleeping in company because of it. And not normal snoring. It's this weird, breathy kind of snoring that's almost as annoying as elephant snoring. I know because my sister once recorded a video of me on her phone. I've been afraid to sleep in a room with another human being since."

He threw his head back laughing, just as I'd intended him to do.

"When I was little I called my dad's great aunt Virginia Aunt Vagina the whole time we were visiting her. My parents were mortified and had no idea how to explain my inappropriate error to me, so I pretty much called her that until I understood the difference."

By this time Scott was choking on laughter. We reached the restaurant and he held up his hands in surrender. "Okay, I'm no longer intimidated."

"Good." I smiled at him as he held the door open for me and we stepped into the warmth of the restaurant.

Scott gave his name to the hostess and she led us through the front dining room and into the back dining room to a cozy table for two.

There was a little awkwardness when we sat down so I resorted to my fallback—teasing. "So, cradle snatcher, how does it feel to be on a date with a sixteen-year-old?"

"It helps that she doesn't look sixteen. And anyway, a little birdie told me you're seventeen soon."

"In a few months."

"We'll be seventeen together then. Late birthday," he explained. "I don't turn eighteen until my first semester at uni."

"Where are you going?"

"I've applied to all the usual, but we want St. Andrews."

"We?"

"My parents are really involved in my academic career."

"That's good. Sometimes—" I stopped talking, the words deserting me as my eyes clashed with Marco's.

What the hell?

My gaze drank him in, taking in the stained apron tied around his waist and the tray of dirty dishes in his hands. Marco was a busboy for his uncle? Since when?

I moved my lips, curling them into a smile that quickly disappeared as I processed Marco's expression. His gaze flicked from me to Scott and back to me again.

His jaw clenched, and his knuckles turned white as his grip on the tray tightened. There was unmasked fury in his eyes.

My mouth fell open in shock as he turned on his heel and marched out of sight.

"Hannah?" Scott asked, drawing my gaze back to him.

"Sorry. I thought I saw . . ." I smiled weakly. "Never mind. What were we saying?"

I worked my arse off to remain present in the conversation because Scott was nice and charming and down-to-earth. He wasn't some huge, brooding American who kept throwing me dirty looks anytime he had to come into the dining room.

After the main course, Scott excused himself to go to the restroom and as soon as he was out of earshot, I twisted my head to look at Marco. The restaurant was too busy for me to shout his name, but I waited until he felt my gaze. He looked at me and I waved him over.

He gave me a slight shake of his head and walked out.

I felt that rejection so acutely I lost my breath for a second.

I never saw him again for the rest of the evening and any attempt at not being distracted was lost to me, as I was lost to thoughts of Marco. I didn't understand what had happened. Was he jealous? And if he was jealous, then why on earth hadn't he asked me out a long time ago? It wasn't like I hadn't made it clear I liked him. Right?

Scott walked me home and I managed some one-word answers. At my door, I gave him a distracted kiss on the cheek and disappeared inside, feeling confused, guilty, and more than a little bit tired of the whole thing.

CHAPTER 5

"Miss?"

"Miss Nichols?"

"Miss!"

I jerked my head up, my unfocused gaze refocusing on the class in front of me. They all stared at me in question.

Shit. I'd completely zoned out. Unfortunately, that had been happening more and more lately. Ever since I'd found that bloody photograph of Marco and me, I kept being assaulted by memories of my time with him. It was beyond distracting and annoying.

I blinked a few times, trying to shake the specter of Marco as I searched my desk and attempted to remember what the hell I was talking about.

Right. *Of Mice and Men* and symbolism.

Pretending I hadn't just taken a nap in the Halls of Forgotten Youth, I pushed on like I was perfectly aware of my surroundings and what we were doing. "So?" I sat down on the edge of my desk. "To end our discussion on symbolism in the book, why do you think Steinbeck titled it *Of Mice and Men*?"

Looking around the room at my third-year class, I saw a lot of brows furrowed in thought. The one brow that was usually furrowed in thought, however, today wasn't. Tabitha Bell was one of my students who continually answered questions. She was bubbly and clever and I could usually count on her to fill any awkward silence. During the parts of the class when I had been fully present that day, I'd noticed that she was just looking down at the table and I didn't hear a peep coming from her. I'd decided not to force her to participate. Something was clearly up.

"Come on, guys, think about it?" I urged.

The bell rang.

"Okay," I said over the sound of their packing up and rising chatter. "Listen," I called out, drawing their attention back to me. "I want you to come in tomorrow with an answer to my question. Why do you think Steinbeck titled it *Of Mice and Men*?" I was more than a bit annoyed with myself. We hadn't been able to discuss it in class because of me, and I knew at least ninety percent of them would Google it and seize on a multitude of right answers they hadn't come up with themselves.

Watching them hurry from my class to get to lunch, my eyes fell on Tabby. "Tabitha."

She looked up at me as she was passing, her eyes rounded in surprise.

I gestured to her and she made her way over to my desk, silently waiting as the room emptied.

"Are you okay?" I asked, concerned. "You were awfully quiet in class today. It's not like you."

Tears suddenly shimmered in her young eyes. "I'm fine."

"You don't seem fine. If you're having any issues with the work, I'd like to know so I can help."

"Class is fine," she sniffed. "It's just . . ." Her lips trembled. "I saw Jack Ryan kissing Natasha Dingwall this morning."

I stopped myself just in time from curling my lip in annoyance. Jack Ryan was in my fourth-year English class along with Jarrod. Whereas Jarrod was merely cheeky, Jack Ryan was a mouthy, disrespectful, women-hating little shit. "Is Jack your boyfriend?"

Tabby shook her head and I almost sagged in relief. "No . . . but I thought . . ." She wiped at the tears that had spilled onto her cheeks and I had to stop myself from rounding the desk to give her a hug.

"Tabby"—I ducked my head to look solemnly into her eyes—"today this feels like the end of the world. Tomorrow? Not so much. You'll be fine. I promise."

Looking anything but convinced, Tabby mumbled her thanks and quietly departed the room.

I stared after her, feeling bad but knowing she'd be okay. I knew because I'd been there. It felt like hell in the moment, but I was pretty sure time healed all.

Sometimes when you came across stupid photographs, however, it nicked the scar a little.

"There you are!" Anisha Patel, a fellow English teacher at the school, rushed toward me as I walked into the department staff room. She was grinning, her dark eyes glittering with excitement. "Please tell me you don't have a date to my wedding because I want to set you up with someone."

I stared at her in confusion. "I'm invited?"

Nish was lovely. In fact, I got on really well with the English department. They didn't act superior to me because I was a probationer; they just welcomed me aboard. Still, Nish and I had known each other only a couple of months so I wasn't expecting an invitation to her wedding. She talked about it every day, just as much as she talked about her gorgeous construction worker fiancé, Andrew, a guy whose boss often worked on projects for Braden and Adam.

Nish looked mortified. "I didn't invite you? Of course I did. Didn't I?" She waved it off. "Well, you're invited to the reception. Of course you are. Here." She strutted back over to her purse, dug around a bit, and pulled out an envelope. "An invitation." She held it out to me.

I smiled as I took it. "That's really nice of you, Nish, but I wasn't expecting an invite."

"Hush. Of course you'll be there. And can I set you up?" She clapped her hands together excitedly. "I know this guy and I've told him all about how gorgeous and smart and funny you are, and after the bad luck he's had in the past he really needs to date someone like you."

Although flattered . . . "Thank you, Nish, but I'm not really—"

"When was the last time you went on a date? I never hear you talking about men. Oh." Her eyes widened and she leaned in to whisper, "Do you like women?"

"No, I'm not a lesbian," I replied, not annoyed that she would think I was gay but annoyed that my perpetual singledom caused people to *assume* I was gay, rather than that maybe I was just happy being alone until I found a guy I could stand to be around long enough to commit to. "I'll bring Cole to the wedding."

"Ah, so something *is* going on there with that boy. Knew it!"

I looked over at my colleague Barbara, who seemed amused by the whole thing, and said, "Why is everyone man crazy at the moment? There is more to life."

Barbara grunted. "Preaching to the converted."

I sighed and looked back at Nish. "Cole and I are just friends, but I'm bringing him to the wedding. No setups."

"Speaking of boys"—Eric, the department head, grinned up at me from his sandwich—"apparently you have a number of admirers, Hannah."

I grimaced. "Are you talking about students?" I shook my head, walking over to the fridge to get my sandwich. "It's just because I'm close to their age."

"I think it's more to do with the fact you wear pencil skirts, high heels, and sexy secretary blouses." Nish sniggered. "And of course you look like that."

My colleagues laughed teasingly at my scowl.

"So do you want to know who fancies you?" Eric grinned cheekily.

"No. Definitely not."

"Jarrod Fisher is in Rutherford's class. He got into it with another boy who said some inappropriate things about you. Both got punishment exercises. And then there's my sixth-year. A kid asked me this morning in front of the whole class whether I thought he had a chance with you."

I groaned into my sandwich, making them laugh, but the truth was it wasn't the most comfortable feeling in the world to know that some of the minors you were teaching were having inappropriate thoughts when they looked at you. "Can we please stop talking about this?"

"Okay. Back to Cole then," Nish said. "You're absolutely sure that it's just friends between you two? Because that picture you showed me . . . if I were ten years younger . . ."

I smiled. "He's good-looking. But he's my best friend. It's not like that between us. Anyway, I'm too busy with this placement for a relationship. No matchmaking, Nish. I mean it."

I sat in my old bedroom on the new single bed, staring at the boxes in the corner where I'd stuffed the picture of Marco. I felt like it had been haunting me, and the only way to stop it was to put it in the boxes I'd eventually store back at my flat.

Hearing a chorus of laughter downstairs, I smiled. It was Sunday. My home had always been a happy one. I was lucky to have two parents who had such genuine affection and respect for each other. They'd rarely argued. Most of the arguing had been between Dec and me as we got older. I gave a small huff of laughter. I guess that hadn't changed much.

I smoothed my hands over the comforter of the new bed. Despite the changes this place still felt safe somehow.

A knock on the door surprised me, jolting me out of my reverie. Jo's head popped around the door, followed by her bump and then the rest of her. She smiled as she looked around, her long strawberry blond hair swinging in its ponytail. "This brings back memories."

When I was younger and Jo and Cole started coming to Sunday lunches, I'd bonded with Jo. Ellie was a great big sister, but she was very overprotective and a little too idealistic and romantic for me to confide in. Admittedly, I'd inherited that same romantic streak from Mum, but I was a little more reluctant to believe in fairy tales. Jo was more like me. She had her feet firmly planted on the ground, even when her head took a wander into the clouds. Before dinner she and I would sneak off to my room and I'd tell her all the secrets I couldn't tell my overprotective family.

"Do you remember Marco?" I found myself asking.

Jo stopped and turned to me, her green eyes round with surprise. "How could I forget? Your first big crush."

It was so much more than that.

I looked away, ignoring that flash of pain.

"Hannah?"

I glanced back at her to find her frowning.

"What made you think of him?"

I shrugged, attempting casual and hopefully not failing. "Mum asked me to throw out some of my old things. I found a photograph of Marco in the boxes. It brought all the old memories back, I guess."

Looking pensive, Jo strode toward me and lowered herself onto the bed next to me. "That's not surprising," she said quietly. "I imagine you have a few regrets where Marco's concerned. He left Scotland before anything could happen between you."

I felt a flip of unease in my stomach. I hated keeping things from the people I loved.

"You really changed after he left," Jo continued softly. "You became serious even before . . ."

My eyes found hers. "I guess that's what regret does to a person."

Jo took my hand. "You're only twenty-two, Hannah. Plenty of time to find 'the one.'"

Forcing the pain away, I smiled at her. "I know that."

The fragments of the past can become restless ghosts, relentless in their haunting, unless you decide to take a stand against them to exorcise them.

I think I'd just needed to say Marco's name out loud to someone, to admit that I'd been thinking about him. It probably would have meant so much more if Jo knew the entire truth, knew the whole story between me and Marco, but it was enough for me to realize that what she'd said was true. I was too young to be haunted. I couldn't let this resurgence of a life better forgotten ruin the life I wanted to make for myself.

I determinedly exorcised those memories, leaving them behind in my old room and venturing back into the present as I walked downstairs to join everyone.

My parents' dining room was filled with chatter despite the fact that not everyone had made it to Sunday lunch this week. Ellie and Adam were at home because William had had a fever the night before and the three of them were exhausted. Jo's uncle Mick and his wife, Dee, were on holiday in Las Vegas, so they weren't with us, but Jo, Cam, and Cole were, as were Liv, Nate, Lily, and January. Joss and Braden were with us, too, along with Beth and Luke.

Mum had set up a kiddie table at the end of the room where Lily, Beth, and Luke sat with Mum, who was this week's kiddie table chaperone. She had January in her arms as she watched over the wee ones and tried to feed herself.

"So, I need a favor and it's a bit late notice," I said to Cole over the children's noise. Thankfully he was sitting next to me.

"I'm intrigued." He raised an eyebrow. "Proceed."

I smiled, rolling my eyes. "Well, your majesty, I've had a last-minute invite to my colleague's wedding reception and I need a date. It's next Saturday."

"What time?"

"It's just the after-party, so I guess we don't need to be there until about eightish."

"No problem."

"You're a lifesaver."

"Begging Cole for a date?" Declan grunted at me from across the table. The boy had supernatural powers of hearing. "That's a little pathetic, Hannah."

"Are we in a pissy mood because you had to surgically remove your hip from Penny's?" I gibed in return. "Tell me, Dec, how *does* it feel to be whipped at eighteen?" What can I say? My little brother brought out my mature side.

He glowered at me. "She's at her nana's today."

"With her whip?"

"Ha ha, you're so funny."

"And whiplash-free."

I could hear Cole laughing beside me, which pissed my brother off even more.

"Seriously?" Dec smirked. "When was the last time anyone wanted to date you? If you need some pointers, I'm happy to help. Let's start with your face. You might want to do something about that. Plastic surgery maybe?"

"Oh." I flinched as if I'd tasted something sour. "If we're going to mock one another let's keep it smart. I refuse to go into a battle of wits with the witless. It's too easy. And rather insulting."

"Children," Mum called over to us, tsking. "Don't make me remind you that one of you is an eighteen-year-old and the other is a twenty-two-year-old high school English teacher."

"Elodie, don't spoil the fun," Cam complained. "These two are my weekend entertainment."

"I'm thinking about filming them and creating a weekly blog," Joss agreed.

Before I could think up a clever retort, we heard my mother *tsk* again loudly. "Beth, eat your greens. They're good for you. Come on, eat your peas."

"I don't want to," she whined, and we turned to watch her push her plate back. "They're little fuckers."

The room stilled, my mother's gasp the only sound.

The laughter built up inside me and promptly exploded as Cole gave a bark of laughter. I collapsed against him, my face in his shoulder, and laughed until my belly hurt.

I could hear everyone's laughter, and looked across the table at Joss to see that she was the only one mortified.

Wiping tears from my eyes, I asked, "How?" hoping she understood the question.

"I said it once," she lamented. "Now she won't stop saying it."

"Mummy?" Beth asked, confused by our reaction.

"I still don't understand." Mum pinched her mouth together in affront.

Joss sighed. "I dropped a jar of peas and I thought I got 'em all, but I found some renegades later on and forgot Beth was there when I did."

"Little fuckers," Beth said promptly, obviously remembering the moment when Joss encountered the renegade peas.

That set us off again.

I had tears streaming down my cheeks.

"Baby, I told you, you can't say that word," Joss told her softly, ignoring the rest of us. "It's not a nice word and Mommy was wrong to use it."

Beth gave Joss a hilariously sly look that suggested she was intrigued rather than cautioned.

We were off again, Braden's laughter louder than anyone's. "Christ, next she'll be repeating it in school." He rubbed his eyes, his expression smoothing out from hilarity. "If she does, I'm leaving you to explain it."

"What happened to being in this together?" Joss grumbled.

"She gets it from you, so you're best equipped to deal with it."

The look Joss cut him was not one of amusement.

"She's definitely your daughter," I said, picking my fork back up.

"Jocelyn's?" Braden asked as Joss asked, "Braden's?"

"Exactly."

CHAPTER 6

T he next week flew in with work and volunteering, the gym and my book club. By the time Saturday rolled around I was looking forward to taking some time off, spending the night with Cole surrounded by people we didn't know, cracking jokes and making up life stories for the strangers we'd be sharing a reception hall with.

When I got into the cab he'd hired to drive us to the reception just outside the city center, my eyes roved over Cole in approval. He'd gone conservative for me this evening, wearing a three-piece suit that covered most of his tattoos. He gave a nod to his own personal taste with the chain that dangled from the front of his waistband, looping down and up to the back of it.

"You look great," I said with a grin.

"You look stunning," he murmured, giving me a quick kiss on the cheek.

I was wearing a black dress, molded to my figure, and bright blue pumps with platform heels. "Was Stephanie okay about you escorting me tonight?"

Cole quirked an eyebrow at the mention of his girlfriend, appearing annoyed. "Nope."

I winced. "Sorry."

"Don't be. She's been acting crazy jealous lately. Not just about you, but girls at uni, even clients at the studio. I don't think it's going to work out."

"Cole, I'm really sorry." I cuddled into his side as the cab drove out of town. "Wouldn't it be so much easier if we were attracted to each other?"

"So much easier," he agreed. "But alas, you are immune to my charms."

"As you are to mine." I sighed dramatically.

Cole chuckled and put his arm around me. "One day you'll meet someone you can stand to commit to, and I'll meet someone who isn't batshit crazy."

"Oh, you dreamer you."

The wedding reception was in full swing when we got there. Someone I didn't know directed me to the table where all the wedding presents were and I put my gift there before tagging Cole by the hand and leading him into the main hall. Tables and chairs had been pushed to the edges of the room and the lights had been dimmed. Guests danced on the floor to the DJ's playlist, while others mingled at the tables and at the bar at the far end of the room. I spotted the bride easily and we made our way over to her.

"Oh, my gosh!" Nish cried out happily upon seeing me. "You look amazing."

I laughed. "I say that to you. And you do. You look beautiful." I gestured to Cole. "This is Cole."

"The famous Cole." Nish hugged him, sharing her joy. Cole patted her back awkwardly and politely tried to disengage. "Oh, my word." She grinned into his face. "You are even more gorgeous in real life." She frowned at me. "What is wrong with you? Just friends. *Pfft.* Anyhoo"— she flung herself around—"Andrew!"

A good-looking bloke in a kilt turned at her yell and grinned, swaggering over to us.

Nish grabbed his arm and yanked him close. "Hannah, this is my husband, Andrew."

After the introductions, we left the happy couple to their mingling and Cole and I made our way over to the bar. I passed the table with my colleagues and waved at them.

"Do you want to go over?" Cole asked, following my gaze.

"Nah. Let's just hang out. Mock people. Mock love," I joked.

"I'm starting with you, Miss Cynical."

I rolled my eyes as he ordered our drinks. As soon as we had them I moved us over to an almost empty table. I'd forgotten how awkward it could be to be in a room with a bunch of strangers who knew one another but didn't know you. "We'll leave soon," I promised.

Cole shrugged. "It doesn't bother me. Nish seems nice."

"She's a kook." I shook my head, watching her drag Barbara onto the dance floor. I sank a little lower in my seat, hoping she wouldn't demand the same of me.

We sat there a while, just laughing and joking and catching up on each other's lives. Some time had passed when I began to feel a burn on the left side of my face. Skin tingling, I turned my head to look across the room. My eyes moved over the guests, not recognizing anyone. *Don't know him, don't know her, don't know her, don't know him, Marco, don't know hi—*

My eyes dragged back, my heart suddenly in my throat as my gaze connected with Marco's.

I felt as if someone had just swung a bat at my chest.

I couldn't breathe.

It was Marco.

He was older, more filled out, if that was even possible, but I'd know that face anywhere. It was hard to mistake.

"Hannah?" Cole's concerned voice tugged at me and I glanced back at him in shock.

"Are you okay?"

"I'm f-fine," I stammered, slowly rising to my feet. "I'm just . . . I need to nip to the ladies'. I'll be right back." I shot out the side door near our table into the cool air of the hallway. I inhaled deeply in an effort to get some of that air inside me.

I studied the hallway a little stupidly, looking for signs for the ladies'.

Finding one, I followed the arrow, my brain on overload with questions.

"Hannah."

His deep, gravel-rough, accented voice drew me to an abrupt halt.

It was him. It really was him. He was *here* somehow.

Slowly, I turned around to face the guy I had pined over for so many years, my eyes greedily drinking in the sight of him, even though I tried to resist. He wore suit trousers and a shirt that stretched nicely across his broad chest. He'd always been athletically built, but he'd put on bulk, his biceps clearly much larger than they used to be. His face had filled out a little too, but was no less angular, his cut jawline and sharp cheekbones such a contrast to his exotic eyes and sensual lips. He was utterly striking.

I wanted to hate him.

"What are you doing here?" I asked sharply.

When he didn't answer me, I studied him more closely and only then realized how stunned he was to see me. Finally he cleared his throat and took a step toward me. I took a step back. Something like annoyance flashed in his eyes as he noted my retreat. "Andrew is a colleague. We work construction together. Real estate mostly."

It occurred to me that meant he'd probably worked for Braden. Good thing I'd told neither Braden nor Adam of Marco's existence. Marco D'Alessandro wasn't really a common name in these parts.

"I meant in Scotland," I said flatly. "Last time I checked you'd gone back to Chicago."

Marco nodded and my heart pumped harder as the surrealism of the moment dissipated. He was really in front of me. Really there. Touching distance. "For a while. But I came back."

My stomach flipped unpleasantly as a question came to mind and quickly spilled from between my lips. "When? When did you come back?"

He shifted uneasily. "A year after I left."

This revelation winded me.

Five words and the betrayal he'd dealt me quadrupled in size. "You've been back for four years?" I asked incredulously, unable to keep the anger out of my voice. "You never thought to call?"

He took another step toward me. I took another back. Marco rubbed his hand over his head in that way he did when he didn't know what to say. His gaze bored into mine, almost pleading with me. "Back then you were better off without me, Hannah. After what I did . . ."

Disgusted, I suddenly stopped retreating and took a few steps toward him. "Better off? You bet your arse, I am." Unable to take one more second in his presence, I moved to stride past him, only to be surprised by the warm curl of his hand around my bare arm. He halted me and I stared up at him in shock, ignoring the intriguing spice of his cologne and the fact that he was the only man who had ever made me feel feminine and fragile.

I used to like that feeling.

Not so much anymore. I tugged my arm, but Marco pulled me toward him.

"Let me go," I bit out.

"Hannah, at least talk to me." He bent his head toward me and I felt that traitorous flutter of butterflies as I looked into his eyes. "It's so fucking good to see you," he whispered, his expression soft on me.

I shook myself out from under the spell he was trying to cast over me. "Pity I can't say the same. Now let me go."

"Hannah—"

"Is there a problem here?" Cole's voice made me sag with relief. I looked over my shoulder to see him glowering at Marco. He was younger and he wasn't nearly as built as Marco, but Cole's tall, athletic body was coiled with hard muscle. Not to mention that he studied judo and kickboxing. Definitely nothing to sneeze at.

Marco reluctantly let me go. "No."

I didn't spare him another glance. I couldn't. Instead I marched away from him, putting my hand on Cole's chest in thanks. He threw Marco one last warning look before sliding his arm around my waist to lead me away.

"You okay?" he asked softly.

I nodded. *Lie, lie, lie!*

"He looked familiar."

"I knew him in high school. I had a crush on him."

"I think I rem—" Cole sucked in a breath, hardness settling over his features. "Is *he* the guy?"

"No," I lied convincingly. "He just rejected me, that's all. I'm not in the mood to be reminded of that tonight."

"Do you want to leave now?"

I drew in a deep breath, knowing I couldn't sit in that reception hall with Marco. "Yeah."

Cole got me out of there, reluctantly dropping me off at my flat. I could tell he sensed there was more to my story and didn't want to leave me alone, but I *needed* to be alone.

I kicked off the heels that were pinching my toes and sat down in my sitting room in the dark.

I couldn't believe Marco had been living in Edinburgh all this time. All this time . . .

The pain I'd shoved deep down inside me all those years ago came back with a vengeance. Tears burned in my eyes and in my throat as I remembered *that* night.

The night it all changed . . .

Walking into the flat I knew I shouldn't be here. It was cloudy with smoke and the thick scent of marijuana. There wasn't much furniture, and what was there was dingy and old. Not that I could see much of any of it, since the flat was packed wall to wall with people.

It was the start of our final year at school and Sadie wanted this year to be the best. How that translated into crashing some loser's party on India Place, I didn't know. As I followed her through the crowds, I slapped at hands that touched my hips and patted my arse. Great.

"I see Dave!" Sadie shouted over her shoulder to me. Dave was the reason she'd dragged me to the party with her. He was a few years older and she had a crush on him. "I'll be right back."

Before I could say anything she'd disappeared and I was left standing in the doorway of the living room. I felt the vibrations from the music speaker thrum unpleasantly in my chest. Where were the neighbor complaints? The police?

I was shoved somewhat forcefully into the room as more people streamed in, and while I tried to squeeze back into the crowds on the outskirts, my eyes caught sight of three lines of white powder on the glass coffee table.

I stared wide-eyed as a girl I didn't know snorted a line.

Fuck, I needed to get out of there.

I turned to flee, only to slam up against someone's chest.

My eyes rose to meet unfamiliar dark ones. The guy's eyes swept over me, glittering with sexual intent, and just like that I found myself pinned between the wall and him.

"I've never seen you before," he said loudly into my ear, his mouth touching it.

I ducked my head, shivering in revulsion at the feel of his lips on my skin. "I'm just leaving," I yelled, attempting to duck under his arm.

He stopped me and I closed my eyes, trying not to panic. We were in a room filled with people. It wasn't like he could do anything. Still, I cursed myself for borrowing Sadie's figure-hugging blue dress—this was not the kind of attention I'd wanted when I'd chosen to wear it.

"Aw, stay a bit." He grinned, pressing in closer. "Get tae know me."

"I don't want to know you. I want to leave. Move."

"That's no very nice." He bit his lip in a way I assumed he thought women found sexy. He assumed wrong. "You look nice. Play nice."

I glared at him. "Get. Off. Me."

Before he could reply, a large fist gripped his shirt and he was suddenly pushed away. He tripped over a girl's foot and crashed to the floor. My eyes went from him to the large guy beside me and a wave of relief and giddiness moved through me.

Marco scowled down at the stranger. The stranger got up without a word, his expression fearful, and disappeared into the room beyond.

Marco quickly turned on me, and my thanks and "hello" caught in my throat as he wrapped his hand around my arm and none too gently shoved me in front of him out the doorway and down the hall.

I could feel the anger emanating from him.

Confused, I stayed silent, watching him take a key out of his jeans and unlock the door at the end of the hall. He shoved me inside and followed me. He closed the door behind us and I heard the lock turn. The music was a muffled throbbing pulse beyond it.

My eyes wandered over the small space. There was a bed, a worn-out desk with an old laptop on it, and a chest of drawers.

"What are you doing here?" Marco asked gruffly, his eyebrows drawn together in annoyance as his gaze roamed over me.

Equally annoyed by his attitude, I crossed my arms over my chest. "Hello to you, too."

I hadn't seen Marco in weeks. After the whole Scott date fiasco, with the help of Jo and Liv I managed to ambush Marco in D'Alessandro's again and got him to agree to hang out with me. We did, but the tension between us had intensified somehow, and he began to make excuses not to see me.

I missed him all the time.

Hiding my hurt, I looked around the room. "Do you live here?"

"Like you didn't know that."

Stung, I gave a bitter snort of laughter. "Contrary to what you might think, I know when I'm not wanted. I didn't know you lived here. How could I? I haven't heard from you in ages."

I watched his eyes soften. "Sorry. That was a shit thing to say."

"Why do you live here?" I couldn't keep the distaste out of my expression.

Marco grimaced and sank down onto the edge of his bed. "I had to get my own place, but I don't exactly have a lot of money. My friend knows the guy who owns this place. The rent is cheap. My roommate, however, isn't worth it." He gestured to the door and everything that was going on beyond it. "I'll be moving out as soon as possible." His eyes narrowed on me. "Doesn't answer the question of why the hell you of all people are at a place like this?"

"Me of all people? I'm at a party, Marco. I've been known to do that sometimes."

"No." He shook his head. "Not this kind of party. Hannah, you need to go. You can't be here."

"I came with Sadie."

"Of course you did." Marco wasn't a big fan of Sadie. "We'll find her and go."

"Or . . ." I took a step toward him and noted his eyes lowered, moving over my legs before he could stop them. "We could stay. Hang out. We haven't done that in a while."

His jaw clenched. "Hannah, just leave."

I had weeks of being pissed off to fuel my anger. "Fine! You stay here and I'll go back to the party."

"Don't you dare." He stood up abruptly.

"Or what?" I taunted him. "Are you going to throw me out? Just like you're throwing me out of your life?"

"You don't belong here!" he yelled, taking me aback.

I flinched but stood my ground. "If you're here, I'm here!"

Marco seemed stumped by that.

He hung his head, staring at the floor.

"I miss talking to you," I whispered sadly.

His eyes flicked to me and he couldn't hide the remorse and tenderness in them. I almost closed mine in relief.

"How have you been?" he asked gruffly.

I shrugged. "Fine, I guess. School is good. I got an unconditional offer from Edinburgh University."

Marco smiled a little. "That's awesome. I'm proud of you."

I smiled back, feeling warmth course through me at his praise. I took another step toward him. "How's work?"

"It's fine. I still work shifts at the restaurant."

I'd told him months ago how surprised I was to discover he was working for his uncle. I asked him why he'd hid it from me. He said it was a shit situation and not worth talking about.

"You've haven't broken away from them?"

He shook his head. "They adopted me so I could live in the UK. I owe them for getting me out of a bad situation in Chicago. I owe my aunt. She's been good to me."

"But you're not living there anymore?"

He looked up at me, his expression solemn. "I worry what I might end up doing if I stayed there. I had to leave."

"Marco," I breathed, aching for him and wishing I could just wrap my arms around him.

"I don't want your sympathy. I never have," he snapped.

"Oh, get over yourself, you big baby. I'm allowed to be upset for you. It comes with the territory of caring about you."

He grunted. "Just say it how you feel it, Hannah."

As our eyes clashed the air felt suddenly electric between us. "Are you sure you mean that?"

He knew where I was leading. He shook his head. "Don't."

"Why?" I asked softly, trying to fight my frustration and failing. "You know I care about you, and you know . . . you know I want to be with you. You can't keep avoiding that." I sucked in a breath. "Why did you react the way you did to seeing me with Scott? Why did you say what you said to me in Douglas Gardens all those months ago? In fact, why have you looked out for me all these years if you didn't feel the same way back?"

He squeezed his eyes shut tight, pinching the bridge of his nose. With a groan, he hung his head.

I almost laughed. "That's not an answer."

"Hannah"—he sighed, still not meeting my eyes—"I looked out for you be-

cause you're a good girl and I didn't want scum like Jenks touching you. I said what I said in the gardens that night because I meant it. Because you're important to me. You're my friend and I don't have a lot of those. As for Scott . . ." He shook his head. "Fuck knows."

I moved toward him, my pulse throbbing in my neck. "I think you know."

His eyes blazed. "It's not what you think."

I closed the distance between us, my body brushing his as I tilted my head back to look into his face. He didn't step back. I took that as a good sign. "It's exactly what I think."

The muscle in his jaw ticked and something powerful and perhaps dangerous emanated from him. "You need to leave."

"Don't."

"Hannah, leave now."

"Marco—"

"Hannah, leave!" he growled, his body heat burning me.

I flinched, rejection and anger molten within me. "You are such a coward!"

"You are such a pain in my ass!" he yelled back.

"Fine! I'll go out there and be a pain in someone else's arse!" My breathing felt out of control. I felt out of control. "I don't need this. There are guys out there who actually want to kiss and touch me." I swung around on that grand, arrogant statement, intent on storming out of the room.

Instead Marco's viselike grip tightened around my upper arm and I was suddenly hauled back, my body crashing flush against his. I didn't even have a second to compute what was happening before his hard mouth was on mine.

I melted instantly into his kiss, relieved and lustful, my hands relaxing on his strong chest, my body leaning into his while my lips parted to let him devour me. The kiss was rough, desperate, and turned me on in a way I'd had no idea a kiss could. I loved the rich taste of him, the erotic feel of his tongue against mine, and the fact that I wasn't just feeling his mouth on mine; I was feeling his strength all around me. His arms were steel bands holding me tight, his hands clenched the fabric at the back of my dress. I slid my hands up around his neck as his kiss slowed but deepened, and I thrilled at the feel of my breasts pressing against his *muscled chest. I could smell him, taste him, feel his hot skin. He was everywhere, everything. It was sensational.*

I didn't know how long we stood there kissing. It felt like forever. My mouth was swollen, and my body was screaming for more. In a bid for more I ran my hands down his chest, around his waist and then under his shirt, groaning into his mouth at the sensation of his smooth, hot skin beneath my touch.

Abruptly, I was pushed away.

Panting, Marco stared back at me as if he'd never seen me before. Shock seemed to immobilize him for a second and I was too busy trembling with unfulfilled lust to string a sentence together.

I watched as he stumbled back against his bed and sank onto the mattress. He hung his head again while he tried to catch his breath.

Knowing that he was berating himself for some stupid reason I had yet to work out, it occurred to me that if I didn't escalate things between us now I wouldn't get this moment back with him. So I took small steps toward him.

I stopped, my legs almost touching his knees. My hand reached for him before I could stop myself and I stroked my fingers over his close-cropped dark hair. He lowered his hands at my touch, tilting his head back to look up at me. There was a warning in his eyes, his expression taut with restraint and perhaps a little anger.

I ignored his warning. "I'll make you a promise," I said. "I'll keep being your friend and I'll never mention this again . . . if you can look me in the eyes after what just happened and tell me you don't want me."

"Hannah." His voice was thick as his eyes began to burn again.

My breathing grew shallow. "We've always been honest with each other, right?"

He gave a slight shake of his head. "I can't."

"Why?"

"I can't . . . I can't tell you I don't want you." His eyes studied my face before moving slowly down my body, and everywhere his gaze touched I came alive.

I'd never done much more than kiss a boy, not because I wasn't ready to explore sex, but because I didn't want to explore sex with anyone but Marco. I'd heard

Ellie, Joss, Jo, and Liv's crappy losing-their-virginity stories and I'd promised myself that the moment I let someone truly inside me, I'd make sure that someone was someone I loved.

And I loved Marco.

I'd been in love with him since the day he rescued me when I was fourteen years old.

Excited, thrilled, I forced bravery upon myself and reached for the hem of my dress. I pulled it up slowly, revealing my body to him bit by bit until it was up over my head. I shook my hair out and dropped the dress on his floor.

I stood there in front of him in nothing but cute turquoise underwear and a pair of heels. I'd never felt more vulnerable in my whole life.

And then he touched me. His fingers skimmed my belly and I felt a bolt of desire hit me between the legs as he caressed my skin. Suddenly he gripped my hips in both his large hands and I tottered toward him on my heels.

Our eyes met and the expression on his face made me feel more beautiful and desired than I'd ever known I could feel.

"Look at you," he whispered hoarsely, almost reverently. "Look at you."

"Marco . . ." I reached out, cupping his face in my hand.

His eyes closed at my touch, his expression so tender I wanted to melt all over again. I sighed as he pulled me closer to press sweet kisses against my stomach. His kisses went lower, following the waistband of my underwear, and I shivered at the touch of his fingertips coasting along my lower back.

I braced my hands on his shoulders to steady myself.

Seconds later I felt a tug on my bra and it parted, falling down my arms. Heat suffused me. No one had seen me naked before.

One look into Marco's eyes, though, and all embarrassment fled.

Marco groaned, his eyes ravishing me, and I found myself guided toward him until I had to put my knees on the bed on either side of him to straddle him. Lowering my bottom to his lap, I felt his large erection through his jeans and a rush of overwhelming sexual awareness crashed over me. My breasts swelled, my nipples tightened, and Marco took it as an invitation.

His mouth wrapped around my nipple and the feeling . . . the tingles, the sudden urgency that made me rock my hips against his . . . I wanted more. I wanted so much more . . .

I whimpered his name as I burned.

Marco pulled back, his heavy-lidded gaze on my face, his strong arms holding me tight. "I shouldn't be doing this."

I took his face in my hands and looked deep in his eyes. "Would you rather some other guy was?"

And that was when I saw it. The dark flicker of anger, of possessiveness that had made him kiss me in the first place. Triumphant, I pressed my lips to his, moaning in pleasure as he kissed me back. Hard. Our tongues touched, sending sparks of growing arousal through me. The kiss turned searching—months, years even, of longing in it. We broke apart briefly so I could yank his T-shirt over his head, my hands roaming and memorizing every hard contour of his beautiful torso.

Suddenly I was flipped, my back on the bed, and Marco pulled away.

I stared up at him, panting, praying he wasn't going to stop this.

My prayers were answered.

He towered over me, a fantasy come to life. His beautiful caramel-toned skin, the powerful shoulders, the abs that made my mouth water. I felt a flush of heat at the sight of the sexy definition in his hips and the way his hard-on strained against the zipper on his jeans.

There was an intensity in his blue-green eyes that made me shiver all over.

He reached for my foot, gently pulling my shoe off. And then the other one. His eyes followed the length of my legs as he stroked my calf. "I've thought about this," he admitted quietly. "A million times more than I ever should have."

Before I could respond, he put a hand on the mattress by my knee and leaned over me, his other hand hooking into my underwear. His eyes asked the question and I nodded, lifting my hips to help him.

He tugged my underwear down my legs and then took a minute to gaze at me.

I felt my cheeks flush under his hot gaze.

"Marco . . . ?"

He pressed a kiss to my ankle and then nudged my legs apart. My lower belly fluttered wildly, but I moved my legs, anticipation making me slick.

His breath fanned warmly over my skin as he crawled between my legs. He lifted one over his shoulder and kissed the inside of my thigh. Then he kissed me there.

I arched my back, groaning at the sensation of his mouth on my sex, his tongue circling my clit for a time before moving south and licking inside me. I pushed up against him for more, my cries of pleasure drowned out by the party outside the little bubble of private heaven we'd created in his room.

Marco tormented me with his tongue, his own growl of pleasure vibrating through me in the most delicious way.

I felt it build, my body stiffening as the tension grew and grew and grew . . . and then shattered.

My first orgasm.

Delight and a weird sense of liberation flowed through my limbs as they melted in relaxation against Marco's mattress. I opened my eyes on a soft smile to watch Marco divest himself of his jeans.

I froze at the sight of his erection.

It was huge.

How would that . . . ?

"Ssh." He hushed me reassuringly, urgently, as he caressed my hip. He kissed me as his body came down over mine and I wrapped my arms around his back, pulling him closer.

Nothing had ever felt more perfect than feeling his hard body against my soft one. I wanted to be inside him and I wanted him inside of me. In every way two people could be.

He touched me, two fingers sliding into me.

His breath hitched. "So ready. So tight." He groaned and buried his head against my neck, kissing me there.

I jerked my hips up toward his, suddenly feeling very impatient. "Marco, please."

He lifted his head and our eyes met.

There it was. That tether. That connection.

He moved, hips gliding against mine and I felt the hot throb of him nudge between my legs. I clutched his hips with my thighs, bracing myself. He surged forward, pushing into my tight, resisting body.

I tried to catch my breath at the overwhelming feeling of fullness.

Marco gritted his teeth, grasping me by the back of the thigh. It changed his angle and he pushed harder.

I cried out at the burn of pain, my whole body tensing.

"Hannah," Marco panted, his concern breaking through my shock.

My eyes opened. He watched me, something like guilt on his face.

That buried the pain.

"Don't stop," I begged, not wanting him to ever regret this.

He shook his head. "You're so tight."

"Keep going." I pulled his head down to kiss him, the kiss desperate and deep.

This hot, rumbling sound growled from the back of his throat as he began to move his hips against mine.

There was some residual pain, but the discomfort eased as all my awareness focused on the thrusts of his throbbing cock inside me. His grip on my thigh tightened, his lust-filled eyes on mine the whole time as he began to move faster, pumping in and out of me, creating the tension again.

"I can't wait," he panted, shaking his head. "I'm sorry . . ." He gritted his teeth again, the muscles in his neck straining as his hips stilled against mine seconds before he shuddered his release inside me.

Marco collapsed against me, his face buried in my neck, and as I stroked his back I felt the wonder of that moment cascade over me, leaving me absolutely content.

I smiled, tears pricking my eyes. "I love you," I whispered.

The muscles in his back tensed.

Wariness moved through my chest, ugly and dark, and I waited, holding my breath.

He pushed up off of me, staring at me incredulously. "What the . . ." He scrambled off me as though I'd burned him. "We didn't. What . . ." He hurried to dress.

"Marco?" I sat up, my lips trembling with vulnerability.

His eyes moved over me, and whatever he saw made him squeeze his own shut in despair. Despair!

My tears fell.

"We shouldn't have."

"Marco."

"I shouldn't have." He yanked his T-shirt on and quickly stuffed his feet into his trainers. He looked back at me as he turned the lock on the door. "I'm sorry, Hannah. God, I'm sorry."

And then he left me there.

Crying, I stumbled around the room through blurred vision, pulling on my clothes before someone came in. Dressed, I stared back at the bed, my eyes zeroing in on the spot of blood on the blanket.

Despair? Despair in this moment was mine, not his.

I never saw him again. Not until a few hours ago at a random wedding. My first love. My first time.

My first heartbreak.

The tears shimmered in my eyes, but I didn't let them loose. I'd shed all those tears years ago.

CHAPTER 7

I think more than anything I was angry. Not just at what Marco had done to me by leaving, but at what his reappearance was doing to me. I'd felt lost for a long time after he left. It had taken me a while to find my strength and independence again. It had meant hardening my heart and creating little locked doors in my soul so that only the people I trusted implicitly could ever make it inside to touch it.

Standing opposite him, staring into his handsome face and those eyes that seemed even more soulful than before, I was that seventeen-year-old girl again. Totally lost.

That pissed me off.

How dare he walk back into my life and make me feel that way? I wasn't that person. I was my own person and I knew who I was, I knew what I was about. I had family and friends and students and colleagues who knew and respected me.

This person, this aching, bruised, lost person . . . that wasn't the person they knew.

That enraged me.

Twisting and turning through the night, the anger eating away at me, I knew when I finally slid out of bed that Sunday that I couldn't face my family. They'd take one look at me and know something was going on. Cole was already too suspicious. So I texted Mum and told her I was bogged down with work and couldn't make Sunday lunch. In truth, I needed time to cool down, reflect, to get back to being me again.

To do that I set myself up in my living room, surrounded with schoolwork, and spent the entire day catching up on my marking. Somewhere along the way the anger began to cool.

I was so caught up in my marking I almost jumped off my couch when the doorbell rang. It was past six o'clock, the sky was darkening outside, and I'd had to switch my lamps on to see my work. I couldn't think who would be visiting me. With my crazy, overprotective crew it could have been anyone. I didn't know why I was surprised. This would be the fourth time I'd missed Sunday lunch in as many months. I should have known it would start to concern someone.

That someone was Ellie.

"What are you doing here?" I asked, following her into my living room.

I watched her take in my work, her expression pensive.

"Ellie?"

She frowned at me. "You missed Sunday lunch. Again."

I gestured to my work. "I told Mum I had loads of marking to do."

Despite the evidence staring her in the face, my sister didn't seem to buy it. She knew me too well. "Are you sure that's it? Cole seemed worried you weren't there."

Ellie would dig until she found the truth, so I outmaneuvered her by opting for a version of the truth. I sighed, crossing my arms over my chest. "Fine. When Cole and I were at Anisha's wedding reception last night, I bumped into a blast from the past. Marco D'Alessandro."

My sister's blue eyes grew round with surprise. "My God. How did that go?"

Any attempt to keep the bitterness from my face clearly failed as I curled my lip in disdain. "I found out he's been back in Edinburgh for four years and didn't bother to get in touch."

"Not good." Ellie winced sympathetically.

"What do I care, right?" I flopped down on my couch. "It's just . . ." I shook my head in pained bemusement, watching Ellie lower herself into my armchair. "I found a photo of him last week and it was the first time in a long time I'd thought about him . . . and then poof! Suddenly he's right in front of me. It knocked me off balance. But I'm okay now."

Ellie narrowed her eyes on me, scrutinizing me. "I hope you're telling the truth."

I made a face. "I am."

"Hannah, I'm your sister and I love you. You have an entire family who loves you. Five years ago you started shutting us out, putting on this front, determined to take care of yourself without our help. You need to stop that. Not just for you but for us. We're here if you need us, and frankly *we* need you to need us."

Feeling guilty, I glanced away from her, staring at my work. "I'm not shutting you out, Els. I promise I'm okay."

"I don't believe you," she replied quietly. "I haven't forgotten our talks back then. I haven't forgotten how much you felt for him. Marco is your Adam. You were devastated when he left. I know you're not okay."

I didn't say anything. I didn't know what to say or if it was possible to force words out of the burning, painful ball of tears clogging my throat. At my prolonged silence, Ellie sighed unhappily and promptly left. The fact that she didn't say good-bye told me she was hurt and annoyed at me.

I went right back to being pissed off at Marco.

I stewed for a while, until my phone rang and jerked me out of my daze. With a sigh, I reached for it, not recognizing the number. Hoping it wasn't a salesman, not just for my sake but for theirs, I answered.

"Hannah, it's me." Marco's familiar deep voice hit me with the force of a cannonball.

My whole body shuddered away from the phone in shock and I stared at it for a second, fury quickly building in me at his audacity.

I heard him say my name in question.

Putting the phone back to my ear, I snapped, "How did you get this number?"

"From Anisha. I explained we were old friends. I just want to talk. I need a chance to explain."

Over the past few years I had imagined this moment, and every single time I hung up on him immediately or I walked away. In actuality I found myself hesitating because the reality was that he didn't sound like the boy I'd once known. It wasn't easy to describe, but even with me, someone whom he'd considered his best friend, he'd kept a guard up around his words all the time.

There wasn't a guard up now. I couldn't say how I knew. I just . . . felt it.

And it stunned me for a few seconds. A few seconds filled with curiosity and indecision.

But following those seconds were the memories of what I'd been through.

"Hannah?"

"I don't want to hear it," I answered. "I'm over it."

Before Marco could say another word, I hung up and switched my phone off.

"It looks like I need to get a new number," I said flippantly, but I wasn't fooling myself. My hands shook and my heart pounded as I placed the phone back on my table.

Probationary year was often difficult—the days were sometimes stressful and I was busy all the time. For once I was thankful for that over the next few days. I was also thankful for the adult literacy course and for the book group I'd joined that gathered every Wednesday evening at St. Stephen's Centre. If it kept me active and focused on anything but Marco, it was a godsend.

I had my fourth-year class that afternoon, and they were definitely helping to keep me busy. It would seem that not all of them were happy to be reading the play *Pygmalion* by George Bernard Shaw.

Throughout the period, Jack Ryan, the little pain in the arse that Tabitha Bell had been so upset over, had repeatedly sighed heavily as we read scenes and discussed the play. Five times I'd asked him to sit properly at his desk after he pushed his chair up onto its back legs, balancing it precariously. I had visions of the chair tipping him and his head cracking off the corner of the desk behind him and me being blamed for his stupidity.

He was driving me nuts, but I was doing my best to ignore him and teach.

"Aw come on, man, whit the fuck is this shite?" he grumbled, loud enough for me to hear him.

Before I could reprimand him, Jarrod got there. "Why don't you shut the fuck up, you whining wee bastard?"

"Jarrod," I warned.

"What?" Jarrod grimaced at me. "He's being a dick."

"That doesn't mean you have to lower yourself to his level."

Jack's chair thudded to the ground. "You calling me a dick, Miss?"

I gave him a lengthy stare in answer. Jarrod relaxed, chuckling in triumph at Jack.

Jack flushed, but fortunately the bell rang before I could receive his sure-to-be-disrespectful retort.

As the kids got up to leave, I called Jarrod over to my desk, something that seemed to be becoming a regular occurrence. He swaggered over to me with his cocky assuredness, grinning at me. "If you're going to give me a row, don't bother."

I raised my eyebrows at him. "Don't bother because you know you were in the wrong?"

He shrugged. "I just said what *you* wanted to say."

That was so terribly true it took everything in me not to give that fact away. "Jarrod, the point is that you're a bright kid, and a good kid, and you need to learn to stop retaliating against idiots who aren't worth it. Keep your lips sealed and walk away."

"From who? Ryan and Mr. Rutherford?" he sneered.

I shrugged this time, and Jarrod smiled as if he knew I agreed with him. I wanted him to rein in that temper of his so guys like Jack Ryan and Rutherford didn't get the best of him. I said this to him and he stared at the floor thoughtfully.

A few seconds of contemplation passed, and since I didn't want him to feel like I was coming down on him all the time, I pushed another topic. "Did you look at my notes on your personal essay?"

He nodded.

"Making any progress?"

"I suppose so."

"As good as it is, I just feel it would have more impact if the reader had insight into your parents and their influence on your relationship with your brother."

Jarrod's eyes hardened. "Well, it's just Mum, me, and the wee man. Dad bolted just after my brother was born."

Feeling instantly uncomfortable and knowing I couldn't really say anything helpful since I fortunately didn't have personal insight into parents who abandoned their children, I offered a lame "I'm sorry to hear that."

"Doesn't matter." He shrugged with fake nonchalance.

"It does. Try writing it in. It might help."

He rolled his eyes, giving me a sad smile. "See, why did you have to go spoil a perfectly nice moment with the personal essay crap, Miss Nichols?"

Giving him a look that told him I didn't buy his pretense at cool, I opened my mouth to dismiss him just as a loud knock on my open classroom doorway drew our gazes.

I sucked in my breath, my body freezing in shock.

Filling the entire doorway was Marco. He was wearing a dark fleece hoodie and dark jeans tucked into construction boots. My eyes flew back up to his face, and I felt that painful wince in my chest at his handsomeness.

What the hell was he doing here?

Jarrod sensed the sudden tension. "You okay, Miss Nichols?" His eyes swung to Marco and instantly narrowed in suspicion.

My heart racing, I turned to my student and attempted to sound calm as I replied, "I'm fine. I'll see you next class, Jarrod."

"I can stay," he said stubbornly.

I smiled at his protectiveness but shook my head. "I'll be fine."

He didn't seem convinced or too happy about leaving me with the large, brooding man in the doorway, but he gave me a chin lift in good-bye and strode across the room, his eyes holding Marco's in warning despite Marco's size.

Marco watched him leave, his gaze following him out of the classroom. When Jarrod was out of sight, he turned back to me with an amused look in his gorgeous eyes. "You've got a loyal one there."

No, no. There would be no pleasantries in this ambush. "What are you doing here?"

At my question, determination swept across his face and he walked into the room, somehow managing to fill the entire space with his more powerful than ever presence. I watched warily as he came to a stop a few feet from me. "Nish left my name with Reception so I could get in. My foreman let me cut out of work early. I was guessing that my only chance to see you would be in school."

My pulse was literally throbbing, probably visibly in my neck, so I was glad I was wearing my hair loose. As dogged as he was in his attempts to talk, I was equally determined to prove he didn't affect me. I stuck my chin out stubbornly. "Why? I told you I'm not interested in anything you have to say."

He shrugged, jamming his hands in his jeans. "I think your attitude suggests otherwise."

I glowered. "What's that supposed to mean?"

If that was a lip twitch of amusement I was going to kill him. He waved two fingers in the direction of my forehead and its frown lines. "That does."

Time to change tactics. "Why the hell do you want to talk? You hate talking."

Marco chuckled. "I'm not that guy anymore, Hannah. I just want a chance to explain that. But also to explain the past. And apologize for it."

There was a part of me that was desperate to give in, like I would have done when I was a kid, eager for his respect and affection. But I wasn't her anymore. He'd helped see to that. I leaned back against my desk and crossed my arms over my chest. "You're sorry?"

His eyes glittered with obvious remorse. "Of course."

"And you once did genuinely care about me?"

Something else entered his eyes, something more intense. His voice was deeper as he answered, "Yes."

"Okay. If that's true, you can prove it by turning around and walking out that door."

Displeasure replaced the intensity. "Hannah—"

"Prove it," I insisted fiercely.

Marco stared at me for a long moment, the muscle in his jaw working just like it used to when he was unhappy about something. To my surprise, my relief, and my disappointment, he gave me a jerky nod and turned around. I watched him walk away, my throat dry with thirst and hunger and heartache.

CHAPTER 8

On Thursday evening after the adult literacy class, I did what I always did and went to my local gym. I didn't have time to work out as much as I had done when I was at uni, but I always felt better if I got in at least two sessions a week. Sometimes, when things were particularly crazy I managed only one. That was always on a Thursday evening. Like my book group evenings, I looked forward to my Thursday nights at the gym because for a whole hour I switched off from work, friends, and family and just concentrated on sweating it out.

There were times, although not too often, when guys who thought they were so attractive they were rejection-proof would hit on me while I was just trying to enjoy my workout. I found that silence usually discomfited them and they'd quickly evaporate.

I was on the treadmill, working my way up from a walk to a run, when in my peripheral vision I saw the large figure of a guy step onto the treadmill next to me. My skin burned under his appraisal, but I ignored him.

However . . . my skin wouldn't stop burning because he wouldn't stop looking.

Annoyed, I chanced a scathing glance at him and nearly went flying backward off the treadmill when I realized it was Marco.

He reached out to steady me, but I flung my hands out and caught the rails. I almost sighed in relief that he hadn't touched me. I quickly reduced the speed on the machine, drawing to a stop so I could turn a full-strength glare on him.

He stared back at me, not saying a word, while I tried to process what the hell was happening and the fact that he looked beyond amazing in his white T-shirt and track bottoms. He definitely visited the gym often.

But not my gym!

"What the hell are you doing here?" I hissed, smoothing strands of hair back into my ponytail, painfully aware of how gross I must look.

Marco flashed me a boyish grin. "Working out."

Ignoring the flutterings caused by that grin, I narrowed my eyes and said through clenched teeth, "I've never seen you here before."

"That's because I've never been here before. I joined today."

I was pretty sure a nerve under my right eye had begun to tick. "Why? And answer in full this time."

He grinned again, crossing his arms over his chest so his biceps flexed. *Oh, mamma.*

It was official. I hated him.

"Speak!" I snapped, trying to control my wandering eyes.

Chuckling, Marco replied, "Anisha told me this is your gym, so now it's my gym."

"You're stalking me?"

"I prefer to call it 'actively pursuing you.' I told you, I just want a chance to explain."

Shaking my head in disbelief, I asked, "Who *are* you?"

"I'm not the guy I used to be."

"Forget I asked, because I don't care!" I yelled, instantly regretting it when one of the trainers shot me a warning look. I didn't like the triumphant expression on Marco's face. I was making it much too clear that he was affecting me. I sniffed haughtily and stepped off the treadmill. "I don't want an explanation and I don't care what gym you go to. I'm here to work out. You do as you please."

With that stick up my butt, I wandered away from him, trying to remember if these were the shorts that made my arse look flat. I swear my butt cheeks flushed beneath the fabric at the thought of him checking me out.

I got on the cross trainer and attempted to put Marco out of my mind. That wasn't so easy when he followed me and stepped up onto the cross trainer beside me. I did a valiant job of ignoring him . . . Ignoring him when he followed me like the stalker I'd accused him of being, around the gym so that we looked like we were working out together.

"If you want to do some weights I'll spot you." He grinned at me as I finished on the rowing machine.

I gave him a look of derision. "I'd rather have an elephant with a flatulence problem sit on my face."

Marco choked on a burst of laughter, swallowing what I was sure had been a gust of amusement. *Had* he changed?

Hmm.

No! Not hmm. You do not give a rat's arse if he's changed!

"Descriptive," he answered, mirth in his light eyes. "You still writing?"

I crossed my arms over my chest, cocking my hip in attitude. "Actually, I am still writing. What do you think of my latest story? It's about this brooding, issue-riddled American boy who slept with this nice Scottish girl. She told him she loved him and it disgusted him so much he flew across an entire ocean to get away from her, leaving nothing behind but a broken heart and virgin blood on the sheets."

All amusement fled from Marco's face. He took an uncertain step toward me, lifting his hand as if he was going to touch me, comfort me.

I flinched, warding him off, all that pain and rage concealed beneath a false calm. I don't know where I got the strength to find that calmness, but I thanked God for it. "Don't. I don't care if you've changed. I don't care who you are now. I don't need or want your explanations because what you did, you didn't do it to me, you did it to that girl you left behind. And I'm not her anymore. You made certain of that. *She* might have needed answers and an apology, but me . . . I don't know what you're talking about. You're just someone stalking me in my local gym."

With that I turned around and walked away from him, hoping he didn't see my legs trembling.

The first thing I did when I got to the locker room was to send a text to Nish, who was on her honeymoon in the Maldives. It pretty much warned her to stop giving Marco my weekly schedule and permission to the receptionist at school to let him in. Or else.

I used the f-word *a lot.*

Even though I had time to visit the gym the following Monday, I didn't. I hadn't received any more calls or surprise visits from Marco, but I wasn't chancing the gym again. It didn't matter, though. He'd won. He was inside my head, just where I knew he wanted to be. I kept expecting him to appear everywhere, and I hated that I was at once relieved and disappointed whenever I got through the day without seeing him. It would seem my mind knew exactly what it wanted, but my body and my heart just wouldn't agree with it.

I tried relaxing by going to dinner with Michaela and Colin on Saturday, and visiting with my family at Sunday lunch. I must have done an okay job of at least pretending relaxation and calm because I wasn't peppered with concerned questions. I'd even managed to convince Ellie so she'd stop being annoyed with me.

School was particularly busy because it was only a few days until Halloween and the kids were hyper. This meant I was really looking forward to my book group because it was relaxing and interesting and a total escape from my real life. It was a group of eleven of us, but usually only eight or so ever turned up on the night. We ranged from twenty-two years old (me) to fifty-eight (an outspoken dental receptionist called Ronnie). We were reading *The Help* and I knew the subject matter would make for some opinionated chat. It would take my mind off *things* for a while.

I walked into the room we used in the community center that evening feeling like tonight would be the night to put Marco and his strange behavior of the last week behind me for good.

I smiled hello to the only guy in our group, Chris. Chris was forty-five years old and a high school history teacher. He'd joined the book group as well as a chess club and bowling team in an effort to move on from his divorce. I settled down in my usual seat between Chris and Laila, a twenty-five-year-old book blogger who had a photographic memory and had read more books in her short time on the planet than all the rest of us collectively.

"Oh, Hannah, come meet our newest member!" Ronnie called.

I glanced up from pulling my copy of *The Help* out of my bag to look across the room at Ronnie. Disbelief crashed over me.

Marco towered over her, grinning at me.

"Oh, my God," Laila murmured, devouring Marco with her eyes. "He's totally my latest book boyfriend."

I shot her a dirty look before getting slowly to my feet. I walked toward Ronnie and Marco, wondering how to handle this new situation, and also wondering how the hell to stop the tingling between my legs at the way Marco was looking at me.

I felt his eyes roam over me, lingering on my breasts, following the curve of my hips and skimming my legs, before traveling back up again. When our eyes met, his were filled with the kind of blatant heat I would have done anything for five years ago.

"Marco." I greeted him flatly, deciding not to hide the fact that I knew him.

Ronnie's eyes widened. "You know Marco already?"

"Yup." I raised an eyebrow at him in question and he gave me that grin again. That was a new grin. And it had an immediate effect on my lady parts.

Damn him.

"Well, what a coincidence." Ronnie smiled, her eyes moving back and forth between us.

"Mmm." I rounded my eyes in mock agreement. "Coincidence indeed."

Marco laughed outright.

Ronnie appeared suddenly confused.

"So, Marco . . . I didn't know you liked to read." I puckered my brow in fake confusion.

"Yeah." He nodded innocently. "I'm a big reader."

"Or a big liar," I muttered under my breath.

"Sorry, Hannah?" Ronnie leaned in to hear me better.

I ignored her as politely as I could, my saccharine smile directed at Marco. "It's nice to welcome you aboard. How did you find out about us?"

He chuckled. "Anisha. Apparently, she doesn't do well with threats. Know anything about that?"

Nish. Of course. I should have known better—threat tactics would make her do the opposite of what I wanted her to do. "I don't know what you're talking about," I lied. "And I'm going to kill her."

Ronnie sighed. "I'm very confused right now."

I sighed too. "Let's just start, shall we?"

We took our seats and Marco sat next to Ronnie in the chair directly opposite me in the circle. All eyes were on him as Ronnie introduced him, and not just because he was new to the group, but because he stood out in so many ways. One, he was gorgeous; two, he was American; and three, he just had that special something about him that drew people to him.

I'd have thrown my book at him if it wouldn't have gotten me kicked out of the group. I even seriously contemplated it for a moment and by the silent laughter parting Marco's lips he knew exactly what I was thinking about doing.

I glared at him and looked away.

"Have you read *The Help*, Marco?" Ronnie asked him, clearly enamored with him.

"Nope, can't say I have."

"Oh, that's okay. Just follow along with our discussion."

"Sure thing."

Sure thing. I made a childish face in mockery and his snort brought my gaze swinging back to collide with his. He was laughing at me. He found me amusing.

He was enjoying himself!

I attempted to join the discussion, attempted to say all the intelligent things I had to say about the book, but with his blue-green eyes boring into me the whole time, my brain wasn't cooperating.

Thirty minutes later, Chris was shooting me concerned looks and Ronnie was preening because she'd brought up most of the talking points this week. She turned to Marco. "Is there anything you might like to add, now that you've heard a little something about the book?"

I froze, my eyes glued to him despite myself. My heart sped up in anticipation.

Marco didn't disappoint. He looked straight at me and replied, "I think it sounds like a book about determination, about pursuing what's right, what feels right, despite the odds stacked against you or the possible fallout. It sounds like my kind of book."

I was frozen in that moment, looking at him as he looked back at me with all the determination he had mentioned. My palms began to sweat, I couldn't hear over the rushing of blood in my ears, and I wondered where the hell I was supposed to go from there.

He was telling me he wasn't going to give up.

I think I believed him.

Clearing my throat, I abruptly stood up and stuffed the book in my bag. Without a word, I hurried out of there, ignoring Ronnie's concerned call of my name as the others murmured their bafflement.

CHAPTER 9

"*When I'm with you it feels like everything's going to be okay. I can't explain it.*"

I couldn't get Marco's voice out of my head, those words he'd said to me so long ago. They had meant so much to me then because I knew that he wasn't the kind of guy who expressed his emotions well, and that day he'd let himself be vulnerable with me.

Despite everything that had happened, despite him leaving me and breaking my heart, I couldn't stop those words from haunting me.

Standing alone on the small patio at the back of the house where I grew up, I stared at the ground and I fought with myself, calling myself foolish for dwelling on the sweet when it was the bitter that had done so much damage. But in a way, I guess, the bitter wouldn't affect me so much if the sweet hadn't been so damn sweet.

"Nanna."

I glanced up at the now open French doors that led into my parents' dining room to see Cole gazing at me in concern. The noise from the front of the house filtered toward me now that the door was open. Although Joss, Braden, Beth, and Luke weren't with us because they had tickets to a children's musical, the house was still crowded and loud. Liv and Nate had made it this time, along with Lily and January. Ellie and

Adam were there too with William, and Jo, Cam, Cole, Dec, and Penny had joined us.

I smiled at Cole. Ever since Lily started calling me Nanna, Cole used it playfully. "What's up?"

He stepped outside, closing the door.

I frowned at the thin T-shirt he wore. Although it exposed his artwork, it also exposed him to the spiky November cold. "Go back inside and put on a jacket."

One corner of his mouth pulled up into an amused smirk. "I'm fine, Mum."

"You'll catch a cold."

"I'm fine," he insisted. "You? I'm thinking not so much."

It was getting harder and harder to pretend with my friends and family that I wasn't in a mood. I'd spent the last week completely discombobulated, living inside my own head. I didn't know how I felt about Marco's persistence and because no one else knew the whole story I didn't even have anyone to turn to. And in the end that was my own fault.

"Hannah, seriously." Cole's smile slipped, a deep frown line appearing between his brows. "You've been quiet all week and you're out here by yourself, looking like you have the weight of the entire world on your shoulders. I'm worried. Tell me what's going on."

I sighed, not wanting to piss him off with an obvious lie. "Do you remember Marco from the wedding?"

He nodded and waited for me to continue.

"I used to be in love with him."

Cole's eyebrows rose at that little bomb of information. "How did I not know this?"

"You and I weren't as close back then. Jo, Ellie, Joss, and Liv know about him. We met when I was fourteen and by the time I was seventeen I was mad about him. He's older, so we were just friends. Sometimes I tutored him. But I always wanted more. We kissed when I was seventeen"— I diluted the information—"and just when I thought maybe he felt the same way about me, he went back to America. The wedding reception was the first time I've seen him since then and . . . he told me he's been back in Edinburgh for *four* years."

My friend's eyes glimmered with sympathy. "I'm sorry, sweetheart. I wish I'd known. I would never have left you alone that night."

"I needed to be alone," I reassured him.

"His reappearance is obviously messing with your head."

"No, actually he is."

Cole's face instantly darkened. "What does that mean?"

"It means he wants a chance to explain why he left the way he left, and he's been turning up everywhere I go in an attempt to get me to listen." I went on to tell him about the school, the gym, and the book club encounter.

His glower cleared. Now he just looked amused. "So, listen."

I jerked back in anger. "No. He doesn't deserve it."

"Hannah, you were kids. If he's taking the time to pursue you, then he clearly feels bad and wants a second chance."

"He's had that chance for the last four years."

"Maybe he didn't know what to say."

"Whose side are you on?"

"Yours," he said with a laugh. "But, Christ, you're working yourself into knots over him when all it might take to give you a little closure is a better understanding of where his head was at. He's offering you that chance."

I gave him a low-lidded look of displeasure. "If I wanted a voice of reason I would have asked for it."

Cole chuckled. "I'm just saying, unless there's more to this than you're telling me, I think he deserves a chance to explain." Some dark suspicion suddenly entered his gaze. "There isn't more to this, is there?"

I shook my head with faux calm. "No . . . but he is the reason I made a stupid decision back then. So . . . there's that."

Understanding settled over Cole's features and he replied kindly, "You can't hold your own actions against him."

Feeling guilty for lying to Cole and angry at Marco and myself for the predicament I found myself in with my family, I nodded glumly. There was no way I'd get the right advice without my friends and family having the full story, and I had no intention of rewriting the history I had given them with the truth. "Let's stop talking about me." I waved the subject away. "How's you? How's Steph?"

He made a face. "Steph and I ended it last night."

My lips parted in surprise. "And you're only just telling me this?"

He shrugged. "There's not much to tell. We were out after work last night and we bumped into some of my friends from school and she started a catfight with one of the girls."

"Catfight?"

"Her jealousy is ridiculous. She has major trust issues. It was time to end it."

"We all have issues, Cole. Relationships aren't easy. Sometimes you have to work at it."

"Agreed. But I didn't want to work at it, so what does that tell you?"

"She's not the one for you."

"Exactly." He turned and opened the door. "Now that we've beat our relationship issues out for the day, let's get fed."

"You're sure you're okay?" I asked, following him inside.

"I'm fine," he promised. "I'm relieved, actually. Steph's problems were exhausting."

Although I wanted him to be happy and that was what mattered most, I couldn't help but feel for Steph and sympathize with her. Cole's words depressed me and I took them far more personally than he would ever have wanted me to. But the truth was, I was like Steph. I wasn't insanely jealous, but my own insecurities came from a lack of trust in the opposite sex. It was crazy, I knew it was. I was surrounded by good men who didn't stray from their wives, but what Marco had done to me and the consequences of that night had cut deep. It had left ugly scar tissue I'd been able to ignore until he was suddenly back in my life. Part of the reason I never bothered trying to find anything serious was because of that feeling Marco had left behind, but also because I suspected that most men would react to me and my issues like Cole had to Steph: with ambivalence and impatience. So what was the point in trying?

"Something's going on," Jo mused, staring at Liv and Nate across the table. She waved her fork at them. "What's wrong with you?"

Cam snorted beside her. "Maybe that's their business, sweetheart."

"Well, it would be their business if they'd managed to pretend they weren't fighting, but things are feeling a little icy," Ellie added.

Liv rolled her eyes. "Nate's being a tool."

Nate didn't lift his gaze from his plate as he ate. "Nate's not doing anything," he murmured back.

Nate was definitely doing something. He was barely talking to his wife, and anytime he was forced to, he wouldn't look at her.

"Keep the domestics at home, people," Cole pleaded.

"It's not a domestic." Liv made a face. "It's an example of man's inescapable immaturity."

"Oh, do tell," Ellie leaned in eagerly.

"I was clearing things out of the house and I specifically asked him to make a pile of things he didn't want to give to charity and a pile of stuff he did want to give to charity. It is not my fault that *he* got the piles mixed up."

"I did not." He glared at her, finally looking away from his plate. "Why the hell would I give away every single one of my favorite T-shirts? Did you not think when you were looking through them that it was a bit strange they were *all* in there?"

She sniffed before responding. "I didn't look through them. I just assumed you gave me the right pile and I put them in the charity bag and gave them to the lady who comes to collect the stuff."

"Some of that shit was irreplaceable."

Lily gave this cute little girlie gasp and Nate closed his eyes, wincing.

Liv scowled at him.

With a sigh, he turned in his seat to look over at Lily, who was sitting with Ellie at the kids' table. "That's a bad word, honey. Don't use it. Daddy shouldn't have and he's sorry."

Lily gave him this cute, serious nod of agreement. My God, was it possible to die from her adorableness?

Nate turned back to Liv. "Happy? Can we not discuss this in front of the kids?"

"Of course." She shrugged nonchalantly, returning her gaze to her plate. "But I don't know why you're so upset. If you'd bothered to look in the bag I put at the side of the bed yesterday afternoon, you'd have seen I called the charity, explained the mistake, and went and collected your irreplaceable crap." She glanced over at him. "I would like to remind you, though, that the only things in your life that are irreplaceable are sitting in this room with you."

"Hear, hear," Mum murmured.

Nate's expression slackened with confusion. "You got it all back?"

"Of course I got it all back."

"Why didn't you tell me?"

"Because now I have leverage against you anytime I screw up. I'll just remind you of the past forty-eight hours where you acted like a petulant schoolboy because I accidentally gave your Borg T-shirt to charity."

"It was the T-shirt I was wearing when we met," he told her quietly.

Her eyes narrowed. "Oh, no, you're not pulling semi-romantic excuses for your behavior out of your petushy to screw me out of leverage."

"Leverage?" I asked. "Marriage is about leverage?"

"Yes." Every single married person at the table answered.

I wrinkled my nose.

Ellie waved her fork at me. "When you screw up, and if you're married you're bound to screw up at some point, it's good to have detailed notes of your partner's screwups because that way you can remind them, and forgiveness for your screwup comes much more quickly. Peace reigns."

"In this case," Liv said, her eyes alight with triumph, "I screwed up a little but Nate screwed up more, so the next time *I* screw up, he'll forgive me way faster."

"It sounds . . . mature," I answered sarcastically.

"What it lacks in sophistication it more than makes up for in effectiveness," Adam attested.

"Married people are weird." I turned to Cole. "Remind me never to do that."

"To do that, you have to agree to go on a date with a man," he reminded me instead.

I shot him a filthy look, but before I could say anything, Adam said, "Hannah, that reminds *me*, you didn't tell me you knew Marco D'Alessandro."

Jo tensed at the name, her eyes swinging to meet mine.

"What?" Adam asked softly, picking up on the sudden change in atmosphere between us.

I drew in a deep breath, unlocking my gaze from Jo's and turning to Adam. "I didn't realize you knew him."

"He's a joiner in one of our construction crews. The foreman, Tam, speaks highly of him and is absolutely convinced he'll be foreman himself in a few years' time. I don't doubt it. He's always on hand when Tam isn't and knows almost everything that's going on on-site. I've known him for a couple of years. He seems like a really good guy. Hardworking and responsible. He didn't realize we were related. Your schoolteacher friend's husband told him."

"Oh," was all I managed.

"Oh?" Adam's eyebrows puckered. "From the way he spoke you two used to be close."

I looked at Ellie, wondering if she'd known Adam was going to ambush me with this, but she looked just as surprised as I was. Not really wanting to discuss it in front of my parents, I shrugged. "We were really good friends in school."

Adam still looked confused. "Isn't he older than you?"

"A few years."

"Well, he says he's been trying to get in touch with you."

Cole snorted at my side.

I ignored that, giving Adam another innocent shrug. "I got a couple of his messages." A deeper snort from Cole. "But I've been really busy."

"You didn't tell me he was in touch," Jo piped up, concern in her gorgeous green eyes. "Are you okay?"

"Who is this boy, Hannah?" Mum quizzed suddenly.

"How long has he been back?" Jo asked.

"He couldn't have been a boyfriend." Mum shook her head at the idea. "Because you would have told me, right?"

Jo leaned toward me. "When did you meet? Did he explain anything?"

"Where's he from? Where did he go? I'm so confused. Is—"

"Hannah, will you help me with dessert, sweetheart?" Dad asked loudly, standing up.

I pushed back from the table, throwing my dad a grateful smile. "Of course." I hurried out of the room, happy to escape the questions as I followed him into the kitchen. "You're a lifesaver."

Dad gave me a soft smile and began pulling bowls out of the cupboard. "No problem."

We were silent as we dished out the trifle.

And then . . . "Hannah." Dad stopped what he was doing, staring at the table, his body tense. "This Marco . . . he isn't . . . ?"

I swallowed, my heart beating hard against my chest. "Dad." I didn't want to lie. Not to him.

He glanced at me sharply, anger in his eyes. "Does he know?"

I shook my head.

"Why is he back?"

"He wants a chance to explain why he left so abruptly. After . . . he went back to America before it . . ."

Dad exhaled, the anger melting. "How long has he been trying to get back in touch?"

"We met at a wedding a few weeks ago. He's been persistent ever since."

"Before . . . what kind of man did you take him for? Was he kind to you?"

For some reason the question opened a flood of emotion in me, my throat constricting, my nose and eyes stinging with tears. "Yes. He was very kind to me. We met because he was protecting me from this really horrible boy that was bullying me. Anytime I missed the bus Marco would walk me home, make sure I got there safely."

God, I'd loved him so much. Maybe the foolish, naïve kind of love, but I'd felt it deeply nonetheless.

Dad slid his hand across the table, covering mine in comfort. I looked up into his eyes. "Maybe he deserves a chance to explain, then."

I was surprised. "I thought you'd be angry at him."

"I'm still angry at his choices, but I can't be angry at him for what happened afterward. He didn't know what you went through, Hannah. If he explains and it's a terrible explanation, we can go back to being mad at him. But maybe he's got a reasonable explanation for leaving you."

"I don't know how you can be so rational."

"Well," Dad said with a sigh, "I didn't know him, so I don't understand everything that happened. What I do know is that I have a strong daughter who's rarely fazed by anything. If this man knocks you off balance a bit, then maybe there's something to that. When I met your mum I was knocked on my arse."

I laughed gently and nudged him with my shoulder. "All these happily married couples are making you soft, Dad."

"Nah, that's just old age," he joked, and grabbed a couple of bowls to take through to the dining room.

"Dad." I stopped him from leaving. "Don't tell anyone. No one else knows."

Dad nodded slowly. "Okay, I won't. But I want you to ask yourself why you're protecting him if you don't care about him?"

More confused than ever, I watched my dad walk out of the kitchen, pondering his question. No answer came. With shaking hands I picked up a couple of bowls and ventured back into the dining room, glad when I got there that Marco was no longer the topic of conversation.

CHAPTER 10

A lull in the discussion during the night's adult literacy session made me smile. "You know, for people who complain that this is the worst part, you certainly had a lot to say."

Duncan smirked while the others laughed. With the exception of Lorraine, who'd barely said a word all class.

I'd found that a good way to help along the class reading skills was to have them read something for homework and come in and chat about it as a group. These guys had very basic reading skills, but they were coming on by leaps and bounds. I found that in discussion they unearthed a better understanding of the words they'd read because what one didn't understand, another did, and they helped one another out without even realizing it.

"Well done, folks." I stood. "Read chapter six for next week, please, and I shall see you all then."

We bade one another a good night, the class filtering out until only Lorraine remained. Since the night I'd spoken to her, she'd turned up for every class. Still, she stubbornly refused any one-on-one assistance, and the reading challenges I set them made her uneasy. I'd quickly discovered that she was the kind of woman who preferred someone to be straightforward with her, rather than pussyfooting around her.

"Is it me?" I asked her.

Her head jerked up from her bag and she frowned at me. "Is whit you?"

"Am I the reason you don't want to speak up in class?"

She shrugged.

I raised an eyebrow. "It's not the others. It can't be. You've seen them struggle, and you've witnessed how patient and kind the class is with one another. You yourself have shown patience. Kindness. So if they're not the ones who make you uncomfortable, who make you afraid, is it me?"

"I'm no afraid," she snapped.

I strode toward her and gently took the book out of her hands. Opening it up to the chapter we'd just been discussing, I handed it back to her. "Read the first two sentences out to me."

Lorraine looked at me incredulously. However, I saw what she was so desperately trying to hide. I saw the fear.

She snatched the book out of my hands and pulled it toward her face. She swallowed. Hard. With painstaking care she began to read to me. Almost near the end, she faltered on a word. Glancing up at me warily, she flushed.

I kept my face perfectly blank. "Sound it out."

The anger flashed in her eyes and yet she looked back at the page. "It's no a word." She frowned. "Fuh-ri-gid," she said, pronouncing it almost like "frigate."

"Do you remember the rules for hard and soft *g*'s? Usually, when *g* meets *a, o,* or *u* it's a hard *g.* The guh sound. Like *gap.* But usually when it meets *e, y,* or an *i,* it's a soft *g.* The juh sound."

Lorraine stared at the word. "It's an *i.* Fuh-ri-gid. Fuhrigid." Her eyes scanned the sentence that preceded it and the tension melted out of her as she said, "Frigid." She shrugged. "I always thought that word wis spelt wi a *j.*"

I took a step back from her. "That was well done."

She ducked her head. "Aye, whitever." Abruptly she grabbed her bag and brushed past me. "See ye next week."

I stared after her in thought for a while after she left the room. Lorraine was definitely rough around the edges, lacking in good manners and social graces, but I couldn't help but respect someone who pushed through despite her fears.

With my heart pounding and my stomach roiling with waves of nausea, I settled onto my window seat in the living room, staring out at the dark, glistening street. Pools of light glimmered here and there where streetlights glanced off puddles made from the recent rainfall. I clutched my phone in my hand and sucked in a deep breath.

Scrolling through my recent call list I found the number, and with Lorraine's perseverance and Dad's question at the forefront of my mind, I pressed the CALL button.

It rang three times before . . . "Hannah?" Marco answered, pleasant surprise in his deep voice.

"Hi," I replied quietly, willing my heart to slow. "I . . ."

His voice was filled with a concern I remembered all too well as he asked, "Are you okay?"

I exhaled slowly. "I've decided I do want to know why you left me that night."

He was quiet for a moment and I was just about to break the silence when he said, "I want to ask why the sudden change of heart, but I'm not going to in case I scare you off. I'm glad you called, but I'd rather discuss it in person. Would that be okay with you?"

"If I say no you're only going to turn up at my next dental appointment, right?"

He laughed quietly, a seriously delicious sound that made my scalp tingle. "Whatever it takes."

"I still can't believe you came to my book group," I muttered.

"It got you to call me, didn't it?"

"Tread carefully, Mr. D'Alessandro," I warned.

He chuckled. "Fine. I'll be good . . . if you invite me over to your place tomorrow night to talk."

Trepidation shot through me at the thought of us being alone in my flat. "I don't think that's a good idea."

"Hannah, what we have to discuss is personal. What I have to tell you is personal and I don't particularly feel comfortable with the stranger behind us in a café listening in."

I processed that, and unfortunately had to admit that he was right. I didn't want a stranger listening in on us either. "Fine," I grumbled, giving him my address. "Six o'clock."

"Does it include dinner?" he asked hopefully, a boyish cheekiness in the question that surprised me.

"We'll see." I hung up without saying good-bye.

I felt much too hot all over and suddenly restless as adrenaline pumped through my body. I hadn't felt this awake in a long, long time.

School was a blur. I was so preoccupied with the thought of Marco being at my place that night that I don't even know how I got through the lessons. Somehow I made it, and with my stomach a jumpy, jittery mess, I hurried home after work and began preparing dinner. I didn't know what to cook because I didn't want Marco to think I was trying to impress him, but I also didn't want to poison him with something he was allergic to.

I'd settled on pasta and salad. Surely you couldn't go wrong with pasta and salad.

It went against the manners of being a good hostess (which my mother had ingrained in me from the age of three) not to dress the table when I was having someone over for dinner, but I also didn't want Marco to think this was something it wasn't.

Who was I kidding? I didn't even know what this *was.*

I changed from my work clothes into a pair of well-worn jeans and a long-sleeved thermal top. Twisting my hair up into a messy bun, I looked in the mirror and nodded, pleased with my reflection. The jeans made my arse look great, the top was form-fitting and made my boobs look good, but overall the outfit said "I'm just hanging at home and I could give a shit what you think about me."

"Perfect."

I spun around, marching out of my bedroom toward the kitchen, and my door buzzer sounded, drawing me to a halt.

I was going to throw up. I was going to upchuck all over my nice hardwood floors.

"Deep breaths," I coached myself, turning back toward the door.

"Hello?" I asked upon lifting the receiver.

"It's Marco."

Yup, definitely going to upchuck. I pressed the entrance door key, letting him into the building.

With blood rushing in my ears, I attempted to prepare myself to see him again, and drew on my powers of indifference. Opening my door, I listened to his footsteps as he climbed the stairs to my flat.

I saw his head appear as he ascended the staircase and my stomach dropped. His eyes lifted from his feet to my face as he climbed higher, and he gave me a small smile in greeting. *Damn it.* Why did I have to be so attracted to him? Why did I have to have so many good memories of him?

His gaze drifted down my body and back up again, and I got the distinct feeling he wasn't disappointed by my outfit. Not at all. Pretending I didn't give a crap, I stepped back. "Come in."

He moved inside, making me feel tiny, and despite his defection, safe. "Did you get taller?" I grumbled, moving away from him and the attractive cologne he was wearing.

He shut the front door behind him and shook his head. "Not that I'm aware of."

As my eyes took him in, it occurred to me that it had nothing to do with his height. It was his muscle. I gulped at the sight of his biceps, nicely displayed in the form-fitting hooded Henley he was wearing. "This way," I almost wheezed, abruptly turning my back at the sight of his amusement.

He followed me into the sitting room, where I'd set the dining table at the back of the room. "Nice place." His eyes hit the piles of books that I had in nearly every corner, and he gave me that familiar half smile that made me feel things I didn't want to feel. "You need bookshelves, though."

Ignoring that comment, I gestured to the table. "Take a seat. I'll get dinner."

Marco raised an eyebrow. "You cooked after all?"

I narrowed my eyes. "Only because I'm hungry."

"Of course."

Pissed that I was doing a very shitty job of coming across as being unaffected by his presence, I marched out of the room and into my kitchen, where I clutched the edge of my countertop, taking in a deep breath.

You can do this. He's just a boy. He's just a boy. He's just a boy. I chanted that mantra over and over in my head while I grabbed the bowls of pasta and salad.

"This looks great," Marco said after I strode back into the sitting room to dump them on the table.

I made a *harrumph* sound and then grunted, "Beer?"

His lips quirked up at the corners and I could see the laughter dancing in his stunning eyes. "Sure."

I returned with the beer, slammed it down in front of him, and then shoved myself ungracefully into my seat opposite him. I gestured to the bowls. "Eat."

Not hiding his amusement any longer, Marco grinned as he reached for the salad bowl. "You seem agitated."

No, do I? Outwardly, I just shrugged. "Well, I'm fine."

His look said he didn't believe me for a second. I took the salad bowl from him, dumping vegetables onto my plate as he scooped pasta al pomodoro onto his own. We were silent as we served ourselves and started eating.

I felt like any second I might just jump out of my skin and throw my skeleton arse out of my bay window. I kept waiting for him to start speaking, to start explaining himself, since that was the whole point of him being here in my sitting room, eating my food and affecting my girlie bits. Finally, I'd had enough of his seemingly comfortable silence. "Four years?" I snapped, glaring at him.

Marco contemplated me, appearing to memorize every inch of my face in a way that made my skin feel hot and tingly. He laid his fork down and sat back, twisting the cap off his beer with little effort. He took a sip, his eyes never leaving me. "Maybe we should start with the night at India Place."

Unexpected pain shot across my chest at the mention of India Place. It stole my breath, that pain. Ever since I'd lost my virginity to Marco, the pain and humiliation of that night had really only ever belonged to me, because he hadn't been around to face afterward and no one else knew about it.

Discussing it with him for the first time made it feel like it had just happened.

I must not have been able to keep that pain out of my expression, because Marco tensed, and something like regret flickered in his gaze.

He set the beer down, his entire focus on me. "I want you to know that being with you that night was one of the best nights of my life."

I froze at that shocking confession, only for anger to quickly unfreeze me. "Don't you dare try to sweet-talk me with bullshit and pretty words. I just want the truth, Marco."

His features hardened. "That is the truth. You can be pissed off at me all you want, but don't question what I tell you tonight because I've never lied to you."

"For all I know."

"No, you do know. I've never lied to you, Hannah. Not once."

"Well, if that night was so amazing how come you couldn't get out of there fast enough afterward? How come you left me lying there in that skeezy flat, feeling used and absolutely worthless?"

Looking pained by my questions, Marco suddenly drew a hand down his face.

I waited.

"I hate myself for making you feel that way," he whispered. "I'm sorry."

My heart was beating so hard against my chest it hurt. "Why, then?"

Understanding my question, he sat back in his chair, his jaw taut. "You were Hannah. You were this great girl who made me laugh and looked at me like I was worth something, and every year you got more beautiful."

His words made my heart flip over in my chest.

"You were too good for me. I knew that the first time I walked you home. Pure class from the tips of your fingers to the tips of your toes. Not for me."

"I don't understand."

Marco exhaled heavily. "I told you I didn't get along with my grandfather or my uncle. And what I meant was that I *really* didn't get along with them. From the moment I could walk Nonno made sure I thought I was a piece of scum, worthless. He told me I was nothing and that I would never amount to anything. He said I was just like my mom and dad, and that every life I'd touch, I'd ruin. He drilled that into me."

I couldn't help myself. Even after everything, I was hurt and angry on his behalf when he said those things. "He sounds like a bitter old bastard."

Marco gave a huff of laughter. "You'd be right. But he was the only father figure I had. So, despite Nonna's attempts to soften my grandfather's blows, I believed him. It got so I was almost trying to prove him right. I grew up with this kid in my neighborhood. His stepdad was kind of a prick to him too. We were friends mostly because of our mutual hate for them. As we got older, Jamal started doing stupid shit like breaking into people's homes, stealing stuff, vandalism, and all that crap, and I went along for the ride. Then when we were almost sixteen he got recruited into a gang."

My eyes widened. "A *gang* gang?"

"A *gang* gang." Marco's eyes were dark with the memories. "He told me some of the stuff they made him do and it pissed me off, but at the same time I kept thinking how much it would really piss off Nonno if I got mixed up in that shit. I think the only thing that stopped me from taking it that far was Nonna and the rest of our family. Still, I did think about it.

"But then one night I was hanging out with Jamal and a couple of the guys from his crew, and they were trying to convince me to join. They waylaid this neighborhood girl Jamal liked." His gaze drifted off over my left shoulder and I knew he was re-seeing it all. "I didn't want to believe it . . . that he was going to rape her, but he started touching her and she was crying and he wouldn't . . ." His eyes flicked back to me, hard now. "I jumped him and she got away, but his friends started in on me and it was three against one. I think if Jamal hadn't convinced them to stop they would have killed me. As it was, I ended up in the hospital and I told my grandparents what had happened. That's when they got on the phone to my uncle Gio and somehow convinced him and Aunt Gabby to adopt me and bring me over to the UK to get away from it all. They tracked my mom down and got her to sign the papers and by the time I turned sixteen it was all done and I was suddenly in Scotland."

"And your grandfather? Didn't he think what you did for that girl was heroic?"

Marco scoffed. "Heroic? No. He called me a worthless, stupid, ignorant piece of shit. He said a father's blood always tells and my blood was telling."

My own blood turned red-hot. "Your grandfather's a dick of the highest order."

"My grandfather's dead."

I tensed. "What?"

He sighed, leaning forward again. "The morning after we slept together Nonna called to tell us Nonno had died of a heart attack. I flew back to Chicago that night with my aunt and uncle."

"That's why you left Scotland?"

"Yeah. My aunt and uncle returned to Scotland but I didn't come back for a year because I wanted to make sure Nonna was okay and I . . . I had a difficult time letting go of the fact that I was never going to get closure with my grandfather. I was never going to get an apology or whatever validation it was I was looking for from him. I tried to find peace, but I couldn't, so I decided to come back here."

I pushed my fork around my plate. "I understand all that, Marco, and I'm sorry he ever made you feel that way, I am. I'm truly sorry. But that doesn't explain why you left me in that room after I gave you my virginity and told you I loved you. It doesn't explain why you never tried to look me up since coming back."

The sudden intensity in Marco's gaze captured me. His voice sounded even rougher than usual as he replied, "I left you because I thought I didn't deserve to touch you. I felt like a selfish bastard for having sex with you because . . . I felt like I was nothing because *he* told me I was nothing, and scum like me didn't deserve to touch you, let alone take what you gave me. But I got so caught up in you and how much I wanted you I forgot all that . . . until you told me you loved me."

I felt cold, remembering the moment well.

"When we met . . . at first the situation with Jenks just reminded me of Jamal and the girl. It didn't matter if I didn't know you. I was there, I saw that shit happening and I knew what Jenks was like, so I wasn't going to stand there and let that happen to you. I walked you home because I didn't want him to circle back on you.

"I stood outside the school gates to make sure you were okay because after I walked you home that one time I thought you deserved someone looking out for you. You were a funny, smart, kind girl, and you looked at me in a way no one had before. Like I had something interesting to say and you wanted to hear all about it. That felt better than you can imagine. I wanted to feel that way again. I got addicted to feeling that way whenever you were around. I even started hoping for reasons for you to miss that bus home. I let something happen that I thought I shouldn't have. I let us get close.

"I didn't want you to love me, Hannah, because I was terrified I'd hurt you, and, yeah, I know that sounds fucked up now since I hurt you by walking out on you, but at the time I thought I was doing you a favor."

"A favor?" I guffawed. "I thought I was in love with you. I let myself be vulnerable with you in every way I could and you scrambled off me as if you couldn't bear to be near me. You broke my heart."

Marco clasped his hands into a fist, resting his chin on them. "I know," he whispered back. "I've never regretted anything more in my life. It was fucked up and stupid and if I could take that moment back I would."

"All of it?" I found myself asking.

His eyes drifted to my lips and then back up to my eyes again. "No," he replied, his voice thick. "Just the part where I left you."

"If you feel that way, why didn't you come back to me when you returned to Scotland?"

"Because I didn't feel that way then. Nothing magically changed when Nonno died, Hannah. I still felt worthless for a very long time."

"When did it change? Why?"

Marco's gaze lowered and he gave a tiny shake of his head. "I don't know. It was nothing. Everything. I grew up, I worked hard, and I began to find value in myself. Somewhere, bit by bit, day by day, I found self-worth. I found it by proving that bastard wrong."

"I'm glad you found that," I told him honestly. "But that still doesn't tell me why after that you didn't come find me."

"Because by then years had passed, Hannah. I didn't know what to say and I didn't know if I could stand to have you look at me like I was nothing after it took me so long to feel about myself the way you *used* to look at me."

"Until the wedding?"

"Until the wedding," he agreed, heat entering his eyes now. "It was a shock to see you there, but seeing you again . . . God, I thought I knew how much I missed you until I saw you again. I know I came on strong trying to get you to talk to me, and I'm sorry if I freaked you out . . . but you didn't look at me like I was worthless at the wedding. You looked pissed, but it wasn't this fucking awful thing I'd built up in my head. With that fear gone, I just really needed the chance to apologize and I was willing to do anything I could to get that chance."

Something inside me, something I wanted desperately to ignore, exalted at his confession. "And now that you've explained everything . . . what do you want from me?"

"Forgiveness," he answered sincerely. The sincerity quickly dissipated under the weight of the intensity that entered his expression. That look filled the whole room until I felt stifled by it. "And a second chance to get to know you."

With my body physically responding to him, I narrowed my eyes and fought to ignore that response. "In what way?"

"Not just as friends, if that's what you're thinking."

I jerked back in my seat at his blunt reply. "You're not even going to pretend to want to be just friends so you can try a sneak attack for more?"

Marco stared at me with serious determination. "I'm not going to hide that I want to get to know who you are now. I'm also not going to hide the fact that I think you're still the classiest, most fucking beautiful woman I've ever seen, or the fact that I remember the taste of you and it still makes me hard."

I couldn't breathe.

"Hannah?" He frowned at my silence.

I reached for my beer and took a long swallow, trying to collect myself.

"Hannah?"

My eyes clashed with his. "What do you want me to say?"

"I want you to say 'Marco, I forgive you and, yes, I want to get to know you again.'"

"I don't know if I can do that," I whispered.

For a minute I thought he wasn't going to say anything, but suddenly he stood up. I tilted my head back, watching warily as he strode around the table to tower over me. I sucked in my breath as he leaned down, his heat hitting me, his cologne wafting over me, and I couldn't suppress the shiver that cascaded down my spine when he pressed his warm lips to my cheek. My eyes round with surprise, I gaped at him as he straightened and said, "I'll give you a couple of days to think about it."

CHAPTER 11

I stared woefully at the wall in front of me decorated with Cole's tattoo art. The buzz of the tattoo needle next door played a sound track to Saturday lunch with my best friend. Cole was working at INKarnate and I'd stopped by with food so we could hang out on his lunch break.

I could feel his eyes burning into me.

Giving in to his silent question, I turned to meet his gaze.

He sipped his coffee and continued to stare at me without saying anything.

"What?" I shrugged before biting into my sandwich.

"As grateful as I am for you bringing me lunch, I am wondering if I should count on silence from you from now on?"

Swallowing my food, I rolled my eyes. "What, we can't just sit in comfortable silence?"

"You didn't come here to sit in comfortable silence." Cole relaxed into his seat, putting his feet up on the part of the tattoo chair my arse wasn't covering. "You came here to talk, so talk."

"But that would make me the whiniest best friend on the planet."

"I'll take whiny over mute."

I snorted, and turned slightly to face him. "You know exactly what I'm going to say."

"Hmm." He crossed his arms over his chest with a mock pensive look on his face. "Is it Marco in the drawing room with the candlestick?"

"Har-de-har-har." I made a face at him.

Cole grinned unrepentantly.

"I had dinner with Marco a week ago."

My friend's eyebrows rose. "And I'm just hearing about this now?"

"Well, I've been taking some time, going over and over everything he said. He wants a second chance. At everything."

"Everything as in . . . a relationship, not just friendship?"

"Yes."

"Did he explain why he left?"

"His grandfather died. He went back to the States to be with his grandmother. He has a lot of self-esteem issues because of his grandfather and he just thought . . . basically he thought I was too good to be in his life and that's why he never told me he was leaving, and that's why he never got in touch when he came back."

"So why the change of heart now?"

I sighed. "*He's* changed, Cole. He's not the guy he was back then, and he says he misses me."

It was Cole's turn to sigh. "I'm just going to say to you what I said before. Everyone deserves a second chance. It's not like what he did was so awful. He left without saying good-bye, but you weren't together. I think you're making this more complicated than it is."

We bloody well had sex!

I frowned. "We were friends, and he knew I cared about him."

"And he explained his reasons. You may not like them, but that's the way it is sometimes. We all do stupid things. Marco is trying to make up for his mistakes. He's been pulling out all the stops to see you. Surely that counts for something."

Yes—I want it to count for something.

I need it to count for something.

"I just don't want to get hurt again."

Cole surprised me with a warm smile. "Then just try the whole friends thing first. It's not like anyone is forcing you to offer him more than that."

"Hannah."

I shivered involuntarily at the rich sound of Marco's voice in my ear. My hand tightened around my phone. "Hi."

"I'm glad you called. I was beginning to think I'd need to go to Plan B."

"Plan B?"

"Much like Plan A but with increased work hours."

I smiled despite myself. "Well, no need. Your stalking days are over."

"That sounds like good news." He practically purred it, and my eyelashes fluttered closed before I could stop them.

Damn him!

"Just as friends!" I found myself blurting out.

"Excuse me?"

"I'm willing to try to be friends again."

He was silent a moment.

"Marco?"

"Friends," he finally answered. "But with the hope of becoming more."

The butterflies were back in my belly. "No, no, no, no, no, no, no."

"Fine. Friends will do for now."

"Marco—"

"You can't take it back. We're friends. We're officially spending time together."

I sighed, willing the crazy fluttering inside me to die down. "How does next weekend sound?"

He hesitated. "I can't do next weekend, I'm sorry. How about this Tuesday, after work, for drinks? I swapped shifts with a colleague. He's doing my Wednesday shift if I do tomorrow for him."

"That's good for you. You can have a drink and not have to worry about work the next day. However, a weeknight doesn't really work for me."

"Oh, come on, it's not like you're surrounded by heavy machinery. We'll have one drink. Or are you too old to go out on a weeknight?" he teased.

I grimaced. "You're such a child. Fine, Tuesday night. One drink."

Walking into the bar on George Street on Tuesday evening, I almost tripped over my own feet at the expression on Marco's face when he saw me.

He stood up from the small booth he was sitting at, his eyes moving from my face, slowly down my body and back up again. The funny thing was there was nothing much to see except for my legs ending in a pair of fur-trimmed ankle boots. I was wearing my favorite green military-style winter coat with fur-trim cuffs. It fitted my body well, but it wasn't exactly sexy.

Marco's gaze made me feel sexy.

Damn him.

When I reached him he surprised me by bending slightly to press a kiss to my cheek. My cheek was rosy and cold from the freezing wind outside, but as soon as his lips touched my skin a blaze of heat radiated out from the spot. I must have looked befuddled because he seemed amused and pleased with himself.

Self-consciously I shrugged out of my coat, glad I was wearing a conservative navy wool dress underneath. However, I might as well have been wearing a nightdress for how hot I felt in close quarters with him.

Sliding into the booth beside him, my whole body hyper-aware of his, I knew I had to at least be honest with myself: I had never stopped being attracted to Marco and I'd once been in love with him. Despite the complicated past between us, despite the truths I was withholding, I knew that I could never just be friends with him on the inside, even if I could pretend it on the outside.

Our arms brushed and sparks shot through me like I'd touched a live wire. I couldn't stamp out that feeling of excitement. That feeling was utterly addictive. From the age of fourteen until the age of seventeen, I'd had that feeling inside me whenever I was around Marco.

I'd missed it.

"How are you?" I gave him a small, hopefully platonic smile.

"I'm good." His gaze was intense on me, his eyes deliberately trying to hook mine.

For the first time ever with him, I felt shy. I glanced away quickly, searching the bar.

"Can I get you a drink?" he asked.

"Sure. I'll have a glass of rosé, please."

As soon as he slid out of the booth my breathing steadied.

You are being such an idiot, I berated myself. This was Marco. So what if he was hot? When I was younger, I'd still been able to carry on a conversation with him!

Pull it together, Nichols.

My eyes followed him as he strode up to the quiet bar, powerful, graceful. He wore a dark blue knit sweater with a shawl collar and a pair of dark blue jeans. He was effortlessly stylish and comfortable with himself in a way he hadn't been when we were at school.

Momentarily sidetracked from my study of him, I picked up on the lust aimed at Marco emanating from the other end of the bar. Two women sat on barstools, speaking quietly to each other as they watched him with hungry eyes and come-hither smiles.

Marco wasn't even paying attention.

I relaxed somewhat at his utter lack of interest, jealousy slowly seeping out of me.

Yup. Definitely not just friends.

Damn him.

"So," he said as he slipped back into the booth beside me, putting my wineglass gently down in front of me as he lightly gripped his pint of lager, "How was work?"

Small talk. Yes, I could do small talk.

I opened my mouth to speak but was immediately distracted by the arm he slid along the back of the booth we were sitting in. I felt surrounded.

What the hell did he just ask?

Work! Right, work. "Good." I took a quick sip of my wine, hoping the alcohol would help me relax a little. "It's busy and stressful, but I love teaching."

"And you were always good at it."

Not wanting to take another trip down memory lane so soon after our last one, I shrugged and then smiled coaxingly into his handsome face. "You seem to be doing well. Adam speaks highly of you. Says you'll be a site manager one day."

"That's the goal. You work hard, you learn, you get there."

I smiled softly. "You say you've changed, but you had that attitude when we were kids. You took those classes when you didn't need to. You were always challenging yourself to be better." *Except when it came to me.*

"Not always," he replied pointedly, as if he'd just read my mind. "In that way I've changed. I go after what I want now, no matter what."

I looked away before we ventured into dangerous territory. "How's your aunt Gabby?"

"She's good. Real good. Gio eased up on me a lot over the last few years and I know it's mostly because of Gabby. I'm pretty close to her. It's nice having family over here."

"Do you still talk to your family in Chicago?"

"Sure. Magic of the Internet."

"Of course. I'm glad for you. I'm happy that, for whatever reason, you're not carrying around all that stuff your grandfather piled on you."

"Thank you." His eyes did that intense roaming of my face thing again and I had a sudden vision of throwing myself at him. I mentally slapped my wrist. "And what about you? How's your family?"

"Really good. Ellie had a little boy, William. She's pregnant with their second child. "

Marco raised his eyebrows. "Full house, huh?"

I laughed. "You have no idea. Joss and Braden have two kids now, Beth and Luke. My parents' house is a zoo every Sunday."

He grinned. "It sounds nice."

"It is."

"And your parents and Dec? How are they?"

"They're well. At least I know my parents are. I wouldn't know about Dec. He's eighteen now and spends most of his time in his room with his girlfriend."

"He's got a girlfriend. He's ahead of the curve."

"Yeah, don't tell him. He's brainy and cute and an arrogant little bugger." I groaned, but Marco smiled at the obvious affection in my voice.

"You always had a nice family, Hannah."

"Yeah," I agreed softly.

Marco tensed suddenly. "And Cole?"

I glanced up at him in confusion. "Cole?"

"The guy you were at the wedding with." Marco shrugged. "Anisha told me who he was."

"You certainly did your homework," I murmured, taking another sip of wine. "Cole is Jo's little brother. He's my best friend. He's . . . been there for me."

Marco frowned at my answer, not seeming to like it much. "But you're not together."

"No, it's not like that between us." I put my glass down, my gaze on the table. "Maybe we should steer clear of relationship talk."

"That's fine with me." He tilted his head to the side, eyeing me through his narrowed gaze. "Is *Finding Nemo* still your favorite movie?"

I laughed at the randomness of the question, relieved by the subject change. "You remember that?"

"Of course."

I shook my head. "I don't know what my favorite movie is anymore."

"We'll need to do something about that."

"I don't know. I quite like not having an exact favorite. Is *Training Day* still yours?"

"Nah, that movie *Lawless*. Now that is a fucking movie."

"I don't think I've seen it."

He smiled and even before he said the words I knew I'd just fallen right into his agenda. "Thursday night, your place, me, you and *Lawless*."

I opened my mouth to shoot him down, but stalled when I saw the glimmer in his eyes. He was expecting me to say no, and it suddenly occurred to me that my refusal might reinforce the idea that I was scared of spending time with him. And he could only assume that my fear of spending time with him stemmed from my attraction to him.

I jutted my chin out defiantly. "It'll need to be later on in the evening. I teach an adult literacy class on Thursday after school."

Marco chuckled. "I know that. And there's no need to sound so excited about spending time with me, by the way."

"Spending time with you doing what?" a familiar voice asked.

I whipped my head around, tilting it back to stare up at Suzanne. I hadn't seen her since our last night out together, but I wasn't surprised to bump into her out on the town on a work night.

She raised an eyebrow. "Hi, stranger." Her eyes moved quickly to Marco and lit up. "So who's this then?"

"Suzanne." I hurried to think of something to get her to leave. She was the last person I wanted around Marco. She had no filter whatsoever. "Uh . . . aren't you with someone?"

"Date." She jerked her head in the direction of the bar and I saw a good-looking blond guy watching us. Her gaze was still fixed on Marco as she leaned across the table, deliberately showing off as much of her cleavage as possible. Holding out a hand for him to shake, she said in a faux husky voice, "I'm Suzanne."

Marco quickly shook her proffered hand. "Marco. I'm an old friend of Hannah's."

I stiffened as Suzanne froze at the name.

Right then I cursed our nights at university together, especially the night we got rip-roaring drunk and Suzanne asked me if I was a virgin because I hadn't slept with any boys at college yet. Drunk and overly emotional I told her about my night with Marco and how I never wanted to let myself be vulnerable with the wrong guy again.

Suzanne's gaze swung back to me, surprise in her pretty eyes. "No fucking way."

"Suzanne." I pleaded silently for her to shut the hell up.

But did she pick up on my signals?

Nope.

She shot Marco a dirty look. "You've got a lot to answer for. My girl has so many issues because of you."

Floor, open up and swallow me. Please.

"Suzanne," I leaned forward, my voice thick. "Now's not—"

"No, he should know." Her eyes widened. "Oh, my God, is he the reason you've been such a complete and utter boring bitch lately?"

I was suddenly very disappointed in my taste in friends.

"Watch it," Marco growled, and Suzanne and I both snapped to attention as if we'd been bitten by the crack of a whip. Marco's eyes had darkened. I could feel the irritation vibrating from him. "We're in the middle of a private conversation. You should leave."

Affronted, Suzanne's lips parted. Her eyes flew to mine, as if she expected me to stick up for her.

Unfortunately, I didn't take too kindly to being called a boring bitch in public or in private. In my teacher voice I said, "I'll speak with you later, Suzanne."

She made a small *harrumph* sound, then turned sharply on her five-inch heels and marched toward her date, grabbing his arm and hauling him out of the bar.

"She's a friend?" Marco asked quietly, incredulously.

"We met at uni. I grew up. She didn't."

He pushed his half-empty pint absentmindedly away from him. "Issues?"

I shrugged. "I honestly don't know what she's talking about."

"Anisha told me she didn't think there was a guy in your life and that you haven't spoken about any from the past. Maybe that's what she was talking about?"

My blood was suddenly hot with anger. I took a moment to calm. The last thing I wanted him to believe was that he'd done such a number on me I hadn't been able to move on. I hadn't been with anyone else by choice.

Sort of.

I exhaled slowly. "No guy at the moment."

He appeared to relax at my reply.

I stared at him, letting my eyes connect with his and I felt the power of my attraction to him take hold. He was beautiful in a masculine way, sexy, charismatic. There had to have been many women in his life these last five years. The thought depressed me. "I'm guessing with the way you've been with me these last few weeks that there's no one special in your life at the moment, right?"

Still holding my gaze, Marco's lips turned up at the corner and I realized I wanted to kiss them right there on that seductive spot. "There's someone. I just have to convince *her* of that."

Yup. Definitely wanted to kiss him.

I narrowed my eyes on him, doing unimpressed convincingly. "I thought I told you we're just friends."

His eyes dropped to my mouth in a way that made me squirm. "I heard you." His heated gaze returned to meet mine. "But I don't think you heard me."

CHAPTER 12

That Thursday evening Marco *did* come over to my flat with takeout and the film *Lawless* and we *did* sit and watch the film together and it *was* brilliant and Marco's company *was* fantastic and I *was* already weakening in my resolve to keep him at arm's length.

Breathe, Hannah.

"I don't know." Ellie shook her head at me. "I can see the resolve still there in your eyes. We need to chase that off."

That following Saturday I ignored my pile of marking to hang out with my sister, Jo, and Liv at Joss and Braden's town house on Dublin Street. They used to live in a flat downhill from the house, but when Joss fell pregnant with Luke, Braden bought and renovated a larger home a few doors up from the old place. We had the house to ourselves—Braden had taken the kids out for lunch—and I'd pretty much been ambushed with questions about Marco as soon as I walked in the door.

I grimaced at Ellie. "I'm guessing you're on Team Marco?"

"I think we all are." Joss handed me a cup of tea. "We haven't heard you talking about a guy like this since . . . well, since Marco. That's got to mean something."

"He's been back in my life three weeks. I can't just give it to him."

"No one is saying you have to," Jo assured me. "But at least admit to us that you're considering it."

"Am I?" I argued. "Does my weakening of resolve mean that I'm considering it? No. It means I'm horny."

"Ew." Ellie put her hands to her ears. "Big sister still in the room."

She really should know by now that only made me want to torment her more. "Seriously," I continued, "I've worn out, like, three vibrators."

"Meanie!" She threw me a horrified look.

"Meanie?" I snorted. "Ellie, that kid growing in your belly is depleting your brain cells."

"Stop torturing your very pregnant sister," Liv told me. "And answer this: Putting aside the attraction to him, would you consider really giving him a second chance?"

I gazed around at them all as they waited. Finally, I sighed. "I've already admitted to myself I would. But I'd be plagued with doubt every step of the way, so . . . it would be doomed from the start."

"You don't know that," Joss replied quietly. "You'll never know that until you take the chance. I was your age when I took the chance on Braden. And sure, there are days I want to kill him, but more often than not, I kind of like having him around. And the kids he gave me aren't bad either. You should take the chance, Hannah."

From the expression on Ellie's, Jo's, and Liv's faces I could tell they agreed with Joss. Knowing her dry wisdom, and how she adored Braden and her kids, I didn't doubt her or her words of experience. But still, I doubted Marco.

Thankfully we moved on to the topic of Beth and school.

We were discussing the fact that Christmas was now less than seven weeks away when the doorbell rang. Joss got up to answer the door, returning with Nate.

Liv's eyes widened with pleased surprise at the sight of her hot husband, and, honestly, I didn't blame her. "What are you doing here?"

He slouched against the doorjamb, grinning at her with those sexy dimples of his. "I just dropped the kids off at Mum and Dad's. I thought you and I could do date night. Starting now." He smiled at us. "If that's okay with you, ladies?"

"Uh, they don't get a say." Liv shot to her feet. "No offense." She threw us an apologetic look. "But no kids and a hot husband? You cannot blame me for ditching."

We snickered. No, we could not.

Liv grabbed her purse after pulling her boots on. "Nate"—she glanced over at him thoughtfully—"remember that time you broke my heart but then proved yourself to me with your perseverance and I gave you a second chance?"

Nate gave her a droll look. "Yes. And thank you for bringing it up. Good times."

I laughed and shook my head at Liv. "You're subtle."

Nate sighed from the doorway. "Was there a point to revisiting a painful time from my past?"

Liv strode over to him, cupping his face in her hands. "Aw, babe," she said as she tenderly pressed her lips to his, "I was making a point to Hannah. Marco wants to be more than friends and she's on the fence about giving him a second chance."

I found myself pinned beneath Nate's soulful dark gaze. "Liv filled me in about this guy and trust me, Hannah, a man doesn't stick around, continuously trying to win you over, just for the chance to sleep with you. I'm guessing from the way my wife talks about him, this guy could get laid easily?"

I made a face at that but nodded.

"Then he likes you." Nate shrugged, as if it were just that simple. "If you still don't trust that, keep him hanging for longer. If he genuinely cares about you and knows there's something between you, he's not going anywhere."

I processed this.

It seemed like sound advice. And it came from Nate Sawyer, once a player, now a devoted husband and father. It was a good source to hear it from. I nodded slowly. "Okay. Thanks, Nate."

"No problem." He grinned at me, saluted two fingers to Ellie, Jo, and Joss, and then grabbed Liv's hand. "Now if you don't mind, I'm stealing my wife."

CHAPTER 13

Unmarked essays were piled on my coffee table while I sat on the floor beside my stack of marked ones. Every now and then I'd reach for my cooling mug of coffee and glance over at Marco, who was stretched out on my couch, dozing.

Dark and cold outside, it was warm inside my flat as the fire crackled in my grate. I couldn't believe it was almost December. It had been a crazy few weeks. A crazy few weeks of hanging around Marco. A lot.

After thinking over Nate's advice I decided that holding out on Marco longer was the only way I'd know for certain if he was genuinely interested in me and not just in sleeping with me again. My gut told me that wasn't the type of person he was. Not with me anyway, but that nagging doubt, that memory of him leaving me alone on India Place that fateful night, held me back from believing in him all the way.

Only time would tell.

The weekend after our movie night together, Marco had had plans. However, the following Monday he turned up at my door after work, carrying a bag of groceries and film rentals. He quickly set himself up in my kitchen and I watched in bemusement as he threw together homemade meatballs and spaghetti. I don't know why I was surprised that he could cook. His uncle owned and ran a restaurant.

We had fun that night, keeping it friendly, although Marco couldn't help himself—he tried to flirt a little despite my lack of any outward response. He called me on his lunch break that week, he texted me a lot, and tried to tempt me to meet him for drinks on the Friday. It was a busy week, so I told him I had too much work to do. Not to be rebuffed, he asked me what I was doing that weekend and I explained I was going Christmas shopping in Glasgow. I liked to be organized about the whole Christmas presents thing.

To my utter surprise, Marco invited himself along.

That Saturday we met at Edinburgh's Waverley Station and boarded the train to Glasgow together. For fifty minutes we sat across from each other and barely said a word. Although Marco was definitely more loquacious than he used to be and he wasn't exactly broody anymore, he was still that guy who was comfortable and happy to sit in silence with me.

He caught me studying him as we passed through Falkirk and he smiled at my scrutiny. "What?"

"You've changed, but you haven't."

There was recognition, an understanding, in his eyes that told me he knew what I meant. "You too."

Although I wasn't willing to admit to my attraction to him, I wanted him to know I still remembered how good our friendship had been and that so far it had been good again. "We always had this, though. Being able to just be quiet and not have it feel awkward. Not needing to feel like we had to fill the silence. I have that with Cole, but . . . I mean, he's like a brother, so . . . but other guys, we've never had . . ." I trailed off, realizing I was perhaps giving him more than I'd meant to.

I looked over at him when he didn't reply, and tensed at the sudden stillness around him.

He leaned toward me. "I know I asked if there had been anyone special in your life but, honestly, Hannah, I don't want to hear about other guys." His jaw hardened and he looked out of the window.

That pissed me off. I was definitely not impressed with his display of alpha man possessiveness. But not wanting to have a fight in public, I stayed quiet, slowly allowing the burn of anger to dissipate. After ten minutes of now awkward silence, I replied quietly, "You and I are just friends." And if he continued to be a possessive idiot, that's the way we'd remain.

Marco looked at me sharply. "But you know I want more," he answered. "So you also must understand why I don't want to hear shit about other guys you've been with. Guys that got all that I've wanted since I fucked it all up."

The weight of our history, of our feelings and confusion, wrapped around me with a sense of longing then, and I felt fearful. Of us. Of our future. Or lack thereof. Without thinking, I whispered, "Maybe we shouldn't hang out anymore."

"You can handle it," he said stonily, his tone brooking no argument.

I forced myself to meet his hard gaze. "But can you?"

"As long as you don't talk about the guys you've fucked, or Cole too much, then, yeah, I can handle it."

I narrowed my eyes. "Cole's my best friend."

He ducked his head, bringing us closer. "*I'm* your best friend," he answered roughly. "You've just forgotten. My fault, I know. I can help you remember."

Honestly, I didn't know how to reply to that. It made me ache so much for what we had been and for what I was terrified to have again with him.

So I remained quiet. It wasn't until we were pulling into Glasgow Queen Street that Marco broke the silence, saying casually, "Gabby wants something called a Jo Malone for Christmas. Please tell me you know what that is?"

I stared at him and his proverbial olive branch.

And then I made a decision. I laughed. "It's a store. Did she say what she wanted from Jo Malone?"

Marco stared at me blankly.

"Okay." I patted his shoulder as we moved to get off the train. "We'll go with a general gift box."

Somehow, despite the hairy moment on the train, we had a great time together that day. After shopping for a bit, we stopped for lunch at a pub. There, I impulsively offered, "You know, if we don't get everything this weekend, I'd be happy to help you shop next weekend."

Marco's gaze softened at my suggestion. However, his quiet answer was a rebuff. "I can't next weekend."

I tried not to feel stupid for putting myself out there. I'd never have felt stupid about something like that when we were kids.

His eyebrows drew together at my silence. "It's complicated, but, uh . . . I'll explain it to you soon," he promised. "When the time is right."

My stomach flipped unpleasantly and I did my best to ignore the feeling. "That's cryptic."

"It's just a long story. One I intend to tell, like I said, when the time is right."

Hypocritically, I didn't like that Marco was keeping something from me, even though I was keeping something from him. To cover that feeling of possessiveness I'd been pissed at him for only hours before, I shrugged casually. "It's not like we're . . . You don't owe me anything."

"Yes, I fucking do," he said abruptly. "Whatever this is"—he gestured between us—"it's important. And I will tell you when the time is right."

How did I respond to that? Pulse racing, I tried for honesty again. "I don't want you to think I'm leading you on, Marco. I'm trying to give you my friendship, but I don't know if it'll ever be more than that. I need you to acknowledge that you understand that."

"I do. More than friendship or not . . . I'm not going anywhere."

And just like that, the ache was back, but this time the burn of it was almost sweet. After a moment of charged silence, I ventured into small talk, asking after his aunt and uncle and the restaurant.

"Good." He shrugged, going with the subject change. "Like I mentioned before, Gabby kind of softened Gio up a little. Somewhere along the line he decided I wasn't a waste of space."

Remembering that night in the gardens, the swelling bruise under his eye, I still couldn't help but feel a deep anger in my gut toward Gio. "Does that make up for how much of a dick he was to you?"

He sensed my emotion, and his expression grew tender. "No, Hannah. But he's not that man any longer. He was carrying around his own shit from Nonno. Their relationship wasn't an easy one and it spilled into ours. Gio apologized for the way he treated me." He smirked. "He *was* drunk when he apologized, but it still helped."

I guessed if Marco was willing to forgive, I should be, too. "I'm glad."

We had lunch, the air lightening between us. We joked and talked and then wandered back out into the crowds for more shopping. That night Marco finagled his way into my flat. I fell asleep watching a movie and when I stirred it was because Marco was carrying me into my bedroom. He gently eased me into bed and I fell asleep with the touch of his lips on my forehead.

The next morning I woke up to find him asleep on my couch and when I asked him why he had stayed instead of going home to his bed, he said he slept easier knowing I was safe. That morning I made him breakfast. I made him breakfast with a tiny fraction of my resolve much weaker than it had been the day before. I thought when he left that day that he wasn't coming back, but he did; he returned with materials he'd ordered for me. I canceled Sunday lunch at my mum's to watch Marco build bookshelves in my sitting room. My resolve weakened even more.

That following week we were both exceptionally busy with work, but Marco found time to call me every other night. As promised, I didn't see him that weekend, as he had made other plans.

While he was gone, I realized something slightly terrifying.

I missed him.

Missed him deep-in-my-bones-missed-him.

It was a relief to see him at my door that Monday night after his disappearance. He broke his silent vow to give me as much physical space as possible by stepping into my flat and enveloping me in a hug I felt in every inch of my body. He kissed my cheek, reluctantly pulling away from me. I was glad for the thick sweater I wore because the combination of his cologne, his heat, his strong arms around me and his hard chest brushing against my soft one, all mixing in with the fact that I was giddy to see him, made my body physically react to his hug.

Attempting to shrug off my sexual attraction to him, I made dinner for us as if everything was perfectly normal.

Three times that week Marco turned up at my flat for dinner.

I asked him why we never hung out at his flat, not because it bothered me, but because I was curious. His answer was that my place was nicer. Although he'd once lived in that shithole on India Place, I couldn't imagine him living somewhere like that now, so I presumed his flat was acceptable for hosting guests despite his denials that it wasn't.

Still, I shrugged off my questions, my curiosity, and my doubt, intent on enjoying the present with him.

Deciding to leave the flat for once, we went out to the movies that Friday night. That clearly wasn't enough time spent together, and Marco insisted on crashing my babysitting duties the next evening. We went to Joss and Braden's and babysat Beth and Luke for them while they had date night. This meant Marco met Joss. He'd already met Braden while working construction on a few of Braden's builds. To my complete and utter shock, Braden was congenial with Marco. There was no intimidating older brother in sight. He appeared relaxed with the whole idea of Marco's presence in my life. Perhaps the macho alpha in him recognized it in Marco and respected it in some weird male psyche thing I would never understand. As for Joss, she made it clear when both Braden's and Marco's backs were turned that she thought he seemed great.

The biggest surprise of the evening, though, wasn't Braden's laid-back attitude—it was Marco's way with the kids. Beth and Luke loved him and he had a never-ending well of patience with them. Although thrown a little by these surprises, I felt like the night had gone well . . . until things escalated out of my control. Joss and Braden returned late that evening when the kids were already in bed, and Joss did the unbelievable—she invited Marco to Sunday lunch the next day.

My expression must have been one of horror because both Marco and Braden burst out laughing.

Of course Marco said yes to lunch.

To my increasing dismay my whole family took to him. I didn't know whether to be happy or devastated. I knew my mum and the girls thought he was fantastic—they pulled me into the kitchen to go on and on about his sense of humor, his easy, quiet way with the kids, the way he listened to everything I said as if it was the most important thing he'd ever heard . . . and of course they teased me mercilessly about how great-looking he was.

As if I didn't know that already!

The guys' reaction to Marco was possibly worse, because they were always so hard to please when it came to the boyfriends of their female relatives. They seemed to like Marco's quiet confidence, respected his careful answers, and enjoyed his dry humor.

I was fucked.

Even Cole liked him, and Marco was definitely much more reserved with Cole than with the others.

The only person who was somewhat aloof was my dad. He was generally a lot more laid-back than the other men in my life, and his reaction would have taken me aback if it weren't for the fact that Dad was the only one who knew the truth. I watched as Dad studied Marco, and I knew him well enough to know that he was trying to gauge whether Marco was worthy of that second chance he'd advised I should give him. If anyone else noticed Dad's unusual behavior, I was certain they put it down to overprotectiveness.

The only really awkward moment during the visit was after lunch when Beth came to stand beside Marco's armchair. She tilted her head to the side, inspecting him curiously as Marco smiled back at her in amusement. And then everyone heard her ask loudly, "Are you Hannah's boyfriend?"

Hannah wanted a black hole to suddenly open up in the middle of the sitting room and swallow her whole.

Worse, Marco's reply was, "Nope. She won't let me be."

Beth had immediately turned her cute look of consternation on me. "That's really rude, Hannah."

And that was so adorably funny even I laughed through the blazing heat in my cheeks.

A little while later Joss and Ellie got up to make coffee and tea and I ignored Marco's gaze, as I shot out of the sitting room after them into the kitchen. "What the hell are you all playing at?" I asked quietly. "What happened to Braden's and Adam's overprotectiveness? What happened to *all* of your overprotectiveness?"

Joss shrugged. "We like Marco. He seems like a solid guy."

I didn't even know what to say to that.

I looked at my sister. Ellie frowned at my expression of disbelief. "Hannah, we all just appreciate how much effort he's putting in with you. We want you to be happy. It's obvious to everyone you two are more than friends. I mean, we've hardly seen you for three weeks and when we do all you talk about is what you and Marco have been up to."

"Friends, my ass," Joss grunted, stirring sugar into someone's coffee. "The sexual tension between you two is off the charts." Her grin turned smug. "Reminds me of me and Mr. Carmichael."

"No details." Ellie held up a hand, her eyes pleading.

"I wasn't going to," Joss assured her, but we knew where her mind had wandered by the still smug smile curling her mouth and by the heat in her eyes.

I sighed, leaning back against my mother's kitchen counter. "I thought I could at least rely on my family to help keep things platonic between me and Marco. But you're practically spoon-feeding me to him."

Ellie snorted, a long, drawn-out, sarcastic snort. "Be serious, Hannah. You spend nearly every waking moment with him. If anyone is helping him with you, sweetheart, it's *you*."

Gazing at him sleeping on my couch, I was overwhelmed with my feelings for him. Feelings deep in my gut, throbbing in my chest, and tingling at the ends of my fingertips. The past week, after Sunday lunch, I'd seen Marco once for dinner, but work had kept us busy and at the weekend he once again had a mysterious family commitment. I came to the not-very-hard-to-deduce conclusion that this family thing occurred on alternate weekends.

It was difficult not to push him on that subject.

But I didn't. Mostly because of the aforementioned hypocrisy.

So . . . we hadn't seen each other for a few days. The whole missing-him thing had gotten worse. That's why when I opened my door that night and saw him there I was flooded by my emotions. Whatever the mysterious disappearance was about at the weekend, Marco proved to me that he missed me as much as I missed him, because there he was on my doorstep the night after. He couldn't even wait a day to see me.

I told him I had essays to mark but that didn't deter him. We ate dinner and then Marco camped out on my couch and let me get on with my work.

My resolve had weakened.

I could feel it.

He just had to push me and . . .

I dropped my gaze from his handsome, sleeping face and resolutely attempted to concentrate on my work. The next essay I picked up was Jarrod's, which made ignoring Marco even harder. But I did it, because Jarrod deserved my focus.

His revised personal essay moved me. For all Jarrod's seeming laziness with the other teachers and obvious issues with the father who had abandoned him, he had found strength that not many boys his age had by looking after his little brother, Harvey, and helping to raise him. For Jarrod, the aim of his essay was to show his growth in getting over childish fears and becoming a young adult. But the reader easily discerned from the multitude of situations he posed to us that Jarrod overcame his own fears in order to make Harvey feel safe, in order to help Harvey not be afraid.

It wasn't easy for someone with Jarrod's pride to put all that on paper, and he'd made me promise that only I and the examiner would read the essay.

It was a shame that I'd made that promise. I wanted to shove the paper in Rutherford's face and demand that he see that the boy he thought so little of wasn't a boy at all. He was a boy in age, but he'd been forced to become a man in spirit in order to give his brother the emotional support he himself had never had.

I sighed heavily, wishing there was more I could do to help Jarrod see his self-worth.

"What's wrong?"

I lifted my head from my work at Marco's rough voice and question. His eyes were open, his low-lidded gaze affecting me emotionally as well as physically.

That rush of tenderness I felt clearly translated in my returning gaze because Marco suddenly grew more alert.

Resolve weakened further. Just one push . . .

My heart was pounding hard, but I tried for nonchalance, tapping my pen casually against the papers in my hand. "I've got this kid in my fourth-year class. Jarrod." I set the essay aside with the others. "He reminds me of you."

"Yeah?" Marco slowly sat up, his elbows resting on his knees as he leaned toward me. "You must have a soft spot for him then."

I laughed. "So sure of yourself these days."

Marco didn't answer; instead, his eyes darkened, glittering in the low light as he lowered himself onto the floor. The thundering heart banging away in my chest sped up even more and I unconsciously licked my lips as he moved toward me.

My breathing grew shallow, my mind screaming *Stop him!* while my body happily gave in as he nudged my legs apart, putting himself between them, and moving his torso into mine so I was forced to lean back on my hands to create space between us. Marco wasn't having any of that. Instead he leaned farther into me as my head tilted back, one hand flat on the ground at my hip, the other sending the hair on the back of my neck up as he cupped my face.

"I know you still care." His words whispered across my lips, his mouth almost touching mine. I shivered, my breath stuttering. "And, babe," he continued, "I don't think I can pretend any longer that I don't think about being inside you nearly every hour of every day."

His words were almost the equivalent of his mouth between my legs.

I wanted him. I wanted him so much I was struck mute with the fear that if I spoke I'd deny myself.

Marco took my silence as acquiescence.

His thumb stroked my cheek in tenderness, his eyes dropping to my mouth.

Breathless, I waited.

His head dipped, crossing the minute distance between our lips, and my eyes fluttered closed at the brush of his mouth over mine. My lips tingled, and I sighed, excited for more.

His kiss continued in gentle seduction, a touch of lips against lips, the pressure increasing in increments as my skin grew hotter and hotter.

I'd never been kissed like this. No guy had ever taken such sweet time with me, as if needing to sample every last inch of my mouth. Every time I thought he was going to deepen the kiss, he pulled back, dusting butterfly touches against the corner of my mouth or nibbling on my lower lip.

The tingling was delicious. "Only yours," I pulled back a little to say softly, sounding almost desolate and wondering if in amongst the lust there wasn't some truth to that tone.

Marco watched me as if he were trying to read me. Tenderly, he tucked my hair behind my ear. "Only mine what, Hannah?"

"Your kiss. My lips tingle when you kiss me." I smiled sadly. "Real, honest-to-God tingling. No one else has ever made me feel that."

A dark triumph entered Marco's eyes. "Good," he answered gruffly, before lowering his mouth to recapture mine.

My breathing grew steadily more and more out of control as he returned to torturing me with slow, seductive kisses. I longed for him to touch his tongue to mine so I could taste him. I *remembered* the taste of him. There was nothing quite like it. I needed that back.

Pushing up off the floor, I reached for him, my hands gripping his shoulders when the sudden movement pressed our mouths harder against each other. I moaned in need and Marco crushed me to him, his other hand in my hair holding me to him as I opened my mouth against his. My lower belly dipped as his tongue moved against mine, as his heat and taste filled me.

Yes.

This is what I've been missing.

CHAPTER 14

"Put your legs around my waist," Marco ordered, his voice thick with need.

I immediately did as he asked, my arms encircling his shoulders as he held me fast and stood with ease. I gasped at the feel of his hard-on, our eyes locking and creating imaginary sparks of molten embers at the collision. Marco carried me, our breaths mingling as we panted in anticipation.

I was barely aware of moving through the flat until he was lowering me onto the soft duvet on my bed, his body sliding over mine.

He held himself up, his hands braced at either side of my head. "No turning back," he murmured.

Pushing his shirt up, feeling his hot, smooth muscle under my hands, I shivered with excitement. "No turning back," I agreed, completely taken over by the sexual promise in his eyes.

Marco tugged his shirt up over his head and tossed it somewhere behind me.

"Oh, my God," I whispered before I could stop myself, immediately reaching for him, needing to touch all that glorious skin. He was powerfully built, sculpted. "You're beautiful."

The words were almost muffled because Marco was peeling my own sweater off me, throwing it in the same direction as his own. "No, but you are," he answered quietly, his hands skimming up my waist to cup my breasts over my bra.

I arched my back, pushing them into his hands.

Marco accepted my offer.

He kissed me, deep and hard, as he deftly unclipped my bra at the back.

My hands traced every inch of his chest while we kissed, reluctantly letting go when he gently pushed me back on the bed and slipped my bra straps down my arms.

The bra disappeared.

Marco's gaze drifted from my face to my naked breasts and the heat in them made my breasts swell, my nipples tightening. I felt that roller-coaster dip in my lower belly and knew that if he slipped his hand between my legs he'd find me wet and ready for him.

He touched me, cupping my breasts again, squeezing them gently, thumbs rubbing over my nipples as he learned the shape of me. His breathing had grown heavier and I could feel the hard press of him through his jeans.

I arched again, silently asking for his mouth.

He didn't deny me.

I sighed at the gentle brush of his lips against first my right breast and then my left. He tormented me, kissing near my nipples. And just when I thought I'd have to beg out loud, he licked my right nipple before closing his mouth around it and sucking it.

A larger ripple moved through my belly and I cried out softly, throwing my head back against my pillow.

Marco lavished attention on both nipples until they were swollen, until I was desperate for him.

He pressed a sweet kiss to the outer curve of my breast and sat up.

I swear to God I almost came just at the sight of him straddling me with that dark hunger in his eyes—a hunger that would make any woman in the world feel combustible.

Our eyes locked, with thick, heady silence between us. Marco hooked his hands into the waistband of my leggings and underwear and he tugged. I lifted my lower body, giving him better access, and he raised my legs to peel the garments off. Once he'd divested me of them, slowly, gently, caressing my calves and outer thighs, he lowered my legs, spreading them as he did so. I'd never felt so exposed, or, to my surprise, so turned on as I felt with him looking at me.

With jerky movements, his jaw taut with dwindling control, Marco unsnapped his belt buckle and drew down the zip on his jeans. Every inch of me was on fire, my inner thighs were trembling, and I couldn't control my breathing as my inexperienced body screamed for his much more experienced one.

He pushed his jeans and boxer briefs down and I was faced with his huge, raging, throbbing hard-on. He was perfectly in proportion to his size but . . . I found myself tensing, my back stiffening against the bed.

Marco removed his jeans, pushing them to the side before moving into me, nudging my legs even farther apart as he lowered his torso over mine. He kissed me gently, trailing his fingertips up my outer thigh in a way that caused renewed shivers and my body to relax a little.

"I'm checked out," he whispered against my mouth. "I'm guessing you are too. You on the pill or do we need a condom?"

I hesitated, thrown by the question.

"Hannah?" He nibbled my earlobe as his hand continued up over my belly until it found its destination at my breast. He squeezed it, his thumb rubbing my swollen nipple. I found my eyes fluttering closed.

"I'm on the pill," I whispered back in a daze, coming out of it only when his hand disappeared from my breast and found a new, even better location between my legs.

My hips jerked at the first touch of his thumb on my clit, and he made deep, soothing noises from the back of his throat. And then he was kissing me, wet and drugging kisses as he played with my clit. I touched him too, caressing his shoulders, his back, his abs, strumming at his nipples in a way that made him growl into my mouth and press hard on my clit.

When he slipped two fingers inside me, I broke the kiss, moaning as my neck arched.

"Baby . . . " He peppered kisses along my jaw as he thrust his fingers in and out. "God, babe, you're fucking soaked."

I made whimpering sounds, my eyes fluttering open to meet his.

"You want me?" he murmured darkly against my mouth.

I nodded, jerking my hips against his fingers, needing more.

"Say it, Hannah."

Mindless, I dug my fingers into his back, urging him closer, the sound of my panting filling the room. "I need you," I admitted breathlessly. "I want you inside me."

Just like that, I watched his control snap.

His fingers slipped out of me, he gripped my thigh as he braced his other hand at the side of my head. Looking deeply into my eyes, he moved. I felt him hot and hard against my center and then suddenly there was pressure as he pushed inside.

I stiffened, the feeling not quite as uncomfortable as I remembered it from the first time.

Marco wasn't even all the way inside me when something new entered his eyes, an incredulous question. His jaw clenched with control, he slowed to a stop. "Babe . . . ?"

I shook my head, not understanding what was wrong.

"Babe . . . " He dipped his head closer, his hand cupping my face. "You're tight as a virgin," he whispered hoarsely.

Oh, no. No, no, no!

I swallowed hard, the arousal slowly dissipating as reality intruded. "It's just been a while." I pushed absentmindedly at his shoulders.

Marco's answer to that was to thrust deeper into me. I gripped his shoulders instead, my hips jerking up for more.

"How long is a while?" he asked, the muscle in his jaw flexing with tension.

I sought for a plausible lie. "First year, uni," I panted. "I've been busy since then."

Marco stilled. "You've not had a man in four years?"

Five, actually.

I shook my head again.

He suddenly shuttered his expression so I couldn't read his reaction. And then I didn't care about reading him because he pushed all the way inside me before pulling back and then slowly thrusting in again.

The discomfort melted away as my inner muscles clamped around his cock. "Oh, God, Marco!" I tried to pull him in deeper.

"Yeah?" He thrust a little harder and I cried out his name again.

He made love to me. Our eyes stayed connected as he glided in and out of me slowly.

"Come for me, babe," he growled, taking hold of one of my hands and pinning it to the bed while his other hand gripped my thigh harder. "Hannah, I need you to come."

The feeling inside me was building upward in a spiral, coiling tighter and tighter until my whole body tensed over a precipice.

"Yeah." Marco thrust harder. "Come for me."

His cock moved inside me a few more times, desperate to light the match . . . and then it did.

It sparked, the tension inside of me exploding, an orgasm unlike any I'd ever had before flowing through me. I think my eyes even rolled back in my head as I cried out to God.

I shuddered against Marco, opening my eyes to watch as he stiffened, his neck arched, his teeth gritted, and his eyes fierce as his own climax rolled through him.

He jerked against me, his hold on me almost painful as he came. He collapsed on me. His body still shuddered as he buried his head in my neck.

My muscles were warm and languid and for a few glorious seconds I just lay there enjoying the aftermath of the most amazing orgasm I'd ever experienced, and exulting at the feel of Marco's warm, hard body covering mine.

Those seconds quickly passed, however.

When he raised his head, his features relaxed, and his eyes filled with affection, a dark, heavy feeling began to sneak into my gut. He kissed me softly and I kissed him back, but . . .

He pulled gently out of me and rolled off me. The feeling in my gut grew bigger as he got out of bed. My eyes took in his long, muscled back, zeroing in on a line of raised skin on the left side of his lower back. A scar.

A new feeling of unease met the one that was already growing inside me. I watched as his magnificent body, bite-worthy arse and all, crossed the room and disappeared into the hall.

A few seconds later he returned, completely at ease with his nakedness. Wishing I could believe in the softness in his eyes as he looked at me, I watched on, a little perplexed, as he crawled back into bed with me. And then he pressed a wet washcloth between my legs.

Surprised by the sweet gesture, I bit my lip to keep myself from saying anything as he took care of me. Afterward he disappeared for a few seconds again, returning to draw down the covers that were under me so he could put them over me. He slipped into bed, lying on his back, and his arm came around me. Without saying a word he pulled me into his side and I rested my head on his chest, my heart racing again.

"I don't know if this changes anything."

Marco replied on a huff of laughter, "Of course it does."

For some reason I wanted to cry. I didn't understand myself at all. "I should be lying here feeling happy, but . . . I'm not."

The air in the room grew chilled. Marco sat up, turning so he could look me in the eye. I could tell by the hardening of his jaw that he was more than a little pissed off by my reaction to us having sex. "What the hell does that mean?"

I went for honesty. Well . . . sort of. "I have this sinking feeling about us." I looked away. "I haven't told you everything, and I don't know if I'll ever be able to."

I felt the press of his fingers against my chin and he slowly turned my head so I had to meet his blazing gaze. "You will, eventually," he said with a certainty I just couldn't feel. "I haven't told you everything either, but we'll get there. And that feeling . . . I'll make that go away. I'll make that go away by proving to you that I'm *not* going away. I'm here, Hannah. And I *want* to be here."

I wanted to argue further, I wanted to run far away before everything between us imploded and left me devastated. But when he kissed me, pushing me back against the pillows, determined to make love to me all over again, I understood that there was a much bigger part of me that had nothing to do with my brain and everything to do with my emotions, and it wanted *this* here with him even more.

The staff room was emptying out with only five minutes to go until lunch was over. I'd just walked to the sink to rinse my mug, still in a daze (and exhausted) from last night's sexathon with Marco, when Nish hurried over to my side.

She ignored my questioning gaze to look over her shoulder. As soon as the last teacher walked out of the staff room she turned back to me, her dark eyes sparkling with excitement. "I heard things are going well with you and Marco."

Annoyance made my pulse speed up. "And where did you hear that?"

Nish shrugged, looking weirdly smug, almost triumphant. "Well, Marco sent me a text this morning and all it said was 'Thank you.' Seeing the dark circles under your eyes, the flush in your cheeks, and putting it together with the cryptic text message, I can only conclude you two had sex."

Great. "Are you an English teacher or a private detective?" I grumbled.

Nish laughed. "I don't know what that grumpiness is for. If I was getting some from Marco D'Alessandro I'd die a happy woman."

"You're a *married* woman," I reminded her, throwing my sandwich packet in the bin as I headed toward the door.

"That doesn't mean I can't appreciate a gorgeous specimen like Marco."

I was admittedly confused over whether or not giving in to Marco the night before had been the right thing to do, but I had definitely enjoyed everything about his body. I shivered just remembering it.

"So." Nish reached past me, putting her hand on the staff room door so I couldn't escape. "Andy says he's known Marco for a few years now and he's never chased after a woman before." Nish grinned at me. "He's usually a love 'em and leave 'em kind of guy."

I stared back at her impatiently. "Was that a question?"

"Well, yeah."

Sighing, I pulled at the door so she had to move back to let me out. "We have history."

"I'm getting that. What I want to know is, is it serious? Will I be hearing wedding bells soon?"

My shoulders hunched at the absurd question. "I'm not even sure if we're together, Nish. Marco's never been one for permanence."

Cole was in his kitchen, grabbing me a glass of soda and some snacks, and I was just relaxing when my phone vibrated. I pulled it out of my purse, that unease back in my stomach when I saw it was Marco.

He'd called me five times and I'd ignored every single one. I'd also ignored the text message he'd sent. Instead of going home, where I was sure he'd only ambush me and force me to work out my feelings before I was ready, I'd gotten the bus to Cole's flat on Leith Walk. It was a small place that he shared with a roommate. The furniture was worn and in need of replacement, the walls were yellow-stained, and it was perpetually cold because the old sash-and-case windows needed replacing

Shoving my phone back in my purse, I looked up as Cole returned to the sitting room. "Do you miss living with Cam and Jo?" I asked, gratefully taking the food and drink he offered me.

Cole shot me an "are you serious?" look. "I like the privacy. For all of us. Cam can't keep his hands off my sister, as evident by that huge bump she's carrying around these days, and that's just something I'm glad I don't have to walk in on anymore."

I chuckled, glancing around the room. My gaze stuck on a plaque that hung above the old fireplace. On the plaque was a singing fish. "Still, your flatmate has the dodgiest taste."

"Bigsie is dodgy, full stop." Cole stared grimly at the fish. "Luckily I don't see much of him."

"Yeah, where is he?"

"Fuck knows. He pays the rent on time, that's all that matters."

"You could ask him to take the fish down."

"The fish?" Cole snorted. "I take it you haven't seen the blow-up doll in my bathroom?"

I burst out laughing. "No way."

Cole closed his eyes as if he was in pain and nodded.

Giggling, I put my Coke down and scampered out of the sitting room and down the hall into the pokey wee bathroom at the back of the flat. As soon as I opened the door I was confronted by a life-size blow-up doll. She was sporting a cartoon face and a majestic bosom, and someone had covered her lower half with a hula skirt.

"Her name is Lola!" Cole called.

Laughing, I took a photo of it on my camera phone and then strode back to the sitting room.

Cole rolled his eyes at my expression. "It's funny for you. You don't have to live with it. I'd seriously consider deflating her if I wasn't worried about Bigsie's retaliation."

I giggled harder.

"Come on." Cole huffed. "Where's the sympathy? How am I supposed to explain that to a woman if I bring her back here?"

I shrugged. "You have a weird flatmate."

"Nah, if we're being serious here they'll be out the door before I even get the *chance* to explain. Would you not be if you saw that in some guy's bathroom?"

I sniggered. "Oh, God, yeah."

"Fucking great," Cole muttered into his coffee.

My phone vibrated again and I studiously ignored it, reaching for my Coke.

"Are you not going to answer that?"

I shook my head.

"Okay." Cole eyed me carefully. "We've barely hung out in weeks, which is fine because you seem to be making progress with Marco. But now you're here, after work, avoiding phone calls. What's up with that? Is it him?"

"You don't want to know."

I felt Cole's scrutiny intensify. He sighed, putting his mug down on the chipped coffee table. "You slept with him."

My lips parted at his perceptive deduction. "Annoying."

"So you slept with him. It was that bad you're ignoring him . . . like the mature adult you are?"

"It wasn't bad," I muttered, feeling my cheeks blaze at just the memory of it.

"Ach, I don't want to hear that." Cole's face scrunched up like he'd just popped a sour apple candy into his mouth.

"I didn't say anything."

He waved his hand. "Forget the details. Why are you avoiding him?"

"I'm just trying to figure things out."

"And what is there to figure out? I thought you were giving him a second chance?"

"Am I?" My brows drew together.

Cole smiled kindly. "Hannah, you let him back in."

I nodded, knowing that was true and that, yes, I was preparing myself to give him a second chance but . . . "I just have this feeling. I can't get past it. It's this feeling in my gut that this time I'm going to get crushed to the point I can't get back up again."

My friend exhaled heavily. "You want to know what I think?"

"Always."

"I think that feeling in your gut . . . that's just the past talking."

I should have expected it. But I didn't.

I'd spent the last five weeks watching him infiltrate my life, pursuing me, spending time with me. Yet somehow I still couldn't get Marco the boy out of my head, and Marco the boy would have broodingly shrugged off my avoidance of the past day and waited for me to come to him.

To my ever-increasing confusion, relief flowed through me to see him sitting on the steps at the front entrance to my building as I returned from Cole's. He was wearing a warm jacket, but it was freezing outside and he didn't have a hat on or a scarf. Guilt immediately needled me.

Cole was right. Avoiding Marco today had been immature. And here he was waiting on me in this bloody Baltic weather.

Was he telling the truth? Was he really not going anywhere?

"I'm buying you a scarf." I sighed, coming to a stop in front of him.

He lifted his head, his hands dangling between his knees, and my muscles locked at the expression on his face.

"Pissed off" didn't even cover it.

I waited for him to say something, to yell, to question my childish behavior, but instead he stood up and turned his back on me. My mouth dropped open with more confusion, and I watched as he took the last few steps up the front stoop and waited.

Realizing that he was waiting for me to let him in, I hurried up the steps and passed him, my hands shaking a little as I unlocked the door.

I felt his intimidating presence behind me as I attempted not to rush up the stairs to my flat as if a debt collector was on my heels. He got so close to me when I was inserting the key into my lock that his chest brushed against my back.

The butterflies had returned to my stomach with a vengeance by the time I got the door unlocked. As soon as the lock clicked, Marco reached over my head, one hand shoving against the door to throw it open. I was unceremoniously shuffled inside, and sensing the anger practically pouring from him, I scooted out of his grasp and strode into the sitting room to get some distance. I began jerkily unbuttoning my coat.

"So this morning"—his fucked-off tone made me stiffen as I slipped my coat off—"when I kissed you good-bye before I left to get ready for work, that sweet you gave me . . . it was bullshit?"

He was referring to the fact that I'd pulled him back for a deeper kiss, reluctant to let him go. The thing was, when he was right there in front of me, the unease I felt was harder to hold on to. By the time he was gone and I was getting ready for work, I'd let that unease win.

I turned to face him. The fact that he was shrugging out of his own jacket suggested to me he was angry but he wasn't angry enough to leave. Why the hell did I feel so relieved again?

"I'm just confused," I answered honestly.

"That's your answer?" He threw his jacket on my armchair and prowled toward me. "I've had the worst fucking day and that's your answer?"

Unwilling to be intimidated when I was just trying to be truthful, I refused to back up, even when he stopped so close I had to tilt my head back to look up at him. "It's the truth," I snapped.

"So you're confused. That gives you the right to treat me like shit?"

The guilt was back. "No." Without even thinking, I brushed my fingertips over his chest, a gesture of reassurance. "I'm sorry for today. It wasn't fair. I'm just . . . *confused*."

For a moment I wasn't sure how he was going to react.

Then slowly the tension seemed to ease from him despite the hardness that remained in his eyes. "I don't ever want a repeat of today. We got problems, we talk. You don't leave me standing out in the cold like a fucking idiot."

Feeling like one of my scolded schoolchildren, I crossed my arms over my chest and answered somewhat petulantly, "Were you always this bossy?"

A dangerous glint entered his eyes. "Oh, babe, you haven't seen bossy."

I let out a gasp of surprise as he pushed me against the arm of the sofa so I had no choice but to sit on it, and shoved my skirt up to my waist in one rapid, smooth movement.

I clung to the sofa, feeling a heady mixture of apprehension and excitement as he roughly yanked my underwear down my legs. He pushed in between my legs, gripping my nape with one hand and tugging at his zipper with the other.

His kiss was hard, desperate, and that plus the torturous press of his throbbing cock against my sex was too much. He rubbed against me, stole me out of myself with his erotic kisses, and teased me until my skin was inflamed.

By the time my mouth was swollen from his kisses, I felt his fingers slip inside me, testing my readiness. He practically growled in satisfaction before he removed his fingers and thrust his cock inside me.

I cried out in pleasured pain, holding on to Marco for dear life as he gripped my hips and fucked me on the arm of my couch. It wasn't like before. It wasn't slow and deep and driven by longing. This was driven by frustration, confusion, desperation, and lust. It was ragged. It was intense. And I was so hot for him I came fast and I came hard.

Coming down from my climax, I felt my inner muscles spasm as Marco growled, "Fuck, Hannah. Fuck, feels so good," before groaning as he came inside me.

Panting for breath, feeling somewhat bewildered by how different and yet exciting that had been, I waited for Marco to make the next move.

His next move was to kiss me slowly, sweetly, and pull back to ask in belated concern, "You okay? I wasn't—"

I covered his mouth with my hand, smirking in satisfaction. "I might have to piss you off more often."

He rewarded my humor with a wicked grin. "My baby likes it hard."

"I like you," I whispered, feeling that ache in my chest expand.

He brushed his knuckles along my jaw, tenderness burning in his eyes now. "Does that mean you're going to give this a real shot? No more avoiding us?"

I thought about him sitting out on my front stoop in the winter cold.

"Yes." I slid my arms around his neck, pulling him close. "This is me officially giving us a shot."

CHAPTER 15

Years ago, when I was attempting to understand the rings Joss made Braden jump through before finally admitting they were meant for each other, Joss had told me that she had been so happy for the first time in so long that it paralyzed her with fear.

Instead of being able to enjoy what they had, Joss was thinking one hundred miles down the road in front of them, fearing a bend in that road, one that they'd take too sharply and end up careening headlong into disaster.

I understood how she could feel that way, now more than ever.

The next week with Marco was exhilarating in its simple beauty. He spent every night at my place, including the weekend, and we made love. Sometimes it was sweet and sometimes it was wild, and every time it was mind-blowing. When we weren't going at it like teenagers who'd just discovered the power of sex, we hung out like always. It was addictive. *He* was addictive. I felt so content I was scared of it.

Distracted by Marco, distracted by my tumultuous emotions, I was behind on work.

The following Thursday I knew I had to skip out on lunch and use that time and the free period I had next to catch up on my marking. My head was down, my stomach was growling, and I was lost in papers when a knock on my door brought me out of them.

Although my heart jumped at the sight of Marco standing in my doorway, I frowned. "What are you doing here?" My eyes ran the length of him. He was wearing his work clothes. I tried to ignore the fact that I found him sexy like this.

Marco shrugged, taking long-legged strides toward me and I noted the brown bag in his hand. "Anisha let me in at Reception." He pulled a wrapped sandwich out of the bag and placed it on the desk in front of me. A bottle of water followed it. "You sounded stressed this morning." Grabbing a chair he put it opposite my desk and sat down, pulling another sandwich out of the paper bag. "I just wanted to make sure you ate something." A pucker appeared between his brows. "You've lost weight recently."

Touched by his thoughtfulness, I smiled as I picked up the sandwich. "The weight loss is because of all the sex. *Someone* hasn't left me alone for the past week and a half."

He grunted. "Like you're complaining."

I shrugged noncommittally and he smiled before biting into his sandwich.

"FYI, I got my period this morning, so no sex for us for the next few days."

"Nice timing. I've got my family thing this weekend."

There was that sinking feeling back to piss me off some more. "Family thing. Right."

Marco shot me a knowing look. "Soon," he promised. Changing the subject quickly, he gestured to my marking. "You can work, babe."

He sat quietly, eating his lunch, while I ate mine and did my marking at the same time.

An hour passed in perfect, comfortable silence and by the end of it I couldn't help myself.

I felt *it*.

· · ·

That night I felt *it* even more. After I'd told him about my period, a small part of me (okay, a large part of me) assumed I wouldn't see him that night since we couldn't have sex.

If I'd bet on that I would have lost big.

After my literacy class, I returned to the flat to find Marco waiting for me. He cooked dinner. I read a book while he watched a movie. And when it was time for bed, we fell asleep on our sides, my legs tangled in his as he held me tight.

It was weird not to have Marco stay the night on Friday, nor wake up to him on Saturday morning. We'd been in a relationship for less than two weeks, and yet it felt like it had been so much longer. I guessed that was the history between us playing its part.

"I'm so bored," Jo huffed, lolling her head back against the arm of the couch.

I'd chosen to hang out with Jo this weekend. Since arriving at her flat, I was somewhat regretting that decision. "Gee, thanks."

"What?" she frowned at me. "What? Oh, no." She waved my comment away. "I mean in general. Mick made me finish up work almost *four* months ago. I've literally read every book on the bloody planet. I've counted every crack in my ceiling a million times. I've seen more TV movies than I ever wanted to see in a lifetime. This baby needs to get out of me and get out of me soon."

I eyed her baby bump and put a fresh cup of tea down on the table beside her. She was almost eight months pregnant. "Not long now."

"I know." She sighed wearily. "I'm so agitated. Ellie, on the other hand, is all relaxed and sweetness and light. I want to kill her," she growled, and I believed she might have meant it. "Being pregnant together was supposed to be fun, but she's ruining the fun by being normal and rational." She said the word "rational" like it tasted like dirt.

I laughed. "The old hormones getting to you, eh?"

"I am such a bitch." She widened her eyes in horror. "I don't even recognize myself sometimes and I can't stop myself when I'm in the middle of being a bitch. Cam's turned Cole's old room into a sanctuary. I even caught him looking at locks the other day. I think he's genuinely considering fitting a lock to that bedroom door so he can keep me out."

It was difficult not to laugh at the visual and the fact that out of everyone, Jo would be the last person I'd have thought would be crazy with pregnancy hormones.

She was right. Ellie had been very chilled out when she was pregnant with William, and she was just as laid-back this time around, if not more so.

Suddenly Jo blanched. "I'm sorry, Hannah," she whispered. "I don't mean to complain."

"You're allowed to complain. Don't ever be sorry." My phone buzzed before Jo could respond.

Swiping the lock screen, I frowned at the text message that appeared. "Marco?"

"No. It's Suzanne."

So? New guy, no time for your girls?

I held it up to Jo so she could read it. Jo curled her lip in annoyance. "Why are you friends with that girl?"

Shoving my phone back in my pocket without texting back, I shrugged. "The hope had been that she'd finally grow up and become a real person, but so far no such luck."

"I'd just ignore her until she gets the picture."

"I'm not sure if I want to completely cut her out of my life. She was once a close friend."

"*Pfft.* Hannah, she's never been much of a friend to you. Ever."

I exhaled, not really knowing what to do about Suzanne. The truth was, I hadn't seen Suzanne or Michaela in weeks. I'd spoken to Michaela on the phone, and she was cool because she understood—she was just as busy with work and with Colin.

However, after the run-in with Suzanne when I'd met Marco for drinks, my patience with her had frayed beyond repair.

"Okay." Jo shuffled up into a sitting position. "On to a much more interesting subject." She grinned, looking like a mischievous little girl. "Marco: the high school fantasy come to life."

I laughed. "He's definitely a fantasy."

Jo's eyes lit up. "I'm guessing he knows what to do with that fantastic body of his."

Feeling more than a little smug I replied, "Oh, yes. Definitely."

"You should bring him over for Sunday lunch again."

"Now that we're actually seeing each other I think it might be a little weird with you guys there . . . being all nosy."

Jo rolled her eyes. "We're not nosy. We're grown adults. We've got better things to do than spy on you."

"Liar."

"Okay, we probably would. Some of us have been cooped up for months, though. Your lusty romance with Marco is our only form of entertainment."

"Great," I muttered.

"So are you seeing him tonight?"

At the reminder that I wouldn't be seeing him because of his "family thing," I felt my mood sink. "He disappears every other weekend. He says it's a family thing and that he'll explain when the time is right."

"Withholding information." Jo raised an eyebrow. "How do you feel about that?"

"What can I do?" I smiled sadly. "He's not the only one withholding, remember."

Jo's expression turned sympathetic and concerned. "Right."

Thankfully, the sound of the front door opening broke into the suddenly gloomy atmosphere. "It's me!" Cam called, his footsteps growing louder as he strode toward the sitting room. He smiled at me as he entered the room, carrying a white plastic bag. "Hannah, how are you, sweetheart?"

"I'm good." I smiled back. "You?"

His eyes flicked to Jo. "Uh, aye, good."

It took everything in me not to burst out laughing at his hesitation. I was guessing Jo wasn't the only one who wanted this baby to come out soon.

"Did you get me them?" Jo asked him, her eyes riveted on the plastic bag.

In answer Cam pulled out a packet of pickled onion crisps and a multi-pack of Kit Kat biscuits. Jo frowned at the biscuits. "They're ordinary two-finger Kit Kats."

"Aye?" Cam asked in wary confusion.

"I like the king-size Kit Kats." She pouted at him. I'd never seen Jo pout in my life. "The four-finger Kit Kats. They taste better."

His answering smile was tight. "Fine. I'll go back and get them. It's *only* an hour's walk to the supermarket and back."

"You don't need to be snippy," she snapped.

Cam closed his eyes as if he was trying to draw patience from somewhere, anywhere. He opened them, looking at me. "Remind me that I love her."

Laughing, I did as asked. "Cam, you love Jo. The pre-hormonally challenged Jo. And give or take a month she'll be back."

With renewed determination Cameron nodded and stalked out of the flat.

I shot Jo a look of chastisement.

She blinked in confusion. "What?"

"You're being irrational to Cam."

"Eh . . . no. I told him before he left that I wanted the king-size Kit Kats, not the ordinary kind. It's not my fault he didn't listen."

For Cam's sake, I shuffled over to Jo and placed my hands on her bump. "Cool it in there, Pipsqueak, before your mummy is left alone to see out the rest of this pregnancy with only a king-size Kit Kat for company."

CHAPTER 16

To my delight and surprise, that Sunday afternoon Marco turned up at my door. He offered no explanation other than there had been a change of plans. It thrilled me that he'd come to see me immediately upon said change of plans, even if it bothered me that I didn't know what said original plans had been.

It thrilled me even more when he absconded with me down onto Princes Street to the German market. It was there every December for Christmas, along with the small fairground and the ice rink. We ate iced pastries, drank coffee, and held hands as we shuffled through the crowds. As we were walking through the gardens, the light fading, the Christmas lights twinkling all around, I smiled down at the ice rink in the distance.

"That looks fun."

Marco pulled me tighter into his side. "That looks cold."

"I used to ice-skate in the gardens every Christmas when I was younger. I don't know why I stopped."

"Because it's cold."

"It's worth it." I grinned up into his face. "We should do it."

"There's no way I'm putting my feet on ice."

"You won't. You'll put skates on ice."

"There's no way I'm putting my feet in rented skates."

I stopped, probably annoying everyone who had to walk around us to continue down the pathway. "Please," I pleaded.

He stared at me, completely unmoved.

Realizing this was one occasion where being adorable wouldn't work for me, I changed it up. Instead, I raised an eyebrow at him. "You're afraid to skate."

"Reverse psychology? Really?"

I huffed, laughing half in amusement and half in annoyance as I pushed against his chest. "Come on. I want to skate with you. We'll be like a perfect, romantic Christmas card. Except not vomit-inducing."

Fifteen minutes later . . .

"Hannah, I don't think you should do that," Marco warned, crossing his arms over his chest as I showed off.

For someone who was as big as he was and who hadn't skated much, Marco had great balance. He hadn't fallen on his arse once, although he'd stuck to the outer edges of the rink in hopes that I'd let him disembark soon.

I was surprised by how easily skating came back to me, how quickly my body remembered how to balance on the skates. I glided around the rink a couple of times, passing a slow-moving Marco.

I wanted to show him the spin I used to be able to do, but people kept getting in my way.

"It's fine," I promised him, smiling.

I was having a ball.

Seeing a gap in the stream of skaters I pushed back on the skates in order to give myself space to move forward into the spin. To my shock, however, I felt myself hit something solid.

An *"oof"* sounded and then the solid weight collapsed behind me, taking my balance with it. I stumbled around, letting out a yelp, as I swung my arms to balance myself. When I turned, righted, my eyes bugged out in horror.

Unfortunately, the something solid I'd hit was a girl who'd then crashed into a boy, who'd crashed into a couple, who'd crashed into another young woman.

As chaos reigned and limbs splayed I could only watch in mortification at the ice rink devastation I'd created as other skaters skidded to a stop to watch them all hit the ice like dominoes.

Groans and curse words lit the air as the crashers all sat up. My eyes jumped from one to the next to make sure there were no major injuries.

A warm hand wrapped around mine and I found myself jerked back against Marco. "They're fine," he said through clenched teeth and yanked on my arm. "Let's get you out of here. *Now.*"

Realizing that was probably a good idea, considering the murderous looks aimed my way, I shot an apologetic glance at the casualties, who were regaining their footing quickly, and I ungracefully slipped and skidded as I hurried after Marco off the rink.

With quick efficiency Marco got our skates off, our shoes back on, grabbed my hand, and started hauling me back up toward Princes Street.

We were only halfway up the hill when he suddenly let go of my hand and looked down at me, appearing ready to explode. And then he did.

His laughter was loud and infectious, and he couldn't seem to catch his breath.

My surprise soon melted into shared hilarity and I collapsed against his side, giggling like a madwoman.

"Oh, man." Marco finally calmed, wrapping his arm around my shoulders. "I didn't realize you were such a klutz, babe."

"I'm not! I just . . . don't have the best spatial awareness. Obviously."

His body shook with laughter again. "That's the fucking understatement of the year. Jesus, that was like a skit. You couldn't have rehearsed it better."

"Should I prepare myself for a constant stream of teasing for the next few hours?"

"More like years of it. Any time we see a pair of ice skates . . ."

I harrumphed. "No one got hurt."

He snorted and I could tell he was trying not to lose it again.

I punched him playfully. "You keep up the teasing, you're not getting your Christmas present." I'd bought him a Blu-ray player since he'd said he didn't have one and I knew how much he loved movies.

Marco looked down at me, pulling me in closer to his side. "You'll still get yours."

My eyes lit up. "You got me a present?"

"Of course."

"I like presents."

His gaze turned deeply affectionate. "Duly noted."

Warmth pulsed through me at the expression on his face. I held on tighter to him. "I kind of like you. You know that, right?"

His answer was to stop us in the middle of the crowds again and kiss me like there was no one else around.

After a lengthy, heated embrace, I pulled back to grin up at him. "You're really cool."

He grinned back. "Good thing one of us is."

I narrowed my eyes. "You have two hours to get the skating incident out of your system, and then no more."

"I object. Two hours isn't long enough."

"It's plenty long enough."

"The length of teasing should be in proportion to the magnitude of the incident. Babe, you just took out five people simultaneously on an ice rink. I'd say that's at least the first five years of our lives together. One year per person."

I wanted to argue with the math, but I knew if our roles were reversed I'd be taking the absolute piss out of him for it for years to come. "Fine," I grumbled. "Five years."

He hugged me to his side and started leading me up the hill again. "You do realize you just committed yourself to me for at least five years."

That sneaky little . . . I gave him a look of reluctant admiration. "Nicely played, D'Alessandro. Nicely played."

For the last few weeks, I'd taken to waking just before Marco's alarm was set to go off. Mostly, I would just cuddle in closer to him and close my eyes again.

However, that morning I woke up to discover that we were tangled in each other as we lay on our sides, my outer thigh resting over his, my lower body pressed into him.

Marco might be asleep, but his body was aware of the close proximity of its manly bits to my womanly bits. With his hard-on pushing against my belly, I felt a delicious tingle between my legs that woke me up entirely.

Trailing my hands up his naked back, I delighted in the feel of him. I lowered my head and started kissing my way down his chest.

Suddenly his arms tightened around me and he pushed us until I was flat on my back and he was braced over me.

He looked down at me through sleepy eyes. "First your snoring keeps me awake and now you're trying to make me late?" His voice was even more gravelly than usual. So unbelievably sexy I wanted to touch myself as I listened to him talk.

I squirmed under him until I had my legs wrapped lightly around his hips. "I'm trying to make up for the snoring with sex, but if you're not interested . . . ," I teased, moving to drop my legs.

"That's not a gun pressing against you, babe."

I grinned cheekily and shook my head. "No, that's your cock."

Marco grinned back. "You just like saying that word, don't you?"

I nodded as he lowered his head to press kisses to my neck. "Cock." His kisses turned to love bites and I giggled. "Cock, cock, cock."

Growling, Marco rolled us so he was on his back and I was astride him. He looked up at me, his beautiful blue-green eyes as awake as his hard-on now. His hands flexed on my hips as the sexual heat in his eyes ignited. "Ride my cock, Hannah," he ordered gruffly.

I purred, lifting myself over him until I felt the tip of him at my entrance. I grew wet at just the promise of him. "Just because you asked so nicely . . ."

I was in a great mood. My day had started with earth-shattering sex and now it was ending with one of my favorite lesson plans. I had my fourth-year class and we were discussing villains. In order to illustrate the use of character development and the need for layers in creating a good villain in literature, I was using clips from the film *The Dark Knight Rises.*

Having the visual and something the kids enjoyed as the source actually really helped in getting them to understand the use of history, circumstance, and motivation in creating a villain. The students were really into it. It was probably the most animated I'd ever seen them, and I was in a great mood, enjoying it right along with them.

"Whit's up wi' you?" Jack Ryan, the thorn in my side, sneered and effectively ruined the positive atmosphere. "Someone finally givin' it tae you?"

My blood boiled and while I counted to ten in order to answer the little shit calmly, Jarrod let his eraser fly. It was some throw.

It hit Jack's cheek. Hard.

"Whit the fuck!" He slapped a hand to his cheek and glared in Jarrod's direction. He moved as if he was going to get up, but I was already marching over to him with determination.

"Sit down," I demanded with a chilling calm. The whole class tensed at the anger in my voice.

Surprised by my tone, Jack lowered himself back into his seat.

Reaching his table, I put my palms on it and leaned down so he had nowhere to look but at my face.

My voice quiet and taut, I laid it out for him. "If you ever speak to me like that again, you are out of here. Do you understand me?"

He shrugged.

I narrowed my eyes. "Let me make myself perfectly clear, then. I am not impressed by you. I am certainly not intimidated by you, and, frankly, I am sick of your continuous interruptions in my class. One more inappropriate word from you and you're gone, and I'll keep putting you out of this class every time you do it. Because do you know what? It's no skin off my nose if you don't pass this class. I'd rather everyone else gets the attention they need from me, because they deserve it. If you want to walk out into the real world without even a basic education and then spend your life struggling to make ends meet, then go ahead—say something that will really, *really* annoy me."

Jack's answer was to stare at me sullenly.

But he didn't open his mouth. I took that as progress.

Shooting him one last warning look, I bent down and picked up Jarrod's eraser. I walked over to his table. "I think you dropped this."

Smirking, he reached up to take it back, but I held it out of his reach for a moment.

"I'm asking you not to *drop* it again."

Jarrod's expression changed, the smirk disappearing, a serious note in his eyes. He nodded carefully and I handed the eraser back to him.

We finished up the class but Jack had officially ruined the mood. I gave him another stern look as he left my classroom at the sound of the bell. The kids were filtering out when Jarrod came over to my desk, waiting for his classmates to leave.

As soon as the last one was out the door, he grinned at me. "You do seem really happy, Miss." That grin turned knowing. "Anything to do with that big guy that came to see you a while back?"

"Jarrod," I said crisply, "it's none of your business."

"Right." He grinned. "Just saying. Nice to know a big guy like that's watching your back."

That was kind of sweet, but I didn't let him know I thought that. Instead I said, "As much as I appreciate the sentiment behind you throwing the eraser at Jack today, I need you to start thinking before you act. You've got a short fuse, Jarrod. That short fuse could get you into situations that you might not work your way out of easily and I want more for you than that. So when someone says something you don't like or tries to get a reaction out of you, stop, think, and remember that you're a smart kid with a bright future and a little brother who thinks the world of you."

He stared at me a moment, seeming to process my words.

To my relief he didn't give me a smart-arse retort. He just nodded.

CHAPTER 17

I was coasting along, almost a little smug not only in my present contentment, but in the fact that I'd beaten my issues with the past.

Little did I know that the past doesn't take too kindly to smugness, to disinterest. The past can be spiteful. It can creep up on the present to taunt it with the memories and all the old hurts.

It wasn't snowing. For this I was thankful. Snow was for when you were curled up safe inside with a fire roaring in the grate. It wasn't for when you were driving a rental to some unknown place in Argyll.

Marco had decided he wanted us to get away for the weekend. He said we needed to talk.

I knew it had to do with his mysterious weekends away and I was glad he was finally going to broach the subject. We'd been officially dating each other for a few weeks now. It was definitely time for me to know what was behind his disappearances, and I was preparing myself for the news.

What I hadn't prepare for was the sight of the large old cottage on a hill overlooking the Holy Loch. My lips parted in wonder as the car drew to a stop on the gravel driveway. With its multicolored stone block facade, creeping vines, and old-fashioned windows made up of lots of little panels, the cottage was like something out of a fairy tale. Smoke puffed out of the top of the roof from a chimney, and a fat tabby cat skittered across the front doorstep as the car drew to a halt.

I glanced over at Marco and he smiled.

Before I could say a word he was out of the car and hurrying around to the passenger side to open my door. My feet had just touched the driveway when he grabbed my hand and tugged me gently over to the front door. Bending down, he unearthed a key from beneath a ceramic tortoise and let us inside.

Heat hit us and I followed Marco in a daze as he led me out of a small foyer into a hallway and then to the right. My eyes grew round with surprise as I took in the large sitting room. Antique furniture cluttered the space, but in elegant coziness. There were dark plum velvet sofas in the French style, a mahogany tea chest, and a huge crockery display cabinet with china plates. But best of all was the roaring fire in the massive fireplace on the main wall. Shadows danced around the darkening room as the flames from the fire licked out at us.

My gaze dropped to the chenille blanket that had been placed in front of the fire. On it were a hamper, a bottle of wine, and a red rose.

Marco squeezed my hand. "You once told me this would be your perfect date."

Slowly, I turned to look at him in amazement.

. . . *there was this scene where he takes her to this tiny cottage on his land, away from everything and everyone. They sit in front of a roaring fire, drinking and eating, sometimes talking, sometimes not. It was like there was no one else in the world but them* . . .

"You remembered that?" I asked, my voice choked with emotion.

His head bent toward me, his lips brushing mine. "I remember everything."

"I can't believe you did all this." I moved into him, wrapping my arms around him.

"I had a little help from the housekeeper, Dottie. She's a bit of a romantic, it would seem."

I laughed softly. "As are you, it would seem."

He cradled my face in his hands, his thumb sweeping along my jaw before coming to a rest on my plump lower lip. "Only with you."

I closed my eyes, soaking up the feel of him holding me, the sound of the fire, the heat of it against my skin, and in that moment I was reminded of the girl I used to be, the reluctant romantic who still believed there was something really special out there for her.

"I can never get enough of you," Marco murmured, pressing soft kisses down my neck and across my naked shoulder.

Caressing his back, I made a contented purring sound in the back of my throat. My whole body was warm and languid after the two orgasms he'd just given me.

"I'll be back." He pressed one last kiss to the rise of my breast and then moved off me.

I pouted. "Where are you going?"

He didn't answer. Instead he disappeared from the sitting room and then returned a few seconds later with a washcloth.

I bit my lip and spread my legs.

A predatory look flashed in Marco's eyes as he sat back down on the blanket in front of the fire to press the washcloth between my legs. "You keep that up and you won't be able to walk out of here tomorrow."

"I'm not doing anything," I whispered, smiling innocently at him.

He shook his head, his eyes never leaving mine. "You are so dangerous."

"Me?" I grinned mischievously as I pushed myself up and slid toward him, lifting my right leg over his knees so I could wrap both legs around his waist. He immediately put his arms around me and hauled me up so I was crushed against him. "I've never been dangerous in my life."

"You're dangerous to me."

I pressed closer, my hands coasting down his muscled back. "I like being dangerous to you."

His answer was to kiss me thoroughly and then bury his head in the crook of my neck, hugging me tight, almost like he needed me to ease something in him.

My chest tightened with emotion as I sensed that Marco was feeling overwhelmed somehow. To soothe him I stroked his back, relaxed in his hold.

But then I brushed my fingers across the scar on the lower left-hand side of his back and without even meaning to I tensed.

Marco felt it and pulled away to look me in the eye.

I wanted to ask him, but I didn't want to ruin the moment between us.

He moved as if to disentangle me and I automatically tightened my grip on him with all four limbs. "Don't."

"Hannah, I don—"

"Was it him? Your grandfather?" I asked softly, feeling the burn of anger in my belly as I did anytime I felt the scar under my hands or saw it.

Marco sighed heavily. Thankfully, he didn't pull away again. Instead he gave my waist an affectionate squeeze. "Babe, it's in the past."

"I want to know what he did to you."

"Why? It's done."

"Because . . ." I shrugged helplessly. "I want to make it better somehow."

His face softened. "You already do. You always have. I'm sitting here with you naked and you've got your gorgeous body wrapped around me. Nothing better than that. And nothing can make that turn to shit."

"So if nothing can make it turn to shit, tell me. *Now* is the best time to tell me," I said to encourage him.

He sighed. "Fine. I was eleven. I broke curfew. Nonno had slapped me around a bit before and a couple times he'd whacked me with his belt, but he'd never given me a thrashing. Until I broke curfew—and I didn't just break curfew, I talked back to him. So he made me take off my shirt, shoved me face-first onto the kitchen table, and took his belt to me. He messed up—let his anger get the better of him—and the belt unfolded and cut a gash open on my back. Nonna went nuts at him. He never hit me again after that." He shook his head, seeming to pull himself out of the memories as his gaze connected with mine. "They didn't take me to hospital because of the questions that would be asked, so Nonna did her best to clean it up, but it wasn't stitched up right, so it left a scar."

I pushed into him, closer, as close as I could get, my lips brushing his. "I hate him," I whispered hoarsely, feeling the burn of tears in my eyes. "I hate him so much."

"Ssh, baby." He kissed me lightly, rubbing his hands up and down my spine. "Don't. I've let it all go."

I nodded, but the tears escaped anyway, and I wrapped my arms around him, burying my face against his neck.

"It was all worth it to get this at the end of it," he murmured.

I was overwhelmed by my need to make everything better for him— wishing I'd been there back then, to take his pain away. From here on out, I wanted to make it so he never felt that way again, so that he always felt loved.

Yes, loved.

Because I did, I realized.

I'd fallen deeply in love again with Marco D'Alessandro.

After a day of fooling around in the cottage, followed by a brisk walk down by the loch, we ended up having dinner at a nice restaurant in the local village before returning to the cottage. As we settled in for the evening, the only sound to be heard for miles was the crackling of the fire in the grate. Despite our romantic surroundings I'd been a little on edge, waiting for Marco to finally bring up what it was he wanted to discuss with me.

At last, as I lay against his side on the sofa, my legs tangled in his, I prompted, "You wanted to talk?"

Marco was silent for a moment as he drew circles on my bare shoulder with the tip of his finger. "Liv said something," he replied, his voice low and amused in the quiet room. "It was that Sunday we had lunch at your mom's. She said that you once planned an ambush with her. She took you to D'Alessandro's so you could corner me and get me to talk to you because I'd been ignoring you. Is that true?"

I closed my eyes, every muscle in my body coiled tightly. Why would Liv bring that up to him? Why would he bring that up to me?

Embarrassed, annoyed, and feeling unbelievably vulnerable even though I knew Marco would never want me to feel that way, I stared broodingly into the fire. The night before in bed with Marco had been a far greater moment of vulnerability for the both us. However . . .

That had been about Marco's past and our present.

This was about *our* past.

I was avoiding our past. Reminders weren't good.

"Yeah, so?"

At my tone, his arm tightened around me. "I just couldn't remember why I was ignoring you. I guess I wanted to remember because I'm trying to make up for everything shitty I ever did to you."

Oh, no. We could definitely not go there tonight.

I pulled away from him, throwing him a tight smile in response to his questioning frown. "I feel like I need a shower. I'll be back in a bit." I was gone before he could say a word.

Stripping out of my clothes quickly, I jumped in the hot shower and leaned my forehead against the cool tiles. I tried breathing in and out slowly to ease my anxiety.

It wasn't long before the shower door opened behind me, but I didn't turn around. I felt his heat all around me as Marco stepped inside. I lifted my head from the tiles, my back immediately hitting his chest.

His hands drifted lightly up the curve of my waist, fingertips trailing a featherlight path over my ribs, until he was cupping my breasts in his palms. I sighed, resting my head on his shoulder, arching into his touch.

His thumbs brushed over my pebbled nipples and my lower belly rippled with arousal.

Without saying a word, Marco played my body, touching me, caressing me, kneading me. As I panted for breath, he slipped his hand between my legs and pushed his fingers inside me. I leaned my hands on the tiles in front of me and rode his fingers.

"Fuck me," I groaned in desperation.

Suddenly Marco's fingers were gone, my hips were gripped hard in his hands, and his cock was gliding into me. I cried out at the fullness of him inside me and reared back into his gentle thrusts.

He cupped my right breast again, pressing me back into him as he squeezed it while his other hand moved between my legs. His fingers slid over my clit, back and forth, as he continued to fuck me in slow, tormenting thrusts.

I rested the back of my head on his chest, my hands on his hips behind me, desperate for satisfaction. He pushed me toward it, until my whole body stiffened.

Marco felt it and started pumping harder, faster.

The tension inside me broke apart, the orgasm quivering through my whole body as my eyes fluttered closed in absolute bliss.

I melted against Marco and he held me tighter, his breath hot on my skin, his grunts and pants increasing as he chased his own climax. And then suddenly I felt his teeth on my shoulder as his body tightened a few seconds before his hips jerked hard with release.

He pressed me against the tiles, his body shuddering as he came inside me.

"Fuck," he breathed, caressing my bottom.

I shivered, my heart still racing in my chest.

That had been intense.

And apparently Marco wasn't done with intense.

He pulled out of me slowly, but I didn't even have time to regret the loss of him before he spun me around to face him. I stared up at him to find his expression fierce. His grip on my shoulders was uncompromising. "When we were kids, I was in love with you."

Surprise, gratification, relief, sheer joy . . . it all moved through me as my eyes widened at his abrupt confession.

"That never went away, Hannah." He rested his forehead against mine. "And now that I know you again, I'm even more in love with you."

Oh, shit. My throat closed up. I knew, I just knew, I couldn't say it back yet.

"Ssh," he murmured, feeling my tension. He kissed me gently. "I can wait for you to say it. I just wanted you to know how I feel. Nothing will change that." His eyes searched mine. "Whatever that was out there, stop. I don't want you to be sore about our past anymore. It's done. We can't take it back. But we have now. And now is good."

Too emotional to form words, I just nodded and wrapped my arms around him. I rested my head on his chest, near his heart, and let him hold me as the warm water cascaded over us.

CHAPTER 18

The next morning, I sighed regretfully as I tidied away all evidence of our visit to the cottage. When Marco came in from putting our bags in the car and saw the uncharacteristic pout on my lips, he cracked a smile. "Back to reality."

I wrinkled my nose. "Do we have to?"

His smile disappeared. "We have a lot to talk about when we get back."

My stomach flip-flopped. "Why don't we talk about it now?"

"I'd rather we talk about it back home. It's a pretty big deal."

"It is about your mysterious weekends, right?"

He nodded. "Yeah."

"Okay, let's hit the road now, because the suspense has been killing me for weeks."

Marco pulled up outside my flat. "You go in. I'll drop the rental off and get a cab back."

I leaned over and pressed a soft kiss to his mouth. "Text me when you're nearly at the flat. I'll put the kettle on for you."

"Sure, babe."

I got out of the car, grabbed my bag, and ducked my head back in the passenger door, everything I wasn't quite ready to say but definitely felt shining in my eyes. "Thank you for a beautiful weekend."

His mouth kicked up at the corner. "It's not over yet, Hannah."

I reluctantly shut the door on that rather thrilling comment and hurried into my building out of the cold. As much as I loved my flat, I really did miss the cottage already. Pottering around the flat, putting on the heat, tidying up the mess I'd left in my bedroom after Marco had dropped the surprise getaway on me, I couldn't ignore the kaleidoscope of butterflies in my stomach. I was beyond nervous about Marco's upcoming discussion with me. In fact, it was an understatement to say I was growing a little impatient with the "family thing." I'd even spoken to Joss about it. She reckoned Marco was waiting until I said "I love you" before divulging whatever this unspoken commitment was.

"It's obviously important. It's not hard to guess he just needs to know you two are serious before he tells you," she'd opined.

"But we are serious."

"Have you told him you love him?"

"No."

"Then how does he know how serious *you* are?"

I wondered now, after he had said, "I love you," if there hadn't been some truth in what Joss said. We had grown much closer over the last two weeks. Perhaps Joss was right. Maybe he had just needed to know I was serious about him.

In an attempt to take my mind off it until he returned to finally clear up the whole mystery, I decided to do some housework, starting with my bedroom.

I'd barely begun when my phone went off. Assuming it was the text message from Marco, I was more than a little surprised to see Suzanne's name on the screen. I swiped it, opening her message.

Don't shoot the messenger. I was at the German Market last weekend and saw this. I thought it through and finally decided you needed to see it.

My heart now flipped in a much less pleasant way as I clicked on the photo attachment to enlarge it—and felt the world narrow around me.

The photo captured Marco by one of the market stalls. He was carrying a little boy and smiling at a pretty brunette who was laughing up into his face.

The little boy . . . he had Marco's coloring . . . Marco's smile . . .

The phone slipped from my hand and I felt my knees wobble.

Suddenly I was on the carpet, attempting not to throw up at the implications of the photograph. My heart was racing too hard. I couldn't breathe properly.

I willed myself to calm down, exhaling and inhaling in measured breaths until my heart rate slowed.

Trembling, I reached for my phone and flicked open the picture again.

Suddenly everything began to make sense and I knew, I just knew, what Marco was returning home to tell me. I forwarded the picture to him so he'd know I knew too.

Suzanne just texted this to me.

It felt like forever as I waited on the floor for an answer, but it was only a minute or two at most before my phone rang. I clicked the ANSWER button.

"Hannah"—Marco sounded out of breath—"I can explain. I'll be ten minutes."

"Marco—"

I heard the click as he hung up.

This was bad. This was . . . I knew it. I was right. If it were anything else he would have explained over the phone. I knew what he'd say when he walked through that door.

Just like that, the past blindsided me, taunting me for my earlier smugness.

Not wanting him to find me on the bedroom floor, pale with shock, I got to my feet and walked into the sitting room. I didn't know what to do with myself. I was a jittery mess.

The buzzer went off.

In a daze, I let Marco into the building, opened my door for him, and returned to the sitting room. I frowned at the mess I was supposed to be tidying up. I had books scattered all over the flat because I was reorganizing them into the bookshelves Marco had built for me.

"Hannah."

I whirled around to face Marco as he strode into the room, his eyes glittering, his face flushed. He was coming straight for me. "Don't." I held up my hands to stop him. He froze. "Explain first."

I watched the muscle tick in his jaw. "I was going to tell you."

"Tell me what?"

He cursed under his breath, rubbing a hand over his close-cropped hair. "That I have a son."

The words hung heavy in the cold air. I closed my eyes against the truth.

"His name is Dylan. The woman in the picture is Leah, his mom. I was at the market with them last weekend along with Leah's fiancé."

Breathe, Hannah.

"You have a son?" I opened my eyes, sure the pain of that truth was blazing clear for him to see. "That's what today's talk was supposed to be about?"

Marco's features were strained as he nodded. "He's three."

I did the calculations in my head and they took my breath away. "When you . . ." I was starting to shake. "When you came back to Scotland you . . . you knocked someone up?"

He took a placating step toward me, as though I were a wounded, abandoned dog, unpredictable but needing comfort. "Hannah, Leah and I were friends at school. Sort of. We hung around with the same people. I was back in Edinburgh a couple of months and I was still trying to sort my head out about Nonno, everything, and a friend invited me to a party.

I thought loosening up might help. I got really drunk. Leah was there and she was wasted too. We hooked up." He said it gruffly, like he felt guilty about it. "She got pregnant. We didn't want to be together, but I'd never leave my kid the way I was left."

He was saying it all. Explaining the situation. I heard it. I know I did. But the past was so much louder than his explanation.

"I get Dylan every other weekend and we alternate holidays, but his mom, me, and her fiancé, Graham, are pretty tight. We have a good relationship, which is great for Dyl. And Dyl . . ." Despite my distraction I saw a happiness in his eyes I'd never seen before. "Hannah, he saved me. You want to know why I got over all the shit my grandfather dealt me? Dylan. Everything changed when he came along. I have someone who needs me to have faith in myself so that he can grow up and have faith in *himself*. But also I need to have faith in myself so that he has faith in me that I'll always be there for him." He gave me that half smile of his I loved. "Kid thinks I'm a goddamn superhero . . . but he's the one that saved me. He's the reason I wanted another chance with you. He made me feel like maybe I could deserve you."

I knew that was a good thing. I knew that.

But that feeling of happiness for him, that relief for him I knew was in me somewhere, was buried under a mountain of irrational fury.

"Hannah, baby, please say something. I'm sorry I kept this under wraps, but I wanted to give us a chance first. I thought if I told you right away it would scare you off, and I needed the chance to remind you how right we are for each other. I knew after last weekend that you and I are solid, so I was going to tell you today and then introduce you to Dylan next weekend. Leah already knows about you, but I needed to be sure about us before Dylan meets you. *I'm* sure, babe. You know that. But I had to be sure that you loved me back, that this was serious, and that we definitely have a future."

It was the most he had said in one breath since the first night he'd come to my flat.

I stared at him, keeping my silence while I tried to keep a lid on my emotions. Something like panic flickered in his eyes. Beautiful eyes. Eyes I loved.

Eyes I wanted—no, *needed*—gone.

I searched for a semblance of numbness to get me through the next five minutes.

"Hannah—"

"I don't want kids," I said dully, holding on to the numb sensation.

Marco blinked in confusion. "What?"

I took a step toward him, trying to herd him out of my home. "I don't want kids. Ever."

He narrowed his eyes. "You're a schoolteacher."

"So?" I shrugged, my expression carefully blank. "I don't want kids. Mine or anyone else's."

"Hannah, just take a minute. We need to talk about this. This is *us*."

Looking him directly in the eye, I replied with calm and authority, "As of right now there is no *us*." The calm slipped somewhat. "You should have told me you had a son."

Suddenly my upper arms were gripped in his hands, his body brushing mine, his face close. "Why are you acting like this? This isn't you." He gave me a little shake, as if trying to loosen me up, get back to something that made sense.

It worked.

I wrenched out of his hold, my face twisted in anger. "You don't know me." I shoved him, stumbling away from him. "Obviously."

"Goddammit. I can't believe this shit." His voice lowered to a growl. "You're not even going to discuss this? Just . . . we're over? After everything? After spending the best few weeks in the fucking history of weeks, you're seriously showing me the door without talking it through?"

Struggling not to let my rage and pain explode all over him for fear I might actually do physical damage, I clenched my hands into fists at my sides and held on to self-control. "This isn't a little thing, Marco." The self-control was slipping already, my voice climbing higher on every word. "You kept a son from me. A son! And yes . . . we are over! You lied!" I panted, shuddering from the weeping wounds inside me. "I don't want kids. I certainly don't want yours. So get the fuck out of my life and stay there."

If I hadn't been so tightly clasped inside the past's vicious grip, I might have faltered in my resolve at the expression in Marco's eyes. The incredulity. The loss.

Then his face tightened with his own fury.

He leaned into me, eyes sparking with fire as he hissed in my face, "It's a good thing I did keep Dylan away from you, because I wouldn't want him around whatever shit this is."

Wearing a look of disgust, Marco turned around and stormed out of the flat.

I jumped at the sound of my front door slamming and immediately swayed with dizziness. My hands groped for the couch to steady myself.

I took a few shallow breaths.

My feet started to move, walking me through a fog, cold little pinpricks of nausea covering my face. I reached the bathroom and lifted the lid on the toilet seat seconds before I threw up the past . . .

The wind was bitter and bracing on North Bridge. It whipped my short hair back and stung my cheeks. It felt good.

I smiled at Cole as he walked beside me. Jo was just a little ahead of us, talking on her phone to Cameron.

Three months ago. Well, just under. That's how long since I saw Marco—my last image of him was India Place . . . that horrified look in his eyes as he dressed and then hurried from the room. I didn't expect to hear from him after he'd taken my virginity and then rejected me, but after four weeks of nothing I finally went to ask after him at his uncle's restaurant. Imagine my total and complete heartbreak to learn that he'd left for America weeks ago. Without saying good-bye.

My family and friends had noticed my despondency. They were worried. I was worried. When I didn't feel numb, I felt like crap. I'd had a sickness bug that I couldn't seem to shake, and I had pains. I didn't feel like myself and I knew if I didn't go to the doctor soon, my parents would force me to.

Everyone was taking their turn with me. Trying to cheer me up. Today was Jo and Cole's turn. Cole and I were friends, not close friends since he was a year younger and we went to different schools, but I found his presence soothing. He didn't ask a lot of questions, which was always nice when you didn't have a lot of answers.

Jo grinned over her shoulder at us and murmured something into her phone.

"What do you think she's saying right now?" Cole squinted against the winter sun.

"That we make a cute couple," I answered wryly.

Cole looked surprised. "You think?"

"Something I've learned watching the women around me fall in love . . . it makes them want everyone else to fall in love."

"I'm not sure I like where this is going."

I laughed weakly. "Don't worry. I'm not interested in falling in love. We can fight any attempts at matchmaking together." I felt a stab of pain in my abdomen and flinched.

"I kind of have a girlfriend anyway," Cole confessed, distracting me from the pain. "I haven't told Jo yet."

I smiled. "Yeah? What's her—" Violent pain shot through my abdomen and I bent double, sucking in my breath.

"Hannah." Cole wrapped his arm around me. "Jo!"

More pain. Agonizing. I think I screamed. I felt a rush of wetness between my legs.

Pain. Nausea.

Fear.

Black spots in my vision, hundreds, thousands . . . until all was just black.

There was a beeping sound.

It was bloody annoying.

Pushing through the dark of sleep, that beeping sound grabbed hold of me and pulled me into consciousness. My eyes fluttered open slowly, my vision hazy. I took in the fading cream-colored walls of the room. The polystyrene ceiling.

Where the hell was I?

I felt weird. My mouth dry. My body weighted.

Catching movement out of the corner of my eye, I turned my head on the unfamiliar pillow to find my mum sitting on a chair beside the unfamiliar bed I was in. Her elbow was braced on the arm of the chair, her chin braced on her hand.

Her eyes were closed. Her cheeks pale.

The beeping behind me seemed to speed up.

"Mum?" I tried to say, but it just came out as a croak. "Mum." I tried again, more successfully.

Her lashes fluttered and then she was looking at me in surprise. The surprise immediately disappeared as her face crumpled and she started to sob.

"Mum?" Scared, I lifted my arm a little to reach for her hand and I spotted the IV stuck in the bend of my elbow. "Mum?" My voice shook now.

She grabbed my hand. "Oh sweetheart, you're okay." She smiled through the tears.

"What happened?"

"Hannah?"

I turned my head to see my dad standing in the doorway. His features were strained, his eyes bloodshot. He rushed toward the hospital bed and leaned over me, pressing a kiss to my forehead. "Sweetheart," he whispered hoarsely.

I started to cry. Silent tears. "What happened?"

A little while later a doctor arrived to explain. She introduced herself as Dr. Tremell, my surgeon.

She stood on my right, while my parents stood in each other's arms on my left. Dr. Tremell stared down at me kindly. "Hannah, you had what is called an ectopic pregnancy."

What? Pregnant? No. I turned to look at my parents in denial. "No . . . I would have . . . known."

The doctor shook her head gently. "Sometimes with an ectopic pregnancy there is bleeding, spotting, that is often confused with menstruation." She must have seen on my face that that's exactly what had been happening these last few weeks. "An ectopic pregnancy is when a fertilized egg implants itself outside of the womb. In your case, Hannah, the egg implanted inside your left fallopian tube. Unfortunately, because you were unaware of your pregnancy, any symptoms you might have had were not picked up on."

The sickness. The pain.

I closed my eyes in disbelief.

"The egg continued to grow inside your fallopian tube until it ruptured the tube. You were bleeding internally when you arrived at the hospital. We had to perform surgery immediately. As I explained to your parents, we lost your heartbeat but managed to resuscitate you."

I'd died?

I looked at my parents and saw it written all over their faces.

"Hannah." Dr. Tremell's voice had grown softer. "We removed the damaged tube and you should make a full recovery from surgery. We're administering pain medication to you, but if you feel any pain, please let your nurse know and we'll administer more if needed."

I looked up at my parents and saw in their ragged expressions what the last forty-eight hours had done to them.

I closed my eyes.

This wasn't real. This couldn't be real.

Two months.

I sat on the end of my own bed, staring around at the things in my room, feeling strangely detached from the person who owned them. I didn't feel like that girl anymore.

Nearly dying, weeks of pain and recovery, missing school, dealing with the rumors at school . . . all without him, all without Marco by my side. The one person I needed.

It had been a long two months.

A life-changing two months.

And I still hadn't explained anything to anyone.

I couldn't bring myself to talk about it.

My eyes locked on a photograph of Jo and me last Halloween. I'd convinced her to dress up with me. She was a sexy nurse and I was a mischievous angel of death. I had my arm around her shoulders and I had pouted dramatically at the camera, laughter and joy in my eyes.

Who was that girl?

I blinked away the tears, refusing to give in to any more of them.

A light knock sounded at my door and I looked up to watch Cole slide in. He was taller than Cameron now.

Without saying a word he walked into the room and sat down beside me.

"I know everyone has tried talking to you about what happened and I know you keep blowing everyone off, but today you aren't going to."

I scowled at my lap.

"Hannah, you passed out in my arms. There was blood. Jo and I didn't know what was going on. You were dying. I was scared shitless," he confessed, his words thick with emotion.

Surprised, I looked up at him. Cole cared about me.

Sighing, I reached for his hand and squeezed it. "I'm sorry I did that to you."

"You don't need to be sorry. Just tell me who got you pregnant so I can kill him before Braden, Adam, Cam, and Nate get to him."

Still, despite feeling betrayed by Marco's departure, angry at him, so angry at him for leaving me to deal with all this alone, I felt fear more than anything else. Fear of my family discovering he got me pregnant. Fear they'd hurt him. Fear they'd think less of him.

"Hannah, you almost died," Cole reminded me harshly.

"I know." I closed my eyes, taking a deep breath. "I made a massive mistake. At the beginning of the school year I went to a party with Sadie. I got really drunk." I looked away from him. "I slept with this random guy I met and I took off afterwards because I couldn't believe I'd done it. I don't even know his name, let alone where he lives. And if I did, what would be the point? I had a miscar-

riage. He didn't know I was pregnant, I didn't know. We were both to blame for acting irresponsibly."

"But you're the only one who had to deal with the consequences. How is that fair?"

I shrugged. "I don't think God's a woman, if that's what you're asking."

He choked on laughter. "You're joking about this? Really?"

"It's either that or I cry." I felt my lips tremble. "Shit. I'm going to cry." The tears fell before I could stop them, the sobs shuddering out from the very depths of me.

Cole wrapped his arm around my shoulders and pulled me into him, his T-shirt instantly soaked where I laid my head on his chest. "You'll get through this, Hannah."

"I keep seeing my mum's and dad's faces. I watched them go through hell when Ellie was diagnosed with her tumor and I saw it in their eyes again when I was lying in that hospital bed. Their whole world nearly disappeared along with me and it's my fault." I sobbed harder.

"Ssh," he soothed, pulling me closer. "It's nobody's fault. Everything's going to be okay."

The truth was, I was scared. I was scared one wrong move could rip life away from me. Suddenly pregnancy was something that could do that to me. It wasn't rational. I knew the doctor had told me I could go on to have a perfectly healthy pregnancy, but the fear of another ectopic pregnancy was too great. My fear forced me to grieve too young for what I always took for granted would be in my future.

Sitting up from the cold tiled floor of my bathroom, I swiped at my wet cheeks, and pressed my back against the bathtub, wrapping my arms around my knees to draw them into me.

My miscarriage, my near-death experience, and my grief changed me. It made me a bit of a loner. I lost most of my high school friends and I created a distance between myself and my family. Partly because I felt to blame for it all. I had acted recklessly that night with Marco, and in doing so I scared the utter crap out of the people that meant the most to me. They all became super-overprotective. To the point of suffocating me. That only made me internalize everything more.

I was depressed for months. Heartbroken.

In an attempt to try to pull me out of the dark, my parents were actually the ones who surprised everybody by suggesting I stay in student accommodations at university. They believed it would force me to start living again.

And it did.

Suzanne was crazy. She was never serious. She liked to party, and I found her carefree attitude addictive during a time when I really needed that.

I soon discovered, however, that my parents were worried about me getting pregnant again. Although they'd never admonished me for my stupidity, since nature had done enough reprimanding for the both of them, I knew I'd lost something from them. I'd lost their certainty in me. They worried that I'd make the same mistake all over again and that I'd put myself in danger.

So I went with Mum and I got the pill.

I'd been on it ever since, even though until Marco there had never been any real use for it.

By the time I turned nineteen I'd gotten through the worst of it, and standing on the sidelines, waiting for me to come back to them, was my family.

And I did.

They knew I would.

Waiting at the head of that line was Cole. He was the only positive thing to come out of it all. Since the moment I'd collapsed in his arms, a bond had formed between us, gradually growing until we counted each other as best friends. He had always been there in those dark days to assure everyone else that I was still in there and that day by day I was making my way back to them.

Eventually I moved on.

I tried to let it all go.

Until Marco. He came crashing back into my life. No one but my dad knew he was the one who had got me pregnant and left me. I felt all alone again. I couldn't talk to my dad about it. That was too weird, too uncomfortable, and so it brought everything back.

I tried to fight through the hurt and disappointment to reach for rational thought. Marco hadn't known I was pregnant. If he'd known it would have been a different story. I was sure of that. It wasn't his fault any more than it was mine.

Okay, if he hadn't left me I would have had him by my side when I needed him. Maybe the days wouldn't have been so dark. However, he'd explained why he left. And Cole had been right. I might not like it, but his explanation was a good one.

I forgave him.

My fingernails dug into my knees.

But to know now that he'd not only returned to Edinburgh without looking me up, but that he'd returned and gotten some other girl pregnant and *been* there for *her* . . . It was devastating.

All that pain was back full force again.

It didn't matter if it wasn't rational. I felt it. I felt it scoring my insides.

The hardest thing I'd ever been through and he wasn't there for me.

But he'd been there for *Leah*.

I knew I shouldn't have let him back in.

I couldn't forgive him this.

CHAPTER 19

"The turkey looks burnt." Dec made a face at the dead bird as he approached the dinner table.

Mum had gone all out, just as she did every year, and the table looked beautiful.

The turkey did not at all look burnt.

"What?" Mum squawked as she hurried into the room, carrying a bowl of potatoes. Her eyes flew to the bird in panic.

I shot my brother a dirty look, ready to reprimand him for teasing Mum when she was anxious, but Dad beat me to it.

"Declan, stop being an idiot and go help your mum get the rest of the food through from the kitchen."

Dec grunted at the order but didn't argue with it.

As soon as he was out the door, I made a face at my dad as I rounded the table to take a seat next to Ellie. "Do you think he'll be passing that irritating stage of teenage idiocy anytime soon? He is eighteen—shouldn't he be over it by now?"

"I heard that!" Dec shouted from the hallway.

I bugged my eyes out at Ellie as she giggled. "Ears of an owl."

"An owl?" Joss smiled, amused, as she helped Beth, Luke, and William settle at the kiddie table.

"Yes," I said. "I do believe they have the sharpest hearing in the world."

"I do believe you know a whole lot of crap that no one cares about," Dec said as he returned to the room with a bowl of steamed vegetables.

"Ha." I greeted him with a grimace. "I do believe I know whose Christmas vouchers are getting canceled if he doesn't stop being an irritating d-i-c-k."

"Ah." Adam sighed contentedly, sitting on Ellie's other side. "Now it feels like Christmas."

Ellie giggled into her glass of water.

Mum glared at us both as she set down the last bowl of food and slipped into her seat at the head of the table across from Dad. "Both of you zip it and eat."

"She's the one that started it earlier on," Dec huffed, sitting down next to Braden. "She's been on my back since she got here. I don't understand why she stayed the night when she has her own place. *And* it's not my fault she's in a shitty mood because she got dumped."

I sucked in my breath and everyone with the exception of Braden and Dec tensed. Braden's reaction was to smack Dec lightly across the back of the head. "One, don't swear in front of the kids. Two, she didn't get dumped, she did the dumping. And three, you're eighteen. Grow up and stop being a pain in the a-r-s-e to your sister. Apologize."

I was too busy avidly staring at my empty plate to see Dec's reaction to that. I was attempting to regain control of my breathing after my brother's words had winded me.

All day I'd been doing my best to forget.

The last few weeks had not been easy, to say the least. I'd had to explain to everyone that Marco and I had broken up, but of course I couldn't explain why. I didn't get into it, and I tried my best to appear as unaffected as possible. However, no matter what I said they were all convinced that I was the devastated party in the breakup.

"I'm not devastated," I'd lied to them on more than one occasion. "We were barely together two months."

Yet the truth was I missed him so much I was in pain. All the time.

I was completely at war with myself.

In the mornings I would wake up alone but I would feel the press of his warm body against mine like a phantom in the room. I'd remember Marco was out of my life and that warmth would disappear and I was left alone in my flat. My flat that had once been home and now just felt empty and cold.

Like its owner.

When missing him became too much, I'd reach for the phone, and just as I was about to dial his number, I'd remember. How much it hurt. Why it hurt. And why we were no longer together.

Of course it made things easier that Marco didn't call or come around. I'd packed up the things he'd left at my place and had Nish return them to him. She did it for him. Not for me. Nish and I weren't really speaking to each other, which made for a very wintry atmosphere in the staff room. I discovered she'd known all along that Marco had a son. He'd asked her to stay quiet on the subject until he had the chance to tell me. Nish was equally pissed off with me for reacting to the news the way I had. She was under the impression I was a selfish, coldhearted bitch.

Nish and Marco could think what they liked, as long as I had space to lick my old wounds and try to make sense of everything.

Being around family helped. I'd stayed with my parents on Christmas Eve and I intended to stay with them right through until the day after Boxing Day. Although Liv, Nate, Jo, Cam, and Cole were celebrating Christmas with their own families, my parents' house still felt full, it still felt warm, and it felt safe.

I was doing my best to hide my heartbreak so I wouldn't spoil the mood, and I'd been doing a pretty decent job of it until my little brother decided to be a little shit.

"Hannah."

I looked up at Dec and saw the remorse in his expression.

"Sorry," he muttered guiltily.

"Don't even worry about it," I replied quietly, and then flashed everyone my best faux smile. "I'm starving. Let's eat the crap out of this turkey."

Thankfully the atmosphere at the table lightened and we were able to enjoy a great Christmas dinner together.

Earlier that morning Mum, Dad, Dec, and I had opened our presents, but Ellie, Adam, Braden, Joss, and the kids had yet to open theirs from us, and we hadn't opened ours from them. After dinner, I hurried upstairs to my old room, where I had a Santa's sack with all their presents in it. I was just going through it to make sure everything was there when my phone rang in my pocket.

Thinking it was probably Jo or Cole, I answered it without even looking at the screen.

"Merry Christmas." Suzanne's greeting surprised me. "I thought I better call since it seems you've lost my number."

Just like that, all my pretense at happy Christmas spirit fled out the nearby window and instantly frosted over in the December air. "I didn't lose your number," I told her flatly. "I just don't want to talk to you."

She gave me a loud, dramatic huff. "Because I sent that picture? That was for your own good. I was being a *friend*."

I shook my head at her bullshit, catching my look of incredulity in the mirror in front of me. "No. You were being a bitch because you don't know how to be anything else. You didn't send that photo because you were looking out for me, you sent that photo because you were pissed off and wanted me to be pissed off too. You're spoiled and you're spiteful. Not to mention inconsiderate. I should have broken off our friendship ages ago, as soon as I realized that you aren't capable of thinking about anyone but yourself. Don't bother calling me again. Ever." I hung up before she could respond and instantly deleted her number.

The fact that I felt relieved more than anything else told me I was doing the right thing.

"What was that about?"

I spun around. "Adam?"

He stepped into the room, scrutinizing me. "Well?" He gave a nod toward my phone.

I slipped it into my pocket. "It was nothing."

Adam scowled at my reply. "Did Marco cheat on you?"

"What?" I stared at him in surprise. "Why on earth would you think that? No. He didn't cheat on me. I told you, I just didn't want to be with him anymore."

"Well, none of us believe that."

I heaved a beleaguered sigh, wishing my family didn't pay such bloody close attention. "Look, if he'd done something awful to me, I'd tell you in a heartbeat so you could go and kick his arse. But he didn't. I promise."

It was Adam's turn to sigh. "Sometimes I don't know what to do with you, Hannah. Els is worried."

I opened my mouth to reassure him, but there was a commotion downstairs—

"*Adam!*" Dec bellowed up the stairs. "*The baby's coming!*"

"I don't recognize any of these people." I wrapped my arm around Cole's shoulders and leaned into him as I looked around the room.

"That's because you've had five beers."

"Yet my cognitive functions appear to be in working order, so it's not that."

He glanced at me, a small smile playing on his lips. "And you used the phrase 'cognitive functions.' Okay." He gazed back around the room. "So I guess I don't recognize some of these people. But most of them are from uni."

"Hmm. Should we mingle?"

"Aye." I felt his concerned gaze on me. "You ready for that?"

"You're the one that's forcing me to celebrate New Year's, so I think you already think I am."

"Jesus Christ, leave it to you to be smart when you're drunk."

"I'm not drunk. I'm buzzed." I spotted a bottle of tequila. "But I know a way to get drunk."

Following my gaze, Cole's nodded. "I'll get the salt and the lime." He walked off toward to the kitchen, smiling and nodding hello to people.

As soon as he was gone, I instantly felt despondent. I hated that I felt despondent. This was supposed to be a happy time. Ellie had given birth to another little boy in the early morning of Boxing Day. She and Adam had named him Braden after his uncle, although we'd all already started calling him Bray. While William was fair like his mum, Bray was already dark like his dad. Only time would tell if he'd remain that way.

We were all gaga over Bray, even the kids. Now we were just waiting on Jo, who was due this week.

I tried not to let their pregnancies or the pregnancies that had come before theirs bother me. Never would I resent a family member's or friend's happiness. However, each new baby was a reminder that I would never have one of my own. So I took joy in being a favorite aunt.

I took no joy in the fact that missing Marco hadn't gone away. In fact it had only gotten worse.

"Screw the salt and lime," I whispered, and headed over to the tequila.

With Cole's help and the help of people who were introduced to me but whose names I quickly forgot, I got drunk to the point where I was happy but I could still control which foot went in front of the other. By the time midnight approached, a cute guy around Cole's age was chatting me up. He was flirty and kept touching my waist and bending close to hear what I had to say, and for a little while, at least on a superficial level, I could forget there was a Marco.

Across the room I saw Cole was flirting with a pretty brunette.

It looked like we'd each found ourselves someone to kiss at midnight.

The room grew still upon the countdown and we all started shouting down from ten.

". . . TWO! ONE! HAPPY NEW YEAR!"

Cheers rent the air along with whistles and claps, and I turned to smile up into cute-guy-I-couldn't-remember-his-name's face just as his mouth descended toward mine.

The instant his lips touched my lips, I tensed.

He kissed me. It was perfectly nice.

But there was no tingling.

I felt the burn of tears in my nose and in the back of my throat and I abruptly broke the kiss. I looked up, horrified by the wet in my eyes, and apologized to his neck since I couldn't meet his surely befuddled gaze. Hurrying away from him, I pushed through the crowds of partygoers in Cole's flat and hurried out into the chilly stairwell. It was cold, but it felt nice against my burning skin.

"What the hell was that?" I murmured to myself, brushing my hair off my face with a trembling hand.

As if in answer, my phone rang.

That was a surprise. It was nearly impossible to get through to someone on New Year's since the networks were so clogged with calls. Pulling my phone out of my pocket, I almost dropped it when I saw the caller ID.

It was like the no-tingle kiss had conjured him.

Marco.

Feeling the breath whoosh out of me, I stared at the phone, unsure what to do.

Then, as if someone else had taken over my body, I pressed the ANSWER button and held the phone up to my ear without saying a word.

"I'm sitting here"—he started speaking, and the sound of his gravelly voice in my ear caused me to close my eyes in pain—"and for the millionth time I'm wondering what the fuck went wrong."

Still I didn't speak.

"I want to know what's going on, Hannah. What's *really* going on? I keep going over it and over it in my head, and no matter what my brain tells me happened that day, I refuse to believe the person that broke up with me was you. There's something you're not telling me. There's got to be something you're not telling me." He sounded desperate, and the pain in his voice was like a fist twisting in my gut. "My head's a fucking mess." He sighed, his voice lowering to a rumble. "I miss you."

Frozen, his words like a vise squeezing my lungs, I couldn't say anything in return.

Marco waited a while.

Then he hung up.

I dropped my head, wondering why I suddenly felt like a coward. "I miss you too," I whispered.

CHAPTER 20

A week later school had resumed and it felt good to have something to bury myself in again. Morning classes had gone quickly and I'd now settled at my desk to do marking while I had a free period.

When the phone rang I didn't think anything of it. I answered it and got Neil at Reception.

"Hannah, we've got a Cole Walker at Reception for you."

Wondering what the hell he was doing there, I tried not to let my mind race with the worst possibilities. "Send him up."

I put the phone down and quickly scrambled through my bag for my own phone. Had something happened to Jo? She was past due and maybe . . .

It seemed to take forever for my phone to come on and when it did I had no new messages or missed calls. I shoved it back in my bag just as Cole came through my doorway and slammed my door shut.

Slowly, nervously, I stood up.

Cole was furious and I had not a clue as to why. "What's going on?"

The muscle in his jaw flexed while he looked me over, seeming beyond frustrated and angry. "I bumped into Suzanne half an hour ago."

My stomach dropped.

"Marco has a family?" he asked in disbelief. "A kid? A wife?"

"No." I hurried toward him in denial. "He has a son . . . Cole, we can't do this here."

"Just tell me what's going on and I'll leave."

I wasn't sure I could get through an explanation that would work without breaking down, but I attempted it. "I found out that Marco got someone pregnant when he came back to Edinburgh four years ago. She was an old friend of his. They're not together. But they have a three-year-old son."

He frowned at me in confusion. "You broke up with Marco because he has a child?"

The incredulity in his voice made my anxiety spike even more, but I nodded, hoping my expression didn't give me away.

Unfortunately, the trembling in my hands did. Cole caught the shaking as he scrutinized me from top to bottom, and as soon as he saw it, he stiffened. Understanding flitted through his eyes and he pinned me to the spot with the force of his realization. "It was him," he said hoarsely. Renewed fury roiled in his gaze. "It was fucking him. You lied? It was him! He got you pregnant and fucked off!"

"Cole—"

But he was already marching out of the room.

Panicked, not sure what he might do, I grabbed my bag and ran out of the classroom after him, struggling in my stupid heels. By the time I caught up to him he was striding across the parking lot toward his beat-up old car and he was talking on his phone to someone.

"Cole!" I shouted, but he ignored me and got in his car. "Shit." I hurried after him, chasing him as he pulled out of the school gates. As soon as I hit the main road, I scanned the street for a taxi.

My phone rang. It was Adam.

My gut told me to answer it.

"Hannah, what's going on?" Adam demanded. "Cole just called to ask what site Marco is working on. He sounds beyond pissed off."

Seeing a cab, I threw my hand out, grateful when it slowed. My heart was racing frantically in my chest. "Adam, he's about to do something really stupid. Where is he going?"

Adam gave me the site address and as I jumped into the cab, I relayed it to the driver.

"Hannah, what is going on?" Adam repeated.

"I need to go." I hung up, turning my panicked attention to the driver. "Please, get me there as fast as you can. It's an emergency."

"I'll try my best, love."

I jumped out of that cab at the site entrance ten minutes later and I heard the commotion before I saw it. As I hurried around the office cabins, my heart plummeted at the sight before me.

Marco had Cole by the throat, his face twisted in anger. He thrust Cole away, but Cole barely staggered back before he swung out and clipped Marco in the face with his fist. There were two workers standing behind them, not doing much to stop them, and I could see more running toward the scene.

Marco punched Cole and suddenly I was in action.

"Stop!" I screamed, running toward them, pushing past the crew that was gathering. "Cole, stop i—"

Cole's elbow slammed into my head as he pulled back his arm in preparation to punch. The pain burst down the side of my face, dazing me, and I stumbled back, feeling hands on me, steadying me.

I blinked, trying to refocus, and when I did, I saw Cole staring at me in horror and an enraged Marco behind him, ready to lunge.

"No!" I pushed past Cole and collided with Marco, pressing my hands to his chest. "Marco, please," I pleaded.

Marco's handsome features were stretched tight, his jaw clenched hard. I could tell he didn't want to stop, but he did, taking a step back in silent acquiescence.

Head throbbing, heart pounding, legs trembling, I spun around to placate Cole. I ignored the men who had gathered around us. "He doesn't know, Cole. He doesn't know."

Cole's nostrils flared. "He still fucking left you."

"Yeah. He did. But everything else . . . he doesn't know."

"I don't know what?" Marco asked impatiently behind me.

My shoulders tensed. I'd never wanted this moment to come.

Cole opened his mouth to speak.

"Don't you dare," I snapped.

"He needs to know."

Feeling nauseated at the prospect I replied, "And now he will. But *I'll* be the one to tell him."

"Will someone please tell me what the fuck is going on here?" Marco growled.

"And me."

I turned my head at the unfamiliar voice. A tall man wearing a hard hat and a yellow safety jacket over a suit was glowering at Cole.

"You want to tell me why you attacked one of my men on a worksite?"

"I'd like to know the same thing."

That voice *was* familiar. I blanched as Braden and Adam emerged through the crowds of men. They stopped by the guy in the suit, who I presumed was Marco's site manager. Braden and Adam looked harried. Their eyes blazed with annoyance as they took in Cole and Marco, but their expressions turned concerned when their gazes fell upon me.

"Mr. Carmichael?" The site manager looked surprised. "I didn't know you were planning a visit today. I can assure you this has never happened before."

"Keep your trousers on, Tam." Braden brushed him off. "That's my little sister." He looked back at me. "Hannah, what's going on?"

Feeling my cheeks pale at having all this attention on me, I took a step toward Braden and Adam's comforting presence. "I need to speak with Marco privately. I'll explain everything to you, but first I need to explain it to him."

For a moment Braden was silent as he considered this. It was clear he wanted to know what the hell was going on *now* so he could decide whether he wanted to help finish what Cole had started with Marco. Finally, he gave me a taut nod and then turned to Tam. "My sister needs the use of the office cabin."

"Of course." The site manager gestured toward it. "It's empty."

Before I could do anything, I felt the warm press of Marco's hand on my lower back. He gently guided me forward as the site manager started yelling at everyone else to get back to work.

I wanted to rip away from Marco's touch, hating the ache inside of me, that torturous longing that couldn't seem to get on board with the whole not-forgiving-him thing. However, I let him keep his hand there and I didn't know if I did it for him or if I did it for me.

Once inside the quiet cabin, I stepped aside from the door and watched Marco as he strode toward the manager's desk. He whirled around to look at me, a million questions in his eyes. Ignoring the throbbing in my head where Cole had clipped me, I dipped my gaze to Marco's lip. Cole had split it open. "I'm sorry about Cole," I muttered.

"I could give a damn about *what* he did. I want to know *why* he did it."

It took all the courage I had to meet Marco's eyes.

"Hannah?" he prompted, his patience clearly waning.

The last time I'd felt this sick was after discovering he had a son. Ignoring the cold chills I was feeling, I rubbed a shaking hand over my dry lips and fought the nausea.

"It wasn't because you have a son," I told him quietly.

The air around him instantly grew still, his look sharpening.

"I don't know how to say any of this," I confessed.

"Well, you better find a way because I lost patience with this shit weeks ago."

Exhaling, I nodded. I just needed to say it. *Just say it.*

Breathe, Hannah.

"When you left me five years ago I was in a really bad place. I thought at first I was just heartbroken, that that was why I wasn't feeling great.

But a few months after you left I was out with Jo and Cole and I felt this indescribable pain. I passed out from it."

Marco's expression tightened and I could see in his eyes that he didn't want to hear what was coming but recognized that he needed to. I didn't want to tell him because I knew in that moment that what I was going to tell him was going to hurt him, too.

I fought the tears and powered on through. "When I woke up it was almost forty-eight hours later and I was in hospital."

"Hannah . . ." He seemed to plead with me.

That's when the tears started winning. "I miscarried. But it wasn't just a miscarriage; it was something called an ectopic pregnancy. That means the egg implanted inside one of my tubes instead of the womb, but because I didn't realize I was pregnant, the egg grew until it ruptured the tube and I started bleeding internally."

"You almost died?" he asked, his voice deep and thick with the emotion I could see blazing in his eyes.

"Yes. I had surgery. They removed the damaged tube." Saying it out loud just reminded me of all the resentment I'd been feeling, and without meaning to I let it spill out of me. "I lied to my friends and family about who got me pregnant. I protected you. I protected you, but you weren't there to protect me. I had to cope with having a miscarriage at *seventeen*. And you weren't there for me. And I know you had your reasons and I tried to forgive and I tried to forget." I swiped at my tears, but they were falling too fast for me to keep up. "But you weren't even back in Edinburgh a few months when you got Leah pregnant. You were there for her, Marco, and as much as I know it's not rational, I feel like you betrayed me somehow. You were supposed to be the love of my life, but how can you be? I went through all of that alone only to discover that the supposed love of my life was there for some other girl when he was never there for me."

The small space was thick with a stifling silence, broken only by my labored breathing.

I waited for him to say something. Anything.

Without warning, he turned around and slammed his fist into the cabin wall. "Fuck, fuck, fuck!" He punched it repeatedly, the wall crumbling like paper.

"Marco!" I moved toward him to stop him, but my voice had already done that. He sagged into the wall, his forehead resting against it as his shoulders shuddered.

"Marco," I whispered, my emotions confusing me all the more when an ache inside me begged me to comfort him. I walked over to him and he turned his head to watch me approach.

There was anguish unlike anything I'd ever seen in his eyes as they looked deep into mine. "You were this precious, beautiful gift that came into my life when I needed it the most," he said quietly. "I never felt safe as a kid. I knew what it was like to not feel safe and I hated the idea of anyone I cared about ever feeling that way. I started to care about you pretty quickly, so it feels like I've always only ever wanted to protect you, you know. And I didn't. So I *did* betray you. And I'm so sorry. I'm so, so sor . . ." His voice fell away as he dragged his hand down his face, pushing away from the wall and turning away from me.

The door behind us opened and I glanced over at it to see Braden standing in the doorway. He took in my tearstained face and red eyes, the broken plaster on the wall, and Marco's obviously bad state. Eyes soft with sympathy, Braden asked me gently, "Do you want me to take you home?"

I glanced back at Marco, but he hadn't turned around to face me. He needed time to deal with this.

Me? I didn't know what to feel. I just knew that a man like Marco didn't lose control of his emotions easily.

I just knew that he loved me. Deeply.

And I just knew that it was all one huge painful mess that I couldn't fix.

"Yeah," I whispered, brushing tears off my cheeks and moving over to Braden.

I rested against him as he wrapped his arm around my shoulders and led me out of the cabin. Walking toward the cab he had waiting, I glanced over my shoulder, back up to the cabin. There was still a massive part of me holding back, trying to protect myself from being hurt by Marco again, but that didn't mean that I felt right walking away from him when he needed me. In fact, the guilt plagued me all the way home.

CHAPTER 21

Adam had told Cole to go home, cool off, and give me time to calm down before facing me, but I wasn't mad at Cole. Maybe I should be, since he was the one who forced me into that position, but I couldn't bring myself to feel that way. Braden took me home and I called work, explaining I had a family emergency—there was no way I could return to school and teach when my eyes were swollen from crying, I had a bruise forming on my forehead, my heart hurt, and my head was thumping.

Braden stayed with me, making me a cup of tea with a splash of whisky in it. He just sat on the couch with me, giving me the quiet I needed but also the comfort of his presence. He left when Joss and Ellie turned up at my door, and I knew he'd been the one to rally the troops.

Not long afterward, Liv showed up, and she had Jo on speakerphone. Ellie and Joss had left the kids with Mum and Dad, and Jo was close to popping, so she was at home with Cam, but obviously wanted to be a part of the discussion.

I was exhausted, but glancing around at their anxious faces I dug deep for the energy to explain everything—the past and the present. They had always been there for me, even when to them it felt like I didn't want them to be, and for that they deserved the truth.

Once I was done, Ellie looked at me with tears in her eyes. "You've been carrying all this by yourself? Why, Hannah? Didn't you trust us?"

I shook my head adamantly. "It wasn't that. Please don't think that."

"You were protecting him." Jo's voice reached out to us from Liv's phone on my coffee table.

Somehow she understood perfectly. "Yes."

"Protecting him?" Joss frowned.

I shrugged helplessly, not knowing how to explain it. Somehow Jo instinctively understood, but having to explain it to someone made me feel like a lost young girl who didn't know what she wanted. "I don't know why. Just . . . I didn't want you to think badly of him."

"You love him," Ellie stated simply. "That's why."

"I forgave the fact that he left me after we spent the night together, I forgave him for leaving the country and then not looking me up when he came back, and I did all that because, yes, I loved him. And I know that if he'd stayed, he would have been there for me through the miscarriage and my depression. I know that because the look on his face when I told him what happened to me said it all."

"Then why—" Liv bit her lip, not finishing the question out loud, but her eyes said the rest for her.

I felt that familiar ache throbbing in my chest. "Then why leave him?"

Liv nodded.

Glancing around at their faces I knew they were trying to understand—and to a certain extent did understand—what I was feeling, but there was also sympathy for Marco in those expressions. "It hurt to find out he not only didn't look me up when he returned but that he got some other girl pregnant and he was there for her. I know it doesn't make sense to be mad at him for a situation he wasn't even aware of but . . . I can't help feeling betrayed anyway. I keep thinking if he hadn't left me that night . . . if he hadn't left me I might have been the girl he stuck around for. But I wasn't. Isn't the man you love supposed to stick around for you, to see you through the worst things that can ever happen to you?"

All three exchanged glances, looks that told me they got me because *they* had men who'd stuck around.

"The one time you needed him he wasn't there." Jo's voice echoed quietly into the room. "But, Hannah . . . you know Marco's capable of being that guy."

I was silent because the reason I was in such a confused state was that I *did* know Marco was capable of being that guy. He'd been trying to be that guy for the last three months. Sensing my quandary, Ellie leaned forward. "Hannah, we have the unfortunate commonality of having loved someone who took their merry time getting over their own issues to finally be with us." She scooted closer to me on the couch and wrapped an arm around my shoulders. I snuggled into her as she continued. "So I think you know I get you, and that what I'm going to say comes from a place of experience and the desire for my wee sister to find the happiness she deserves."

I nodded carefully, expectantly.

"You just said it yourself, so deep down I know you know that it wasn't Marco's fault he wasn't there for you. Yeah, he definitely shouldn't have left you alone that night, but you don't know what he would have done if his grandfather hadn't had a heart attack. He would have stayed in Scotland, but you have no idea how things might have worked out between you. I do know that the Hannah back then didn't take no for an answer, so I have a sneaking suspicion you would have gotten your way. But that's not what happened, and as rubbish as it is, Marco had a reason for leaving Scotland. And as much as you don't like his explanation for not looking you up upon his return, frankly I can't be annoyed at a man who stayed away because he thought my smart, funny, beautiful, strong sister was too good for him. I definitely can't be annoyed at him for pulling his head out of his issues and taking time to prove to you he wanted to be with you. He sounds like a good dad, and I've witnessed him with you—

he treats you like you're the most precious thing on the planet. Adam and Braden were pissed off that you broke up with him, because to them, if you had to be with someone, they were happy it was someone like Marco. He was straightforward and he seemed very protective of you. We all liked that about him, Hannah."

"Els," I whispered, almost pleading. I didn't need to hear this. It just confused me more.

"But . . ." Ellie sighed. "Sometimes we just feel what we feel. It doesn't matter what we know is logical, our emotions usually rule. However, I don't think Marco isn't 'the one' because he left and he wasn't there for everything that happened." She nodded to Liv and Joss. "I doubt these guys do either."

Liv and Joss confirmed this by giving me small sympathetic smiles while shaking their heads.

"Hannah, if you don't think he's the one, then he's not. But ask yourself . . . why did you lie to your family to protect him? Why did you race after Cole to stop him from attacking Marco? Why does it matter if you're not in love with him?"

Turmoil. Total turmoil. There was no escaping it. Although Ellie's questions had opened doors I'd been trying to keep tightly closed since breaking up with Marco, I hugged my sister hard because at least I was no longer carrying the weight of the truth on my shoulders alone. There was a simple relief in that.

The girls were gone, returned to their kids and their husbands, but I knew that they were worried about me. I tried to reassure them as they hugged me before leaving that I was okay, but they gave me these looks that showed they doubted me. I couldn't really blame them. After all, I'd just provided them with proof that I didn't always tell them the truth when it came to what was going on with me emotionally.

The quiet wasn't good. I tried watching TV, reading a book, but my mind kept wandering and I was completely restless. I felt like I was preparing for something really nerve-racking—I was all jittery and my heart was racing, like I had too much adrenaline flowing through my body.

When my phone rang just before nine o' clock, I had to wonder if my body had a sixth sense.

Caller ID told me it was Marco.

I could have ignored it, but we both deserved better than that.

"Hi," I answered softly, curling up into a ball on the couch, the phone pressed tight to my ear.

"Hey."

I closed my eyes at the sound of his voice in my ear.

"I don't know what to say."

"I do and I don't," he replied. "I would have come over, but I didn't know if you'd answer the door or not."

"I don't know if I would have either," I answered honestly.

"Yeah." He exhaled and it sounded a little shaky. "Hannah, I get it, but I have to see you. Can we please meet? We need to talk about all this."

"I don't know."

"Baby, this can't be it." His voice lowered, deepened. "We need a chance to work all this out."

His endearment reached out, its hook catching and tugging painfully on my heart. It took me a moment to gather myself and say, "I just need time."

"And after everything you've been through you deserve whatever you need, but I'm afraid if I give you that time all you're going to do is use it to keep us apart." At my continued silence, Marco said softly, "I'll give you time. But not a lot of it. I've lost you twice now, and I'm not losing you again."

I've lost you twice now, and I'm not losing you again.

I've lost you twice now, and I'm not losing you again.

I've lost you—

I shook my head, trying to shake Marco's last words to me the night before. They kept playing on repeat.

It was easier to switch the memory off while I was teaching, but I had only a half day of classes, and although I would usually use the rest of that day for marking and lesson planning, I skipped out of work to head to Cole's place.

He looked like shit.

When he opened his front door to me, I winced, taking in his black eye, pale skin, and guilty expression. Without saying a word, I stepped over the threshold and put my arms around him, hugging him tight.

"You're not mad?" Cole asked in surprise as he held me close.

I kissed his cheek and pulled gently out of his embrace. "For you having my back? No. For the bruise on my forehead . . . maybe." I smiled, a sad smile but a smile nonetheless, so he'd know I was teasing. "I'm not mad. You acted impulsively, but your heart was in the right place."

Cole blew out a breath between his lips. "I've got to say that's a relief. I was expecting you to be so pissed off at me for letting the cat out of the bag with Marco."

"It wasn't fun," I admitted. "But it was probably about time. I actually feel a lot better now that everyone knows the truth."

"I did good then?"

"Oh, I wouldn't take it that far. You definitely owe me coffee at least."

He threw me a crooked grin and started walking toward his kitchen. I followed him, raising my eyebrow at the sheet of paper that had been pinned to his hallway wall. It had the words TOMATOES ARE NOT A FRUIT printed across it.

"I thought tomatoes were a fruit."

"What?" Cole glanced back at me, saw me pointing to the homemade "poster," and shook his head in despair. "Don't even ask. Bigsie is on his own wee planet."

"I don't understand why he feels strongly enough about tomatoes to print a poster about it."

"And pin it to our wall. There goes a percentage of our deposit."

"Cole, you need to get a new roommate, or a new flat."

"Rent's cheap." He shrugged. "Starving artist/poor student and all that."

Right. Some of us didn't have a wealthy brother and sister to buy us a flat. I felt a pang of guilt that I didn't have to struggle like so many people my age.

Cole's eyes narrowed on me as he pulled a couple of mugs out of one of the dingy cupboards in his dingy kitchen. "What's with the guilty expression?"

"Nothing's with it. I'm just a bit of mess right now."

His features softened with understanding. "If you need to—"

I didn't know what Cole was going to say and I never would because at that exact moment we both got a text message from Liv.

Jo's gone into labor!

We both looked up from our phones, eyes widened, and I knew Cole's was the same message because he whispered, "Fuck."

He flew into action. In less than a minute he'd thrown on his boots and coat, grabbed his keys, grabbed my hand, and hauled me out of his flat. We got into his little rust bucket of a Fiat, which was older than Beth, and hurtled toward the hospital.

Nine hours later, Jo gave birth to Annabelle Walker MacCabe, a gorgeous seven-pound baby girl. The entire time I sat in the waiting room with my family, my mind was on Jo and Cam and their new family. When I met Annabelle, or Belle, as we were already calling her, she was all I could think about, and when I kissed an exhausted Jo good night, hugged my family, and returned home to my flat to get some rest, my mind was still on them all.

There was a whisper in the back of my thoughts, a whisper too loud to ignore, that wished Marco had been there to enjoy the moment, to be a part of my family. He'd missed Ellie giving birth to Bray and now Jo to Belle.

There was a part of me that didn't think that felt right.

That part scared the hell out of me.

CHAPTER 22

A little under a week later I was heading out of my flat. It was a Saturday, the ground icy where the snowfall of the past few days had melted with the rain and then frozen over with the newly falling temperatures. I sidestepped a large patch of ice on my porch and started to make my way down the steps.

I was excited to be spending the day with Jo, Ellie, Belle, and Bray and had a bag filled with goodies for both children and mothers.

"Hannah Nichols?"

I glanced up at the question, stopping on the last step of the front stoop to stare at the pretty brunette who stood a few feet from me on the pavement.

My eyes washed over her, wondering why she looked so familiar. "Yes?"

The young woman took a few steps forward, seeming anxious, and that's when I remembered where I'd seen her: the photograph of Marco and his son at the German Market. The pretty brunette at his side. Leah. The mother of his son.

My heart suddenly took off at a gallop.

"I'm Leah McKinley. I'm Dylan's mum."

Eyeing her warily, I replied, "I know who you are."

She stared at me. "You're just like he described."

I frowned in response. "What are you doing here?"

Her expression tightened. "I'm here because I care about Marco. And Marco's a mess right now."

I couldn't ignore the guilt and pain that knowledge caused me. Since we'd last spoken on the phone, Marco had given me time. But he'd been honest when he said he'd give me time but not a lot of it. When five days passed and I didn't contact him, he called me. Having already told him I needed space, I didn't answer.

I didn't answer when he called me three times after that.

I couldn't answer, because my fear had made up my mind for me about us, and I didn't know how to tell him.

"Look, he didn't go into the details, but he explained that something bad happened to you years ago when he left and now he's blaming himself." She crossed her arms over her chest, appearing annoyed. "I knew Marco at school. Not well. But I knew him. I knew he was quiet and seemed a bit pissed off with the world. I watched him change when he became a dad. He got, I don't know, like, sure of himself. And happy. Yet, still, I've never seen him as happy as he was when he was seeing you." She squinted against the winter sun. "He told me all about you, you know. Before. When I was pregnant with Dylan we became good friends and he talked about you. I was even a wee bit jealous of the way he saw you—like you were so much better than every other girl on the planet. I told him countless times that he was good enough for anyone, that he should try to get in touch with you again, but he wouldn't do it. That really fucked me off—that he thought he wasn't good enough. Now I'm even more pissed off because with you not forgiving him or giving him the time of day, it makes him think he *is* to blame for whatever shit went down with you. He's back to thinking he's not good enough. I know him. I know he would never hurt anyone deliberately, so I know whatever happened to you isn't his fault. It would be nice if you'd let him know that, too."

Feeling cornered, remorseful, and pissed off that I'd been made to feel guilty by someone I didn't know, I gave her a look that told her I wouldn't be cowed. "I'm not sure any of this is your business."

Her face grew hard. "Marco isn't just my son's dad, he's my friend. He's a good guy and I don't like anyone hurting him."

"Does he know you're here right now?"

"No." She huffed. "And he'll probably be really pissed off when I tell him I came to see you. But if it gives you a kick up the arse to do the right thing, then I'm okay with that."

"You have no idea what you're talking about."

"Maybe not. But we both know Marco is a good person. He doesn't deserve to be feeling the way he's feeling." She shrugged, shot me one last searching look, and said, "You think on that."

My visit with Bray, Belle, and their mums was somewhat poisoned by Leah's decision to try to force my hand in the situation with Marco.

I spent most of the day worrying about him, until I came to the conclusion I needed to stop being such a coward and call him.

There was no game playing on his part. He picked up on the second ring.

"You know how to keep a guy hanging," he answered quietly.

"I'm just calling to tell you I want you to stop blaming yourself. I don't blame you for what happened to me."

"Easier said than done, Hannah. There's a reason you broke up with me when you found out about Dylan. You said yourself that at least a part of you blames me for leaving you to deal with all that shit by yourself."

"Honestly," I whispered, "I did. I know that it wasn't right, though, and I've worked through that. I know that what happened to me wasn't your fault. What happened to me wasn't anyone's fault. We were both at fault for being irresponsible and not using protection, that's all."

"No. That was my fault. I was the experienced one. But it was *you* . . . and in that moment I was too lost in you to think straight."

"Was that the way it was with Leah?" I asked caustically.

"Hannah, it wasn't like that with her. We were both shit-faced. It's a miracle we had enough faculties about us to get undressed and have sex, if—"

"Okay, I don't want to hear any more," I interrupted.

He was silent for a while and then . . . "It's about Leah, isn't it?"

"No," I answered, and then sighed. "I don't know."

"Hannah, I care about Leah. She's my friend and she's the mother of my kid. But I love *you*."

"Should it be this hard, though, Marco?" I asked. "Should it hurt this much?"

"I don't know. I don't know what the rules are. All I know is that it means something pretty fucking important to feel this way about someone. I'd do anything for my son, Hannah. I'd do anything to protect him. To make sure he knows he's loved. That he makes my universe turn. And I feel that way about you too. I want to protect you, I want you to know that for me there's no one else like you. That *you* make my universe turn."

My heart actually hurt in my chest.

"Hannah?"

"If it was up to how I feel when it's just us and the world is quiet and everything seems so far away," I told him softly, "we'd be together. I'd put it all behind me and we'd move on. But life isn't like that. The rest of the world never goes away. Our mistakes are out there and we can't hide from them. I don't want to mess you around and it's not my intention to hurt you"—my voice cracked—"but I just don't think this is what I want anymore."

"You don't love me?" His voice was gruff, the way he sounded whenever he was feeling something deeply.

I hated that I was hurting him. "Marco, I've been in love with you since I was fourteen. And it's hurt for eight years. I'm just not sure that's the right kind of love."

"I didn't know there was a right or a wrong kind," he whispered hoarsely.

"Perhaps not. But maybe I need a shot at an *easy* kind."

"Or maybe you just need to give us a shot with all this shit out in the open," he argued. "Hannah, when we were kids I was messed up. I didn't give us a chance. But those two months we had before Christmas were the best fucking weeks of my life, and they would have been perfect if we'd just been honest about everything. Now all that is out there, and we can start over. It can be great. It can be *easy*."

I wanted to believe that, but I was too scared. I wasn't even going to lie to myself about it. I was terrified.

Marco could hurt me like no one else could because I loved him with everything I had. I'd allowed his mistakes, our mistakes, to bend me. However, I couldn't let *us* break me.

Wiping the tears from my face with trembling hands, I prepared myself to finally make a decision.

"Hannah?"

"Marco . . ." My voice came out as a whisper and I had to clear my throat to get the volume back. "Because of you I've never given anyone a chance. If you want the whole and absolute truth, there's never been anyone since you. I lied when you asked me when the last time I had sex was. I've only ever been with one man and that man is you."

"Hannah—"

"It's time I gave myself a chance to fall in love with someone else."

"You don't mean that."

"I do. We're not good for each other. You need to move on."

"No," he growled down the phone in a surprising and yet not so surprising response. "You're mine. I'm yours. Don't you dare run from that."

"I'm not running." *More lies.* "I just need a fresh start."

"Hannah, I love you."

"Please don't . . . don't make this harder than it already is."

"No. Don't give me bullshit clichés. I need to see you. We can't do this over the phone. We can talk and we can work it out."

Terrified at that thought because I knew that just seeing him would weaken my resolve, I hurried to deny him. "I don't want to see you. I'm moving on, Marco, and I need you to do the same for me. Do this for me."

I could hear that his breathing had grown shallow. "I can't. It might be the most selfish thing I'll ever do, but I can't give you up. I won't. If I thought it was what you really wanted, really needed, I would. But it's not. You're scared. I know you're scared. I'm going to do everything I can to take that fear away."

"Stop being a stubborn idiot!" I snapped, feeling desperate.

"Pot, meet kettle," he answered, his voice edged with determination. "We'll see which one of us can be the most obstinate, Hannah, because, babe, I'm never giving up on us. If it takes a week, a month, a year, whatever, the future is *us*. I'm spending the rest of my life waking up in the morning with you beside me and getting through each day knowing that when the sky turns dark I'll be spending the night inside you."

His sensual, beautiful words knocked me for six. "You are such a bastard," I breathed.

Marco laughed shortly, harshly. "I see I'm winning already."

CHAPTER 23

"So Beth is having a Daddy's girl day?" Liv asked Joss, her tone telling us just how cute she thought that was.

Joss grinned, putting her cup of coffee down on the table. "After her excitement at the zoo last year, and her current obsession with all things animal, Braden decided to take her to that Safari Park in Stirling but discovered it was closed for the season, so he's taking her to Deep Sea World. He wanted some daddy-daughter time."

I smiled. "He's a good egg, that one."

Joss made a face. "That he is. Makes it really hard to be crabby at him."

Liv, Joss, and I were at an activity center in Morningside that had a café just on the edges of the play area. Since it was in the same building as a full-time day care, there were a number of staff to watch the kids while their parents could have lunch and chat, but still keep an eye on their children. From our table we could see Lily and Luke in the soft play area supervised by a couple of nursery assistants. January was in her pram next to Liv, sleeping peacefully for once.

It had been a week since my conversation with Marco. I'd thrown myself into work and done what I could to distract myself from the wreckage of my love life. That wasn't easy at first because Marco must have updated Nish a little and she came to me in the staff room to apologize. Since then she'd been watching me carefully, as if I were made of glass, and every day she'd ask me in this sweet but unintentionally annoying tone if I was all right.

I'd also had to update Michaela on *everything*. Suzanne had told Michaela her own version of events, and obviously her account had some inaccuracies. Poor Michaela now found herself in the awkward position of being friends with two people who no longer wanted anything to do with each other. I assured Michaela I wouldn't make it difficult for her. I couldn't assure her Suzanne would do the same.

All of this made it hard to put the wreckage out of my mind. Even worse was my flat and those damn bookshelves. This meant I jumped at any opportunity to get out of the flat. I'd babysat for Liv and Nate the night before, and now I found myself hanging out with Joss, Liv, and their kids to avoid my home. Not that it was a hardship to hang out with them.

I looked over at Lily to find her watching us. She waved when she caught me looking.

"I'll be right back." I hopped up out of my seat and grinned at Lily in a way I knew made her laugh.

"Lily Billy," I called out to her as I approached.

I played with her and Luke, letting them crawl all over me before pretend-chasing them. I was probably making them hyper, and Joss and Liv wouldn't thank me for it later, but it felt good to laugh hard with the kids.

"Oh, my gosh," I panted, attempting to catch my breath as I lay on the floor with Lily trying to tickle me and Luke sprawled across my chest in an effort to use his weight to keep me there. They were giggling like crazy. "I can't move, Luke Carmichael. You're too strong!"

He giggled harder. "I'm goin' keep you here, Nanna."

"Forever?" I gasped.

"Uh-huh."

"I think that might be Hannah Nichols buried under those kids, but I can't be sure." An amused voice spoke from somewhere above me.

I tensed at the voice and I knew the kids felt my sudden change in demeanor because they stopped giggling. Turning my head, I searched him out.

An upside-down Marco appeared in my line of sight.

Shit.

Breathe, Hannah.

"Uh, hullo," I managed.

"Need a hand?"

"Come on, Luke," I heard Joss say and then suddenly she was there, bending down to pick Luke up off my chest. I sat up and she shot me a questioning look as she grabbed Lily's hand. She was asking me if I was okay to be alone with Marco.

Um . . . honestly, I didn't know.

But I nodded as I got to my feet. I watched her walk Luke and Lily over to the table with Liv and January.

My eyes moved to Marco, who was standing at the edge of the soft play area. Clinging to his big hand was the most beautiful little boy I'd ever seen. My chest ached looking at him.

Dylan.

He had Marco's coloring, down to the striking blue-green of his eyes, and he had cute, tight black curls. He was tall for three, which could mean he was going to be as tall as his dad one day, and he was wearing this serious, curious expression on his face that was so like one of Marco's expressions that the ache in my chest intensified.

Feeling emotions I hadn't expected to feel, I looked up from Dylan and into Marco's eyes and choked out, "He's beautiful."

Marco's hand flexed in Dylan's and he glanced down at his son with an adoring look of pride. "Yeah."

Just like that, I remembered the awkwardness of being around him and I covered my uneasiness with a glare. "There are hundreds of day care centers in Edinburgh. This one? Really?"

Marco's grin was slightly wicked. "Looks like the universe wants me to win as well."

I would have responded with something cheeky or curt, except for the fact that Dylan was there. Not to mention that Marco couldn't quite hide the sadness in the back of his eyes with those teasing smiles of his.

Not wanting to deal with how that made me feel, I glanced down at Dylan again. He kept looking between his dad and me, clearly wondering who I was.

"Dylan," Marco caught his attention again, "this is Hannah. Hannah, this is Dylan."

I smiled at Marco's mini-me. "Hi, Dylan."

He shifted a little closer to his dad's leg. "Hi," he replied quietly and clutched a soft toy to his chest. On closer inspection I realized the toy was a miniature of Sulley from Pixar's *Monsters, Inc.*

I swear I almost melted all over the floor. "Sulley is one of my favorites." I gestured to the toy.

Dylan's eyes widened slightly.

"Do you like Lightning McQueen too?" I referenced the hero of the Pixar movie *Cars.*

Dylan nodded.

"He loves Pixar movies." Marco smiled softly. "You and he would get on great."

I knew my smile was a little sad when I replied, "He's fantastic. I think everything turned out the way it was supposed to for you, Marco."

Determination etched his features. "It's not all done turning itself out. Obviously."

There wasn't really a way to reply to that, but I didn't have to. An attractive brunette had approached, grabbing my attention. She stopped beside Marco, touching his arm to get his attention too. "You're not leaving just yet, are you, Marco?"

Marco stared at her a second and I knew him well enough to know he was distracted by the unspoken conversation between us, so it took him a while to process what she had asked. "Uh . . . I'm just picking Dylan up for my weekend with him. We have other plans today."

The woman's gaze flicked to me, and I could see the unhappy question in it. "Marco is one of the few single dads we see at the center. As you can imagine, he's very popular." The question suddenly became a back-off warning as she said to me, "I haven't seen you here before. Which little rascal is yours?"

I wanted to vomit at her fakeness, her saccharine tone. "Oh, I don't have a kid. I just come here to see if any of the single dads are looking for a 'playdate.'" I gave Marco an exaggerated wink. "Marco's a good playdate. One of the best."

She looked aghast as Marco did a horrible job of choking back his laughter. "I . . . uh . . ." She looked at him and then back to me, consternation wrinkling her brow. "I, well, I'll . . . uh . . . see you next time then, Marco." She backed off, hurrying across the room toward a little girl.

Marco laughed. "Playdate?"

My eyes still on the brunette, I replied, "She wants a playdate with you." I looked back at him, my gaze turning suspicious. The ugly heat of jealousy churned in my chest like heartburn. "Maybe she's already had one."

"Leah and Graham only moved to Morningside two months ago, and you and I were regular playdates then. Since we stopped, there haven't been any other playdates for me." He raised an eyebrow as he unconsciously reassured an increasingly restless Dylan with a squeeze of his hand. "But it's good to know you're jealous."

"I'm not jealous."

His grin was heated and knowing. It was a grin that reminded me of everything we'd had only a few short weeks ago.

I wrinkled my nose at him. "I have to get back to the girls." My gaze moved to Dylan. "It was nice to meet you, Dylan. 'Bye." I gave him a small wave.

"'Bye," he answered with his serious little-boy expression.

Feeling emotional all over again, I whispered to Marco, "He has your eyes. He has your everything."

The muscles in Marco's jaw flexed, and I knew he was trying to hold himself back from saying something. To help him along, I gave them another small wave and walked away from them toward Liv and Joss.

The girls were silent as I took a seat with my back to Marco and his son.

"Is he gone?" I asked, staring doggedly ahead.

Liv looked over my shoulder. "Yeah. He just left with his beautiful little boy. Seriously? Those two together? Wow."

"You're crazy. You know that, right?" Joss said casually before taking a sip of a fresh cup of coffee.

"Why?"

"For giving up on a man who looks at you the way Marco does. I thought Braden could be all brooding and possessive with a single look, but Marco is in his own league."

My heart skipped a beat, causing an unpleasant flutter in my throat. "What?"

Liv nodded her agreement. "Hannah, the look on his face when you were talking to Dylan . . . oh, my God, he couldn't take his eyes off you."

"It was hot," Joss added. "Possessive. *Hot.*"

"Tender too. Sweet. Kind of adoring." Liv sighed.

Joss smirked. "Best. Look. Ever."

With my heart now banging away in my chest, I threw them both a dirty look and said determinedly, "You won't deter me with talk of hot expressions. Marco and I are over." Now if the rest of me could just get on board with that, life would be fantastic.

I didn't know what to expect from Marco in his attempts to win me back. I guess I expected much of the same treatment as before—unexpected appearances in all the places where I spent my spare time.

A slow seduction.

However, he threw me off guard with his next move. So much so, it tripped me up completely.

I gathered from one of my second-year boy's comments on his essay for *A Midsummer Night's Dream* that he wasn't enjoying our current lesson plan. I think it was the "Puck is a wanker" comment that really tipped me off.

I underlined the comment with a red pen and wrote in the margin beside it, "Give examples to explain why you reached this conclusion." We would discuss in person his inappropriate use of profanity to express himself. We did that on a weekly basis, so that was nothing new.

Feeling an ache in my upper back from sitting on my living room floor marking essays for the past two hours, I pulled my shoulders back and sighed in satisfaction at the soft crack of my bones. Grimacing, I looked at the clock. It was almost nine. I should really get up before my arse fell asleep, but I had only a few more papers to mark before I could say I was caught up.

The flat was so quiet that my heart jumped right into my throat when my doorbell rang. Not my building door buzzer. My front doorbell.

Wondering who it could be at this time of night, I cautiously walked out into the hall toward the door on my tiptoes. Feeling weirdly skittish, I nervously put my eye to the peephole. Looking very far away in the small circle of glass was Marco.

"What the hell?" I whispered.

He knocked. "Hannah?"

I felt confused and wary, but at the same time I felt relieved that it was Marco on the other side of the door and that I was safe.

Upon opening the door I parted my lips to ask him how he'd gotten into the building, but the question was swallowed as he crushed his mouth down on mine, wrapped an arm around my waist and pushed inside. I clung to him in surprise, hearing the slam of my door behind him.

Then, just like that, the taste, smell, and feel of him overwhelmed me and I was kissing him back.

My feet left the ground as he lifted me, only to plant my bottom on top of the sideboard in my hall. He pressed himself between my legs and

I instinctively wrapped them around his hips. His kiss was demanding, hard and drugging, and all rational thought fled as I kissed him back with equal fervor. All my body knew was that it had missed this.

All my soul knew was that it *craved* this.

Marco broke the kiss, pulling back only to grab the hem of my baseball shirt in his hands and yank it upward. I lifted my arms, helping him out. My top went flying behind him seconds before his nimble fingers made quick work of my bra.

Despite the fire between us, I shivered, my nipples turning to hard pebbles that drew a groan from deep in the back of Marco's throat. He cupped my breasts and I arched my back with a sigh as he kneaded them, his touch shooting darts of liquid heat straight through my belly and down between my legs.

The sensation increased when he pulled gently on my hair, arching my neck and back further and lifting my breasts closer to his mouth. He bent his head, his hungry eyes on my low-lidded ones. I shivered again, this time in anticipation, and a smirk of satisfaction quirked his lips before he dropped his gaze and closed his hot mouth around my left nipple.

I whimpered at the molten pleasure that rippled through my lower belly and I clutched the nape of his neck with one hand while the other caressed his upper back. He sucked hard, causing a sharp streak of pleasure/pain, and then he licked the swollen nipple before moving on to the other.

Wanting the feel of his hard muscles and smooth skin under my hands, I started pulling on the long-sleeved T-shirt he was wearing.

He got the hint and jerked back impatiently to remove it. He'd barely dropped it to the floor when I clutched him, yanking him back to me, our kisses hard, hurried, and hot. With one hand I caressed his strong back, with the other his sculpted chest before sliding it down over his hard abs. At the feel of his abs rippling under my touch, arousal pulsed between my legs.

Mind reader that he was, he took his lips from mine to ask breath-lessly, roughly, "You wet for me?"

I looked directly into his lust-fogged eyes with my own lust-fogged eyes and whispered, "I'm one touch away from coming."

His eyes flared. "You'll come with my mouth," he promised.

My belly squeezed deep down low and I knew I was more than wet now. I was soaked. I was always turned on for Marco, I always wanted him, but I couldn't remember ever being this hot and desperate to have him. As he pressed hot kisses against my jaw, my neck, his tongue flick-ing against my skin as he did so, I rubbed my thumbs over his nipples, scored my nails lightly down his stomach, and panted with excitement when he started unbuttoning my jeans. I stopped touching him momen-tarily to brace my hands on the sideboard at either side of my hips so I could lift my bottom to allow him to pull my jeans off.

My underwear quickly followed and, completely unabashed, I de-lighted in the way he pressed my legs apart to stare at me.

There was a primitive need etched into his taut features and it spoke to whatever echoing primitive need there was in me. My heart was racing so hard, I was panting in expectation, my breasts rising and falling as I tried to catch my breath.

"You promised your mouth," I said softly, barely sounding like my-self.

My voice pulled him out of his intense perusal of my body and sud-denly he was kissing me again. He gripped the backs of my knees in his hands and wrapped my legs around him so his jeans-covered erection pushed between the folds of my sex, brushing my clit in a way that made me spasm deliciously. I wrapped my arms around him, my sensitive breasts crushed against his chest. He continued to kiss me, our despera-tion building in that kiss, in the way he stroked my naked back and the way our hips undulated together.

The pressure of his erection heightened my arousal and I tried to press harder, my fingers digging into his back.

Marco growled into my mouth and I swear I almost came, it was so hot.

Then his lips were gone from mine, moving down my neck, across my chest, down my ribs, across my stomach, and he was lowering himself to his knees as his hands pressed my thighs apart.

I watched, lost in my daze of utter need, as he licked me.

"Oh, God," I gasped. I threw my head back, his name a plea spilling from my lips over and over as he tortured me with light licks.

Then his mouth found my clit.

He circled it with his tongue.

I climbed higher.

He pumped two fingers inside me.

I climbed even higher.

I tensed.

He sucked on my clit. Hard.

I reached the top on a scream and then shattered, falling into blissful oblivion.

Still shuddering through the remnants of my orgasm, I was barely aware of Marco standing up and yanking his zipper down. Within seconds he was gripping my thighs, and pulling me to the edge of the sideboard. My palms were flat on the piece of furniture, my arms braced a little behind me. It was a good thing too. I was steady and prepared when he thrust into me. Hard.

I cried out, closing my eyes to savor the rough but pleasurable assault on my senses.

"Look at me," Marco demanded, his voice so thick with sex the words were clipped, the tone guttural.

My eyes opened on command and our scorched gazes collided.

My lips parted as he continued to fuck me, another orgasm building inside me, my arousal only increasing at the way he was watching me as he stroked inside me.

"Yeah?" he panted, his hot eyes never once leaving mine.

"Yeah," I answered breathlessly.

His grip on my legs became almost biting as his thrusts came faster. "You've got to come for me, babe." He panted harder, a bead of sweat glistening on his forehead from the strain of holding back his own climax.

"I'm coming," I promised, jerking my hips in rhythm to his thrusts. "Baby, I'm coming, I'm com—" I tensed. Then over the precipice I fell again, crying out on my second orgasm, this one shorter and sharper than the last but no less brilliant.

I shuddered against Marco as he continued to pump into me, my inner muscles squeezing around him.

He stiffened, his grip on me almost painful.

His eyes never left mine as he groaned through gritted teeth.

"Fuck." His hips jerked against me while he came.

He let go of my right leg to kiss me deeply. I wrapped my legs around his hips, squeezing him closer as we kissed, loving the feel of him shuddering with little aftershocks.

Gradually, as our muscles relaxed and the haze of desire began to clear, reality began to intrude upon us.

I dropped my legs from his waist and pushed on his chest as I pulled my lips from his. I saw the consternation in his eyes but ignored it. "This doesn't change anything," I whispered, feeling the déjà vu of this moment from the first time we had sex three months ago. Except this time around there were no more secrets between us.

Marco went from consternation to pissed. "You sure about that? Because by my count you just came twice. Once with my mouth and again with my dick. I'm pretty sure that means things have changed."

I scowled at him. "I obviously just need to get you out of my system."

His whole expression tightened. Now I'd pissed him *way* off. He put his hands on my thighs again and jerked me back to him, before sliding his hands under my arse and lifting me so I had to wrap my legs around his waist for purchase. I clung to his shoulders as he began to carry me down the hall to my bedroom.

"What are you doing?" I snapped, trying to wriggle out of his grip and failing.

Marco didn't answer until we were in the bedroom and he'd dropped me none too gently on my bed. He pushed his jeans down and started kicking them off and I scrambled to get off the bed. Marco was too fast for me, though, grabbing my hands in his as he lowered his body over mine. He pressed my hands to the bed, holding me captive.

"I guess I'll be fucking you until I'm out of your system, then."

I narrowed my eyes and tried to push against his hold, to no avail. "You have to leave."

"Sex first."

My belly rippled at the thought, my appetite for him clearly insatiable. Sensing it, he looked smug.

"Fine!" I gave in because . . . well, frankly, because I wanted him and I wasn't thinking clearly. "But you can't stay."

"I won't," he promised darkly, eyes on my lips. "But I'm going to make you come again before I leave."

And so he did.

Brilliantly, I might add.

He filled me up with his heat and lust and tenderness.

However, as soon as we were finished, he was good as his word and he left the flat.

Just like that, I was back to feeling empty.

CHAPTER 24

"Marco," I said on a gasp, as he moved inside me.

I was on my side, as was he. His warm hand was wrapped around me, kneading my breast, as he thrust up into me from behind.

I came hard, crying out in satisfaction as I shook through my climax. A few seconds later Marco followed me, his hold on me tightening as he tensed and then groaned against the back of my neck as he found his own satisfaction.

I lay there, trying to catch my breath and get hold of my senses.

The soft touch of Marco's lips on my shoulder drew me back into the room. He slid out of me and I felt the loss of his heat. Turning around, I watched as he climbed out of bed and started to get dressed.

For two weeks we'd been doing this. Marco would turn up at my door, I'd let him in, and then we'd have sex until our bodies were weary and my heart was in even more turmoil than before. I couldn't seem to stop myself from giving in to the sexual heat between us. But every time he left, I felt emptier. What we were doing, just sex, made a farce of what we'd had before.

Tonight, however, was worse.

Marco hadn't even bothered to clean me up, as had become his ritual. It was something that I'd always found sweet.

Watching him fasten the last button on his shirt, I recognized that he was agitated, perhaps even angry. I wanted to ask what was wrong, but I didn't want to encourage him into thinking that there was more here than there was. It was just sex. No matter how much that hurt.

I should end it. I should end it now. But I didn't know if I was ready to cut him out of my life completely. I thought I could . . .

My eyes drifted away from him to stare blankly at my ceiling. It was about time I sorted my head out, it really was.

"You're not even going to say anything?"

I snapped my gaze back to his to see him standing with his hands on his hips, his legs braced, as he exuded major pissed-off-macho-man vibes. Ignoring the threat, I replied, "What do you want me to say?"

Disbelief flashed in his eyes, and he leaned in to answer in guttural tones, "I want you to put a stop to this shit and admit you were wrong and that you love me. This arrangement is total bull and you know it."

Somehow I kept my face perfectly relaxed. "It was all I was willing to give. And now I think it's time to end it."

Despite the disgusted look he gave in answer, he grunted, "Like I'm giving up that easy."

Fine. I sighed, lacking the energy to fight him on this. "I'll see you tomorrow, then?"

Marco exhaled heavily, as if clinging to the last threads of his patience. He shook his head. "I can't. I'm doing a favor for Leah tomorrow. I'll see you Monday after my weekend with Dylan."

I nodded casually, which pissed him off even more. The way I know it pissed him off even more is that he stormed out of the flat without saying good-bye.

I reached for my phone on the nightstand and texted Cole:

I'm a mess.

. . .

"Okay, so your solution to taking my mind off Marco is to take me to D'Alessandro's?" I frowned up at the exterior of the restaurant.

Cole chuckled. "What? I like the food."

"We could go anywhere," I grumbled. "Miscreant."

Laughing, Cole grabbed my hand and led me inside, out of the cold and into the pleasant warmth of Marco's uncle's restaurant. "You know we're going to spend most of the meal talking about him and why you're acting like a hormonally imbalanced madwoman around him, so I don't see why we can't eat his family's food as we do so."

My hand still clutched in his, I warned, "Well, we're going to spend the *whole* of the meal talking this through as payback, just FYI."

He squeezed my hand. "I think I can handle a wee bit of girl talk." We stopped at the hostess's table and Cole gave her his name. She was leading us into the back room of the restaurant and I was about to respond belatedly to Cole's comment with something cheeky when Cole jarred to a stop and I bumped into his back with the sudden loss of momentum.

"What—" My voice cut off when my eyes followed his gaze.

Marco.

And he wasn't alone.

My stomach flipped unpleasantly as I took in the sight of him smiling at some unknown blond woman.

Cole started to move us toward them, holding tight to my hand.

"What are you doing?" I hissed, feeling very close to having an emotional outburst and not wanting that bastard Marco to witness it.

"Trust me," Cole urged.

As we approached the table, I managed to unglue my horrified gaze from Marco and his obvious date to see that they shared the table with Leah and an attractive dark-haired guy I assumed was her fiancé, Graham.

My gaze snapped back to Marco.

A double date.

I was going to be sick. Or I was going to kill him. We were only a few feet from the table when we drew Marco's gaze. His expression softened at the sight of me until his eyes dropped to my hand in Cole's and that expression instantly hardened.

Seriously?

He was on a double date and I was with a friend and *he* was pissed?

"Marco." Cole greeted him pleasantly. "Just wanted to come over and apologize for . . . well, you know . . ." My best friend looked at the pretty blonde at Marco's side. "I hope I'm not interrupting your *date*."

Marco's eyes clashed with mine and I knew he was definitely irritated with Cole. "It's not—"

"We shouldn't have interrupted." I was studiously avoiding Leah's burning gaze as I tugged on Cole's hand. "We'll let you enjoy your dinner. Cole."

Cole gave Marco a tight grin before sliding his hand around my waist and leading us to the waiting hostess. As soon as she delivered us to our table, Cole sighed and said, "You're shaking like a leaf."

"I'm trying not to kill somebody," I said through clenched teeth. "Let's just go home."

"Fuck that." Cole let the anger shine from his eyes. "He can't do this to you."

"He's not. I am. I'm doing this to me," I muttered angrily. "I'm sending him mixed signals, he's sending me mixed signals. It's a whole bunch of fucked-up mixed signals. And I really just want to go home before I end up doing hard time."

Cole leaned into me, pressing his forehead against mine so I had nowhere to look but in his eyes or at my feet. I chose his eyes. "I'm sorry for taking you over there. But he knows that no matter how mixed up you are, underneath it all you love him. And he's here on a bloody date? I wanted to shake him up, not you."

"I'm fine."

"You're not fine. You're trembling."

"I'm trembling with anger. Cole—"

He cut me off by cupping my face in his hands and pressing a soft, sweet kiss to my lips. When he finally pulled back, I stared at him wide-eyed and more than slightly alarmed. "What the hell are you doing?"

"Reminding him he hasn't won you yet and unless he fights harder he'll lose you to someone else. He doesn't need to know that someone will never be me, sweetheart." He grinned unrepentantly.

I loved my best friend. Totally. I leaned up and pressed another soft kiss to his cheek. "You're the best, but part of the reason I'm so messed up is because I don't want him to fight harder. I want us to be over. I just don't know how to let go."

Cole leaned into me again, lips almost touching mine as he said quietly, "You need to stop lying to yourself, Hannah Nichols. You love him. You know you do. Otherwise you wouldn't be in such a state."

Before I could respond in the negative, a shadow fell over us and we pulled slightly apart to look to our right and into Marco's furious face. Anger danced in his exceptional eyes and it was all directed at Cole. "You've got two seconds to move away from her before I fuck you up a million times worse than I did at the site."

I jerked back from Cole instantly, hating the idea of them fighting again. Anyway, if anyone was going to be throwing a punch tonight, it was going to be me. At my movement, Marco's gaze flicked to me, along with his anger. "Nothing going on between you, huh?"

Indignation riled me even more. "What about you?" I leaned into him. "This is you fighting for us? A double date with some blonde and the mother of your child?"

His jaw clenched and he forced the words out between his teeth. "It's a favor for Leah. It means fuck all."

"Then why didn't you tell me last night about it?"

"Because according to you we're just dicking around, so I didn't think it would matter all that much to you."

Oh, my God, how on earth had I gotten myself into this convoluted emotional craphole? I pressed back against Cole, silently telling him it was time for us to leave. "You're right. It doesn't matter."

But Marco wasn't about to let me leave. Suddenly he was so close to me I had to tilt my head back to look up into his face. "What do you want from me? You tell me I'm just something you need to get out of your system and then you act like a jealous wife. Are you proving me wrong about you, Hannah? Does it turn out you're just another woman playing stupid, fucking mind games that I'm never going to understand? Because if that's who you are, maybe I don't want this after all."

A punch to the gut. His words were a definite punch to the gut. Winded, I crowded back into Cole, who was now gripping my arms, as if holding himself back from jumping into this with Marco. "Finally," I said, breathing harshly, "we're on the same page." I turned around and strutted past Cole, hearing his footsteps following quickly behind me.

I hadn't taken five steps when I heard faster, heavier footsteps approaching. My arm was seized in an unrelenting grasp. I gasped, and looked up at Marco's resolute face. He didn't say anything—he just turned and started marching toward the hallway of the restaurant. My cheeks were burning because by now we had an audience. "What are you doing?" I snapped, tugging at my arm and meeting absolute resistance. As I was dragged farther, I glanced back over my shoulder to see that Cole hadn't moved to stop him. "Cole?" I called back into the room.

He shrugged.

Shrugged!

He'd just made it onto my kill list!

In the dimly lit hallway we passed the door to the kitchen, turned a corner, and marched to the very end of it. Marco knocked on the door there and pulled me inside.

We were in a small office. Bookshelves crammed nearly every inch of the wall space and in the center of the room sat a large desk with a computer and piles of papers all over it.

Behind the desk was an attractive older Italian man I'd seen a couple of times around the restaurant. Gio D'Alessandro.

I tensed.

This was a man who had verbally abused Marco. This was a man who had hit him. I felt invisible little claws spring out at the end of my fingers and I narrowed my eyes on Gio.

He looked at Marco and me in surprise. "Everything okay?" He stood up. He was tall and still fit for his age. If he'd been anyone else I would have admired his air of casual grace.

"Gio, this is Hannah. Can we borrow the office for a few minutes?"

Gio's gaze snapped to me and the recognition in his eyes told me that he had heard of me. That surprised me. Marco had spoken to his uncle about me? "It's nice to meet you, Hannah." He gave me another smile and then passed us to let himself out of the office.

I didn't say it was nice to meet him back.

Once the door closed behind his uncle, Marco let go of my arm and I took a few steps away from him. Not wanting to look at him, I looked anywhere but, and my gaze fell on a frame on Gio's desk. In the frame was a picture of Gio holding Dylan and staring at the boy with undisguised love.

"Dylan," I said in realization, unable *not* to look at Marco now. "He's what brought about the change in your uncle."

He watched me carefully. "He finally saw I wasn't my father or my mom. In fact, he thinks I'm a good dad. He loves Dylan."

I was thrilled for him that things had turned out the way they had. That he was able to forgive his uncle and move on and have a real family for the first time in his life. However, I didn't say that to him. I didn't want him to know how much his happiness affected mine. Instead I threw him sass. "Do you have a purpose behind publicly humiliating me?"

"That way you were with him, with Gio just now . . ." Marco took a step toward me, clearly ignoring my question. "That's how I know you still care."

Unfortunately, I couldn't think of a smart answer, so I remained silent.

Marco sighed, rubbing a hand over his short hair in discomfort. "It's just dinner. Me and the blonde. She's Leah's cousin and she's staying from out of town. She's just got out of a bad relationship and Leah wanted to take her mind off it. Nothing was ever going to happen." He took a step toward me. "But it was a stupid thing to agree to when I'm trying to get us back on track. I'm sorry."

I continued to remain silent because I was afraid of what I'd say if I opened my mouth. My emotions were sitting on the surface and I was very close to letting it all spew out in one hysterical rant.

Marco didn't get this, though. I could see he thought I was being obstinate. His eyes hardened in annoyance. "You and Cole?" Okay, more like jealousy than annoyance. "You been lying to me about him all this time?"

I raised an eyebrow at the accusation. "Do you really think if I had something going on with Cole he would have let you haul me away from him like that without putting up a fight?"

"So he was just trying to piss me off?"

"Yes. Not because I asked him to," I assured him. "But I do think sleeping with you has confused things for me because . . . admittedly I was pissed off to see you with another woman. Which is ridiculous! Like I said last night . . . we need to stop."

In answer Marco turned toward the door and my heart jumped into my throat when I thought he was just going to walk out on me. Instead he locked the door.

Something made my muscles relax and I knew it was relief.

What the fuck?

"I'm a mess." I threw my hands up, not even caring that I'd said the words out loud.

Marco prowled toward me. A second later I was in his arms, my whole body pressed against his. He stroked my back and murmured somewhat cockily against my mouth, "You want this to stop? Just say no."

He started kissing me and I could feel myself melting into his embrace.

However, there was this roiling ball of confusion within me and no matter how much I loved Marco's kisses, I knew I was only going to keep on hurting us both.

I pushed hard against him, breaking the kiss. I panted a little breathlessly from the effort it took to do so and I stared up into his confused eyes. "No."

His fingers bit into my waist in reflex. "Han—"

"I've been giving you amazingly bad mixed signals." I pushed out of his grip, creating some much-needed distance between us. "I'm sorry. I'm so, so sorry. But I have to stop. It's not fair to either of us. We have to end this."

"Or you could just admit you're scared shitless and give me one more chance to prove to you that you don't have to be scared. That we can work."

I shook my head, gesturing around me, indicating the situation we found ourselves in. "We're nothing but drama."

"Yeah?" he snapped. "So what? Everybody has drama. They deal with it." He took a step toward me, trying to close the gap, but I only stepped back to widen it again. The anger in his eyes banked at the movement. "You know what? I fucked up five years ago. Big time. And I probably won't ever forgive myself for that. But I can't fight if you're not willing to fight with me. Do you know what it does to me to leave you every night? It makes me feel like that dick kid that walked out on you five years ago. And I can't be that kid anymore." He strode toward me, desperation in his features as he grabbed me by the shoulders. "No more games, Hannah. Please. This is it. You're either taking that chance with me or you're not and I'm gone for good."

His ultimatum paralyzed me.

The fear paralyzed me.

Pain entered Marco's eyes and he gently let go of me. Frozen, unable to stop him, I watched as he walked toward the door and unlocked it. "You better get back to Cole and I better get back to my *date*."

"Marco—" My lips suddenly moved and his name came out, pleading for him to understand. "We just keep hurting each other."

"No." He glanced back at me over his shoulder and I flinched at the anguish in his eyes. "I hurt you and I didn't mean to. Now you're deliberately hurting us both." He sighed, seeming unable to let go completely when he said, "Babe, you come to your senses, you know where I am. But I'll only be waiting there for so long."

The door closed behind him and I was left standing alone in a stranger's office, wondering if I was wrong and Marco had been right all along.

———————

CHAPTER 25

"If she upchucks, Dad, you're cleaning it up," Liv warned Mick as he lifted a giggling Lily above his head for about the fifteenth time.

"She's not going to upchuck." Mick grinned, bringing Lily down into his arms. She was little anyway, but Liv's dad was a big guy and she looked tiny and adorable clinging to him. "Soul of a pilot, this one."

It was Sunday lunch, and this time Mick and his wife, Dee, had been able to join us, so it was a full house. It was actually hard to think, what with the children giggling and chasing one another, Bray crying, which was upsetting a usually docile Belle, and the adults trying to be heard over one another. I loved our huge makeshift family, but on a day when I needed them to take my mind off Marco, all they were able to do was make my head pound with their cheerful but disjointed noise.

In order to escape some of the cacophony, I volunteered to do the dishes and shot my arse into the kitchen. It was still noisy, but at least there was distance between me and the worst of it. There I was able to replay the scene with Marco at the restaurant over and over again, as I had been doing for days. I'd been so sure as I stood there and told him we were through that it was the right thing to do, but as soon as that door closed behind him I was seized with instant panic. The truth was, I didn't know what was right and what was wrong. I wished there was some kind of magic wand I could wave that would give me all the answers. Likely some people would call me foolish—tell me that surely the answer is so obvious. If you love someone, you should be with them.

Was it really that simple, though, when there was so much history and hurt? Could we really work through that? Could I really let myself be vulnerable with him again when there was absolutely no way of knowing what the future held for us?

I was exhausted from going over it all over and over and over again.

I scraped the plates and had started loading them into the dishwasher when I felt another presence in the kitchen. I looked up to see who it was, and my eyes collided with Nate's as he leaned against the doorjamb.

"You okay?" I asked, my eyebrows drawn together in concern.

"I was actually going to ask you the same thing," he replied, walking slowly into the kitchen.

I shrugged. Really, what was the point in lying?

Nate sighed. "Thought so." He leaned back against the kitchen counter, crossing his arms over his chest. "You know that Liv and I were just friends before anything romantic happened between us?"

"Yes."

"Well, when we did go down that road, we both knew what was between us was special. Except I didn't want to admit that because I was afraid of losing her in the long run."

"Because of what happened to Alana?" I asked, tentatively because Nate rarely talked about his ex-girlfriend. She had died when they were only eighteen and Nate had had a really difficult time moving on from her death.

"Aye. I pushed Liv away and I really hurt her, all because I was too afraid to go there with her. I almost lost her for good, Hannah. There was a moment when I thought my stubbornness had destroyed us. It was one of the scariest moments of my life. And sometimes I allow myself to think about what my life might have been like if I hadn't won her back. It doesn't even bear thinking about. How does someone live with that kind of regret?" I felt his hand on my shoulder. He gave it a squeeze and said kindly, "You're a good teacher, Hannah. I just hope a lesson in regret isn't something you'll be able to teach well in the future."

Nate's words of wisdom stayed with me through the rest of the day and well into the evening. I returned home that evening with a box from my parents' attic in my arms. I dumped it on the floor of my bedroom. At first I flicked through the pictures of Marco and me from the last few months that I'd taken with my camera phone. From there, I dug through that box and unearthed all my old diaries.

For hours I pored over the documented history of my teen years, filling myself up with all my old feelings for Marco, and hoping they'd collide with the new and somehow breach the blockade of fear.

Because one thing I did know for certain—Nate was right. That kind of regret was a lesson I didn't want to learn.

CHAPTER 26

I knew there was something wrong as soon as I stepped into the school.

There was a hush in the air.

Walking down the first corridor of the English department, I thought I heard sniffling coming from one of the common rooms. I was about to stop to listen harder when Nish called out to me from the open doorway of the staff room.

As soon as I saw her face I knew my gut had been right. Something was very wrong.

"Can you come here?" she asked softly, looking stricken.

I hurried over to her and she gently guided me into the staff room. Eric, Barbara, and two other members of the staff were in the room. Barbara had tears in her eyes and Eric's features were strained, his face pale. "What on earth is going on?" I asked. My pulse started to race as nervous butterflies took flight in my stomach.

Nish grabbed hold of my hand. "Hannah . . . Jarrod Fisher was killed on Saturday night. We just found out this morning."

I stared at Nish blankly, trying to make sense of her words. "What?" I shook out of her grip, glancing at Eric and Barbara. "Is this a joke?"

"Hannah, I know he was a favorite of yours. I'm so sorry."

"I don't understand." I looked back at Nish incredulously. "I don't . . . I don't . . . no." I shook my head.

Her kind eyes grew wet with tears. "He got into a scuffle with an older boy. The wrong boy. He pulled a knife on Jarrod. Jarrod died in surgery."

A knife? Jarrod?

Smart, charming, funny Jarrod, who I'd told umpteen times that he needed to check that short fuse of his. Jarrod, whose mum and wee brother relied on him. *Jarrod.* A fifteen-year-old boy who had his whole life in front of him.

Gone.

Just . . . gone?

No more?

It wasn't possible.

The sob burst out of me before I could stop it and then I was in Nish's arms, bawling the burning pain of his sudden loss into her shoulder. As I thought about his mum and his little brother and the grief that would gnaw at them, that would ache in every muscle, and hang in a dismal pall over their lives for the months to come, I only cried harder.

The tears finally had stopped. I attempted to catch my breath as I pulled out of Nish's arms. "I'm sorry." I swiped at my cheeks, feeling embarrassed for breaking down in school. One look at my colleagues' faces, though, and I knew they understood. Jarrod had been that kid for me, the one where I really felt I could make a difference in his life. It was hard in our job to feel that way, to feel like what we did mattered. I'd imagined discussing university choices with Jarrod next year, helping him get funding, feeling proud of him and how far he'd come. I'd felt like I saw him when no one else did and I'd hoped that it mattered to him.

It was like I'd stepped into some horrible, surreal nightmare.

Children didn't die in knife fights in my world.

Where were *we* to stop that?

How could it be that he'd been in my classroom just last week, and now I was thinking about him in past tense? How did someone go from being this tangible person to being a ghost, a player in a film reel of memories?

The tears started coming again.

"Hannah." Nish rubbed my arm in comfort. "You're going to have to get yourself together, sweetheart. You've got classes, and you've got . . . you've got your fourth-year today."

Oh, God.

How was I going to make it through that class when his empty chair would be staring at me the whole time?

I blew out a shaky breath and wiped at my tears. "I know," I said, my voice trembling, my lips quivering. "Just give me a minute."

"His funeral is on Thursday," Eric told me. "Thursday, eleven o' clock at Dean Cemetery."

I winced, sucking in my breath to hold back another flood of tears. "Do you think they'll give me time off to go?"

"Hannah, you were his favorite teacher," Eric said kindly. "We'll make sure you get to say good-bye."

I pinched my lips together, my eyes blurring with fresh tears.

"Get rid of it now," Nish said softly. "So you can face the kids."

My first class that morning had not been easy, but it was my first-year class and they were subdued by the news of Jarrod's death, which had already met their young ears as it passed through the school halls, and they quietly put their heads down and got on with the task I gave them.

It was when my fourth-years walked in that I felt myself waver and I had to turn my back, suck in the emotion, and count to ten before I could face them. When they were all settled in their seats, I looked them over, taking in the tearstained faces of some of the girls and the shocked, pale features of the rest of them. Even Jack looked upset.

I knew some of them had never been touched by death, and most of them had never been touched by the death of a peer—someone so young, so vital. There is a general belief in one's own immortality when you're young, that you can see and do anything and you and the world as you know it will still be there in the morning.

I wondered how Jarrod's classmates and friends were coping with their sudden mortality.

My gaze came to a stop on his empty chair and I leaned back against my desk, my fingers curling into the wood.

"I wish I could tell you why," I said, clearing my throat when my voice broke on the last few words.

Staci, a pretty blond girl who sat at the table behind Jarrod and often walked out of class with him, caught my eye as she swiped angrily at her tears.

"Why it is that life can change so quickly?" I continued. "How it's possible for a heart to stop beating so suddenly, instantly breaking all the hearts that were ever connected to it? But the truth is there is no sense in what happened to Jarrod. None that I can see. I wish I had a better answer, but I don't."

The entire room watched me silently and I kept speaking. "I can tell you that it's okay to feel whatever it is you're feeling right now. It's okay to miss him and it's okay to hurt and it's okay to feel lost—just as long as you come to me, or your friends, or your family, when all those feelings try to overwhelm you. Because in amongst all those feelings, some of you are going to be angry, and some of you will need someone to blame. It's okay to be angry. I can't tell you if it's right or wrong to feel blame, but what I can say is don't be angry for too long and don't hold on to the blame forever. That kind of anger can take away a piece of you, a piece of you that you might not get back. Jarrod wouldn't want that. Under the bluster and swagger, he was a really good person"—my lips trembled and my eyes were bright with unshed tears I couldn't and honestly didn't want to hide from them—"and I don't think he would want that for any of you.

"I won't lie to you. This changes things. It may even change you. I know it will change me." I shrugged helplessly, feeling suddenly so young, too young to help them. "I guess it's a reminder of the uncertainty in life and the foolishness of merely existing when the world is pleading with you to live. If you take anything from this, please take that. We take life for granted. We have to stop that. We have to start living." I looked around at them all, catching some of their grief-stricken eyes. "If any of you need to talk to me, even if it's to write it down, to put what you're feeling on a bit of paper, then I'm here."

I smiled sadly through the blur of tears and tapped the pile of books at my side. "Jarrod once confessed that his favorite book when he was younger was *Danny the Champion of the World* by Roald Dahl. His primary school teacher read it to the class. So we're going to honor him today— you can read along with me as I read it to you."

Before class I'd run over to the primary school next door and asked them for copies of the book, explaining why I needed them. They were kind and gracious enough to let me borrow the books. I passed the copies out to my kids and placed the last book on Jarrod's desk slowly, fighting my tears. His friend Thomas, who had always been full of cheek in class, made a choked noise at my gesture and when I looked his way I saw him bury his head on his arms on the desk, his shoulders shaking as he tried to muffle his sobs. I passed him, squeezing his shoulder in comfort before walking to my desk, fighting the burn of emotion in my own throat. The muscles in my jaw, in my gums, in my cheeks, ached with it.

Somehow, I managed to open the book and I started to read.

Feeling as though I were wading through mud, I got through the day. I had e-mailed the teacher I shared the adult literacy class with and explained why I wouldn't make my Thursday evening lesson this week. I got a kind e-mail in response from him and he told me he had it covered. From there I finished up my classes and jumped on a bus to Leith after work. There was one person I wanted to see more than anyone.

I wanted Marco. I wanted to wrap my arms around him and feel his strength, breathe him in, and know that I hadn't given up on living the life I really wanted, the life I needed.

I was determined that someday in the near future I would do just that. The Hannah I used to be, the Hannah from my diaries, wasn't afraid of anything. I didn't want to be afraid anymore, and I didn't want life to pass me by. However, I didn't think it was right to use Marco as an emotional crutch. Things were already so complicated between us as it was. When I went to him, I wanted him to be sure I was coming to him for the right reasons.

So I got off the bus and I strode to Cole's apartment.

As soon as he opened his door I walked into his arms and burst out crying. Thankfully, his dodgy flatmate was out, so I could tell Cole about Jarrod in private. He left me briefly to make me a cup of tea and when he returned he pulled me into his side and held me close.

"I was standing there in front of the kids," I whispered, "telling them that they had to learn too soon how fragile life is and that they should learn from it and really live life. I felt like such a hypocrite, telling them to live life when I'm so scared of living that I pushed Marco away."

"What is it you're afraid of, Hannah? Him hurting you?"

"Yes. But I don't want to be anymore. Once I get through this, I'm going to go to him."

"Hannah, he loves you. You should go to him now, let him help you deal with this."

"I can't." I shook my head stubbornly. "I can deal with this alone. I'll go to him afterward, so it's clear why I'm coming to him. Plus, I have to talk to him about something that could mean he doesn't want to be with me."

Cole frowned. "What could that possibly be?"

"The fact that I can't have kids."

"Since when?"

"I don't want them, Cole. After what happened. I almost died. I can't put the people I love through that again."

"Who says you will? There's a risk?"

I shrugged, feeling stupid but no less absolute in my fear. "There's always a risk of another ectopic pregnancy, but, no, the doctor said I could go on to have a healthy pregnancy."

"Okay, so . . . you don't want them? Or you're afraid?"

I shrugged.

"Do you want kids, Hannah?" He insisted on an answer.

I pinched my lips together and nodded.

"Then one day . . . you'll be brave enough." And he seemed so sure I couldn't help but hope he was right.

Cole wasn't the only one who attempted to get me to call Marco to tell him about Jarrod. Ellie did too. As much as my family was there for me through the hard time of losing a student, they didn't seem to understand that I could handle it on my own.

Thursday morning came all too quickly. I dressed in a conservative black pencil dress I sometimes wore to school and borrowed Ellie's long black wool coat. Jarrod's mother had decided to hold the funeral at Jarrod's gravesite instead of inside the church. When I arrived, my knees almost buckled at the sight of his mum. I didn't know if I'd ever witnessed such devastation.

Harvey, Jarrod's little brother, clung to his mother's side, his eyes wide and haunted.

My tears started to flow freely as I found a place in the crowd of mourners near the front. I recognized some faces of his classmates—Thomas and Staci were both there with their parents. After the minister spoke, Jarrod's coffin was lowered into the grave.

Jarrod's mother threw a rose in. A girl I didn't recognize stepped forward and threw another in. She was followed by Staci, and then an older woman, who hugged Jarrod's mum tightly immediately afterward.

During this, I stepped forward, the paper in my hand biting into my skin. Gently I threw the paper into the grave. On it were words I'd borrowed from Shakespeare.

"Good night, sweet prince.
And flights of angels sing thee to thy rest."

It was my way of saying good-bye, of letting him know that he mattered to me, that I'd seen him for who he really was, and that I wanted him to find peace wherever he was now.

Good night, sweet prince. And flights of angels sing thee to thy rest.

I stepped back into the crowd, taking a shuddering breath as the minister began to say his final words. In my sadness I was vaguely aware of the people near me shifting, but I didn't look up.

I didn't look up until I was startled by the warm, rough fingers sliding through mine to hold my hand tight. My breath left me as I turned to look up at Marco.

Shock, relief, disbelief, and gratitude moved through me.

His kind eyes locked with mine and he held on tighter.

Ellie's words from months ago suddenly came to me in that moment.

Five years ago you started shutting us out, putting on this front, determined to take care of yourself without our help. You need to stop that. Not just for you but for us. We're here if you need us, and frankly we need you to need us.

The truth hit me then that she'd been right all along. I needed them, I needed Marco, and I knew that just like my family needed me to need them, he needed me to need him. So I let him know that I did.

Thank you.

He read the silent message in my eyes and in answer brushed his lips against my forehead in comfort. I closed my eyes, rested my head on his shoulder, and listened as the minister laid Jarrod Fisher to rest.

CHAPTER 27

—————

Marco's flat wasn't anything like he'd described.

It was a fairly new build, a two-bedroom flat at St. Leonard's Hill east of the university. It was small, but it was furnished in a masculine, contemporary style—it captured the idea of luxury on a budget. A large flatscreen TV hung on the wall across from the three-seater sofa in the open-plan living space. A small but modern kitchen was situated in the back of the room. There was a door in the middle of the back wall that I guessed led to the bedrooms.

Marco had told me his place was a dump. He'd told me that because if he'd taken me to his flat he would have had to hide the photographs of Dylan that hung on the walls. He would have had to hide the toy box in the corner of the room, and the action figures set up by the French window that overlooked the gardens.

But he couldn't hide the second bedroom that I had no doubt was decorated for a little boy.

Leaving me to shrug out of my coat and take a seat on his black leather sofa, Marco marched determinedly into the kitchen and started brewing me a cup of tea. My face was frozen from the winter wind, but the chill that ran deep through the rest of my body was from having to watch a fifteen-year-old be buried on a day bright with winter sun and dark with bitter confusion.

"It's not fair," I murmured. "And I have to move past that. You'd go crazy, wouldn't you? If you obsessed over the unfairness of it all?"

Marco poured hot water from the kettle into two mugs and then lifted his gaze to me. "It's times like these it's better to accept it and move on. But, yeah. It isn't fair." He moved back to me with the mugs, handed me one and then sat down close to me. His gorgeous eyes held sympathy and concern. "I'm sorry, Hannah. I know he was a good kid."

I clutched the mug tightly in both hands, allowing the heat to seep into me. "Was it Ellie that told you about Jarrod?"

"Cole, actually."

I raised an eyebrow. "I would have lost that bet."

Marco settled his left hip into the back of the sofa, sliding his arm along it until his fingertips were close enough to touch my shoulder. "My question is, why didn't *you* tell me?"

Perhaps it was too much to have this conversation after Jarrod's funeral, but I knew it was time. Marco was here. He had come to me when I needed him without me even having to ask.

"I hate that it took the death of one of my kids to wake me the hell up," I muttered angrily, not flinching from meeting his gaze even though I felt almost ashamed by my choices these last few months. *Strike that. These last few years.* "I thought if I could just get through this alone, then I could come to you after."

His brows drew together. "Hannah, you broke up with me because I left you alone to deal with a miscarriage that almost cost you your life. Now you're telling me you want me to leave you alone to deal with the shitty things that happen? I'm confused."

"No. I thought I could and should do this alone, that it wasn't fair to want to lean on you, but as soon as you were there I knew I needed you." I swallowed hard and admitted, "And I'll always need you."

I watched as he leaned over to put his mug on the coffee table and when he faced me, his eyes were blazing. "Are you for real? Because I don't know if I can take you turning away from me again."

"The miscarriage . . . I don't know how to explain what it did to me. The worst thing that ever happened to me before it was Ellie's tumor. When we didn't know if it was cancer or not, and even the time in the hospital and how scary it was to see her like that . . . I was thirteen and suddenly I realized we didn't live forever. Of course I knew people died and I'd known people who'd lost family, but I'd never experienced loss for myself before. And then there was Ellie, a huge part of my life, a huge part of what made me happy, and there was a possibility that we were going to lose her. One of the worst parts of it all was seeing what it did to Mum and Dad. It was like they could barely breathe until they knew she was going to be okay."

I felt my chest compress as the memories flooded me. "When I started to feel ill after you left all those years ago, I tried to explain it away to myself because there was this dark part of me, buried deep down, that was scared there was something really wrong with me like there had been for Ellie, and that I was going to put everyone through it all over again. That fear almost cost me my life. And yet . . . I didn't learn my lesson. I put these blinders on, facing the world on my own as if that somehow makes up for the fact that underneath my bullshit I'm utterly petrified. I didn't mean to hurt you because of that. I am . . . ." I shook my head, knowing an apology wasn't enough but giving one anyway. "I'm sorry. But I can promise I won't ever do that you again. Ever."

He made a move toward me as if he was going to touch me. I held my hand up to stop him.

"Before you say anything, you need to know something."

Marco grew still but gave a stiff little nod for me to continue.

I took a shuddering breath for the coming revelation. "I wish I was stronger. I wish I was Hannah before the miscarriage, but I lost a huge piece of her after it happened. Especially the part of her that went after what she wanted no matter the consequences. I want kids, I need you to know that, but if we get back together and somewhere down the road you wanted kids, I don't know if I could actually give you that." I couldn't read his expression. "What I'm trying to say is that I'm frightened to try to get pregnant, and I can't promise I'll ever get over that."

His hands were suddenly on me, pulling me close until our noses almost touched. "Do you love me?" he asked hoarsely, giving me a little shake.

I laughed softly at the question, the answer so obvious—to me at least. Reaching a hand up, I ran the backs of my knuckles along his cheek, feeling the possessive thrill I always felt when I was near him. Because buried under all my crap was the utter belief I had deep in my bones that this man belonged to me. "What I said before was true. I've been in love with you since I was fourteen."

His grip tightened. "Then that's all that matters to me. We'll take the future as it comes. There's no promise that life will ever be easy. It never has been for me. But the moments where all that shit disappeared, where it ceased to matter to me, those moments always had you in them. I know you make me laugh, I know you make me feel worth something, you make me feel needed, and I know I want you like I've never wanted any other woman in my life. All that makes sense.

"I've never been able to explain what it is about you that makes all the bad go away. I don't need that to make sense, though. I don't know why it is that way. All I need to know is that you do, you always have. I'm in love with you. There is no one else for me and I don't know how I know, but I do know that there never will be. So"—he cupped my face in his hands, drawing me closer—"we'll deal with tomorrow, tomorrow."

After he pressed a soft kiss to my lips, he hugged me to his side and we sat there for a while as he comforted me in silence.

Finally I said softly, reflectively, "It changes you. Loss."

I felt his arm tighten around me. "It changed you, babe. But not as much as you think."

"Still, it's always there. Do you think that's okay?"

"In what way is it always there?"

I took a moment, trying to think of the best way to explain it. "When you haven't experienced loss directly, it's like . . . well, you drive the same road home you drive each night. You know it as well as anyone can. Then one night you decide for the hell of it to drive a different road home. You think nothing of it. It's merely a change of scenery.

"But if you're someone who has lost someone or come close to losing yourself . . . and if you take that different road, there's this second after you've made that decision, just a second, in which you wonder, worry, if taking that road means changing your life irreparably—you don't know the curves in the road as well, you don't know the blind spots. In that second you imagine a crash, a collision. Just a second, until you tell yourself to stop being so morbid. Yet no matter how silly it makes you feel, every time you make a decision to take that different road, you can't help that instant of questioning if your choice will end in loss."

He was quiet as he processed my words, and then his lips were in my hair, his whisper a promise. "Life's fragile, Hannah. You know that and that's what those seconds are a product of. You're allowed to have those seconds, just as long as they don't mean you ever shut me out."

Relieved that he understood, I closed my eyes and held on tighter, giving him a silent promise in return.

That night I slept next to Marco in his bed for the first time. He held me close, keeping me warm and safe through my sadness.

I was just drifting to sleep when I heard Jarrod's voice in my head, a memory from weeks before.

"Just saying. Nice to know a big guy like that is watching your back."

From his voice came peace.

CHAPTER 28

"I'll get your short essays back to you next week," I promised my literacy class as they all began packing up for the evening.

"Have a nice weekend, Hannah," Duncan said, throwing me a kind smile as he headed out the door.

The others followed his lead. They'd been somewhat subdued this week and I had a feeling they knew the reason why I hadn't been there to teach them last Thursday.

I was packing up my own things when to my surprise Lorraine made her way over to me. Trying to mask my disbelief at her willingly approaching me, I stilled, waiting for her to say something.

She shifted a little uneasily. "I, eh . . . I heard aboot the wee laddie fae yer class. Sorry tae hear it."

I blinked rapidly at the unexpected condolence. "Thank you."

"Aye, well, ye seem like ye probably give a shit, so, I imagine it hus'nae been easy fur ye."

I nodded in silent agreement, honestly not knowing what to say.

Lorraine shrugged, looking anywhere but at me. "Aye, well . . . thote ye might like to ken that I, eh . . . got a jobe."

"That's brilliant." I grinned. "Where?"

"Fur one eh the sport bookies chains." She flashed me a smile and I was almost knocked over by the extremely rare sight. "It's awright money, like."

"Lorraine, I'm so pleased for you."

She shrugged, shuffling back from me, seeming all too uncomfortable again. "Well, just wanted tae tell ye 'cos I probably widnae huv got it if it wisnae fur this class. I'll see ye later." She dashed out of the room before I could say anything else.

I stared after her. Lorraine was as rough as they came and prickly as hell. She didn't like me, or at least she didn't understand me, but she was the first student since Jarrod's death to make me feel like there was still a chance to make a difference at all this.

Marco's muddy riggers were sitting on a folded-out newspaper just inside the door to my flat. I felt something pleasant shift in my chest at the sight of them, and after I shut the door behind me, I cocked my head to listen for the sound of him.

I could hear the shower running.

To prove to him I was serious about us, I'd given him a key to my flat a few days ago. I knew, despite his determination to keep us together, that *I* had a way to go in reassuring him that I wasn't going to do a one-eighty and come up with another reason for us not to work it out. My suspicion that he wasn't quite over my defection sprang from the fact that this weekend was his weekend with Dylan and he hadn't suggested I stick around for it.

I could live with that.

For now.

Dropping my keys in the bowl on my side table, I kicked off my shoes and then moved into the sitting room. Marco's empty coffee mug was sitting on the table, his jacket was hanging over the back of the armchair. Shrugging out of my own jacket, I draped it across the arm of the chair and began making my way out into the hall, unbuttoning my shirt as I sauntered toward the bathroom. For the last eight nights Marco had stayed with me, but he'd given me space sexually, allowing me to deal with Jarrod's loss, and the ramifications of it upon my kids at school. Marco didn't want to push me into the physical stuff, and that was thoughtful and considerate and, ironically, sexy as hell.

That's why I was done with him giving me space. I wanted a new kind of comfort from him. Specifically in the form of orgasms.

Dropping my shirt to the floor, I pushed open the bathroom door, the steam from the shower hitting me immediately. Marco jerked his head up at the sight of me through the somewhat fogged glass of the shower screen, and then a slow smile that melted my insides lit up his handsome face.

I unzipped my pencil skirt and pushed it to the tiled floor, my eyes devouring my too-hot-to-be-real boyfriend. By the time my underwear was off, Marco was ready for me. I stepped into the shower, eyed his hard-on with a sense of empowerment, and lowered myself gracefully to my knees to help him out with the situation I'd gotten him into.

As I lay in bed, my arm draped over Marco's stomach and my head resting on his chest, I suddenly gave voice to my wandering thoughts. "Do you ever think about finding your mum and dad?"

Marco gave a huff of surprise. "Where did that come from?"

"I was just thinking about you and Dylan and how you managed to turn into this great dad despite your lack of a role model."

"I guess I just don't need my folks anymore, you know? It used to burn in my gut—the rejection. It did for a long time. But once Dylan came along, I slowly began to see it wasn't my fault that my parents didn't want me. You hold your kid in your arms, and if you don't feel an overwhelming need to protect them, then that's on you, not the kid."

I sat up a little so I could look him in the eyes. "You're one of the strongest people I know."

His eyes warmed. "Back at you, babe." His gaze suddenly turned knowing. "I'll introduce you to Dylan as my girlfriend soon. I promise."

Wrinkling my nose, I pulled back from him, disquieted. "Are you a mind reader now?"

Marco grinned and it was cocky enough for me to want to smack it off his lips. "I'm a Hannah-reader and my not introducing you this weekend doesn't mean what you think it does. I just want this weekend to explain stuff to him first."

Appeased by that, I said, "It's fine. I get it." I settled back down beside him and pressed a soft kiss to his chest. "You do what's best for Dylan."

"You mean that?"

"Of course."

"Then I'm sorry, but . . . you're never taking him ice skating. Ever."

Marco's laughter rang throughout my apartment as he attempted to escape the punch that I was aiming for his upper arm.

"So I take it this is permanent this time?"

I turned back from watching Dylan as he chatted quietly to his dad. Marco was down on his haunches, rezipping Dylan's jacket after his son had started to remove it. We were taking him out today, however, and I gathered that was what Marco was telling him quietly, since Dylan kept throwing me quizzical looks every now and then. It was hard to pull my eyes away from them together, but I did at Leah's question.

It was two weeks since Marco had laid down the law and told me I was not allowed to take Dylan skating. He'd revised it to say I was not allowed to take Dylan skating unsupervised, which I thought was rather fair of him, considering what he'd witnessed the last time I was on a rink.

This was my first weekend hanging out with Dylan. Marco had explained to him who I was and what I meant to him and that I'd be around a lot whenever Dylan came to see his dad. I didn't know how Dylan was going to react to that. Although he was used to sharing Leah with Graham, since Graham had been in the picture almost as long as Dylan had been alive, I didn't know how he'd feel about sharing his superhero dad.

Leah had just dropped him off with us. It was early Saturday morning and my stomach was filled with butterflies. I wasn't really in the mood for an inquisition, but when I saw the smile in Leah's eyes, I realized she was teasing me.

"Oh, I don't know," I answered. "As soon as it gets boring, I'll probably move on to another single dad."

She stared at me blankly.

"That was a joke," I explained. "Apparently not a good one. Too soon?"

Leah raised an eyebrow. "You think?"

Awkward. I looked back at Marco, who had stood up and was listening in with mirth in his eyes. "I like her." I raised my arm and gave a mini fist pump. "She's feisty."

His shoulders shook with laughter. Dylan looked up at his dad, saw him laughing, and a small smile played on his lips.

Glancing back at Leah, I found her smiling at her son. Her eyes flicked to mine and thankfully she didn't stop smiling. "I'm glad it all worked out, Hannah."

"Me too," I told her sincerely.

She grinned at her son. "I'll see *you* after school on Monday, honey. Have a great weekend with your daddy."

In answer Dylan hurried over to her and gave her a hug. I got the impression from the surprised look on Leah's face that he didn't usually do that when she dropped him off with Marco. I was guessing the need for reassurance and comfort from her was because there was a strange, tall blond lady in his dad's living room and she didn't appear to be going anywhere. The concern must have shown on my face because Leah said as she caressed her son's hair, "He'll be fine once he gets to know you. He's just a wee bit shy. Ay?" She pulled back from him, looking down into his gorgeous face. "You'll have a good time with Hannah, though. She's Daddy's other best friend, and you know if Daddy likes someone they're usually pretty cool."

Dylan looked at me a little dubiously over his shoulder but turned back to his mum. "Okay," he replied quietly.

The urge to cuddle him was great. He was so adorable. I had to remind myself, however, that he was a little boy and not a puppy. I doubted very much he wanted to be smothered with kisses and cuddles while I baby-talked to him.

"See you later, honey." Leah kissed him on the forehead and gently nudged him toward Marco. "Take care of him."

"Always do," he replied.

She smiled, gave us one last look, and her eyes seemed to be laughing at us like she knew something we didn't.

When she was gone I looked up at Marco and said, "I really do like her."

"She's good people."

Still smiling, I looked down at Dylan, who was watching my interaction with his dad like a hawk. "I heard three-year-olds love the zoo. Do you fancy a day at the zoo, Dylan?"

"I'm nearly four," he answered, holding up four fingers.

Must. Not. Cuddle.

Pushing past the overwhelming adorableness, I replied seriously, "Well, I've heard nearly-four-year-olds love the zoo, too."

His brows drew together. "Will there be lions?"

"They have two lions, I think, and big cats."

Dylan's face closed down at that and he moved into his dad's legs.

"They're in an enclosure. A big cage. They can't get at you."

He still looked unconvinced.

"Your dad will be there with us. Do you think he's going to let a lion get near you?"

It was the right thing to say. He looked up at his dad, contemplated how big he was compared to himself and slowly shook his head.

Marco grinned and smoothed a hand over his son's hair affectionately. "You ready to go, then, buddy?"

He nodded and reached for his dad's hand.

As we were walking out the door, Marco's other hand in mine, I asked, "You won't let the lions near me either, right?"

"It *is* tempting."

"That was definitely the wrong answer." I sighed in mock weariness. "No more searching for superhero boyfriends on the Internet. They always turn out to be duds who'll quite happily let you get eaten by a lion."

Marco hissed in a breath through his teeth. "You *do* roll the dice when you find a boyfriend on the Internet."

"What about penguins? Surely you won't let the penguins get me?"

"I don't know—that might be fun to watch."

I stopped on the stairwell and Marco and Dylan drew to a halt on the steps below me. "No penguin protection? What kind of superhero are you?"

"You're weird," Dylan said quietly to me.

Marco burst out laughing. "Buddy, you don't know the half of it."

Since Dylan grinned in response, I took the "weird" comment on the chin and went with it.

Dylan and I stared at each other across the table.

Marco had left me with him while he went up to order us some food from the zoo café. Everything had been fine while we wandered around the zoo with Marco present as a buffer. When Dylan had gotten close to the lion enclosure and one of the lions let out what I think was really just a yawn rather than a growl, I had easily reassured Dylan so he didn't go skittering off in fear.

But alone? Even if it was only for a few minutes? I felt so much pressure for him to like me that my mind was suddenly blank. I couldn't think of any topics of conversation that were appropriate for a child.

"You were scared of the snakes," Dylan suddenly said, tilting his head to the side inquisitively.

He was not wrong.

I shuddered. I'd hurried away from the snakes as quickly as possible. "I don't like snakes."

"Why?"

That was actually a really difficult question to answer for a small child. "They scare me."

He frowned. "Why?"

"Uh . . . because so many of them can bite you, and the bite can make you really, really sick."

"All of them?"

"Well, no . . ."

"But you're scared of all of them?"

"Yes." I could see where this was going and I didn't like it.

"Why?"

Yup, that's where I thought it was going.

There really was no good explanation other than irrational fear, and I didn't think an almost-four-year-old would understand irrationality as an answer. I didn't want the kid to think I disliked things because they were different, because even at his age that kind of thinking might stick with him. In the end, I replied, "The hissing sound they make."

Dylan stared at me a second and then nodded slowly. I gave an inner sigh of relief before quickly changing the subject.

"What was your favorite animal?"

"Giant panda," he answered immediately.

I grinned and turned the tables on him. "Why?"

He shrugged. "Cool eyes. I wasn't scared. It smiled."

The panda hadn't actually smiled, of course, but when she contemplated us I could have sworn there was something mischievous in her eyes. The fact that Dylan had picked up on that made me feel absurdly proud of him. "All good reasons."

"D'ye live with my daddy now?"

And we were back in dangerous territory. I shook my head. "No. We just hang out a lot."

"You'll be there when I come to stay?"

"Sometimes. Is that okay with you?"

Dylan shrugged again. "Daddy laughs a lot, so okay."

I felt elated by Dylan's analysis of the situation and the blessing he had given me in his cute little-boy way.

Must. Not. Cuddle.

When Marco came back to the table with the food, I was grinning from ear to ear. He smiled in bewilderment at my expression as he sat down and made sure Dylan had his food and juice. "What's going on with you?"

I shrugged. "I just love giant pandas."

Marco's brows drew together and he looked at Dylan as if he would explain. His son gave him a look as if to say, *What? It makes sense to me*, and I burst out laughing.

The last few months had been an utter roller coaster of emotions for me, and after having to go through the ugly past again, and then losing Jarrod, I hadn't known if or when I'd ever be able to laugh that hard again.

But laugh hard I did.

Marco was smiling, but he leaned his head down to Dylan and said, "You were right. Weird."

Dylan gave a world-weary sigh that was far beyond his years.

I didn't care if they teased me for the rest of my life. In that moment, all I cared about was that they'd be there for the rest of my life.

CHAPTER 29

June

The late June sun streamed in through my classroom windows, the light spilling over the kids' empty desks. My last class of the year had already left, but I found myself immobilized. I couldn't take my eyes off Jarrod's desk. It had remained empty for the rest of the year whenever his class came into my room.

I didn't want to forget.

It had been hard the past few months to find myself as a teacher again. Part of me had wanted to fall back on old habits and create a distance between myself and the kids. There was always supposed to be some distance anyway, but it was hard not to care about them, and in the end I decided if I stopped caring about them, I'd stop being a good teacher.

It hadn't started out as the best year, but the past few months had begun to make up for that. One way in which they had was the permanent job offer I received from the department here at Braemuir. I'd be returning as a fully qualified English teacher after the summer. It was one less thing to worry about.

I had thought I would feel relief that the year was over and that I had the summer to enjoy before it started all over again.

But standing there in my classroom that last day, I couldn't stop staring at Jarrod's desk.

Sometimes it still made my breath catch when I remembered that I wouldn't see him next year, that he wouldn't get to grow up and become the amazing man I knew he could have been.

I hadn't realized how hard the last day of school was going to be with that hanging over me.

"Knock, knock."

My gaze jerked away from the desk and my eyes widened in surprised pleasure, my mood instantly lifting at the sight of Marco and Dylan walking into my classroom.

"What are you two doing here?" I asked, grinning happily as Dylan's steps quickened. He reached me and instantly slid his arms around my legs. I hugged him close as Marco bent down to give me a quick, sweet kiss on the lips.

"I thought maybe you'd want some company. Not an easy day for you, babe."

I shook my head in wonder. How had he known when even I hadn't known? "I love you," I murmured.

"I love you, too."

I looked down at Dylan to see him watching us. I scrunched my nose up at him. "Guess what?"

"What?" he returned, genuinely curious.

"I love you, too."

He smiled shyly and ducked his head.

So cute, I could die.

"Dylan, what do you say?" Marco chucked his chin.

Dylan shrugged. "Hannah knows I lu huh." His words became a mumble, but I got the gist.

I gave Marco a look. "He's four and he's uncomfortable saying 'I love you.' I already pity his future girlfriends."

Marco laughed. "He's a man. He has a hard time showing his feelings."

"You're a man and you don't have a hard time showing your feelings."

"In public I do."

"You just said you loved me in front of Dylan."

"It's just Dylan."

"So you're telling me that when we get married you're not going to say you love me in your wedding vows?"

"You don't say 'I love you' in wedding vows."

"You do if you write your own." I was completely messing with him and it was worth it to see the flicker of panic in his eyes.

"Write my own . . . vows?" His grip on Dylan's shoulders tightened.

"Mmm-hmm."

"You want me to write my own vows?"

I turned my mouth down at the corners as I shrugged. "Well, I might let you off with it, if you actually get around to proposing sometime."

The light dawned in his eyes. "You manipulative—"

I grabbed my purse off my chair, ready to leave. "Finish that sentence and I won't say yes."

"I never asked," he argued, ushering Dylan out behind me.

"But you're going to." I glanced back at Dylan. "Your daddy is a slow-coach."

Marco looked at his son for help, but Dylan just looked at him with this "Really, dude" expression that made me love him even more.

"Are you sure he's not my child?" I joked.

"Sometimes I wonder," Marco muttered.

From school we got a cab back to my place so I could change for the evening's event. It was Lily's fifth birthday, and Gio and Gabby had generously offered the restaurant as a place to host it, closing off the back room for our private party.

Outside the restaurant we bumped into Cole and his new girlfriend, Larissa. She was a quiet, pretty auburn-haired psychology student who was clearly one hundred times more madly in love with Cole than he was with her.

"D-Man," Cole greeted Dylan first. The two of them bumped fists, the brightness in Dylan's eyes the only indication that he was thrilled to see Cole. While it had taken a few months for Marco to come around to Cole, his son had latched on to my best friend within a matter of hours after meeting him. They shared an overall seriousness that put them beyond their years and had a seemingly innate understanding of each other.

"What d'ye get?" Dylan gestured to the wrapped gift in Cole's hand.

"Girlie stuff. You?" He indicated the present Dylan was carrying for us.

He scrunched up his nose. "Girlie stuff."

Cole patted him on the back of the head and pulled open the door to the restaurant. "I hear you."

"Hi, Larissa," I greeted her with a coaxing smile.

In return I received a pinched smile. I couldn't quite work out if it was because she was shy or because she, like most of Cole's girlfriends so far, resented my presence in his life. I was sure it was the latter.

Marco and I held back as the three of them walked inside.

"She hates me," I grumbled.

"You're hot and Cole loves you. Of course she hates you." Marco tugged on my hand, pulling me inside.

"Well, thanks for that very comforting and concise summary of the situation."

He gave me a wry half smile as we walked through the front dining room and into the hall to reach the back. "She'll get over it. That better?"

"No, because now you're lying."

He looked up at the ceiling as if talking to God. "I can't win."

"He's not listening."

He cut me a dry look. "Obviously."

"Oh, shut it. You love me and you know it."

"You kill me with your sweetness, babe."

"Ah, there you are!" Liv came hurrying forward as we entered the back dining room. Pink and purple decorations had literally exploded all over the room. There were balloons, ribbons, flower chains, and sparkly confetti everywhere. Liv gave me a quick hug and grinned up at Marco in greeting. "Your aunt and uncle are amazing to do this. I think I've thanked them so much they're ready to kill me."

"It's no problem." Marco shrugged. "You're family."

Her eyes bugged out at me and she whispered comically, "I'm family."

I patted her shoulder. "They're not the Mafia, Liv. Calm down."

"Nanna!"

My nephew William came flying at me, dangerously unsteady with momentum. I grabbed him before he made hard impact with my legs. As soon as I lifted him into my arms, Beth, Lily, and Luke were at my side. I greeted them all before bending down to kiss Lily's silky dark hair. "Happy birthday, sweetheart."

She smiled shyly and leaned into my leg.

Surrounded by the kids, I watched happily as we appeared to magnetically draw everyone else to us. Jo and Cam came over to say hello, Cam holding little Bella in his arms. Holding Bray in his, Adam came over with Ellie, who scooped William from my arms to hers. Joss and Braden sauntered over to join the pack and were quickly crowded in by Mum, Dad, Mick, Dee, Cole, Dylan, Larissa, Declan, Penny, Nate's mum and dad, and Gio and Gabby.

Chatter sparked off all around me as I leaned against Marco, my hand resting lightly on Dylan's head, and I didn't feel overwhelmed.

I felt content.

I felt at peace.

I had just taken a wolflike bite of birthday cake when Gabby approached me. She smiled and I quickly tried to swallow the delicious sponge cake and buttercream icing so I could return the gesture.

"Marco says it was your last day today. You've got the summer now before you go back to school?"

I nodded, putting the cake down, only somewhat reluctantly, to converse with Gabby. I'd met Gabby and Gio officially a week after we took Dylan to the zoo. It had been difficult to be congenial to Gio, despite how charming he was, because I knew what a prize shit he'd been to Marco. However, Marco had moved past all the ugly stuff with his uncle and I didn't want to constantly remind him of it, so I did my best to move past it too. Gabby was a different story. I loved her straight off the bat. She had a dry wit, a warm demeanor, and her fondness for Marco was obvious to everyone. "I'm just glad I've got a job to return to."

"I heard about that." Gio suddenly appeared, smiling warmly at me. "Congratulations on the permanent position."

I gave him a small smile. "Thank you. And thank you both for hosting Lily's party. It's beautiful and the food is amazing, as per usual."

"No problem." Gio waved off the thanks and put an arm around his wife's shoulder. "Lily is your family, which makes her our family."

"She is beautiful." Gabby looked over to where Lily was sitting on Nate's knee and grinning up at whatever Liv was saying to her. "So well behaved too."

"Oh, she's an angel." My eyes darted across the room, where I could see Beth doing what appeared to be a bad job of attempting to talk Dylan into swiping an extra piece of cake. "And some of them are angels with dirty faces."

Dylan didn't look convinced, so Beth reached up to the table to take another bit of cake by herself. Her little hand had just closed around it when Joss appeared. She didn't say a word. She just held out her hand, palm up. Beth wrinkled her nose in annoyance and plopped the cake in her mother's hand. Joss raised an eyebrow at her and nodded her head to the right. Beth followed the direction of the gesture and her shoulders slumped at the sight of Braden. He was sitting beside Adam and Ellie, holding his nephew, Bray, in his arms, but the look of rebuke on his face was leveled at his daughter. At the expression on her dad's face, Beth's shoulders suddenly flew back, and as if she was marching to her end, she strode across the room to her dad with the look of a martyr on her own face.

I could tell it took everything Braden had not to laugh.

My eyes went back to Dylan. Joss said something to him, smiling, and he gave her his serious-little-boy nod and began to move away. I expected him to head toward Marco, who was standing chatting with Cam, Cole, and Mick about something, but Dylan headed toward us.

I assumed he was coming over to Gabby and Gio, who were pretty much beloved grandparents to him. However, Dylan just looked up at Gabby and Gio as he walked by them, before dropping his gaze to me. Without a word he climbed onto my lap and rested his head against my chest.

He probably heard my heartbeat banging away in his ear.

I could tell by Gabby's and Gio's amused expressions that my face was a picture of surprise and absolute adoration. Looking down at the top of his head, I tentatively lifted my hand to stroke his soft curls. "Tired, sweetheart?"

He nodded slowly, and relaxed even deeper into me.

"Do you want to go home and I'll read *Where the Wild Things Are* before bedtime?"

He nodded again.

My chest tight with emotion, I looked up from him to search out Marco. It didn't surprise me to find his eyes were already on us, and there was such intensity in the way he was watching us that my chest tightened that little bit more until I was entirely breathless.

My mum always said it was the simplest things in life that moved you.

My mum had never been more right than she was just then.

"'. . . and it was still hot.'"

I closed the picture book and looked down at Dylan, whose eyes were already closing. Carefully, I extricated myself from the bed, put the book on his bedside table, kissed his forehead, whispered good night, and walked over to the door.

Marco gave me a loving look from his place in the doorway and then strode inside to say good night to his son. I left them, giving them their time, as I had tried to a lot over the past few months. I didn't spend every day of their alternative weekend arrangement with them because I felt it would be an easier transition for Dylan if he at least got his dad to himself sometimes. That was hard for me, not just because I missed Marco whenever he wasn't around, but because those alternate weekends were the highlight of my month. I missed Dylan when he wasn't with us, so I knew Marco must miss him a million times more.

This summer, however, we were getting him for two full weeks while Marco was on holiday. We'd booked into a holiday park in Cornwall, so we were praying for some of the sunny weather it was known for. I couldn't wait to spend so much time with two of my favorite guys in the world.

I was in the sitting room, pushing my feet into my shoes, when strong arms wrapped around my waist and I found myself pulled back against Marco's chest. "Where are you going?" his gravelly voice rumbled sexily in my ear.

A shiver chased down my spine, but I knew I had to ignore it. "Time for me to go home." Not once had I remained overnight when Dylan was staying with Marco. We wanted to take things slow when it came to introducing me into Dylan's life.

Marco kissed my neck as his hand coasted up my side, and over my ribs until he was cupping my left breast.

I sighed in pleasure, arching my back. "What are you doing?"

"Trying to get my girl to wrap those long fantastic legs of hers around me."

Reluctantly, I broke the embrace to turn to look at him in question. "But Dylan—"

"We'll be quiet," Marco murmured hungrily against my mouth. "And I think we're good to start introducing you as a permanent feature to his weekends with me." His lips brushed over mine. Mine tingled in answer. Like always.

"Do you think he'll be okay with that?" I panted, my hands already roaming over his strong chest.

"You make those great pancakes of yours in the morning, he'll be fine." He reached for another kiss, but I grinned, stalling it momentarily.

"Pancakes I can do."

"Good," he growled, crushing me against him. "Now do me."

EPILOGUE

*B*reathe, Hannah.

Breathe.

I sucked in a giant gulp of air and almost choked on it.

My whole body was shaking and no matter how much I tried to push back the fear, it kept surging forth, attempting to wrap its clawed hand around my throat. My gaze bored into the door to my flat as I waited for Marco to come home.

We'd finally decided it made more sense for him to move in with me, and thankfully Dylan had been okay with that, particularly because he had fun picking out all the stuff for his new room. That had only been six weeks ago, the weekend before I started back at school.

It was fast. We knew that. We'd been together less than a year, but considering our history and the fact that we loved each other to pieces, it was the right move for us.

It didn't feel fast.

This . . . this was fast.

And this . . . this was . . .

Terrifying.

I didn't know if I could do it.

The key turned in the lock.

Marco walked in, his head came up, and as soon as he saw me standing there, with the petrified expression on my face, he closed the door. "What's going on?" he asked, his eyes dark with concern.

I was so close to upchucking where I stood.

Pale, feeling the tingles of nausea on my cheeks, I fought for some control. "My period is really late." I held up the pregnancy test, my hand visibly shaking.

Marco's eyes flew from the test to my face, and then suddenly I was in his arms. He could feel me trembling hard and his muscles tightened around me. "It's going to be okay," he told me in his quiet, controlled voice. "Baby, I won't let anything happen to you."

I fought the burn of tears in my throat. "It must have been when I went off the pill to take those tablets for the sickness bug I caught on holiday. I knew we shouldn't have had sex when I was feeling better," I murmured absentmindedly.

"We don't know anything yet, right?" He pulled back to look into my face, and what he saw there made his features taut. "Hannah, don't look like that. It kills me."

My lips quivered as I tried to smile. I didn't pull it off. "I'm scared. I'm trying not to be."

He cupped my face in his hands. "It's understandable, but I promise I won't let anything happen to you. You know that."

Nodding my head again, I clutched him more tightly. "I should take the test so we know for sure."

"Hannah, what's going on in there?" Marco rapped impatiently on the bathroom door.

I'd flushed the toilet seconds before I'd thrown up so he wouldn't hear me being sick. I flushed the toilet again and stood on shaky legs. Marco rapped on the door once more while I brushed my teeth, avoiding the strained, pale face in the mirror that I didn't recognize.

Finally, once I looked as good as I could, I opened the door. He forced it open all the way so he could yank me out of the bathroom and into his arms. "Well?" he asked, his voice deeper, rougher than usual as he stroked my hair off my face.

My lips felt numb. "Test says I'm pregnant," I whispered.

He didn't even blink. "We'll get you in to see the doctor tomorrow, we'll get it confirmed, and then we'll get it all checked out to make sure everything is okay."

I looked away, fighting the panic that was rising again swiftly on the heels of the last wave of it. "I don't know if I'm brave enough."

The little shake he gave me brought my gaze back to his. "You are. You know you are."

"This is too fast."

He gave me a reassuring smile. "You think Dylan wasn't? But Leah and I dealt with it. You and I have dealt with it. You don't think we can handle another kid?" He squeezed my waist and through my panic I sensed his quiet excitement. "This is our kid, Hannah."

I raised my shaking hands and laid them on his chest. "If our kid doesn't kill me, we're getting married."

Marco scowled. "You have a sick sense of humor."

"I either joke and get through this or I start to cry."

He considered the ultimatum and gave a sharp nod. "Sick sense of humor it is, then."

I tried my best at a brave nod in acknowledgment of his acquiescence and I pulled away. "Do you want a coffee? I need tea." I began to make my way slowly down the hallway.

I was just at the kitchen door when he called my name.

"Yeah?" I turned around, feeling exhausted. I quickly grew alert, however, at the dark intensity in Marco's eyes. He often looked at me like that when we were making love.

He took a step toward me. "Kid or no kid . . . this is us forever, and you're right, we should make that official." Another step closer. "Marry me."

The panic retreated along with my breath. "Is that a request or a demand?" I asked breathlessly, laughter in the words.

Marco's lips curled up at the corners. "A little of both."

I cocked my head to the side, contemplating him with mischief in my eyes. That he could make me feel this way when I also felt so worried about the future was one of the reasons I loved him. "If you'd asked me when I was seventeen I would have given my parents both a heart attack by saying yes."

"And now?"

I shrugged and began to turn away. "I'll think about it."

Two seconds later I was hauled into his arms, laughing as he growled, "I'll think about it?" against my mouth.

I nodded, wrapping my arms around his neck to hold on to him.

"Think fast." He nipped at my lip.

"Okay, okay . . ."

"Hannah," Marco warned.

Standing on my tiptoes, I brushed my lips against his ear and whispered, "I'll say yes. I promise."

"Then say it now," he whispered back.

"You're my best friend."

"Hannah."

"Always have been. Always will be." I pulled back to hold his handsome face in my hands.

"I'll take that as your yes," he replied, his voice hoarse with emotion.

Letting all my feelings of tender affection and love shine out of my eyes, I grinned. "You always were good at reading me."

He kissed me, pulling back only to look me deep in the eyes. Understanding passed silently between us. We could do this.

It hadn't been an easy journey to here. We'd tried to fly numerous times since meeting each other, and we'd fallen more times than we liked to count. That was life.

Flying and falling.

Next week, for all we knew, we could very well fall, but in that moment, we were happy because we knew with certainty that if we fell . . . together, we'd get back up to try again.

ACKNOWLEDGMENTS

Hannah and Marco's story made it into readers' hands because of my wonderful, determined, and amazingly supportive agent, Lauren Abramo. As always, thank you for going above and beyond the call of duty, Lauren!

Moreover, I have to thank my awesome editor, Kerry Donovan, for not only loving the ODS world as much as I do, but for helping to make it so much better than I ever thought possible. Working on this series with you, Kerry, is a dream.

I must say a big thank-you to Erin Galloway and the team at New American Library for all their hard work on this series, too. You guys are phenomenal!

Thank you to Anna Boatman and the team at Piatkus for believing in this series and bringing Hannah and Marco's story to the UK readers. Your enthusiasm means the absolute world to me.

To Georgia Cates, thank you so much, not only for being a great friend and part of the amazing support system we call the Hellcats, but for sharing your wisdom from fifteen years as a delivery nurse and for providing me with invaluable advice on the medical information in Hannah's story.

And to Shanine Christoffersen and Kate McJennett, thank you for being such wonderful teachers and such an inspiration. The kids you teach have no idea how lucky they are to have you, and how much it matters that you care so deeply for what you do. Kate, thank you for all your advice as a high school English teacher. Hannah came alive as a teacher as I was writing, and a lot of that came from you. Also, thanks for letting me steal your *Dark Knight Rises* lesson plan. Very cool.

Finally, a massive thank-you to you, my reader.

You know why.

Don't miss this bonus novella in the

ON DUBLIN STREET series!

Turn the page for

CASTLE HILL,

which has previously been available only in digital format.

CASTLE HILL

A Joss and Braden Novella

For all the Joss and Braden fans . . .

CHAPTER 1

The Proposal

My fingers moved fast but quietly across the keys of my laptop, and I'd adjusted the screen light so it wasn't so glaring. I'd woken up in the middle of the night, wide-awake and itching to finish the chapter in my manuscript where my dad finally makes progress in his relationship with my mom. Much of what I'd written was conjecture since I only knew the basic history of my parents' relationship, but their world, or the world I'd given them, had taken me over these past few months and I found myself enjoying writing in a way I never had before.

This often meant late-night type-fests and despite the fact that I was partially consumed by their story, I was also very much aware of my considerate bedfellow and was trying to act as he would and not wake him up.

I'd been typing for just over an hour and finally I'd come to the end of the chapter. After saving the file, I shut down the laptop and stared at it for a while. Breathing in and out, slowly, evenly, I controlled the wound inside of me. Pain slashed me deep across my chest and when I thought on the loss of my parents, of my little sister, Beth, that cut would widen into an agonizing gash. Before my considerate bedfellow, I'd have sewn that cut completely shut and put a numbing agent over it. Now I felt it. I just didn't let it overwhelm me by turning it into a gaping hole.

Braden helped a lot with that.

My considerate bedfellow.

Among other things.

I smiled and turned in my chair to look at him in the dark room. His bare back was uncovered, the sheets drawn up to his waist, his long legs tangled in them in the middle of the bed. We didn't have "sides of the bed." Braden was a cuddler—he insisted we didn't need sides.

He'd had an exhausting day yesterday. He'd called me late, explaining how he'd gone from meeting to meeting, and then he had been pulled into some emergency at his nightclub Fire, which turned out not to be such an emergency but a case of crap management. When he'd returned home I must have already fallen asleep but I wasn't surprised that I woke up in his arms. Or that he'd been so tired he didn't wake up when I extricated myself from his embrace.

Gazing longingly at his muscular back and strong arms, I wanted to slip back into bed and wrap him around me. But looking at his sleeping face in profile I stopped myself. I was afraid I'd wake him up and he obviously needed his rest.

Standing up slowly so my chair wouldn't squeak, I tiptoed in the dark across to the bed and very gently eased myself back into it, checking constantly to make sure I hadn't woken him as I pulled the sheets back up over me. I lay down on my side, my hand tucked under my cheek, and I stared at him.

He was beautiful.

Just looking at him caused a different kind of ache inside of me.

This was a man who'd fought long and hard to keep me, even when I was bent on self-destructing us. This was a man who understood I could be difficult and stubborn and a little bit irrational (okay, maybe a freaking lot irrational), and still loved me. I wasn't the best at expressing my emotions. I'd spent so long guarding them so I wouldn't be vulnerable to heartbreak that even now I wasn't the gushy, emotional type of girl who could tell her boyfriend every single day that she loved him.

But Braden knew I loved him.

Sometimes I wondered, though, if he knew how much. I wondered if he knew that just watching him sleep made me scary happy, breathless even. I wondered if he knew that he was absolutely, without a doubt, everything to me.

Usually that wasn't something I'd want anyone to know because it meant admitting it out loud, and if I admitted it out loud and then lost that person, I couldn't pretend I'd never felt so much for them in the first place. But that was the old me. Dr. Pritchard, my therapist, wouldn't be happy with me if I held on to that kind of thinking.

I wouldn't be happy with me.

Worse, Braden wouldn't be happy with me.

I snuggled a little closer, just needing to feel the heat from his body against my skin. My eyes dropped to his mouth, his beautiful mouth, which said and did a lot of nice things to me.

I was everything to Braden. I knew this because he told me so. He never made me doubt how much I meant to him.

"Is there a reason you're over there and I'm over here?" he suddenly muttered, his eyes still shut.

I'd jerked back at the sound of his voice but was now smiling as I slid closer. "You're awake," I whispered, wrapping my arm around his waist, entwining my legs with his as he draped a strong arm over my back and snuggled me against his firm chest. I sighed. Content.

"I've been awake for the past ten minutes, waiting for you to get your arse back in beside me."

I snorted at his disgruntled tone.

His warm hand slid down over my back, caressing my butt before smoothing back up my spine. "You get what you needed to get down?"

"Mmm-hmm. Finished my chapter."

"Good, babe. Now go back to sleep."

I smirked against his chest. "Okay, caveman."

A minute or so passed and just as Braden was drifting back off I whispered, "You're my everything. You know that, right?"

His arm tensed around me at my words and then I found myself pushed back, his eyes boring intensely into mine. After his search was done, his sleepy mouth curled up at the corners. "You don't need to sweet-talk me to get sex, babe."

My eyes smiled. "Well, that kind of knowledge could have saved me months of uncomfortable expressions of love."

Wide-awake now, Braden tightened his arms around me and as he flipped onto his back he hauled me with him so I was sprawled across his chest, my legs straddling his hips. A note of seriousness entered his gaze as he drew his thumb across my mouth. A shiver rippled through me and I loved that he excited me so much. "I know how you feel about me. I feel the same way. You never have to worry that you don't tell me enough, okay?"

There he went again, being all perceptive to the point of being creepy psychic mind reader guy. "You're creepy psychic mind reader guy."

He raised an eyebrow. "Creepy?"

"In a hot way."

"There's a hot way to be creepy?"

"Slide your hand south and creepy will certainly become hot."

Braden's teeth flashed in the dark, his wicked smile jump-starting my heart. His hand drifted south, down my back, over my pert ass that he liked so much, and under my nightdress.

"Am I hot now?" he asked, his voice low and rumbling with arousal as his fingers slipped beneath my panties.

I arched into his touch, bracing my hands on his chest. "Baby, you don't know how to be anything else."

My words jacked Braden up, his torso lifting from the bed, so I found myself sitting in his lap, our chests pressed close, his arms holding me tight. His lips brushed gently over mine as he shifted me so his erection throbbed between my legs. "You're killing me with compliments."

I shrugged, my reply whispered against his mouth. "I just wanted you to know that just because I don't say it all the time doesn't mean I don't feel it."

This time he kissed me, tongue and all, deep and wet. When he pulled back for air, he promised me, "I know." His hands pushed at my nightgown until he caught the hem and tugged it up over my head. Braden's heated gaze moved over my naked body and I abruptly found myself on my back as he pushed down his pajama bottoms. "Believe me, I know."

The wind was beating against my back and the sad gray clouds above me were giving me this apologetic little pout. When I'd left the flat this morning the sun had been out and I'd dressed weather-appropriate. I had on a thin T-shirt and my best pair of black skinny jeans. Now it was threatening rain and I was shivering in my shirt, wondering how I'd managed to let myself be talked into the trek I was on and trying not to be as pissed as I was feeling.

After the emotionally fueled sex Braden and I had had early this morning, I was a little surprised to find him so distracted when we got up. Sure, he was tired from lack of sleep, but that had never stopped him from paying attention to what I had to say. However, he'd hurried into a shower, shooed me (yes, shooed!) me out of our bedroom while he got dressed, given me a quick kiss, told me Ellie wanted to spend the day with me and I should call her, and then hurried out of the flat.

It left me feeling confused. I felt like I was missing something.

Instead of sitting at home on a Saturday, stewing over it, I'd let Ellie talk me into accompanying her. Sometimes she'd get something in her head that she just had to have or had to do and she'd drag me all over the city to these obscure little shops. This time I'd let her talk me into the thirty-minute walk to Bruntsfield. Way back in my pre-Carmichael years I used to live in Bruntsfield. It was this kitschy little area of the city with kitschy little shops. It was popular with students. I'd say I missed it but it hadn't come with an adorably annoying best friend like Ellie or her brother Braden, the man who was currently driving me to distraction.

The journey to Bruntsfield had a purpose. Or at least that's what Ellie told me. Apparently she'd passed this little clothing boutique that had on sale "the most gorgeous vintage shoes ever" and she was kicking herself for not buying them. We were back, trying to find the shop and hopefully the shoes.

"Are you even listening to me?" Ellie asked, a teasing smile in her voice as she studied me, her short blond hair blowing into her face.

"Of course." I really was listening. Mostly. I knew the discussion pertained to our friend Jo and her new boyfriend, Cameron. "You were telling me you think Cam is moving pretty fast with Jo?" I asked it with a slight hint of a question in my tone, since I wasn't too sure if that was the point she'd been trying to make.

"A little. Don't you?"

Absolutely. "Uh-huh." And I did. However, my gut told me Cam was a good guy. "But I don't think it's a bad thing. In fact, I pretty much think he's the best thing that could have ever happened to her."

Ellie shrugged. "I like him. I do. I just don't want Jo to get hurt."

I raised an eyebrow at her. "Since when did you get so . . . normal?"

"Normal?" She glared at me. "You mean unromantic? I do realize there are times when romance needs to take a back burner to reality. Jo's had it tough. As much as I think Cam's great and as much as I'm rooting for them, I hope he really is going to be there for her. Taking her home to meet his parents this weekend? He's telling her he's serious. I hope he means it."

Although Ellie's caution surprised me, I understood where she was coming from. Our friend Jo had been messed around by too many guys because she'd chosen them for the wrong reason. Struggling to look after her little brother and her alcoholic mother, Jo always chose men who had financial security. Cam wasn't one of those guys. He was a struggling graphic designer who'd gotten a job as a bartender alongside me and Jo at Club 39, this swanky little basement bar on George Street. The sparks had started flying as soon as they met, though, and Jo had finally set aside all her silly little dating rules to take a chance on a man who seemed to want her for *her*.

Despite understanding Ellie's reservations, I didn't share them, and finally I found myself being distracted from my own boyfriend as I tried to convince Ellie. "I think he's serious. I think they have a connection. There's no way to slow that down when you just fit with someone like that. If I hadn't been so stubborn with Braden, we probably would have been a done deal within a few weeks of meeting each other."

A mysterious, secretive smile flirted with Ellie's lips.

What the . . . ?

"What? Am I missing something? Did I say something funny?"

"No," she answered hurriedly, eyes drifting up over the old Evangelical church. Abruptly she stopped. "We're here."

"Where is here?" I looked around. There were no vintage shoes in sight.

Ellie glanced at her watch and then out at the traffic on the cross junction, then back at her watch, then back at the road . . .

"Ellie?" My heart started to thump as the day's events began to fall into place, like pieces of a puzzle. "What is going on?"

Her eyes were wide when they hit mine.

"Jesus C, Ellie, what is it? You're freaking me out."

For once, however, her lips were tightly sealed. Literally. They were pinched closed so tightly the color was bleeding from them. Her eyes swung back out to the road, and as I watched her shoulders deflate with relief, I followed her gaze.

She was smiling at an approaching black cab.

That excited, eyes-twinkling-bright-with-utter-joy smile swung my way. "I'm going to go now."

Uh . . .

I whirled around as she strode past me, heading back the way we'd just come.

Baffled, I threw my hands up. "Ellie?"

She was still grinning as she looked back at me over her shoulder. She pointed behind me and I turned back to see that the black cab had pulled up to the curb beside me.

The door swung open and I was greeted by a surprising but always very welcome sight.

My boyfriend.

"Braden?" I gave him a quizzical smile as he leaned toward me. He was wearing one of his fitted, expensive three-piece suits I loved. This one was a dark gray and was molded perfectly to his broad shoulders and fit physique. The sight of him sitting in the cab in that suit on this spot where we first met—

My heartbeat skittered to a stop as I finally processed the intensity in his gaze and the fact that the floor of the cab he was sitting in was strewn with dark red rose petals. *Fuckity, fuckity, shit, fuck.* His distraction this morning, his shooing me out of our room . . . it all added up, and the breath just whooshed right out of me at the realization of what this meant.

"Get in," he said, his voice low, brooking no argument.

Limbs trembling, I took his offered hand, ducked my head, and let him settle me close to him on the cab bench. "Braden, what is . . ." My words trailed off as he held up a gray suede ring box.

Everything around me stopped.

There was no cab, no rose petals, no nosy cabdriver grinning at us in the rearview mirror, no traffic going by . . . nothing but Braden and a ring box that symbolized so much to me.

Years ago I'd lost everything that meant anything to me.

Losing that left me lost.

Until Braden.

I'd given him the fight of his life when he'd tried to convince me that loving him was the best thing for the both of us, but when he won, when I eventually realized the truth in that, I knew our path wouldn't always be smooth. I'd thought if this moment ever came, I'd be searching for a brown paper bag to stem my panic attack. To my utter surprise, I felt no such thing. Yes, the fear was there. The fear of giving in . . . only to lose him to life's unpredictability. However, greater than the fear was my excitement. My excitement that this impossible, too-perceptive-for-his-own-good, arrogant, stubborn, kind, caring, sexy man was about to ask me to spend the rest of my life with him.

Braden's pale blue eyes shone with emotion as he flipped open the ring box to reveal an elegantly simple platinum band with a princess-cut diamond perched upon a raised prong with small diamonds nestled on either side of it.

It was so me.

Shit, he knew me so well. *Do not cry, do not cry!*

"Jocelyn—" His voice was rough, like he was struggling to get the words out. "You're my best friend. My everything. I love you and I want to be with you always. Marry me. I promise to try not to fuck it up if you promise to try not to fuck it up."

I burst out laughing, tears falling without my say-so as I nodded, completely unable to speak. Braden grinned huge and I reached for him, needing to feel his mouth on mine. My tears mingled with our heated kiss and when he finally let me go, we were both a little out of breath. He took hold of my trembling hand and slipped the ring on my finger. We both stared at the diamond glittering on my left hand. My stomach and heart were jumping all over the place.

Threading my fingers through his, I clasped his hand tight and stared into his beloved face.

"I love you," I whispered hoarsely. "You're my favorite person." The tears blurred in my eyes again. "And if you ever tell anyone I cried during this moment I will withhold sex for a year."

His warm, husky laughter spread through me as he wrapped his arms around me, hauling me close. I tightened my own arms around his shoulders, shivering with delicious anticipation as he murmured against my mouth, "I'd like to see you try."

Cocky, arrogant caveman. "Marriage will drive the cockiness right out of you," I murmured back.

"The only thing that'll drive the cockiness out of me is you faking an orgasm. And I don't see that happening anytime soon."

"Hmm." I nuzzled my nose against his, the tingling between my legs growing more insistent. "You've got a point there, Mr. Carmichael."

"Mr. Carmichael, I do believe I'm tipsy." I threw him a wonky smile over my shoulder as I turned the key in our door.

We'd just returned from having celebratory drinks with Ellie and Adam. Honestly, I think Braden and I would have preferred a quiet night in together on the evening of our engagement, but Ellie was having none of that, and Alistair, my colleague at Club 39, had given us two bottles of champagne on discount, so I wasn't complaining. It had been a fun night.

As I pushed the door open, I felt Braden's strong hands on my hips and his warm breath on my ear as he asked softly, "Tipsy or drunk?"

I grinned, stepping into our flat with him close at my back. "Tipsy."

It was true. I was feeling a little giddy and more talkative than usual, but my vision was clear and my coordination was intact.

"You sure?"

Turning around, I reached past him and shoved our door shut, leaning my breasts into his chest as I turned the lock. I was still grinning as I tipped my head back to meet his heated gaze. "If you're wondering if I'm sober enough to fuck but drunk enough for it to be especially hot, the answer is yes."

Braden fought a smile. "Have I ever told you how much I love that filthy mouth of yours?"

Yes, on many occasions. "Well, I hope so," I teased, "because it's going to be *your* filthy mouth for a long time to come." I smoothed my hand up over his hard chest. "Speaking of coming . . ."

His hand on my hip tightened, drawing my eyes back to his. To my surprise he'd gone from teasing to intense. I knew that look well. My fiancé was in the mood to play "caveman." I shivered, feeling my breasts swell with arousal. "Strip," he uttered quietly, deadly serious.

The tingles started. "Here?"

He nodded to the space in front of him, smack-bang in the middle of our hallway. "There."

"Okay," I agreed. "But I get to be bossy tomorrow."

The intensity in his eyes lightened for a second as he gave me a little nod of acquiescence. Of course he would acquiesce to that. My version of sexually bossy was insisting on being on top, and although it wasn't Braden's favorite sexual position, he certainly enjoyed it and the view.

Eyes locked, I took a few careful steps backward until there was enough distance between us for him to enjoy the show. I shrugged out of my light blazer first, letting it pool at my feet, and then I reached for the first button on my black sleeveless silk shirt.

"Everything but the ring," Braden murmured, his expression all smoldering as he leaned back against our front door, crossing his arms over his chest, and one ankle over the other. His pose said casual, possibly even bored. His eyes, however, were burning my not-even-naked-yet skin.

I shivered at his command, my own gaze dropping to the glitter on the fourth finger of my left hand. Braden had a possessive streak. He hadn't even known he had one until he met me. The thought of me with someone else cut him, just like the thought of him with someone else cut me. It was part of the undeniable connection between us. More than that, I'd made it hard for him to win me over. That had not been intentional, believe me. I got the impression, however, that winning me over not only brought Braden peace, but it made him feel a bit like a conqueror. Not that he would ever admit it, but I knew my fiancé, and he definitely had that caveman mentality.

Thus, I knew that having me stand before him, wearing nothing but the symbol of my promise to be only his for the rest of always, was a huge turn-on for him. And that meant it was a huge turn-on for me.

My fingers drifted from my buttoned shirt to the studs in my ears. I took them out and reached over to the sideboard, the sound of metal clinking against wood as I dropped them there. I then removed the necklace I was wearing, followed by my watch. Once all the jewelry but the ring was off, I went back to my shirt.

Braden's pale eyes were already blazing.

I kept mine on him as I slowly unbuttoned my shirt, shrugging my shoulders so the fabric would slip down my arms and flutter to the ground.

The zip on my pencil skirt was next. I slid it down in increments, enjoying the way the muscle in Braden's jaw flexed at the sound. My eyes lowered.

He was hard already.

My nipples tightened and I felt my breath hitch with anticipation.

Once my skirt fell to the ground, I stepped out of it, marveling at my own stability. I was still tipsy, and tipsy, four-inch heels, and good balance usually didn't go hand in hand. Thankfully, I kept my grace and I bent down to slip the heels off. Flat on my feet, I lifted my eyes to watch Braden again as I reached behind me for the clasp of my bra. I unhooked it but slowly peeled the straps down, teasing the fabric away from my body.

Goose bumps erupted over my breasts and areolas, my nipples hardening to little points. Braden's hard-on pressed against his suit pants and I hid a pleased smile. For someone who had dated a lot of women with small chests, Braden certainly was obsessed with my D-cups. He had gone from being a leg man to a boob man.

Not that he didn't like my legs, because he definitely liked those too.

Unconsciously I licked my lips, watching his eyes flare as I gently pushed down my panties. They were damp with my arousal. I was dying for Braden to touch me, to feel how wet I was with only his eyes on my body.

"Now what?" I asked quietly, my voice thick.

His eyes burned a path that touched every inch of me. "Let down your hair."

I smirked at him as I reached up and unpinned my hair, letting the mass of waves fall heavily down my back. I threw the pins on the sideboard and massaged my head, my breasts rising provocatively with the movement. "And now?"

He stood up from the door, his relaxed pose gone as he replied in his low, rumbling tones, "Now walk into the bedroom, lie on your back on the bed, stretch your arms above your head, spread your legs, and prepare to take me. Hard and deep."

Desire shot through my belly and straight to my core at the imagery. I had to admit I loved how confident and commanding Braden was in bed. Still, I couldn't allow him to be too bossy. "If I'm spreading my legs for you, I want your mouth between them before anything else."

He gave me a slight smile and a knowing nod. "Deal."

"Deal." I smiled saucily back at him and turned around, feeling a surge of empowerment at the sound of his indrawn breath.

As I walked toward our bedroom he said, "Later, I want you on your stomach and that gorgeous arse in the air."

"First your mouth," I replied before disappearing inside our room.

My heart was beating fast with excitement as I crawled onto our cool sheets, reached across, and flicked on the bedside lamp before turning on my back, stretching my arms above my head, and spreading my legs.

My whole body shivered at being in such a position.

Eyes on the door, my pulse raced as Braden appeared in the doorway.

"Fuck," he breathed, moving toward me, stripping much more quickly out of his clothes than I had done. "How did I get so fucking lucky?"

"You were a very good boy this year," I teased.

He smiled devilishly in the low light as he pushed his pants and boxer briefs down. My hungry gaze settled on his huge, throbbing erection as he moved onto the bed, his beautiful hands sliding up my spread legs. "And have you been a good girl, Jocelyn?"

I tilted my hips up, telling him silently I wanted his mouth on me and I wanted it on me now before I combusted. "Yes," I breathed. "I haven't made any grown men cry this year. I'd call it an improvement upon last. Now give me your tongue."

His hands gripped my thighs. "Who's in charge here?"

pite having started the teasing, I was losing patience. I knew one
) speed things up. "Just put your mouth on me, Braden, please."

His growl was the last thing I heard before his head descended and
is tongue parted my labia. I rocked against it, feeling the build start as
he circled my clit over and over before sucking it between his lips. My
panted pleas for more filled the apartment, my fingers curling into the
sheets as his tongue drew down and entered me.

"Braden," I gasped, my hands automatically reaching for his hair.

This halted him immediately. "Hands back," he demanded, looking
up at me with fire in his eyes.

I instantly did what he asked and he returned to tormenting me.

Just when I was on the brink of orgasm, he stopped.

"What are you doing?" I panted as he moved up my body. He'd
promised me his mouth first.

He threaded his fingers through mine, holding my hands firmly to
the mattress. I felt his thumb rub over my engagement ring as our eyes
held. "I want the first time you come as my fiancée to be around my cock."

My inner muscles squeezed and my reaction was surprisingly docile.
"Okay."

As his mouth moved over mine, he thrust into me.

It was hard. It was deep. And it was beautiful.

Just like always.

CHAPTER 2

Mission Accomplished

"I'm thinking of quitting Club 39," I called out to Braden from the bedroom. He'd gotten home from work earlier than usual and was in the kitchen, making us coffee.

"Why?" he called back. "I thought you liked it."

I closed my laptop, deciding to go back later to the chapter I was working on. It wasn't very often that Braden finished a workday at five o'clock, and I was determined to take advantage of that fact.

Wandering into the kitchen, I drew to a stop at the sight of the table. Braden's laptop was open, surrounded by papers and clippings. "Um . . ." I looked up at him as he stirred sugar into his coffee. "I'm sick of missing out on the weekends with you, and Jo's leaving, so . . ." I gestured to the table. "What's all this?"

He handed me my coffee. "Wedding plans."

"Wedding plans?"

Braden sat down in front of his laptop and nodded at me to take the seat beside him. "I said I'd organize this thing and you said you'd help. I'm not finalizing anything until I get your opinion."

Since I was more than grateful he'd decided to take over the wedding plans from Ellie, who was determined to pinkify our wedding, I had agreed to help Braden. Sipping my coffee, I sat down and stared at everything. It didn't look like much, but our decisions were worth thousands of pounds, so we needed to be sure. We'd decided to split the wedding costs, which I thought was very evolved of my fiancé, considering his tendency toward caveman mentality.

"So what have we got?"

"The church is booked, but we have to make a decision on the reception venue." Braden turned the laptop toward me. "I like the Balmoral Hotel. I've priced it. What do you think?"

I was looking over the PDF the hotel had sent him when our doorbell rang, followed by the sound of it opening. That meant it was either Ellie or Adam.

"It's me!" Ellie called. "Before I come any farther, are you both dressed?"

Laughing, I assured her we were. Somewhere along the way she'd gotten the impression that Braden and I didn't do anything together but have wild monkey sex.

His sister appeared in the doorway, smiling broadly. She held up a bag of delicious-smelling food. "Braden told me about the wedding plans. I brought Indian!"

"Even though I fired you from the wedding plans, I'm going to let you stay because you brought takeout." I slid out of my seat to help her plate up the food.

"I know." She smiled sheepishly. "But it's exciting. I just wanted to be here to see what decisions you make."

"No refuting those decisions," Braden muttered, eyeing her sternly. "That's why I ended up as the wedding planner in the first place."

"I'll be good," she promised. "Oh, I brought you these." She shoved a white plastic bag at me as I fumbled with a plate.

"What is it?" I asked warily.

"Candles." Ellie shrugged out of her jacket. "This place is so bare since I moved out. I thought those might make it a bit homier."

Sharing an amused look with Braden, I put the bag on the counter.

Ellie was known to like clutter. Her idea of bare wasn't a normal person's idea of bare. "We're minimalist. But thanks."

"Ooh," Ellie cooed over Braden's shoulder as she tilted the laptop screen. "The Balmoral? What do you think, Joss?"

"I think it's beautiful," I replied honestly, having already decided after looking at the photos that I was just going to agree to Braden's ideas. It would make the process a lot less of a headache, and it wasn't like we didn't share the same taste.

"Yeah?" he asked.

"Definitely." I approached him with a plate of curry and rice, my eyes dipping to the floor. My gaze caught on Ellie's feet. I tried and failed not to smile as I asked Els, "Sweetie, have you looked at your feet lately?"

Wrinkling her nose in confusion, Ellie looked down. She sighed. "Bugger."

Curious, Braden looked down too after accepting his plate from me and immediately choked on his bite of curry.

I laughed.

Ellie was wearing two different shoes. They were flats of a similar style, but one was definitely brown and the other black. "I've been wandering all day over New Town like this."

"I doubt many people noticed your feet, Els."

She kicked off her shoes and we all settled around the table, eating and planning. Well, Braden had done all the planning, so it was mostly just me nodding my head to his suggestions and covering Ellie's mouth when she got too vocal in her opinions about the flowers.

We were just winding down when Ellie's phone rang. It was Adam, requesting her company, although from the way she blushed I doubted the request was that polite or lacking in sexual innuendo.

She got up hurriedly, giving me a smile and her brother a kiss on the cheek. "This was fun. Thanks for letting me crash it. Speak soon!" She floated out of the kitchen, in her mind already out of the flat and with Adam.

"Tell Adam I said hey!" I called to her.

"Will do!" The door slammed in her wake.

I pushed my plate away, cupping my chin in my palm as I smiled at Braden. "Thank you for doing all this."

"You're welcome." His smile turned into a yawn. He ran a hand through his hair, looking exhausted. "The only thing left to plan is the hen and stag nights."

A hen party was what the Brits called a bachelorette party, and a stag night a bachelor party. "Won't Ellie and Adam be organizing those?"

"Aye, at least that's something."

I huffed. "That's okay for you to say. I doubt Adam is going to arrange an elegant tea party for yours."

"Nah." Braden grinned. "Casino night."

I pouted. "I want a casino night."

"Have a casino night. I'll get Adam to nudge Ellie in the right direction."

"We can't end up in the same place for our parties."

Braden leaned toward me, his gaze curious. "Why not?"

Surprised by the question, since I thought the answer was pretty straightforward, I blinked a few times. "Uh, because it's supposed to be a symbolic evening where we celebrate our last night of singledom."

"But we're not single. We're married without the certificate. Let's change the symbolism of it. We'll celebrate together. We'll celebrate how we mean to go on for the rest of our lives."

I loved the way he looked at me. So full of . . . *everything*. "You could charm the pants off absolutely anyone," I told him quietly.

He smirked. "I take it that means you like the idea?"

"I love the idea. I love everything you've said. But I know Ellie's excited about this, so we're going to give our friends what they want."

"Adam mentioned strippers," Braden warned me, his eyes twinkling.

"If Adam books a stripper for you, I'll force Ellie to book a stripper for me."

Chuckling, Braden relaxed back in his chair. "Let's agree to no strippers."

I raised my glass of water and waited for Braden to do the same. "To no strippers."

"To no strippers," he repeated.

"And let's just make that a motto for our marriage."

Laughing, Braden nodded. "I can guarantee it."

I gestured to our plans and gave him a smile. "So are we done for the night? Can we lounge in front of a movie now?"

"Definitely."

Together, we cleaned our dishes and cleared the wedding plans away. Half an hour later we lay on the sofa together, my head on Braden's chest, his arm around my back, as we watched an action movie on pay-per-view.

Forty minutes in, I tilted my head back to look into his face and said, "Sometimes I can't believe that I get to do this with you for the rest of my life."

Surprised at my sentiment, Braden looked at me, eyes glittering with amusement. "What? Watch a movie?"

"Yes," I answered honestly. "Lie in your arms and watch a crappy movie. It might seem simple to other people, but it's everything to me."

The amusement left his expression, quickly replaced with something far more intense as he reached up to stroke my cheek with his thumb. "I'm glad you're quitting the bar."

"You are?"

"Yeah. I've never liked you working there, and I miss you at the weekend."

"Why didn't you say anything?"

"Because you seemed happy. It's sort of my life mission to make sure you stay that way," he teased.

I grinned. "Gotcha. Well, mission accomplished. I have lots of new friends, so I don't need the bar for a social life anymore. And I want to concentrate on my writing and on us. I'll hand in my resignation this week."

Braden nodded and squeezed me closer. "Sounds good, babe."

Snuggling into him, I let out a contented sigh and turned my gaze back on the movie. "Pfft." I mocked the screen as we soaked in each other's warmth. "Like a cop would start shooting in a public place like that. What is this crap we're watching?"

"Something about 'everything to you,' I believe."

"Hmmph. Well, it will be if we become a little more discerning in our rental choices. Oh, God." I groaned at the screen. "This guy is a tool."

"Jocelyn?" Braden tightened his arm around me and I looked up at him to find him grinning. "Just so you know, this is everything to me too." He bent down to give me a sweet kiss before turning back to the television. "Perhaps minus the commentary from the peanut gallery."

CHAPTER 3

The Wedding

Clark, Ellie's stepdad, and thus father figure to Braden and me, tucked my arm through his and patted my hand in a comforting way.

At the gesture, I glanced sharply at his kind face. "What? Do I look nervous?"

He smiled softly at me. "A little."

"I don't want to look nervous," I whispered back.

Although his mouth didn't laugh, his eyes definitely did. "Just take a deep breath."

We were standing out of view of the double doors that had opened up onto the red-carpeted aisle of the church, and my bridesmaids were already walking up it. It was nearly my turn.

I couldn't believe our wedding day was here already. It didn't seem that long ago that I'd woken up the day after my engagement with Ellie knocking on my door with a bunch of bridal magazines in her hands. Although I'd had moments of doubt, I'd fiercely fought them back.

It was kind of a shock then to find myself standing at the bottom of the aisle, freaking out.

Fuckity, fuckity, fuck, fuck.

Deep breaths.

I could not have a panic attack. I wanted to spend the rest of my life with Braden. The problem was I was terrified I was going to find some way to fuck it up. Even after months of proving to myself that I was capable of being in a committed, loving relationship, I was still afraid. I was afraid I was going to hurt him.

"What if I mess this up?" I murmured.

Clark's hand tightened over mine. "It's not going to be perfect because no marriage is. You're going to fight, clash, say things you don't mean . . . When you love someone, these things can happen. But, Joss"—he dipped his head to meet my gaze—"the good you two will have together will always outweigh any bad." He smiled. "And I think Braden's proved there's not much you can do to chase him off."

"True." I squeezed his hand and took a shuddering, deep breath. "Thanks."

"You're welcome. Now let's do this."

The strains of the guitarist and violinist grew louder, their beautiful instrumental version of Paul Weller's "You Do Something to Me" sending shivers down my spine. We stepped out onto the carpeted aisle of the church and at first all I could see was the flowers, the guests who had turned to stare at me, their approving smiles, their curiosity. At the squeeze of Clark's hand around mine where I clutched fiercely to my bouquet of white lilies interspersed with thin reeds of champagne gold, I began to focus. My eyes found my bridesmaids, Ellie, Hannah, Jo, Rhian, and Liv, dressed in their floor-length champagne-colored dresses, looking elegant and happy. The closer we got I could see Ellie was tearing up. I caught Elodie in the front pews along with Cam; Cole; Jo's uncle Mick; his new girlfriend, Dee; Cam's best friends, Nate and Peetie; and Peetie's girlfriend, Lyn. I didn't have any family here, so we'd decided not to divide the room into groom and bride sides. Still, there were just my colleagues from Club 39. Everyone else was associates or friends of Braden and the Nichols family. And of course his vapid socialite mother hadn't turned up. She was feeling under the weather. More like we'd met at Christmas last year and I'd made my distaste for her clear and vice versa.

My eyes found Adam and Dec, who were standing on the opposite side of the altar. They wore the same as Clark and Braden—what was referred to as a Prince Charlie gray jacket and matching three-button waistcoat. Their silk champagne ties were intricately knotted against their dark gray shirts, and because the Carmichaels were associated with the Stewart clan they were wearing a subdued Stewart gray tartan. Adam's kind, bolstering smile finally made me look at Braden.

I almost faltered on the walk up the aisle.

The look in his eyes was like a physical pressure on my chest. The love there caused my throat to constrict and I leaned more heavily against Clark as I attempted to float toward Braden in my wedding dress. My dress was simple. It was strapless with a heart-shaped neckline, and the upper half of the bodice was ivory with crystal beading and lace. The finest white silk chiffon pulled across the bodice in a tight drape, fitted to my waist. From my hips the layers of chiffon, shot through with silver, fell to the floor in simple elegance. I could tell by the look on Braden's face as Clark and I approached that he liked the dress.

Still shaking, I kissed Clark on the cheek, so honored that he'd walked me down the aisle in the absence of my father. I thanked him sincerely, almost choking up at the sheen of wetness in his eyes as he handed me over to Braden.

Instead of turning me to face the minister, Braden took my hand and pulled me into his side, his eyes burning intensely into mine. His head lowered and I felt his warm breath on my ear. "You look stunning, sweetheart, but deep breaths. This is just you and me."

"Tell that to the hundred people sitting behind us," I told him a little shakily.

He chuckled, pressing an amused kiss to my mouth.

When he pulled back, Braden's expression was reassuring as he murmured against my lips, "I love you, you love me, our family loves us and they're right here beside us. Nothing else matters. So no fears for the future, no fear that you'll fuck it up beyond repair. Life isn't perfect, we aren't perfect, but I'm telling you now, Jocelyn, we're indestructible. Stop shaking, and just marry me."

I pressed deeper into him, brushing my mouth over his. "You got it."

The minister cleared his throat, drawing our attention back to the ceremony and out of the little bubble we'd been in. I heard our guests titter behind us and the music stopped.

This was it.

There was something a little surreal about sitting next to Braden at the top table, my wedding band shining prettily against my engagement ring, everyone referring to us as husband and wife, and people being cute and calling me Mrs. Carmichael instead of Joss. It was weird. But the good kind of weird.

Our wedding reception *was* held at the Balmoral Hotel. The banquet suite was this grand hall with tall ceilings, pillars, elaborate chandeliers, and huge arched windows with views of Edinburgh Castle. It was stunning and classy and beyond anything I'd ever imagined for this moment.

After dinner, Clark tapped his champagne flute, drawing everyone's attention as he stood up to give his father-of-the-bride speech. I'd told him he didn't have to, but he said he wanted to. And watching how comfortable he was as he lifted the mic, I knew that as a university professor, he wasn't daunted by having to talk to a large crowd of people.

I didn't know what to expect from Clark's speech. I felt butterflies in my stomach as he smiled down at Braden and me.

"Braden is one of the finest men I know," he began. "He's a son to me. And he's a friend. So when it became clear that what he and Joss had together was something special, I couldn't have been more delighted for him. Because Jocelyn is without a doubt one of the strongest, most extraordinary young women I have ever met."

Jesus C.

I swallowed past the hard lump of emotion in my throat, leaning into

Braden, who automatically wrapped an arm around me without my even having to ask.

"I am sorry that your dad can't be here with you on this day, Joss," Clark continued, his voice low with enough emotion that it threatened to spill the tears over my lids, "but I know that he would be so proud of you for the woman you've become, and so happy that you've found a family in Braden, and in us. I was honored to walk down the aisle with you for him. Tonight"—he lifted his glass, turning to our guests—"I ask you all to raise your glasses to my son and daughter. To Braden and Jocelyn."

As everyone said our names in unison, lifting their glasses to us, I fought back the tears. Just barely.

The truth was I did feel part of the Nichols family. But it was kind of more than a little beautiful that the Nichols family thought of me as part of them.

Next to stand up was Adam as Braden's best man. He lightened the mood, joking about his and Braden's past, about Braden's reputation with women, how different he was with me, and how much fun he had had watching Braden work his ass off to get me. Upon Adam raising his glass to us in a toast, Braden kissed me, waited for his best man to sit down, and then stood up himself.

I looked up at him. More than anything I wanted the reception to be over; I wanted to not be the center of attention anymore. Mostly, I just really wanted to be alone in a room with my new husband.

Braden stood tall in his kilt, looking every inch the delectable Scotsman, and he stared out at the room with a familiar air of intimidating confidence. "Over two and a half years ago," he began, his voice deep, his tone serious, "I shared a taxi with a complete stranger. A young woman with a smart mouth and"—he smirked down at me—"a great pair of legs."

The guests chuckled as I shook my head slightly at him, a small smile playing on my lips.

"I knew then"—Braden spoke loudly to the guests, but his eyes remained on my face—"that my life had changed. I just wouldn't know until you walked out of Ellie's bathroom without a towel on how happy I was with that coming change."

I rolled my eyes, feeling my cheeks burn as everyone laughed.

"I'm not joking." Braden turned back to them. "The second time we met, Jocelyn was starkers. Up to that point it was the best day of my life.

"Even after being caught in the buff she gave me attitude." He grinned down at me again, and I felt the warmth inside my chest turn into a burn of overwhelming emotion. "You've challenged me since the day I met you. No woman has ever challenged me more. Nor made me laugh harder. There is not a moment that passes where you don't make me feel more alive than I ever thought I could, and today you gave me something I thought was lost a long time ago for the both of us. You've given me peace, babe. You've given me everything." The timbre of his voice had deepened with emotion and I swear to God I was close to bawling my eyes out as he lifted a glass of champagne from the table and raised it in the air. "To my wife, Mrs. Jocelyn Carmichael."

The guests repeated his words as he bent down to me, his eyes warming at the sight of my unshed tears. "To my wife," he murmured again, cupping a hand behind my nape to bring my lips to his.

As I made the rounds of the reception, attempting to stop to chat with all our guests, the unsettled fluttering in my stomach called a cease-fire and I was feeling a lot more relaxed. The champagne was helping.

I stood by Braden's side while he introduced me to distant cousins, relatives of Elodie and Clark's, friends and business associates. We'd nearly made our way through the entire guest list when we came upon Jenna and Ed. Jenna was one of Ellie's friends and Ed was her husband. When I'd first met Ellie, Jenna and Ed had been a close part of their group, but after their wedding Jenna fell pregnant and for some reason they stopped hanging out with a lot of their friends. Ellie had been a little put out at first, but Jenna seemed more content to spend time with married friends who had children, and I reassured Ellie that she hadn't done anything wrong. Some people were just like that. Still, it was nice to see them.

"Joss, you look beautiful," Jenna said, giving me a tight hug.

"Who's looking after Andrew?" Braden asked, referring to their baby boy.

Ed grinned. "I talked my parents into babysitting tonight. We haven't had a real night off in God knows how long. I actually had to talk Jenna into coming here, into leaving him."

Jenna frowned at her husband. "I don't like leaving him. There's nothing wrong with that."

Hearing the bite in her tone, I shot Braden a look that suggested we should move along.

He nodded at me and turned to speak, but Jenna cut him off by jerking me toward her.

"So, when are you thinking about having a baby, Joss?"

The Jenna I knew was chilled out, down-to-earth, *uninquisitive.* Whoever this was, I wanted to kill her. "Uh . . ." I glanced around the room, looking for help.

"We haven't had a proper talk about it," Braden offered, his hand resting on my lower back in a way that suggested he knew I was about to run away. "But kids are definitely in the plans."

My shoulders tensed, my stomach cramped, and the champagne sloshed unpleasantly in my stomach.

This morning I'd been optimistic as I'd looked at myself in the mirror. I'd thought about my mini meltdown I'd had a few weeks ago when Braden first mentioned having kids. I'd thought that it was something I'd get over.

But once again, the thought of children paralyzed me.

Worse, the thought that Braden believed they were in our immediate future paralyzed me.

I couldn't have kids yet. I wasn't emotionally ready for that. No. I definitely wasn't. "There's Alistair and his girlfriend." I pointed over Ed's shoulder. "I better go say hello." I pulled away from Braden's touch and almost sprinted away from them, two steps from Alistair when a strong arm wrapped itself around my waist and hauled me about.

I crashed against Braden's hard chest, blinking up at him in surprise. "Was that necessary?"

My husband frowned at me. "Something's wrong."

"No." I shook my head in denial. "I just . . . Jenna bothers me a little now. I just wanted to get away."

As Braden searched my face, I wondered if he believed me. In the end I didn't know if he did or not. But he let it go, bending down to press a soft kiss to my mouth. It was our wedding.

No fighting allowed.

CHAPTER 4

The Honeymoon—Part 1

"Does that say what I think it says?" I asked, leaning my cheek against Braden's upper arm. With his hand clasped in mine, I stood next to him before the departures board in Edinburgh Airport, quietly excited about our honeymoon to Hawaii, and trying not to be deflated by the information on the board.

Braden gave my hand a squeeze. "Yeah. Delayed."

Our flight was delayed by a few hours, which meant being stuck in the airport. Luckily Edinburgh wasn't grimy. In fact it was kind of shiny. We were surrounded by designer shops, restaurants, and an old-fashioned oval bar at one end of the international departure lounge. Still. It was an airport. As human beings we were genetically predisposed to hate them.

My husband let go of my hand to curl me into his side, his hand resting low on my opposite hip. "Do you want to wait in the first-class lounge, get a drink there, or do you want to get a drink at the bar we just passed?" he asked, absentmindedly pressing a kiss to my temple.

This was one of the things I loved about him. After having starved myself of affection for years, it had taken me a while to get used to Braden's tactility, but now I wouldn't know what to do without it. His affection for me came so easily, he touched and kissed me all the time, even when he was half-distracted. I'd gone from being uncomfortable with it to expecting and coveting it.

"Here." I nodded, taking a reluctant step back. "I need to go to the restroom. I'll meet you at the bar."

After I peed, I stood in front of the washstand, searching my face in the mirror. After the wedding Ellie had said I looked different. I hadn't known what she meant at the time but gazing at my reflection I had to wonder if it was something different about my eyes. They were gunmetal gray and tip tilted. They weren't warm, friendly eyes. I knew from photographs of myself that my eyes tended to come off intense, sometimes kind of bedroomy, even though most of the time it was unintended. The warmth entered them only in photographs that caught me laughing. However, staring into my eyes now I could see a shift in them. The intensity hadn't totally left them, but there was definitely something new reflected there. Something good. Something warm.

I ducked my head, smiling as I dried my hands.

My eyes dropped to my legs. They were bare in the sundress I'd chosen to wear in anticipation of the hot weather in Hawaii. My olive skin was ready to deepen to a tan as I lazed by the pool for the next fourteen days. Vacations weren't something I ever bothered about because I'd lost all that stuff when I lost my family. However, I'd never been somewhere like Hawaii before. And I'd be there with my hot husband.

Braden and I had busy lives. This was the first time we'd spend a solid fourteen nights just enjoying each other's company with no interference from work or friends or family. Days by the pool or on the beach, and nights of hot, energetic sex.

My smile turned smug.

Strolling out into the departure lounge I wandered slowly toward the bar, glad at least not to be rushing around in a sweaty, flustered mess as some late passengers were. Eyes drifting over the quiet bar, I found Braden's back facing me as he sat on a stool. The female bartender kept throwing him surreptitious looks as she pretended to be busy.

Braden wasn't a classically handsome guy, but he was rugged, sexy, very tall, well built, and he wore his suits better than an Armani model. Since the moment I'd met him I'd been struck by his natural confidence. It was hot. Even when it veered into arrogance, annoying the hell out of me, I still found it hot.

So it didn't surprise me that a lot of people found my husband attractive too.

When we first started our no-strings-attached relationship I'd pretended not to care when I saw other women flirting with Braden. Afterwards, once I stopped putting him through the wringer and admitted that I loved him as much as he loved me, I'd found it hard not to chase the obnoxious flirts away from him. In fact, sometimes I lost my cool and wasn't very diplomatic about telling those women that Braden was mine. Of course, he found this amusing and a total turn-on.

Not so much when the shoe was on the other foot.

Still, as our relationship had grown, so had my confidence in us, as had Braden's, and together we'd mellowed somewhat. Not completely, but enough that right at that moment I didn't want to stride up to Braden in front of the bartender and stake my claim.

I was going on my honeymoon. I'd taken a huge leap toward putting my issues behind me by even getting married. I was in a damn good mood.

I wanted to play.

Hiding my mischievous grin, I smoothed my features until they were perfectly blank and sauntered toward the bar. However, I didn't take the stool next to Braden. My heels clicked on the hard, shiny floor as I sashayed onto a stool that gave me a good view of Braden . . . on the opposite side of the bar.

"What can I get you to drink?" the female bartender asked politely.

"A glass of red wine, please."

I felt Braden's eyes on me as the bartender turned to get me my drink. Flicking my gaze his way I saw his eyes dancing at my mischief.

He knew exactly what I was up to.

The bartender slid the glass of wine toward me as I attempted not to laugh.

"Hi," I greeted him casually down the bar. "I'm Jocelyn."

He eyed me for a moment with those intimidating, gorgeous pale blue eyes of his. And then he obviously decided to just go with it when he slipped off his stool and made his way over to the one next to mine. He gave me a smirk as he reached out to take my hand in his. I felt his thumb rub over my wedding rings. "Braden."

I gave him a small, flirty smile. "Can I get you a drink?"

"I really should say no." He held up his ring finger with his wedding band on it. "I'm married."

"Oh?" I hid my smile, feeling a rush of excitement go through me at our little game. "I didn't realize. I take it your wife isn't with you this evening?"

"Apparently not," Braden answered, his mouth twitching with definite amusement now as our eyes met.

Pretending we weren't at a bar in an airport but at home, my gaze turned heated in a way Braden understood. "That's good news."

"It is?" He glanced down at my left hand.

I turned my diamond so that it sparkled beautifully in the light. "Yeah, I'm married too."

Eyes staring into mine again, Braden's reply was thick with a sincerity that somehow managed to be as emotional as it was sexual. "He's a very lucky man."

I tilted my head flirtatiously. "That's what I hear."

Braden leaned into me and I knew he didn't even realize he was doing it.

My smile grew. "So *can* I buy you a drink?"

"I actually think I'd like that."

The air was charged between us as he waited for my next move. I looked away and called the bartender over. After ordering him a drink, I waited to see if Braden would keep up the pretense with me.

"So, where are you traveling to?" he asked, his tone amused but slightly rough.

I didn't have to look into his eyes to know he was aroused, but I looked anyway because I needed to.

"Hawaii." I pressed my leg against his thigh, wishing we weren't in a public place. I wanted his hands on me.

"Me too."

"Your drink." The bartender slid Braden's drink to him.

We took hold of our glasses and clinked them together.

"Business or pleasure?" I asked saucily.

"Oh, I'm definitely hoping pleasure," he said as I took a sip of wine.

Slowly I licked a drop of wine off my lower lip, triumphing over the suffocated groan it produced from the back of Braden's throat. "That makes two of us."

Eyes still on my mouth, Braden's hand tightened around his glass. "My wife wouldn't be too pleased to find a strange woman flirting with me at a bar."

"Is your wife the jealous type?" I teased.

My amusement was stifled by the intensity of our connection as our eyes held. "She can be," he murmured.

I sucked in a breath. "Are you the jealous type?"

"Abso-fucking-lutely."

I smiled. "So you're both a little possessive, huh? I don't suppose she'd like what I'm thinking about doing to you, either."

Braden ran his gaze over my face before replying. "No, she definitely wouldn't. But, you know . . . you remind me of my wife."

Chuckling, I pressed my leg harder against his. "Yeah, you remind me of my husband."

Eyes glittering with laughter, Braden asked, "What would your husband do if he were here right now?"

"Well, he's a little possessive himself, but a gentleman, so he'd be polite when he made it perfectly clear to you that I wasn't yours to flirt with."

"Smart man."

"That's what I hear."

His laughter always made me feel like I'd won something.

I stared, relishing everything about him. Slowly, his laughter faded and we were staring at each other like we were about to start going at it right there on the bar. "Then what would he do?"

The tingling between my legs flared to life and I felt my breasts swell against the thin material of my sundress. Shifting closer, inhaling his familiar scent, I wished we were somewhere we could do something about being this turned on.

"Jocelyn?"

I cleared my throat. "He'd probably kiss me. And then he'd insist on hearing about all the things I'm going to do to him when I get him alone."

Braden's eyes instantly darkened, his head descending toward mine before I could blink. His kiss was deep and hot, and I found myself clinging to him. I shivered at the feel of his hand sliding discreetly under my dress, his touch making my nipples pebble with need. I gasped, breaking our kiss.

Barely cognizant of anything around us, I drew his ear to my lips. "As soon as I get you alone," I whispered, "I'm going to let you fuck me as hard as you want." I then went on to elaborate until my breathing grew hitched and the muscles in Braden's jaw were tense.

In fact, every line of his body was. His hand was clamped tightly around my thigh. I dropped my forehead to the side of his jaw, trying to control my breathing.

After a few very long minutes, Braden's grip on me loosened and he pulled me into a hug. I nuzzled his neck, feeling the burn of unsatisfied lust. "Sorry," I murmured against his skin.

He stroked my back in comfort. "Don't be. It was hot."

"Too hot for an airport."

I felt him shake slightly, obviously laughing. "Probably. I'll take care of you later, though. And, hey, at least you don't have a hard-on in public."

My turn to laugh now. Pulling back I glanced down at his lap, hidden under the bar, to see he was not lying. Glancing up into his face, I said, "Your mother. Naked."

A look of distaste took the heat out of his eyes.

He took a swig of whiskey and eventually muttered, "Thanks."

I looked down at his lap. The erection was gone.

Trying not to smile, I looked away casually and asked airily, "What do you want to talk about until the flight is called?"

"Cold wind. Sleet. The ugly doorman at Club 39. Porridge."

I burst out laughing. "You mean anything that won't give you an erection?"

He smiled at me, his eyes roaming my face lovingly. "Maybe we should just stop talking altogether. And put a bag over your head. And cover your legs."

"Just don't look at me."

"I can still smell you."

"I could move."

"Dare move away from me and I'll put you over my knee, Wife."

"That doesn't sound so bad."

Braden cut me a dirty look and I covered my mouth with my hand so he couldn't see my grin.

We were silent for a few minutes and then I leaned my elbow on the bar, resting my chin on my palm as I told him softly. "I'm loving our honeymoon so far."

He took my other hand in his. "I am too."

I shifted closer to him, resting my knee against his. "Do you want to wait in the first-class lounge? I'm sure it's filled with stuffy businessmen types who will certainly shatter the very sexual mood we've got going on here with all their stiff-upper-lippishness."

Braden's mouth twitched. "Stiff-upper-lippishness?"

"Stiff-upper-lippishness."

He nodded, laughing softly now as he got off the stool and helped me down from mine. Wrapping an arm around my waist, he said as he walked us toward the lounge, "Maybe we should stop using the word 'stiff,' since apparently being married to you means losing control over my body and any self-respect I might have."

"Grounds for divorce?" I teased as we showed our boarding passes to an airline attendant at the lounge doors.

"Grounds for a marathon fucking," he answered dryly, not caring that the airline attendant had turned purple at his reply. "You won't be able to walk for a while when I'm done with you," he continued, gently guiding me into the lounge, leaving the gasping attendant behind.

I determinedly tried not to show my embarrassment, as I was used to him sometimes saying hot, blush-inducing shit like that to me in public. The key was to not let him know he'd flustered me.

"I'm happy with that as long as we're talking *multiple* orgasms."

Three suits turned their heads toward me from the small bar in the lounge, their eyebrows raised.

Braden and I stopped and I felt his hand squeeze my hip. "We're going to get thrown out of the first-class lounge."

I smirked. "You started it."

"Actually, *you* started it."

I heaved a sigh and glanced at my watch. "Well, unfortunately we've got about ten hours before we can finish it."

Not looking too happy about that, Braden swept the room with his eyes, a glint entering them when they stalled on the restroom door.

"No," I said immediately.

He threw me that boyish grin that was very, very difficult to resist.

Shit, fuckity, shit, fuck.

"Braden, no," I hissed. "There's no way we can do that discreetly."

"So?"

"Braden—"

He let go of my hand. "Follow me in after a minute."

I grabbed his hand back. "No, we're acting like teenagers."

His grin widened as he leaned his head toward mine. "We're on our fucking honeymoon, babe. That's the whole point." He glanced back at the restroom and squeezed my hand. "I'll go and then you follow me after a minute. Pretend I'm ill or something and you're just checking up on me."

Before I could refuse again, Braden strolled away from me, disappearing into the restroom.

I looked around the lounge. There were only four men in it and one woman and not one of them was watching me. Still . . .

"I've never been in first class," I muttered, "and I'm going to get thrown out before I even hit the plane."

Frowning, I waited what felt like a millennium but was only a few seconds, then wandered over to the restroom door. Feeling like a total idiot, I knocked on it and asked, "Baby, you feeling okay?"

When no answer came, I slipped inside like I was a concerned spouse and nothing more.

We so couldn't be fooling anyone with that crap.

Once inside I discovered there were separate doors for men and women.

I knocked on the men's, and my knuckles had barely left the door before it opened wide enough for Braden to haul me inside, slam it shut, lock it, and press my back against it.

I slid my arms around his shoulders as he leaned his hard body into mine. "We're so getting kicked out of first class."

His hand caressed my ass before coasting down my thigh and then back up under my dress. His talented fingers slipped beneath my panties and he whispered hoarsely, "Then let's make it worth it."

CHAPTER 5

The Honeymoon—Part 2

From the moment we stepped into our plantation-style villa in the luxury resort Braden had booked for our honeymoon in the Pacific, I didn't want to go home.

A few minutes' walk from the main resort, up a landscaped, lamp-lit path, sat our villa. A huge deck with a plunge pool and a cabana overlooked the ocean. Inside was a huge, airy, beautiful living room with white furniture I was almost afraid to touch and a gorgeous bedroom with a walk-in closet and a four-poster bed draped in white voile. The final touch of beauty was the marble bathroom, which must have been bigger than Olivia's entire flat.

Braden and I had been there for three days. We'd spent our days lazing by our private pool, enjoying spectacular views that filled me with the kind of contentment I wished every day would bring. At night we'd choose from one of the three amazing restaurants, head off to one of the bars to have a few drinks, and then we'd head back to the villa, where we made love for hours.

Best. Honeymoon. Ever.

For a change of scenery, we'd left the villa on the third day and grabbed a couple of sun loungers under a cabana on the beach. Every now and then a courteous staff member would approach us and ask us if we wanted anything to eat or drink while we both lay there, reading on our e-readers and soaking up the sun.

Just an hour earlier, Braden had finally managed to coax me into the sea. I hadn't been too keen on entering the water, but it was so beautiful, its tranquility and Braden's persistence finally got to me and I decided to wade in.

Lulled by Braden's patience, I was completely taken off guard when he dunked me.

You did not dunk Jocelyn Butler Carmichael and get away with it.

Thus commenced a water wrestling match that had children swimming out of the way to avoid us while their parents shot us dirty looks. Braden was cracking up. He would be. He was winning. It was only after he lifted me and cannonballed me into the water so hard that I almost lost my bikini top in front of the entire resort that he decided the game had hit its peak. I spluttered and coughed as he swam up to me and retied the strings of the bikini around my neck.

"Happy now?" I'd slapped water at him, throwing him a mock dirty look.

He'd kissed my neck and wrapped his arms around my waist under the water. "Always."

There really was no way to be crabby at an answer like that, so I'd let him off the hook, letting him lead me back to our loungers, where we were currently drying out. Braden was lying on his stomach, his tall body too big for the lounger, but he seemed comfortable enough. I had turned onto my side, watching him doze in the afternoon sun. Everything about the moment was perfect—the sound of the water lapping gently to shore, the cries of happy kids, the soft chatter of couples, the smell of suntan lotion and seawater, the tiny flutter of my husband's lashes as he dreamed beside me . . .

I should be terrified.

It was a lot to lose.

That fear niggled at me and I determinedly pushed it back out.

"Why are you staring at me?" Braden asked quietly, eyes still closed against the sun.

"I've never seen you relax for this long. It's nice."

"It's actually nice to be relaxing."

Raising an eyebrow, I teased, "You're telling me you're not missing keeping busy?"

His eyes opened slowly, blinking in the sunlight. He shifted up onto his elbows. "I have uninterrupted access to my wife for the next two weeks. Believe me, I'm not missing a thing."

A delicious shiver rippled through me and I leaned over so my mouth was almost touching his. "Them be fighting words." I brushed my lips against his. "I think someone is trying to get into my bikini bottoms."

"What do you mean, 'trying'?" Braden grunted as he cupped his hand around the nape of my neck so his next words were muffled against my lips. I got the gist of it, though. Some cocky comment about having un-hindered access to what was beneath my bikini bottoms. I bit his lip gently in retaliation, which only made him groan into my mouth and deepen the kiss.

As always, the world disappeared and I found myself balancing pre-cariously half on, half off my lounger, clinging to Braden's biceps as he drugged me with kisses that still knocked me off-kilter.

The sound of a sharp, playful child's scream broke us apart, and I smiled ruefully as Braden brushed my lower lip with his thumb. He glanced over in the direction of the scream and my gaze followed his. A young boy was chasing what appeared to be his little sister, his delighted laughter and her mock-screams annoying a young couple that lazed near the spot of their antics.

Braden looked back at me. "We can return to the villa, lie by the pool, if the kids are bothering you."

Frowning, I shook my head. I didn't mind the kids. Their excitement and joy only added to the overall atmosphere of the resort. "The villa seems a long way away right now and I honestly don't mind the kids."

My reply caused Braden to tilt his head and ask in obvious surprise, "Really?"

I snorted and lay back down. "Really."

"Well, that's a good sign."

The smile in his voice for some reason caused my stomach to flip. And not in a good way. "What's a good sign?" I asked, not really sure if I wanted an answer or not.

"You. Not minding the kids."

Yup, I definitely didn't want the answer.

"If you don't mind the noise of other people's kids, then you'll definitely not mind the noise our kids will make."

He might as well have wrapped his hand around my throat. I tried to swallow past the constriction his words had caused and I knew I had to get up, walk away, do anything, so that I didn't have a panic attack. So it wouldn't be obvious he'd freaked me out, I waited as long as I could before saying, "You want a drink? I'm going to get a drink."

I felt his eyes on me as I shoved on my flip-flops and sunglasses, hurriedly tying my sarong around my waist. Not once did I look at him, but I knew from his quiet "Sure, babe," that I hadn't been successful in keeping my freak-out to myself.

The whole time the bartender was making up our drinks, the guilt clawed at me. I'd left Braden back there wondering what the hell had happened and if I was shutting him out. That was something I'd promised never to do to him again, and I had to keep that promise. With that in mind I took the drinks back to him and settled back onto my lounger.

After a few minutes of quiet I said, "Let's go lie on our deck at the villa."

Glancing over at Braden, I found him staring at me, his brow puckered in consternation. "Why?"

I held his gaze and answered pointedly, "Because I like the peace and quiet. I want that for a while yet."

Braden drew in a deep breath and slowly sat up to face me. Resting his elbows on his knees he leaned in and asked, "But one day you'll want the noise, right?"

My heart started to bang around in my chest at the thought, but I nodded tremulously. "Yes. But I just want it to be us for a while."

Something dark that I didn't quite understand flashed in his eyes, but he kissed me, cupping my face in his hand, and he murmured against my lips, "All right."

When he pulled back his eyes moved behind me and he frowned at something. Feeling like there was definitely something off about his acquiescence, I asked, "You okay?"

I got a reassuring nod and he pulled back, standing up to gather his things.

Turning, I did the same, shoving my flip-flops back on and bending down to find my e-reader, which I'd hidden under my lounger in the shade.

"Do you fucking mind?" Braden snapped.

My head jerked up at his tone and my eyes collided with my neighbor. He was an older man, perhaps in his late forties, early fifties; he wasn't with anyone, and he was staring in mild amusement over my shoulder at my husband. His eyes flicked to my boobs and then back to Braden.

Great.

I didn't need to look around to know that Braden's sharp aggression had drawn all of our neighbors' gazes.

"Your woman is very beautiful," the stranger commented in a thick accent.

I tensed and quickly turned around to face Braden, giving him a shake of my head. "Leave it."

He didn't leave it.

He gently took hold of my wrist and pulled me behind him so he could lean into the stranger's face. "My wife is very beautiful. But to you she's invisible. Understood?"

The stranger nodded. "Understood."

I understood too. I understood I was mortified.

Not wanting to cause more of a scene, I let Braden hold my hand as we walked up the beach, but as soon as we were out of sight I tugged out of his hold.

"You're pissed off." He sighed.

"Yes, I'm pissed off. There was no need to speak to him that way. It was embarrassing. You were peeing all over me."

I heard his snort of laughter but didn't dare look at him because I was afraid I'd kill him.

"That arsehole was ogling you all fucking day and ignoring every warning look I gave him. I don't appreciate another man staring at my wife like he's imagining fucking her when he knows I'm standing right fucking there."

"Is dropping the f-bomb three times really necessary?"

He sighed, *heavily* this time. "You're still pissed off."

Yes, I'm still pissed off. "I'm confused. You overreacted and you know you overreacted. I'm just thinking the overreaction had nothing to do with that idiot staring at my breasts."

Instead of agreeing, instead of telling me he was bothered by the unspoken issue that was on our minds, Braden shook his head impatiently and began striding toward the villa without me.

Dinner was a quiet affair.

I'd spent the rest of the afternoon lying by the pool with my headphones on, listening to Bastille, while Braden took a walk around the resort. By the time he came back I was in the shower. When I got out of the shower to get ready for dinner, he got in. Afterward, he attempted conversation with me. I grunted answers at him, not so much pissed at him anymore as pissed that he'd given me reason on our honeymoon to be pissed at him.

He'd scowled at me when I strode out of the walk-in wearing a figure-hugging blue dress. The fabric was a thin, stretchy jersey, so although it covered me, it pretty much left little to the imagination. It was a hot dress and I'd bought it for my hot husband.

At the time the thought hadn't been to torture him, but I was pissed, so now it *was* about torturing him.

Our walk to dinner was quiet. The night before, we'd dined at the Oceanview, a restaurant situated on the beach. Tonight I silently led us to the Great Room in the main house of the resort.

That silence reigned all through dinner.

The tension between us was thickening and I could tell Braden was losing patience with it. Or with me, rather.

Deciding the best thing for us was to get a good night's sleep and put the stupid argument behind us, I quietly suggested we leave out drinks tonight and just return to the room. I took his brusque nod as agreement.

Dinner over, we strolled back to the villa. I kicked off my heels to sink my feet into sand, only reluctantly trailing back onto the landscaped path to our villa, all the while secretly dreading a quiet night in with annoyed silence and no sex.

Inside the air-conditioned heaven, I threw my heels to the floor and padded on cool tiles toward the bedroom. I heard Braden's footsteps behind me seconds before I found myself jerked back against his body.

I gasped at the sudden movement, my breath hitching as one hand coasted roughly up my stomach to cup my breast, while the other gripped my hair lightly. Braden gently tugged my head back, exposing my neck. Those familiar shivers tingled through me as he kneaded my breast and pressed hot, wet kisses down the side of my neck.

Just as abruptly as he'd pulled me to him, Braden pushed me forward until I hit the bed. My torso bowed over the end of it as he nudged my legs open with his feet. In the same motion he slipped his hands under the hem of my tight dress and shoved the fabric upward until it hit me at midback, baring my ass to him.

By this point my breathing was as hot and heavy as his.

Cool air touched my skin as Braden tugged my panties down. I stepped out of them and kicked them aside, quickly widening my stance again and biting back a moan at the feel of Braden's erection pressing against my ass.

His fingers dug into my hips as he tormented me with the promise of him.

"Braden," I whispered, his name a plea.

He rubbed his cock between my legs, teasing me mercilessly. I rocked back and forth against him until it was too much.

"Please," I whimpered.

I lost his heat, but it was quickly replaced with his strong fingers slipping between my legs and deep inside.

He groaned to find me already wet, and just like that his fingers were gone, a zip sounded, and his cock slammed into me. I whimpered again, my chest pressed to the bed, my hands gripping the sheets as Braden held me tightly by the hips and thrust roughly in and out of me.

The build started quickly and I found myself rearing back against his dick in desperation.

"Harder?" he growled.

"Harder," I gasped.

He pumped harder into me and just as I was on the cusp of coming, he pulled out, flipped me over onto my back as if I weighed nothing, and took hold of the hem of my dress, pulling it up over my head. He tossed it aside, hurriedly removing his own shirt before gripping my thighs, spreading my legs, and jerking me toward him so only my back was pressed against the bed.

Our eyes locked and we both moaned as he slid back inside me.

As he fucked me toward oblivion we kept our eyes locked, the connection heightening our arousal, shooting us toward climax faster. His panting breaths and my gasps filled the night air until his cock drove deep, shattering the fragile tension inside of me.

"Jocelyn," he groaned as my inner muscles squeezed him. He jerked hard against me, shuddering as I felt his release inside of me.

After a moment he wrapped his arms around me and I wrapped my limbs around him, allowing him to drag me farther up the mattress. As soon as I was fully on the bed, Braden collapsed over me, his mouth nuzzling my neck as I squeezed my thighs around his waist and stroked the damp skin of his muscular back.

He lifted his head to press a soft kiss to my mouth, asking as he pulled back, "Did I make my point?"

I raised an eyebrow. "That you're still a freaking caveman? Yes."

His chuckle made him shake against me in a way I loved and I was disappointed when he rolled off of me. That disappointment quickly faded when he pulled me into his side.

"I should clean up," I murmured.

"In a bit." He sighed. "I didn't like the way that guy was looking at you. I made a point."

"It was embarrassing . . . also . . . was it really just about the guy? Honestly?"

"Of course." He kissed my hair. "And . . . maybe the bikini. Maybe you shouldn't wear that one again."

"I thought you liked that bikini."

"I do like that bikini, but so does every man on this resort with a dick he knows how to use."

"Hmm, okay."

He snorted. "You know I hate to point this out since we're speaking again, but you've acted worse when you've found women flirting with me."

Dammit.

"Okay, true. But I thought we were trying to be grown-ups now that we're married."

"Is that what you were doing at the airport?" He chuckled again. "Being a grown-up?"

He had a freaking answer for everything. "Fine," I grumbled. "I'm sorry for being pissed. I guess I was a little edgy . . ."

"Because I mentioned kids again?"

I tensed against him. "I just . . . I want to wait a few years, but I don't want you to be upset about that. I don't want to disappoint you."

I quickly found myself on my back, my husband braced over me. "You're not," he promised. "We'll wait."

In answer I kissed him.

Thinking back on it, I realized I kissed him so I didn't have to see the disappointment he was trying so hard to hide.

CHAPTER 6

The Homecoming

Something nudged me into consciousness, but I refused to open my eyes. Instead I kept my face buried in the warm, familiar skin of Braden's neck.

It became clear that the thing that woke me was my husband. I could feel him trying to extricate himself from my hold as gently as possible.

I held on tighter.

Braden shook against me, his voice rumbling with laughter as he asked, "Am I not allowed out of bed this morning?"

"Nope," I mumbled against his skin. "If you move, I'll have to move. If I have to move it means facing the fact that we're no longer in Hawaii. I don't know if I'm ready to deal with that."

He rolled me onto my back, laughing at the fact that I refused to open my eyes. "So is the plan to stay here forever?"

"Yes."

"That might become a problem."

I shook my head against the pillows. "I don't foresee any problems. It's a sound plan."

"Well." Braden sighed. "We will eventually start to smell. And needing the toilet might become a problem. And with your issues with flatulence—"

I punched him on the arm, opening my eyes so I didn't miss. My husband fought me off, laughing as though he was the funniest man on earth.

"One year," I growled at him. "All I'm asking for is one year without you bringing that up!"

"You getting adorably embarrassed when you fart in front of me?"

After throwing him a narrow-eyed glare, I rolled off the bed. "I am not adorable," I snapped, stomping out of the bedroom.

"You're fucking adorable!" he called to me as I made my way into the kitchen. I rolled my eyes. Braden could be pretty adorable too, but he'd like it even less than me if I told him that.

I reached for the kettle, about to call through and ask if he wanted coffee when a wave of nausea caught me completely off guard and I found myself swaying against the counter.

"Babe, you okay?" Braden rushed to my side, grasping my hip in his hand.

Breathing through my nose, I fought to hold the sickness down. After a moment I rested my forehead on his chest. "I don't feel so great."

I felt his lips in my hair. "Jet lag. Sit down." He ushered me toward the kitchen table and planted my ass at it. As he began to make the coffee the nausea rose again and I knew this time there was no fighting it. Without a word I shot up from the table and rushed out of the kitchen to the bathroom.

The toilet lid was barely up when I heaved everything inside me into it.

"Jocelyn?" I could feel Braden behind me.

I waved him off. "I'll be okay."

Sensing I wanted privacy, he left.

After waiting a few moments to make sure the nausea was dealt with, I got up on shaky legs and washed and brushed my teeth. Seeing my pale face in the mirror, I glowered at it.

Home sweet freaking home.

"Better?" Braden asked as I entered the kitchen.

"Yeah," I smiled, gratefully accepting the coffee. "Much."

Sitting in the waiting room, listening to people cough and sniffle, I felt breakable for the first time in a long time. My chest was heavy, like the air all around me was much too thin, and my thoughts were too harried, making me feel like a crazy person.

I just needed to know one way or the other.

If I knew . . .

I just needed to know.

"Jocelyn Carmichael, Room Five, Dr. Orr."

Here we go. . . .

Braden was sprawled in the armchair, his shirtsleeves rolled up, his tie askew, and he was staring at the television as if he was only half-interested in what was going on.

He'd had a long day at work.

I'd just had a long day.

And now I was terrified. Terrified of answers. Terrified of fucking up. Of losing . . . *everything.*

We'd been home from Hawaii for almost four weeks and I'd been hiding my sickness from Braden ever since that first morning. After a visit to the doctor's that day I was almost sure of the diagnosis, but I wouldn't know until they called to confirm the results.

"Jocelyn?"

I turned my head to look at my husband.

He was frowning at me in concern. "What's wrong, babe?"

"Nothing," I whispered, my heart beating hard against my ribs.

"It's not nothing. You've been quiet. Tense."

I shrugged. "I'm just on tenterhooks waiting to see if that lit agent in New York wants to sign me."

After months and months of rejection letters I'd gotten an e-mail back from a lit agent from one of the top agencies in New York asking me for the first three chapters of my manuscript. When she e-mailed back asking to see the rest, I couldn't believe it. I'd been trying not to get my hopes up, and my secret worry was helping keep my mind off it.

"You sure that's all it is?"

I felt sick lying to him. So I didn't. Instead I got up slowly and sauntered over to him, climbing onto the chair with him so I was straddling his lap. "I wish we were back in Hawaii," I whispered against his mouth as he ran his hands down my back. "I wish, I wish, I wish . . ."

"Joc—"

I cut him off with a hard, desperate kiss, and that night I made love to my husband as if I knew what was coming next could change everything.

Ellie and Adam had fallen in love with a property on Scotland Street, and in a bid to distract me, I let Ellie set up another viewing so that the girls and I could check it out. Jo, Liv, and I followed Ellie and her estate agent around the Georgian-period flat, and for a while Ellie's exuberance and exciting plans for the flat took me away from my problem. For a moment I even forgot I had a problem, so it was a bit like being jolted back into reality when my phone rang as we were leaving the property.

My stomach churned.

I gave the girls an apologetic smile and wandered off to the side to answer.

"Mrs. Carmichael, this is Dr. Orr. We have the results of your pregnancy test. I'd like to be the first to say congratulations. You are pregnant."

The world skewed to the left.

"Mrs. Carmichael?" Dr. Orr asked softly. And then his tone became more careful. "I'll give you time to process the news. Please do call as soon as possible to arrange your prenatal care. We'll set you up with your first appointment with a midwife."

"Thanks," I somehow managed to mutter, every nerve trembling like I'd just run the New York City Marathon. I hung up and slipped my phone back into my purse.

I could hear someone trying to speak to me.

I'm going to be a mom.

Someone was questioning me.

I'm going to have a child.

"Joss, what is it?" Ellie's frantic voice finally broke through.

I looked up at her, her pretty face a little fuzzy in my distress. "I have to go."

"Go where?"

"I just—" The world skewed to the right. "I have to go."

"Seriously, you're scaring me. What's going on?"

She was scared? *She* was scared! "Ellie," I snapped, feeling an invisible hand wrap around my throat and constrict my breathing. "Just . . ." I stopped cold at the unadulterated concern in her eyes. "I need to be alone for a little while."

I waited for her nod and as soon as I got it, as soon as I knew she understood I wasn't shutting her out—I just needed space—I turned on my heel and started walking, almost running, toward the castle.

Somehow a thirty-minute walk was over in a flash. I was buying my ticket into the castle, I was hoofing up the Lang Stairs, and striding up onto the elevated section of Edinburgh Castle where St. Margaret's Chapel was situated. And right outside the chapel was my place.

My place with the cannon, Mons Meg, and the best view of Edinburgh.

I leaned against the cannon for a moment, ignoring the tourists who were trying to get a photograph of it. Feeling its cool cast iron under my hand, I drew in a deep breath.

I was going to be a mom.

Limbs still quivering like a mess of jelly, I walked over to the parapet, leaned my elbows on the wall, and gazed out over my home.

Here was where I found my calm. For whatever reason, this place on Castle Hill allowed me to sort out my feelings, to process them, to deal with them. It was my special place. And I hadn't needed it in a while.

But now that I was going to be a mom . . . now, on top of having Braden and Ellie and all of my family and friends to lose, I had something miraculous to lose. My child.

The tears burned in my throat, the fear becoming something raw inside of me.

"Jocelyn?"

I whirled around at the sound of Braden's voice, knowing that everything I was feeling had to be written all over my face.

Ellie must have called him and he'd guessed exactly where I'd go.

Braden's features grew alarmed at the sight of me and he hurried toward me, gripping my arms in his hands. "Sweetheart, what happened?"

"I'm pregnant," I blurted out, the tears spilling down my cheeks.

Braden jerked back like I'd hit him. He stared at me for a long time, as if trying to figure me out. Just like that, he looked like he'd been punched in the gut. "So you came here?" he whispered incredulously.

I didn't know what that meant, but I realized quickly it didn't mean anything good.

"Braden—"

"Don't." He cut me off, turning from me. "Not here."

There was an uneasiness, a new fear, in leaving my place before I'd gotten a chance to work through everything in my head. I'd just wanted that chance before Braden and I . . .

We walked in tense silence back down the hill and out of the castle. Braden had a taxi waiting for us on the esplanade. I was so out of it I didn't even realize he hadn't touched me. He opened the door for me but he didn't put his hand on my arm to help me in. He didn't scoot near me once we were inside. I'd realize all this later, when my brain wasn't a tumult of thoughts and my stomach and chest weren't awash in too many feelings.

Not a word was spoken between us, not until the door to our flat was closed behind us and we stood facing each other in the kitchen.

Braden's features were hard in a way I didn't like. "You're pregnant with my child and that's such fucking awful news you go to the castle?"

I couldn't believe he thought . . . That wasn't it at all!

"Braden—"

"Are you happy or are you unhappy?" he snapped, his eyes glittering with desperation.

My heart was pounding so hard in my chest, I thought I might vomit. "Braden." My lips trembled, my nose stinging. "It's not that simple."

He jerked back again, with a pain in his eyes that he quickly banked. "Let me—"

I didn't get a chance to finish. He was out of the flat too fast.

Trembling, I sank into a chair. Not only hadn't I been given a chance to process my own feelings, I was left confused and afraid of Braden's. He was the kind of man who gave you a chance to explain, but he'd obviously taken my reaction to the pregnancy the wrong way, and now he was too hurt to listen.

I just needed to explain.

He *had* to listen.

It was late, but I left a message on Dr. Pritchard's work voice mail asking if I could schedule an appointment that week. Dr. Kathryn Pritchard was my therapist and she'd helped me come a long way in dealing with my post-traumatic stress disorder. She'd helped me grieve for my family and she'd helped me work through my fears. I hadn't scheduled a session with her in a while, but I needed someone impartial to talk to.

Braden stayed gone for hours. I got a text from Ellie asking me if I was okay. It was a dead giveaway that Braden had told Adam about my pregnancy and Ellie knew. She was trying to figure out how to deal with me. I knew this because normally she'd call me or even come around to the flat. A text for news this huge . . . Yeah, she didn't know how to handle my reaction.

Staring down at the photo of me with my family that Braden had framed and given me for Christmas, I tried to force my insides back together again. I gazed at Beth, my baby sister, who I held tight in my arms, and I attempted to do this by understanding exactly what it was I was feeling. The fear was coloring everything, I wasn't even sure that I was unhappy with the idea of being a mom. It was soon. Sooner than I'd wanted, but if I could just get past the fear, maybe I would see it wouldn't be such a bad thing. Not such a bad thing at all. This baby was a product of Braden and me. A part of him. A beautiful piece of him. A gift we'd given each other.

As much as I loved the makeshift family I'd created in Edinburgh, this was my chance at my very own family again.

That clawing pressure pushed and ripped at my chest, but I fought through it, taking deep, even breaths.

Now I just had to explain all this to Braden so he'd see I wasn't pulling another "Ellie moment," pushing him out when things got tough like I did when Ellie was diagnosed with a brain tumor. I just wanted him to understand what was going on inside of me.

See? I had come a long way.

I jumped at the sound of the door opening and shutting. My pulse throbbed harder beneath my skin as Braden's footsteps grew louder the closer he got to our bedroom.

He stood against the dark backdrop of the hall, the soft light in our bedroom barely casting him out of the shadow, but I could see his expression was tired. Grim, even.

I sat up, waiting.

"Today was supposed to be the happiest day of our lives."

Guilt gnawed at my stomach and I winced apologetically.

"I need an answer," he demanded softly. "I need to know if you're happy to be pregnant with my kid. After everything we've been through, I need that answer."

I shifted, reaching out to him. "Please, just let me explain. I'll—"

"Wrong answer," he uttered bitingly, his expression shutting down. "I can't believe you . . . after everything . . . that we're back here again." He turned, leaving me shocked, openmouthed as he stormed down our hall. A door slammed and I hopped off the bed and dashed into the hall to watch a light come on, shining under the guest bedroom door.

Tears choked me and I swallowed the hitch in my breathing as I tiptoed back into our bedroom. My husband and I had fought quite a few times in the last few years, but not once had Braden let it come between us. He always slept in our bed with me and he always pulled me close at night.

The hot tears slipped down my cheeks.

I'd hurt him.

And for the first time in a really long time, he'd hurt me too.

That whole night I tossed and turned, my eyes on the hallway. A big part of me wanted to go into our guest room and shake Braden awake and make him listen to me, but the more I lay there and the more I thought everything over, I thought it best to let him sleep so we could have a rational conversation in the morning.

Except I was exhausted from lack of sleep. I got up just before six in the morning and sat in the kitchen, drinking coffee and attempting to read a book. Just before Braden's alarm was set to go off, I made some fresh coffee for him.

Not too long after, he wandered into the kitchen in his pajamas, his hair in disarray, and I ached with hurt and love as he avoided my eyes.

"I made you coffee," I told him quietly, trying to gauge whether or not this would soften him up.

"Thank you," he muttered, taking hold of the mug. He leaned against the counter, staring at the wall.

My stomach flip-flopped unpleasantly.

I had to explain so he'd stop thinking the worst of me.

"Braden—"

"I have to shower." He walked out of the kitchen abruptly.

"We need to talk!" I yelled at him angrily.

His answer was to slam the bathroom door.

This was a whole new side to my husband. And I did not like it one bit.

I got up, ready to do battle, when a knock at the door stopped me. That knock was followed by a key turning in the lock, and I knew then it was Ellie.

Bracing myself, I wondered if I'd be able to handle two of my favorite people being so mad at me. Three years ago that would have been a piece of cake. But these idiots had softened me up, whether I liked to admit it or not.

Ellie appeared in the kitchen doorway, her blue eyes instantly finding me.

Whatever she saw in my face made her pale and she came straight at me, arms wide open.

I relaxed into her hug, not even realizing until right then how much I needed it.

"I don't even know if I should say congratulations."

I tensed.

Ellie pulled back, peering at me cautiously. "Braden's really upset."

I couldn't speak. I wanted to. But I was afraid if I did I would scream.

"Look, I'm here, Joss." She rubbed my shoulder in comfort. "I'm here if you need me."

Swallowing past the gust of screams, I nodded and thanked her hoarsely.

We were quiet as I made her a cup of tea and we sat down at the table together. It occurred to me as we sat in silence that maybe if I told Ellie everything I was feeling, Braden would listen to her. I didn't know what was going on with my usually understanding and compassionate husband, but what I did know was that he was angrier than I'd ever seen him, and clearly unwilling to listen to anything I had to say. He might listen to Ellie.

I opened my mouth to speak when the sound of the bathroom door opening halted me. Both Ellie and I turned to watch for Braden and as he passed the doorway he gave his sister a taut nod of hello and continued on into the bedroom to get ready for work. On a Sunday.

Ellie turned to me, her eyes questioning.

I took her hand and squeezed it. "He slept in your old room last night," I whispered. "He's never done that before."

My friend's expression grew pained. "Joss . . . talk—"

Nausea hit me before Ellie could finish her sentence and I was up, bending over the kitchen sink. I felt her hands in my hair, holding it back. After spitting up the last of my morning sickness, I sank back against Els, glad for her comforting presence. A flicker of movement out of the corner of my eye drew my gaze and I froze at the sight of Braden staring at me, a muscle ticking in his jaw. He turned to Ellie. "Give Elodie my apologies for missing Sunday dinner. I'll be in meetings all day. And, uh"—he cut me a look before glancing back at his sister—"stay with her until she feels better."

Anger burned through me as Braden walked out of the flat, ignoring Ellie's shocked and questioning calls of his name.

Ellie's pitiful and sympathetic looks suddenly became painful rather than comforting.

I pulled out of Ellie's arms. "I'm sorry, hon. I just . . . I'm going back to bed."

She nodded carefully and let me go.

I couldn't sleep. I kept playing everything over and over in my head, trying to work out what to say to Braden first to make him stop and talk to me. I had it all planned, but dinner passed and he still didn't turn up.

Then evening.

I texted him and didn't get a reply. I called. No reply.

I texted Adam, but he wasn't with Adam.

Finally, just after two in the morning, our front door opened. Fury propelled me out of our bedroom and I stormed into the hall as Braden shut the door behind him. His eyes moved to me, but it was like he was staring right through me as he started toward the guest room.

Oh, no! Not again!

"Where have you been?" I snapped, grabbing hold of his arm so he'd look at me.

He jerked his arm away from me like he couldn't stand to be touched by me. "Out," he told me simply, his tone cutting. And then he disappeared into the guest room, not even aware that I probably looked like he'd run me over with a car.

I had theories as to why he was so angry. I knew he thought I didn't want his kid. I wondered if he was questioning everything about us. I wondered if he was scared. I wondered why he couldn't just tell me all that. I thought we had come further than that. No . . . I guess I'd just, probably unfairly, thought he'd see me through anything.

A long time ago he'd almost left me for good for shutting him out. And now *he* was shutting *me* out. He'd dived inside his head and he wouldn't let me near him.

He didn't even want me touching him, and that hurt and scared me so much I didn't want to feel anything. I'd sleep to help with that, but sleep was eluding me. Instead I shut myself in the bathroom and undressed. I switched on the shower and stepped into the freezing-cold water, allowing the shock to dissipate into numbness. My mind adrift, my hands covered the small of my stomach protectively, and I closed my eyes. I could be numb everywhere but there.

I thought I heard a muffled "Fuck" and it brought my eyes open just as Braden was sliding the shower door open. He reached in, his features like granite as he switched the nozzle to warm. His eyes cut to me. "Are you trying to catch fucking pneumonia?"

Chittering, I blanched. I hadn't been thinking. Obviously.

"Stay in there until you warm up," Braden snapped.

Where was my husband?

Everything I'd been feeling suddenly broke out of the numbness. All the fear, the guilt, the anger, the loneliness of the past few days, and most especially the hurt.

Braden jerked back, confusion and something like fear entering his expression.

But since this man was a stranger . . . I couldn't give a fuck how he felt.

I reached over, staring at him blankly, shut the shower door, and turned my back on him.

CHAPTER 7

Castle Hill

"It's been a while, Joss. What's been happening?" Dr. Pritchard asked in that careful voice of hers. She had mastered the art of not sounding concerned. Nor too breezy. Just calm. Soothing.

It used to bug the crap out of me. There was a time I would have given anything to hear her yell at her kids for some wrongdoing just so I could hear a little bit of raised blood pressure in her voice. I wanted proof she was human.

Now I knew she was human. She could be a little on the sarcastic side. That's probably why I liked her so much.

"Braden and I got married," I informed her quietly, my hands resting on my stomach.

She smiled. "Congratulations."

"Thanks."

Dr. Pritchard raised an eyebrow. She gave good eyebrow-raising. "Anything else?"

Easing into the reason for my visit, I avoided the subject altogether. "I got an agent." It was true. Dana had called at the beginning of the week and I'd signed with her. It should have been one of the most exciting moments of my life. "She has a publisher interested in my manuscript." Already. Again, it should have been one of the most exciting moments of my life.

"That's great news."

Dr. Pritchard also seemed to fear hyperbole and expressions of excitement. Again, another reason I liked her so much.

"I'm pregnant."

The good doctor was quiet for a moment as she processed my blurtage. "Is that why you're here?"

I nodded, trying to ignore the lump of tears in my throat as I thought over the last few days. Our home had been a silent, cold place recently. My whole life had. Ellie and Adam had refused to get in the middle, so they were staying out of it completely. I think Ellie must have talked Elodie into staying out of it too because I hadn't heard from her. I'd gotten tentative texts from my friends but no one wanted to bring the subject up. "It's slammed up this huge wall between me and Braden."

"It has or you have?"

"Actually, *he* has." I shrugged. "I was scared when I suspected I was pregnant. I was terrified when I found out that it was true. But I knew that wasn't all. I just . . . I had to get away, go to my place to process. Before I could, Braden got there, I told him, and he took one look at my face and assumed . . . the worst."

"The worst?"

"That I'm unhappy. That I don't want a child with him. He's so mad, so hurt, he wouldn't and still hasn't let me explain."

"And what would you tell him if he gave you the chance?"

My hands pressed tighter against my stomach. "That our kid means more to me than anything ever has before. That it scares me to feel that much for anyone. It always will. But that I'm working through it now. That I'm still scared, and I'm scared about screwing it all up, but that I want this with him. I just needed time to work out what I was feeling."

"And that was?"

I smiled at the irony. "So happy I was paralyzed."

"You still believe that everything good will be followed by bad?"

"I haven't for a long time." I shook my head. "But this is a huge deal. I had a relapse."

"Joss, you're allowed to feel this way. You recognized it and you're working through it. That's all anyone can ask."

We were quiet for a moment as I studied my wedding rings, twisting the bands on my finger. "He hurt me," I whispered, not wanting to admit it out loud.

"Braden?"

I nodded.

"He's not perfect, Joss. You've always known that he was a family man. It must be hard for him to wonder if he's married to a woman who could be unhappy about carrying her own child, his child."

"But he won't let me explain."

She cocked her head to the side, giving me a small, reassuring smile. "Maybe he's afraid to hear what you have to say. So make him listen."

"I would . . . but . . ."

"Joss—"

"When he's gone I blame myself," I admitted. "The way I reacted . . . I can see why he would feel this way, act this way. But when he's right in front of me, looking through me, not wanting me to touch him, unable to bear my touch, I almost hate him. I feel so alone." The tears spilled down my cheeks. "And he promised I wouldn't feel that way again."

Dr. Pritchard leaned over and pressed tissues into my hand, giving it a comforting squeeze as she did so. "You have to try to get past that feeling long enough to talk to him. This is a case of total miscommunication, and you two have come too far to let that derail you."

I nodded as I wiped the tears.

"And, Joss?"

"Yeah?"

She smiled kindly. "Congratulations."

She was the first person to say it to me in person, and although I understood it was my own fault that no one else had, it was still nice to hear it. "Thank you."

I shut down the laptop after having just bought up every self-help book Amazon had on being a first-time mom. After my session with Dr. Pritchard I'd come home to an empty apartment and gone into this hyper mode, cleaning and tidying, throwing things out. I'd also ignored reminders that Braden and I weren't sharing the same bed when I went into the guest room to measure it for nursery furniture and saw his stuff scattered everywhere. I stared around the room that would be the future nursery. I was thinking yellow or green for a color scheme since those were both gender neutral.

I'd then opened up my laptop to an e-mail from my new agent, telling me she'd sent off my manuscript to the publisher, and she would like me to start thinking up concepts for a new book. For a while I typed up notes for several ideas that I would come back to, to flesh out later.

And then I'd started freaking out that I knew nothing about being a mother and began an online shopping spree.

Nerves frayed, I stood in front of the mirror in our bedroom and lifted my T-shirt.

No bump yet.

I smoothed my hand over my stomach, thinking how weird it was that there was a little person inside of me whom I already loved beyond reason.

Now if only my husband would give me a chance to tell him that.

I glanced at the space between the window and the bed and wondered if there was room to put the baby's crib there for a while. I wanted him or her to be close to us. I already knew I'd find it difficult to sleep if I didn't know our kid was safe and at arm's reach.

After a few minutes of fruitless search for the measuring tape, I wandered back into the guest room to see if I'd left it in there. I found it on the bedside cabinet, but as I moved away, the address on a letter half-hidden under a book drew me up short.

With my heart beating obnoxiously loud, I slipped the letter out from under the novel and fear prickled my skin in cold shivers as I read it.

My fingers went numb and the letter fluttered out of my grasp to the floor.

It was a letter to Braden's tenants, asking them to vacate the premises in one month's time. It was his bachelor penthouse on the Meadows. The one he'd put up for rental when he moved in with me.

The one he could take back from tenants on short notice if he needed it for personal usage.

My doorbell rang.

A welcome distraction from the pure fear running cold in my veins.

"Liv?" I said, after I opened my front door, surprised to see her on my doorstep.

Olivia and I were good friends, but for some reason she wasn't the first person I expected to see. Jo and I were closer. Liv and I only knew each other because of Jo, but we'd quickly banded together as fellow Americans and book enthusiasts.

Liv's eyes washed over me in concern and I instantly tensed. I knew what she was seeing. Dark circles under my eyes because I hadn't been sleeping; a pale, icky complexion; and hair that was all over the place.

"Is Braden here?" she asked casually as she barged right past me and into the flat.

There was no need for barging. I welcomed her presence as long as we talked about anything else but Braden and my pregnancy.

"No, he's at work," I replied as I followed her into the kitchen.

When I got there she was already making coffee. She frowned at me. "You need to take better care of yourself."

"I've been busy." I hopped onto a different subject quickly. "A literary agent in New York now represents me."

Liv smiled in excitement. "She loved your book?"

"She loved my book."

"Joss, that's amazing."

I smiled back, knowing that out of everyone Liv would be the one to really get how cool it was. Liv was a librarian. Books were her passion.

When her eyes dipped to my stomach, uncertainty entering their depths, I cut off her obvious next question.

"She thinks I should start working on another."

To my relief, Liv let me get away with the distraction, listening to me yammer on about my different ideas as we settled in the sitting room with coffee and biscuits. Anything, *anything*, to forget the letter I'd just found.

I was in midsentence about this crazy dystopian idea I had that was completely not what my agent had in mind when she asked me to think up new concepts, when the front door opened.

Braden.

I felt my whole body lock with tension as I stared, waiting with this horrible sick feeling in my stomach, for him to appear in the doorway and crush me.

He appeared, looking just as tired as I felt, and stopped in the doorway. "Liv," he greeted her before glancing at me. His eyes instantly narrowed at the sight of me. "Did you sleep today?"

Are you leaving me? "I couldn't."

Appearing annoyed, he sighed. "You need to get some sleep." Tugging on his tie, he strode out of sight.

"Joss?" Liv's whispered anxiety brought my attention back to her. She looked so worried for me. "Girl, what are you doing?"

What am I doing? What am *I* doing? "Don't." She didn't know shit.

We sat in taut silence, sipping on coffee.

"I've got a late meeting with Adam," we heard Braden say as he wandered down the hall. Another lie. The front door slammed behind him. I flinched and desperately tried not to cry. This pregnancy was turning me into an emotional black hole.

"Oh, honey." Liv stood up as if she was coming to hug me.

I held up a hand to stop her. "You hug me and I won't stop crying. And I need to not cry."

She froze, looking helpless and angry that she felt that way.

I knew exactly how she felt. "It's not me." I needed someone other than Dr. Pritchard to know that. "I haven't shut him out. I'm just having a really hard time right now and I ruined it. I ruined this for him."

"He's the one not talking to you?"

"He talks. But it's . . . it's like he can barely stand to be in the same room as me. He hasn't asked me how I feel about it now that the shock has worn off. He doesn't want to know. He doesn't want me to touch him. . . ."

"I'm sorry, Joss."

"He's never been like that." The letter came back to mind and I felt that panic swallow me whole. "I think I've fucked up." My hysterical laughter immediately turned into loud, hard sobbing I couldn't control. I couldn't even be mortified that I was breaking down. I was crying too hard to care.

I felt Liv's comforting warmth as she gently nudged me aside on the chair and snuggled in beside me so she could pull me into her arms. And then everything just disappeared as I let her comfort me, the tears soaking her shirt a testament to the fact that I wasn't alone.

I wasn't aware of the shaking stopping, or the tears drawing to a halt. Everything was just black as I finally fell into the deep relief of sleep.

My eyes felt crusty as I tried to open them, consciousness coming to me, and with it the feel of a heavy warmth resting on my waist.

As I opened my peepers I realized they felt swollen and that's when I remembered why. I tensed at the memory of crying in Liv's arms at the same time I looked into my husband's sleeping face.

The heavy warmth across my waist was his arm.

We were lying in bed together.

I didn't know how we'd gotten there.

I started to cry again.

Braden's arm tightened around me and through the blur of tears I saw I'd woken him.

"I wasn't not happy," I whispered, licking the salt water off my lips. "I was so happy I was terrified."

His warm fingers brushed my chin and I felt the gentle pressure of his touch as he tilted my head back so I would meet his questioning eyes. "Terrified?"

I nodded. "Just because I've come a long way doesn't mean I don't still feel that way. You wouldn't let me explain. I'm still terrified of losing all the good we have together." *Had* together.

Braden frowned as he sat up. "You're afraid of losing our baby, so you shut me out before I—"

"No!" I sat up, glaring at him. "You shut *me* out."

"I thought we were past all this."

"Then let me fucking explain!"

He glowered at me but shut up.

I glowered back. "You know I'm afraid of losing the people I love. But my kid, our kid, I already love this kid so much I can't breathe. The thought of something happening . . ."

Braden shook his head slowly. "You kept avoiding talking about having kids . . . I started to worry that you didn't want them. I thought with you running off to the castle it meant you were gearing up to shut me out because . . . you didn't want our kid. Then when you tried to explain, I was . . ." He sighed.

"You were what?"

"Scared," he admitted softly, his eyes locked with mine. "My mother never wanted me, Jocelyn. Never. I was not a happy kid and I would never wish that kind of childhood on anyone, let alone my own kids. I promised myself if I ever had children I'd be the kind of father mine never was and I certainly wouldn't marry a woman who wouldn't treat them like they were her whole world. So I didn't know how to feel about my wife not wanting our kid. I didn't know how to react to that and what it meant for *us*."

A knifelike pain cut across my chest. "Is that why you're moving out?"

"What?" he asked incredulously, his eyes darkening. "What are you talking about?"

"The letter." I lifted a shaky hand, pointing out to the hall. "I found the letter in the guest room. The one asking the tenants of your old apartment to move out within the month."

A thick silence fell between us.

Braden slipped out of bed, staring at nothing for a moment before turning to me with a very familiar anger. "That's the second letter to those tenants. The first one told them they were being evicted because of the complaints I'd received from residents of the building. The letter you saw was a standard notice telling them how much time they had to get out."

Oh.

Fuck.

"You thought that without talking to you, or trying to work this shit out that I . . . that I . . . was leaving you!" he yelled in disbelief.

Oh, no, he did not get to be angry anymore. I got out of the bed on the opposite side. "You froze me out. I was scared and confused and you left me on my own!" My voice cracked as I yelled back at him, and the break lowered my voice. "You wouldn't let me touch you. You flinched from me." I watched his face soften. "You promised me I wasn't alone anymore, but instead you made me think you hated me. And I think I hate you a little for that."

I turned away so he wouldn't see me cry again.

Two seconds later he was turning me into his arms. "Fuck, baby," he whispered hoarsely. "You could bring a man to his knees."

There was so much relief in feeling his arms around me, his chest beneath my cheek. Inhaling his scent. Soaking him in. But I didn't hold him in return.

"I'm so sorry," he said gruffly, desperately, in my ear, easing me back to stare into my eyes. He brushed my hair off my face before cupping it in his hands. There was something like panic in his eyes. "Jocelyn, I will never make you feel that way again. I promise. I'm so sorry." He kissed me hard, tasting my tears. "I was scared. I acted like an idiot, but it was just because this is our kid. It means more to me than anything ever has. I fucked up. I fucked up this time, but I'm sorry. I'm so sorry, sweetheart. I love you. You believe me?" He pulled me against him, his hands running down my back. "You believe me?"

I took a deep breath, trying to let go of the last few days. It would be so easy to hold on to the hurt and anger. But instead I looked back a few years when I was lying in Braden's arms, grateful that he'd forgiven me for everything I'd put him through.

I lifted my arms and wrapped them around his back. "I believe you."

He kissed me again, this time slower, deeper. When he pulled away, he was frowning. "I fucked up," he repeated quietly.

"Well, it was your turn."

"There will be times," he murmured against my lips, "when we don't like each other very much, but I need you to know that I will never stop loving you. This time it was me who was terrified of losing you, and I pushed you away because I was afraid to hear what you had to say. If, God forbid, I ever hurt you again, tell me. Don't lock me out. Don't shut the shower door in my face. Scream at me. Don't let me get away with it until you're storing that shit up and looking at me like you're haunted. Because . . . I swear to God, that look in your eyes that night, it almost broke my fucking heart. We need to stop doing that to each other. Right now."

I nodded, clinging tighter to him, relief and forgiveness melting my body into his. "I promise. And not just for me, and not just for you. We have a baby to think of now too. Congratulations, by the way."

Braden's eyes brightened. "Congratulations, sweetheart."

I laughed. "Oh, Jesus C, that took us long enough."

He pulled me up into his arms, so my feet left the ground. I automatically clung to his neck and wrapped my legs around his waist, only to find myself being lowered to my back on the bed.

Braden lay over me, his loving eyes staring straight into mine. "I've missed you."

I slipped my hands under his shirt, feeling his warm, muscled back beneath my fingers. "I've missed you too," I told him thickly. "I love you so much. Even when I didn't like you very much, I loved you completely."

His thumb brushed across my cheekbone. "Back at you, babe. And I won't ever stop loving you. But just in case you have your doubts"—he threw me a quick, heated smile as his fingers curled around the waistband of my sweatpants—"let me show you how hard and deep . . . and desperately I love you."

I tilted my hips, giving him better access to slowly peel the sweatpants off. As soon as they were gone I wrapped my legs around his back and my arms around his shoulders. "Let's do this in the shower," I murmured hungrily against his mouth.

Holding me tight, Braden stood up and cupped a hand to my nape, bringing my mouth to his. We savored each other in that kiss, tasting each other, our lips growing swollen from the passionate makeout.

"I love making out with you," I confessed, nuzzling his neck as he began walking us toward the bathroom.

He smiled in agreement and slowly lowered me to the floor once we were inside the bathroom. I pulled off my T-shirt and reached in to switch on the shower while Braden undressed, then divested myself of my bra and panties. My hungry eyes roamed my husband's body as he slipped off his boxer briefs. My lower belly clenched with need as he pulled me gently to him, his pale eyes burning with desire and his hands stroking down my spine, to caress the curve of my bottom.

I sighed, running my own hands over his chest, before pressing soft kisses across his pecs, stopping to tease his nipple with my tongue.

He squeezed my ass, groaning and pressing his erection deeper into my stomach. I continued to explore him, my mouth trailing kisses across his skin, while my own hands brushed across his hard abs, smoothed around his narrow hips, and grabbed his taut ass.

In retaliation, Braden let go of my bottom, stroking up my sides until he cupped both of my tender breasts in his hands. A pleasant pain shot through me when he kneaded them and I gasped, arching my neck. "They're tender," I whispered, reminding him of my pregnant state.

He kneaded them harder and I felt a rush of arousal shoot between my legs.

"Braden," I moaned, pushing deeper against him.

To my disappointment he eased his hold on me.

I eyed in him question and he smirked, silently answering by arching me over his arm and lifting my breast to his hot, wet mouth. I cried out at the sensation of his teeth gently scraping my nipple and then I was holding on for dear mercy as he sucked it deep into his mouth.

My breasts had never been this sensitive before.

"Oh, God, I think I'm going to come," I panted in disbelief, my hips undulating against him.

As if to test that theory, Braden sucked harder, circling my nipple with his tongue while he squeezed and kneaded my other breast.

I was on fire, my whole body hot and stiff.

And then I felt the ripple in my stomach and the slick wetness between my legs. I'd just had a mini-orgasm from Braden playing with my breasts.

He lifted his head when he felt my body relax, his eyes questioning.

Breathing heavily, I smiled languidly, brushing his hair from his face. "Yes."

Braden coasted his hand down my stomach and I shivered, my sex clenching in anticipation. He slid two fingers inside me easily and his eyes darkened.

"You're soaked." He pumped his fingers and I rocked against them. "This is going to be fun, babe," he muttered darkly.

I held on to his shoulders, moving on his fingers. "Baby, don't stop." I was close again.

"I want to taste you," Braden said, stopping the penetration. "I want you to come on my tongue."

I wasn't going to argue with that.

In seconds I found myself inside the shower, my back against the wall, Braden on his knees. He hooked my leg over his shoulder and I dug my fingers into his hair as he lowered his mouth and the shower water sluiced down his back. I was consumed with pleasure, with chasing orgasm, and nothing else mattered but his tongue circling my clit, his fingers pumping inside of me. My body stiffened as the climax came rushing for me. I cried out my husband's name as I shuddered my release against his lapping, talented tongue.

Drowsily, languidly, my hands slipped to rest on Braden's shoulders, moving down his chest as he stood up, kissing me in a wet, erotic kiss. With one hand he gripped the back of my right thigh, with the other my ass, and I somehow managed to hop up, wrapping my legs around him so he could ease his hot, throbbing dick inside of me. My inner muscles quivered at the pressure of him pushing deep and he groaned against my lips.

Our eyes held as he moved slowly in and out of me, our breathing growing steadily more shallow. "I missed you," he growled, his grip on me hard as his thrusts came a little faster.

"I missed you too." I kissed him. I kissed him with everything I had and Braden bent his knees, his cock thrusting so deep into me as he surged up that my cry broke our lips apart.

My fingernails dug into his skin as he continued to fuck me with a slow intensity that was sure to kill me. All my muscles were stiff as he worked me toward another climax.

Braden's warm breath puffed against my mouth. "Come for me, babe," he gasped, his hips flexing faster as it approached. "I need you to come, Jocelyn."

As if on cue the pressure in my lower body blew out and I shattered on a muffled scream, my sex rippling around Braden. "Fuck," he grunted, pressing his face into my neck as he fucked me harder, faster, until his own shout of climax was muffled against my skin. His hips jerked against mine, shuddering hard as his cock flooded my womb with his warm release.

I stayed there, locked around him for a while as we tried to gain control of our breathing.

Finally, Braden lifted his head and before I could say it he smirked and murmured, "Best. Shower. Ever."

Braden stared out at the view and then turned back to me with a pucker of confusion between his brows and a hint of annoyance in his eyes. "And we're here why?"

Standing beyond Mons Meg at Edinburgh Castle, I wrapped my arms around my husband's waist and pressed in close, tilting my head back to meet his eyes. "Somewhere you got the impression that I only come here when I'm in despair. I think that's why you shut me out. You were angry that I came here when I found out about our baby."

He nodded, his grip on my hips tightening. "We don't need to rehash this, Jocelyn."

It was a week after our reconciliation and things since then had been tentative, a little fragile, but good. We were finding our feet again but this time as a pregnant couple. Braden was so excited to be a dad that he was really helping me work through my fears. I also talked to him about seeing Dr. Pritchard again and we'd agreed to see her together, so he'd understand what I was going through even better. Seeing a therapist was not on the list of things Braden ever wanted to do, but he was doing it for our family.

"I'm not rehashing," I promised him. "I need you to know that I don't come here when I'm in despair."

He frowned. "You don't?"

"No." I smiled, shaking my head. "I come here whenever I need quiet. Some peace and quiet to process stuff. When I found out I was pregnant everything just filled my head. My mom and dad. Beth. You. Ellie. Elodie. Clark. Everyone I love. And the baby, our baby. I didn't know if I was scared or happy or sad or excited. It's an uncomfortable feeling to have all that crap colliding without focus. I came here to focus it so I could work out what I was feeling. But you showed up before I could."

"And jumped to conclusions."

"Yup. Then I wanted to talk it out with you. I really did. I wanted your help."

"And I was a complete bastard."

I laughed. "That's not why I brought you here. I brought you here so you'd know that this isn't three years ago. When I need to work something out I won't run from you. But if I come here I need you to know that it's just a place I like to come for peace and quiet. I'm not shutting you out of it. I want to share it with you."

He bent his head to speak quietly against my mouth. "This is your place. You don't need to share it with me. Just as long as you share what's going on with you, I'm happy."

"I can definitely do that."

Smiling, Braden ducked his head as he opened his coat and pulled a small package out of the inside pocket. It was a weird shape and very badly gift-wrapped. "For you."

Bemused, I took the present. "What is it?"

He shrugged, still smiling. "Just something to remind you of who you are and what a great mum you're going to be."

Grateful that he thought so, I quickly unwrapped the gift, my heart flipping over in my chest when I recognized it. It was a silver baby rattle and if I turned it I'd find my name engraved on one side and my little sister Beth's engraved on the other. It had been my rattle and when Beth came along I had my mom get Beth's name engraved on the other side so I could give it to my little sister. My mom had kept it in a silk-lined box, in the hopes that we'd started a new tradition of passing it down through the family. It wasn't a story I'd told Braden, even when I'd rescued it from the storage facility in Virginia when we went there to clear out my family's belongings.

Even without knowing the story, he'd known it meant a lot to me.

"I got it out of the box with all the things you've kept from your family, had it polished up." He turned it in my hand so Beth's name was facing upward. "I was thinking if we have a wee girl, we could name her Beth."

Swallowing past the lump of emotion clogging my throat, I nodded. "I'd like that. Thank you." I threw my arms around his neck, the rattle clenched tight in my fist, as I kissed him.

We kissed, sweet brushes of our lips that grew quickly heated. My breathing was heavy as I pulled back, my forehead pressing against his. "Do you think we've finally made it through?"

"Made it through?"

"All the crap." I grinned cheekily. "Do you think we finally get everything about each other?"

Braden shook his head, pressing another kiss to my lips as I clung to him. "No, babe. We're going to spend every day growing up. We'll learn new things about ourselves, never mind each other."

I pulled back. "Did anyone ever tell you that when your fear doesn't get in the way of your perceptiveness, you are an incredibly wise man, Mr. Carmichael?"

He rolled his eyes. "Am I ever going to live this down?"

I snorted, threading my arm through his as we started to stroll back down the castle hill. "When I fucked up you joked about it inappropriately for months and then pulled it out every now and then when you wanted to make a point."

He grunted. "I'll allow you to emotionally manipulate me with it for a week."

"A year."

"A month."

"A year."

"Six months."

I thought about it. That was a fairly lengthy period of torture and it probably fit in better with our pregnancy time frame. "Okay, six months. But I should warn you that it'll include more than emotional manipulation."

"Elaborate."

I smiled up at him. "I'm pregnant. My requests, cravings, they may get a little outrageous."

His body shook with laughter. "You're carrying my child. I'd probably take the blame if you murdered someone."

"You'd probably do that anyway, pregnant or not."

Braden smiled softly down at me. "No 'probably' about it."

Chuckling, I held on tighter. "I'm going to make you come shopping with me for maternity clothes."

"I can handle it. In fact, I'm rather looking forward to you having a bump." He smoothed a hand across my stomach, something he'd taken to doing a lot.

"My bump? Why?"

"It's a caveman thing," he joked.

"Elaborate." I repeated his word back at him.

"I'm not sure you want to know. You've just recently stopped being pissed off at me."

"Braden . . ."

He stopped just as we were about to walk outside the castle entrance onto the esplanade. I let him pull me against him as he bent to whisper his answer in my ear. "When every man sees our bump, they'll know I was the one you let inside you, they'll know you're mine and I'm yours, and that growing inside you is our kid."

My lips parted as I pulled back to meet his eyes. "The idea of the bump turns you on," I said more succinctly.

He grinned unrepentantly.

I shrugged. "That's fine with me. I'll start showing during my second trimester, and I've heard that's also when I'll get horny as hell."

Braden grabbed my hand as we began walking down the esplanade. "I'll do my best to accommodate you."

"I'm expecting a lot," I teased. "Filthy comments in restaurants, sex in bathrooms, cars, elevators, the changing rooms of maternity clothes shops . . ."

My husband laughed, letting go of my hand to wrap his arm around my shoulders and draw me into his side. "You missed the couch, the kitchen table, the shower, the bathtub—and the bed could work, too, you know."

"We need to get a cab." I began walking faster down the Royal Mile.

I felt Braden grinning at me. "Pregnancy hormones?"

"Braden-induced hormones," I grumbled, flagging down an oncoming black cab. I turned to him, my eyes glittering with anticipation. "Since you fucked up last week, I'm in charge. And on top. We'll see how it goes from there."

He sighed heavily, as if it was such a hardship. "Ah, and so it begins."

ECHOES OF SCOTLAND STREET

Shannon MacLeod has been a bad-boy magnet since she was a teenager. Tattooed musicians, pierced biker wannabes, and even ex-cons decorate her past. And unfortunately, not a single one ever treated her kindly. When her latest boyfriend upends her life in Glasgow, Shannon attempts to run from the devastation he's caused by escaping to Edinburgh to start over.

Despite her aversion to anything resembling her old life, beggars can't be choosers. In a case where miscommunication meets fate's twisted sense of humor, Shannon accepts employment as a receptionist at INKarnate, Edinburgh's most popular tattoo parlor. At first she's reassured by the owner's easygoing demeanor . . . until day one on the job, when she discovers the owner is semiretired and INKarnate is actually managed by the talented Cole Walker.

Cole is everything Shannon wants to avoid. Gorgeous, tattooed, charming, and cocky—and worst of all, he makes his interest in her obvious. Falling back on rudeness to keep him at a manageable distance, Shannon's behavior quickly creates an antagonism that makes their jobs difficult. That is, until it becomes clear to her that while Cole Walker may look and talk like a bad boy, there's so much more to the tattooist than meets the eye. He inspires such loyalty and love from his friends and family.

When Shannon offers to help him rid himself of a persistent ex-girlfriend, Cole catches an enticing glimpse of the real Shannon. And he likes what he sees. Not one to shy from a challenge, Cole begins a campaign to get to know her, in every way he can.

Soon the chemistry sparking between them turns from attraction into something that runs much deeper as he begins to uncover her secrets.

But just when Cole thinks they may have a future together, Shannon's past comes blasting into the city to destroy everything they've been building together. . . .